"NAY ... !"

He silenced her protest with a final kiss. Then he set her back, dark eyes glittering with either satisfaction or icy triumph, perhaps both.

"There. A taste of a true scoundrel, Mistress Tanner." Ran's mocking voice rang in the hall, or mayhap 'twas Merry's own shame and despair which made it seem so.

"I despise you, sirrah! You are naught but the lowest cad to e'er walk the earth."

"No doubt, you are quite right." Ranald's cold glance was dismissing as he turned away, his boot heel echoing with finality. He paused near the stairs and cast a final word at her. "You wonder if I intend turning you over to Wickham on the morrow. The answer is nay. You will be my guest at Auchmull until I say otherwise."

"I will see you in hell first!" Merry cried after him.

"So be it, madame. So be it."

BOOK YOUR PLACE ON OUR WEBSITE AND MAKE THE READING CONNECTION!

We've created a customized website just for our very special readers, where you can get the inside scoop on everything that's going on with Zebra, Pinnacle and Kensington books.

When you come online, you'll have the exciting opportunity to:

- View covers of upcoming books
- Read sample chapters
- Learn about our future publishing schedule (listed by publication month *and author*)
- Find out when your favorite authors will be visiting a city near you
- Search for and order backlist books from our online catalog
- Check out author bios and background information
- Send e-mail to your favorite authors
- Meet the Kensington staff online
- Join us in weekly chats with authors, readers and other guests
- Get writing guidelines
- AND MUCH MORE!

Visit our website at http://www.zebrabooks.com

SNOW RAVEN is dedicated to the dreamers.
You know who you are.

Life is mostly froth and bubble;
Two things stand like stone;
Kindness in another's trouble,
Courage in your own.

—Adam Lindsay Gordon

Prologue

Summer 1598
Auchmull Castle
the southeastern Highlands

"Come away, lad. There's naught to be done here."

Gently but firmly, Hertha Cobb interrupted the laird of Lindsay's stricken vigil. She reached up and laid a wrinkled hand on the man's broad shoulder, squeezing her fingers, letting him know she shared in the grief of his loss. Together, the two regarded the tartan-wrapped figure lying upon the cold stone bier.

"Blair," Ranald Lindsay whispered, reaching out to trace his wife's beloved features for the last time. He ran calloused fingers over a sweetly curved cheek, then closed his eyes in anguish as he remembered the first time, and the last, he had seen her. *Look at me, my love!* he begged her silently, wanting— nay, desperately needing—to gaze into those soft blue eyes one last time.

It seemed a dream now, yet just a short week ago, Blair Lindsay lay beside her husband in their huge carved bed, the pair of them snuggled happily under warm fur pelts, whispering of the bairn to come in the spring. Blair seemed so certain 'twould be a son; God would surely bless them doubly, she said, after so much disappointment.

Ran remembered her giggle as she teased her lord husband 'twould serve him right if there were twin lassies instead, both as feisty as their sire. He had growled and playfully swatted Blair's behind for such impudence, then rolled her over and made gentle, fierce love to her again.

Ran's gaze slowly refocused on the woman lying so still and pale before him. Blair's dainty hands were cross-folded over her midriff, the slight bulge of a future forever lost still visible. Her fingers curved about the hilt of the jeweled hilt of the dagger he had given her, an ornate piece no less deadly for its feminine decoration and swan's-head design.

He did not weep. He felt naught but a deadly calm, a resolve almost frightening in its starkness. Somewhere in the distance he was aware of voices, hushed whispers echoing in the great hall, but 'twas as if a shroud of mist separated him from reality. His attention did not stray from his Blair.

Even in peaceful repose of death, she soothed him with her presence. Her bright flaxen hair was dressed with white heather, as she had worn it when they had wed, and rested unbound in maiden fashion over the deep scarlet of her kirtle. Earlier, his shaking fingers had fastened the sprig of rue and crest badge to her cape. For a second, Ran's gaze focused on the Latin inscription surrounding the swan rising from a coronet proper *Endure fort.* Endure With Strength.

Ran glanced away. A tremor ran through his frame, a piercing white-hot stab of emotion, prompting one word.

"Wickham."

The name hissed from his lips banished the silence, and it seemed nature released its breath, for a sudden gust of wind through the half-open window made his tartan stir. Spring's kiss lay in the cool wind, in the pale sunlight dappled upon Blair's cheeks. How different 'twas from the Lammas day he and Blair had wed, bright with sunshine and laughter, as she had swirled in her plaid beside her young husband, threading the needle 'tween the other dancers. Their wedding music was a spritely reel, dubbed "Gay Lindsay" in honor of Ran's ancestors, once known as "The Lindsays light and gay . . ."

"M'laird?"

His reverie was shattered. The wail of bagpipes faded to the hushed stillness of a vigil beside a stone bier. Ran glanced over his shoulder at the elderly woman, his expression distant, as if he dreamed not of dancers, but rather *this* was the dream.

Hertha observed the lad she had nursed at her own bosom. Her heart ached for the depth of Ran's loss; 'twas no less than her own. She knew his senses must be dulled by shock, for his dark eyes swirled with emotion. After they had received word of Blair's death, Hertha had expected their lord would grieve. But he had endured the news in terrible silence, and she realized this icy restraint was far more dangerous than if a hell-hound of fury like the legendary Cu Sith had raged through Auchmull's halls.

Hertha's voice was husky with emotion when she spoke again.

"Ran, lad, 'tis time to come away. The others hae arrived from Edzell, Lady Deuchar and the boys. Father Pettigrew is here to attend to the rites."

Ran blinked, as if her words slapped him into reality. His hand rose from where it had unconsciously dropped to rest upon the hilt of his claymore at the name of Wickham and raked with sudden agitation through the deep brown waves of his hair.

"God's blood, Hertha, I cannot deal with Darra today."

Hertha sighed. "Yer sister will nae be put off fer long, m'laird."

"I know. See to their hospitality, Hertha. Keep them distracted as long as you can. Give me but a moment more with my bonny Blair . . ."

"Ye canna help yer poor lady-wife. She serves a higher laird now."

"Then I will avenge her."

The sudden vow was no less deadly for its quiet delivery.

"Hist, Lord Ran! Ye dinna ken what yer saying in yer grief. The others look to ye now, to set an example and lead them through these dark days."

Ran nodded. Hertha sensed his capitulation came too easily, and frowned a little. She wanted to clasp him to her breast, soothe and croon at him in a motherly fashion, but long had it been since any touched this proud man in aught save passion or battle. Always, always was the barrier there, though Blair had seen many a stone removed during their brief marriage.

Hertha had only seen Ranald Lindsay tremble thrice in his life. Once, when he wed Blair, and gazed into her loch-blue eyes as he spoke the binding vows; the second when word came from Edzell his father, the Earl of Crawford, had died; and lastly when he had returned from hunting stag in the Grampians and learned of his wife's fate.

All three within less than a year. Ran suddenly turned from the bier and faced Hertha. Raw emotion had replaced the bleakness in those dark eyes. Hertha felt a sudden chill that did not issue from any spring breeze, and knew the wolf was back.

Chapter One

Auchmull
Two months later

"What is the excuse this time? How dare he hide from me like some Lowland churl!"

The crisp, impassioned voice of Lady Deuchar rang throughout the great hall, and her gaze focused on Hertha almost accusingly. Darra shared her elder brother's keen dark eyes and the infamous Lindsay penchant for rebellion. She was renowned for her wit and beauty and was a favorite at James's Court. Married to Kinross Deuchar, a baron of some prominence and excellent reputation, now the mother of two young sons, Darra was quite content with her lot and thus had an inordinate amount of time on her hands for meddling in others' affairs.

"Ran is acting like a mummer gone mad," Darra said curtly, before Hertha could even think to reply. "Well, he is! 'Tis not as if this outcome was not unexpected. I should think he would at least acknowledge Blair brought such ill fortune upon herself."

Hertha shuddered at the matter-of-fact statement, though she knew Darra spoke with no true malice. This Lindsay lass had been a spoiled, willful bairn and had yet to grow out of it. Her talents outweighed her shortcomings, for Darra Deuchar née Lindsay was a devoted wife, mother, and chatelaine at the family estate of Edzell. Hertha could only fault the lass one thing, and that was her oft too merciless attitude toward her eldest brother.

"His little Blair is but hardly gone, lass," Hertha said with equal bluntness. "Surely ye would nae deny yer brother private time to grieve."

"Brooding does not suit any Lindsay."

To be certain, Hertha had never seen this lass brood. Ran was the moody one, Darra the ever-practical lass, and young Gil the charmer. All three bore the dark hair of their Crawford maternal kin, and the fair skin of their Anglo-Norman Lindsay ancestors. Darra was eloquent and striking in her black velvet mourning, which she still wore out of respect for her sibling. The fact her looks were attractively foiled by such a stark hue was but a benefit. There was no question as to why the lady enjoyed such popularity at Court. Hertha restrained herself from going to adjust the train of the gown. She was too accustomed to fussing over all the Lindsays in mother-hen fashion. 'Twas hard to accept the fact the Lindsay bairns were nigh all grown.

Och, poor Mistress Darra, Hertha mused. The lass had never understood Ran anyway; his secretive nature and moody reveries had never mixed well with Darra's incessant curiosity and inherent desire to control every situation.

Hertha sighed, wishing Darra's boys had come along, for she would have welcomed their noisy distraction at present. She still held the tray of cakes and heather ale she had brought out for the unexpected guest, and she regarded it with sudden weariness. Lady Darra was above such humble offerings anyhow, and young Gil and his older sidekick Hugo had grabbed handfuls of cakes before dashing off to practice tilting in the yard. Hertha set the tray upon the sideboard, noting Darra's gaze had instantly marked the slight tarnish on the silver.

Darra's lips thinned. "Ran has enough funds to run a proper

household,'' she said. ''Bad enough he refuses to occupy the high seat at Edzell. One must marvel that he cannot comply with even the meanest concept of civilization here.''

''Perhaps because I've yet to find any guests worthy of the effort'' came a cool reply from the top of the stairs, and Darra frowned. Only with the greatest of restraint did she manage to turn and regard Ran with what might have passed for indifference.

''High time you faced me,'' she rebuked him as the elusive chief of Clan Lindsay descended the stairs to the hall, clad in his red-and-black Lindsay tartan, with the ceremonial key to Auchmull pinned at his left shoulder. Ran's shoulder-length, wavy dark hair was loose, spread across his broad shoulders. He was thinner since she had seen him last, but Darra glimpsed a familiar, feral glint in his eye.

Darra eyed her brother's appearance disapprovingly. She had willingly surrendered the clan plaid when she wed Kinross, and it annoyed her Ran still clung so stubbornly to the past, especially when it amounted to naught but misty legends and myths of Lindsay glory.

He seemed not the slightest perturbed by her remark.

''Indeed'' was all he said, and his lips curved slightly. Darra suspected he mocked her and this prompted another gambit to regain control of the situation.

''I have been here nigh an hour, Ran, and yet you cannot be bothered to greet your own kith and kin. D'you suppose I traveled all the way from Edzell to cool my heels in your humble hall, awaiting your pleasure?''

Ran looked at her. His boot heel hit the main floor with a ring of finality. When he spoke again his voice was so deceptively soft as to give the illusion of gentleness, where there was, in truth, none.

''Nay, lass. As I hardly presume you came to weep over Blair's grave, either.''

Darra flushed at his remark, and hugged herself, her hands rubbing up and down her arms. '' 'Tis too cold in here by half,'' she complained.

Ran said nothing then, but crossed the hall to the huge, empty hearth where a fire had not blazed since his wife's death. He leaned against the mantel and folded his arms, regarding his sibling with something akin to dark amusement.

"I prefer it cold."

Sensing the impending storm, Hertha saw opportunity to escape. She gratefully seized upon the excuse of the tray as she picked it up again and bustled off for the kitchens. After her departure, nothing was heard for a long time but the distant shouts of the lads as they thundered their ponies across the inner ward. Their laughter and good-natured taunts rang off the keep's stone walls, underscoring the daunting silence in Auchmull's great hall.

Finally Darra spoke. She could not bear the tension. Nothing was more chilling than Ran's icy silence when he chose to use it as a weapon.

"Ran," she said abruptly. "I realize you and I have never gotten on famously, but there is no need for further adversity at such an hour. Gilbert looks to you now, more than he ever has. You must set an example. You are the Earl of Crawford now."

"A *Sassenach* title with all the attached unpleasantries of duty, I see," Ran said, punctuating his words with a chuckle containing no mirth whatsoever. His flinty gaze never wavered from his sister's face.

Darra felt cornered, and raised her chin. She was but five foot three to her brother's strapping height, but enough High-land blood coursed through her veins to make her every bit as dangerous as male Lindsays when her ire was roused.

"Duties, unpleasant or otherwise, are a fact of life, Ran. Best grow up and accept it."

"I need accept nothing I do not choose to."

"Pray tell, how does refusing to accept Blair's death aid or benefit any of us?"

Darra's inspection of her brother's residence had not failed to note the fact none of the late Lady Lindsay's personal items had been removed. Indeed, the woollen Blair was mending around the time tragedy struck was still neatly folded upon a low table beside her favorite fireside chair, as if waiting for its mistress to return any moment and pick up the darning needle again.

Darra was not certain why this piqued her so; she valiantly resisted the urge to walk over and gather up the kirtle and yarn, crumple and toss both into the hearth. Had it been blazing as she wished, she might have done so. Ridding Auchmull of the last taint of Blair Maclean could not come soon enough.

Ran finally replied, in such cold vein she knew he had read her thoughts. '' 'Tis not death itself which I refuse to accept, but rather the means by which 'twas inflicted.''

''Blair's death was an accident, Ran.''

''Was it?''

''Aye. Had she not been so foolish as to set out in the rain on some misplaced mission of supposed mercy—''

''Enough, Darra.'' Ran's voice was like a whipcrack in the room.

She heeded the warning but could not resist one last retort. '' 'Tis a pity you insist upon being so foul-natured, Brother, because methinks there must be a bright mind behind the roar and bluster.''

He arched an eyebrow, and actually chuckled a little, to her surprise. ''Coming from you, lass, I am not sure if that is a compliment or an insult.''

Darra shrugged. ''You always were difficult,'' she said with a sigh, and shook her dark head. She looked at Ran with what seemed sympathy for a moment. ''I know how much you loved Blair . . .'' she haltingly began.

Something shifted in Ran's expression, and when he spoke his voice was cooler than ever. ''As I know you never cared for my wife, is this your roundabout way of saying you're sorry for my loss anyway?''

''I suppose 'tis.''

He nodded curtly at her. ''More than I expected. Thank you.''

" 'Twas nothing personal, Ran. Blair would have made the right man a good wife."

"Right man?"

Ran looked at her, his dark eyes blazing again. At moments such as these, Darra knew why her brother was called the Wolf of Badanloch, with a measure of awe and respect and no little fear. Any ordinary mortal would have quivered where they stood. Lindsay women, however, were renowned for being just as courageous as their menfolk, and legend said the females of the line had inherited the powerful aura of the Ceasg, a Scottish Highland mermaid whose temper was as dangerous as any fathomless loch. Darra stood her ground and matched her brother glare for glare.

"Aye, the right man. Even Father tried to dissuade you from the notion of wedding a Maclean. Whenever tradition is broken, there are consequences to pay."

"Consequences. Is that how you define Wickham's actions?"

Ran's voice was harsh, his eyes narrowed with rage. Just the mention of Wickham was enough to set him on edge again.

"I do not deny Sir Jasper is vulgar beyond belief," Darra said, hesitating when she encountered Ran's scowl. " 'Twas unfortunate he was the one Blair turned to in her hour of . . . need. However, the plain fact is, 'twas Blair's and her family's meddling which led to all the trouble in the first place."

"Enough!" Ran's snarl was that of a wounded wolf, and had Darra not been kin, she sensed he would have rent her in half with the great fists clutched at his sides. She did not feel inclined to press her luck further.

For a long moment, the siblings stared at each other, a familiar impasse broken only by the abrupt entrance of a third party.

A slim, handsome youth dashed into the great hall, somewhat breathless, his dark hair disheveled. Garbed in a sober black tunic, black braies and cloak, his boundless energy was nonetheless readily apparent, unchecked by the brooding atmosphere overlaying the room.

"I'm hungry," Gilbert Lindsay began without preamble, his

newly deepened voice both wheedling and matter-of-fact all at once. "Cook said nothing will be ready until this eve."

Ran glanced at the younger man, seeing a reflection of his own self, light contrasting the dark. A grudging smile curved his lips. 'Twas impossible for anyone, serf or lord, to remain impassive in the face of Lindsay charm. Fifteen-year old Gil had inherited his elder brother's portion, and the deep dimples tugging at his cheeks betrayed both a mischievous nature and a *joie de vivre* that was contagious.

"We'll feast after chapel," Darra said, a motherly note entering her tone as she turned toward Gilbert. She, too, seemed relieved by the distraction he offered from an uncomfortable subject.

Ran chuckled a little as he looked at Gil. "Hmm, I distinctly recall you and Hugo feasting quite heartily on Hertha's stove tatties and black buns not an hour ago."

Gil's violet-blue eyes twinkled. "Did we?" he shrugged affably. "Lud, I cannot recall. I feel as though I'm wasting away by the moment." He patted his lean waist for dramatic emphasis, and extracted smiles from both onlookers.

Ran did not care to pursue a heated argument before young Gil, though there was much left between him and Darra as yet unsettled. "Mayhap after sup, I can show you a bit of sword-play, lad."

He reached up and lifted a gleaming blade from the mantel, gripping the leather-wrapped hilt of the claymore almost reverently. He detected Darra's flinch from the corner of his eye, and chose to ignore it. By contrast, Gil perked up, stepping forward for a better view.

"Scathach," Gil breathed, looking at the steel now balanced across the flats of his brother's upturned palms. " 'Tis been a long time since she graced us with her presence."

Ran nodded. He had not held the weapon since . . . och, maybe it was better not to remember. He brushed a thumb across the dusty steel and remembered how it looked when it was coated with blood instead. How long had it been since Scathach sang a tune of simple vengeance?

Vengeance, aye. Ran thoughtfully slid the double-handed claymore into the scabbard at his side, adjusting himself to the feel of its weight at his side, absent for so long. Far too long. It felt like an old friend come home to stay.

Darra looked on with disapproval, distaste reflected in her eyes. Yet she held her tongue in check, either for Gil's sake or simply to maintain the fragile truce of peace. Instead, she sighed.

"We must attend your appearance first," Darra said to Gilbert as she stepped forward, reached out and smoothed his hair by habit. She ignored Gil's attempt to duck and evade the hands straightening his collar and checking his laces, and she even untied and briskly relaced his shirt until it met with her approval.

"Such disarray!" Darra clucked her tongue as Ran looked on, smiling a little, and Gil squirmed in unabashed misery. "One might suppose you have been living in the mews, Gilbert, not with the mighty Earl of Crawford."

"Would I lived here at Auchmull always," Gil muttered, either to spite his sister or express his unhappiness with his current status, a lad subjected to motherly fussing.

Ran chuckled, and felt the impact of Darra's piercing glance.

" 'Tis what comes from letting a lad run wild without measure. . ."

"Gil asked if he might stay on after the funeral, and you and Kinross agreed," Ran reminded her. "Would you change the tale now to ease your conscience, lass?"

Darra frowned. She hated it when Ran called her lass; it made her feel younger than he, when she was the elder by fact of maturity. Also, she did not care for the niggling truth behind his words. He was ofttimes so blunt it startled her.

"Pierce and Thierry miss their uncle" was her somewhat evasive reply. "Gilbert kept the boys well occupied. I note there is nothing here at Auchmull to similarly engage young minds. Gilbert's education has clearly suffered."

"Rather you imply there is nothing of import here to learn," Ran said. "I would disagree."

" 'Tis your prerogative, of course." Darra nodded curtly.

"Yet you must admit Gilbert has benefited from sharing Thierry's tutor over the past year, and in my opinion his progress and his manners have noticeably declined whilst he's been here."

Gilbert made a protesting noise. "There is more to learn of life than Latin and theology."

"Well said." Ran smiled at his little brother, and their gazes met in a moment of perfect understanding. Darra noted the exchanged glance and felt a twinge of envy and a sudden compulsion to bring them both back to earth.

"Ross and I have spoken, and we are agreed upon one thing. We wish Gilbert to live with us at Edzell . . . permanently."

Ran looked at Darra as if she'd slapped him. Whether he was appalled or simply stunned, it was clear he was not pleased by the prospect.

"Nay."

The flat, harsh reply left no room for negotiation. Darra hesitated, doubting he deserved any explanation and yet feeling compelled to provide one.

" 'Tis not any reflection upon your character, Ran," she said. "However, Gilbert needs a stable family, a permanent place where discipline and love are measured in equal doses."

Gilbert protested at the mention of discipline. "Am I allowed no say in this? I have seen fifteen winters, and being Highland winters, they should count even more."

Ran gave a grudging chuckle, but Darra shook her head. "Go find Hugo, Gilbert. Ran and I must needs talk alone."

"No."

"No?" She looked at Gilbert sharply, not only hearing defiance but seeing it in his dogged stance, an imitation of Ran's. Her gaze traveled from brother to brother, frustrated. "Even Father Pettigrew agrees 'tis the wisest decision. You would not gainsay your own confessor, I trust."

"Neither will I allow a churchman's meddling to disrupt Gilbert's future," Ran replied. "The lad is in dire danger of becoming a useless ornament, a courtly decoration with neither mind nor courage. The greatest danger to this land is her lack of true defenders. Gil must learn the gentle art of war from the only warrior remaining in the Lindsay clan.''

Darra laughed. ''Gentle? You?''

Even had her short laugh been twice as cutting, 'twould not have made an impression. Ran was used to insults; they bounced off his armored emotions like so much chaff. He regarded his sister, his gaze coolly assessing.

''Gilbert will not join the legions of mealy-mouthed courtiers, Lady Deuchar. I forbid it.''

Darra bristled at his faintly sarcastic emphasis of her title.

''Oh, I see. *You* forbid it . . .''

''I am the laird of Lindsay, am I not? As you so oft remind me. Therefore my word is law, and I hope you take it to heart gracefully, for I do not intend to sit back and watch you and oh-so-gallant Ross turn a bright mind into some hideous mocking caricature of masculinity. If a man was meant to bow and scrape, surely Destiny would have sewn altar cushions to his knees.''

Darra gasped. ''Ran! 'Tis blasphemy!''

He shrugged. ''I speak not of the Church, though I suppose it may be applied there as well. I refer to those ill-favored fops like Wickham who drip lace from every edge and gush compliments as ceaselessly as a burn.''

''I was not aware compliments were out of fashion,'' she replied shortly, still ruffled by his cavalier comments about courtiers and the Church. Honestly, sometimes his manner was so devilishly cold. She might respect Ran, but she could not fathom him raising Gilbert alone. Gil needed to secure position at Court to keep the family in a favorable light. Ran disdained the entire ritual of pomp and circumstance, and although Darra was graciously acknowledged whenever she appeared, she did not wield the power of title Ran so contemptuously ignored.

Already he had dismissed the topic as unimportant and turned to Gilbert. ''What of the riding wager with Hugo?''

Gil perked up. ''I won!'' The youth began to dig in his surcoat to show off his winnings, while Darra frowned in disapproval.

''This is the sort of example you would set?''

"Aye, and why not?" Ran did not even spare her the courtesy of a glance, but chuckled as Gil, flushed with pride, displayed the glint of gold against his palm.

Darra whirled and left the great hall in a rustle of skirts. The slamming of the double doors behind her caused Gil to jump, but Ran was used to his sister's fits of pique and did not even flinch.

" 'Twould appear the grand Lady Deuchar disapproves of my influence, Gil."

Gil's violet-blue eyes darkened. "Dar would keep me tied to her apron strings forever!"

"Now, you cannot blame her, lad. She took over the care of you when we lost Mother. I was away too much to be of any help, I fear. However much she might irk us both, she has a good head and heart. I know her to be a far better chatelaine than I shall ever aspire to."

"She rules her own home like a self-righteous tyrant," Gil said unhappily. "I think she has been reading far too much of the Virgin Queen and fancies herself a similar Scottish termagant."

Ran laughed at Gil's wry observation. He would admit a secret admiration for Elizabeth Tudor, and aye, his sister as well. It did not mean he agreed with their strong-arm tactics, but an intelligent lass was to be admired. If only from a safe distance.

Chapter Two

A fortnight later
near Cardigan, Wales

"What d'you mean, the road is impassable?"

Meredith Tanner sounded petulant as she poked her auburn head from the window of her uncle's fine coach, and regarded her driver and the man he was speaking with with frustration and dismay.

The serf quickly doffed his hat, visibly awed by her elegant and no-nonsense demeanor, while Jem merely nodded at her statement.

"Aye, miss. The spring rains have washed out the main route. The streams are bursting, running amuck. We must choose a safer course."

Merry's gray-green eyes flashed, and Jem braced himself for a familiar flurry of brisk orders. Mistress Tanner had a sweet, even temperament when content, but proceeding cross-purposes to her wishes was never wise. Already he recognized the stubborn set of her lips and inwardly sighed, resigned to another fruitless argument.

"Jem, y'know I must return to Court directly. Her Majesty will be cross enough as 'tis, since I lingered overlong at Falcon's Lair. Her permission to visit Kat was granted with the clear provision that I return to London and resume my duties as soon as possible."

Jem nodded. There was nothing he could say to counter her statement. He knew their monarch's infamous temper well enough from having served as the Tanner driver for years, whilst his master Sir Christopher danced attendance upon Henry Tudor's little virago often enough. He bit back a smile, however, as a mental comparison between the two redheads came to mind. Mistress Tanner was far younger, of course, and fresh as a hawthorn blossom in comparison to Elizabeth's time-worn Tudor rose, but there was some intriguing likeness between maid and monarch. A keen wit, ready laughter, and a love of dance, mayhap.

Merry impatiently rapped her jeweled fan upon the window-sill of the coach, and Jem's fleeting muse passed under his lady's summons. He almost laughed. A comparison of the two redheads' volatile natures was bound to be accurate, as well.

"How much extra time will a detour cost us, Jem?"

Jem looked to the peasant he had waylaid for directions. The other man provided a hedging estimate which only increased Mistress Tanner's anxiety.

" 'Twill never serve," Merry fretted aloud. "We cannot risk so great a delay. A missive came from Father before I left Falcon's Lair, and my betrothed is at Whitehall. He may head home any day. I cannot risk the chance of missing him."

"Surely he would linger long enough to make your acquaintance, miss." Jem knew she had never met her intended. Tanner curiosity being a natural trait, he knew the prospect of not meeting her future lord husband until the day of the wedding did not rest easy with Mistress Merry.

"Aye, I am sure he would if he could, but the borders are so dangerous nowadays, and he daren't leave Braidwood unattended err long." As she spoke, Merry absently toyed with a flaming curl which had escaped her coiffure, and Jem saw the peasant's cautious if somewhat dazed admiration. Mistress Tanner was no beauty by Tudor standards, red hair accounted unfashionable and her features a trifle sharp for a woman's, but there was no denying her sheer force of presence. She did not blend into the background, but rather dominated it. Her traveling gown of cream-and-rose velvet suited her fair complexion, as did her fawn-colored cloak, though her coloring was presently heightened in proportion to her distress.

"It simply cannot be endured," Merry stated firmly. "Jem, we must press on. Proceed cautiously if need be, but I remind you we must needs make haste once the road has cleared."

Jem frowned at this order. "There is great risk the coach might become bogged, miss."

"Far greater risk of Her Grace's wrath should I fail to appear by the appointed hour. You should know by now our queen's moods flux with the wind, Jem."

He nodded. "Yet Her Majesty has always been most benevolent with you, miss."

Merry smiled at Jem's words. 'Twas true she stood high in Elizabeth Tudor's favor. She had followed in her paternal grandmother's footsteps, carving out a cozy niche for herself among the ranks of the chosen few. Only Essex and perhaps her uncle occupied greater favor at present, merely because they were men and so could lavish Her Grace with jewels and romantic sonnets. She had also heard rumor before leaving Whitehall that Elizabeth was annoyed with Robert Devereux. Something to do with Ireland. A tiresome topic in itself, at least in Merry's opinion, who, although half-Irish herself, was never desirous of being reminded of it.

Reluctantly, Jem bowed to her demand. He had learned long ago never to argue with a Tanner. By virtue of blood or by sheer tenacity, somehow they always won.

As the coach set off with a bone-jarring lurch through the thick spring mud, Merry settled back into the plush velvet cushions with a sigh. Bad enough she had darted hither and yon upon her sister's whims over the past months, finally coming to Wales in order to effect a truce between Lord Trelane and her dear, proud, stubborn little Kat, but now her own future was at stake because she had lingered overlong.

Merry shuddered. The miserable, wet weather did not aid her mood nor her outlook on life in general. Despite her happiness for her twin, something in her nature prompted a twinge of envy for Kat's position. Not just the title she had claimed by the act of wedding Morgan Trelane, but the love itself. It shone so clearly in Kat's beautiful green eyes whenever she spoke about her dark Welsh lord.

Merry was cut of far different cloth from her twin sister, however. She would never risk life and limb to sail upon the high seas like some feckless pirate wench, nor brazenly go into a house of God disguised as another woman so she might wed the man she loved. Part of her had always envied Kat that fearless stance. 'Twas the Irish showing through, Merry reasoned, for all their maternal kin were as feisty and daring, their mother Bryony no exception.

Merry had never felt she belonged among the boisterous clansfolk. Despite her flaming hair, and her birth name, Erin, she was like a delicate English rose among the brooding, brawling lot at Raven Hall. Her practical nature longed for manners and order and a good, stiff dose of cleanliness. On her first visit to England she felt she had come home.

Hence Merry, a misfit among the brash Irish clan of relatives, seized upon her sensible English relations with relief. Caution, practicality, and common sense were something she understood. So were wit and the ability to entertain, for if she had inherited nothing else from her Irish ancestors she was quick with a line and clever to a fault. In this respect she resembled her beloved uncle Kit, long one of Elizabeth's favorites.

Sir Christopher Tanner wielded more than a little influence at Court, and was able to win his niece audience with the queen upon her very first visit. The two redheads in tandem had charmed Her Grace so thoroughly that Merry was offered a position as maid-of-honor right then and there. A rare honor for one so young and untried. Merry prettily begged her doting sire to let her remain at Whitehall and serve the queen, and since Slade Tanner could refuse his daughters nothing, Merry had entered the dazzling world of the Tudor Court at the tender age of fourteen.

Like her paternal grandmother before her, she quickly became one of the few trusted females surrounding the proud, vainglorious Elizabeth Tudor. Merry's practical nature had long ago accepted the fact she was no beauty; hence Her Grace did not feel threatened, either, though Bess was known to make a pert comment or two about Merry's youthful inexperience.

A trusting nature did not equate with naïveté, however. Merry was used to courtly intrigue and the ofttimes cruel little plots which simmered beneath the lively, colorful Tudor arena. Surely Rome herself had never seen the like of so many bishops, knights, and petty pawns always jockeying for position and influence and wealth. Merry found it all thrilling and terrifying and so very suited to her curious and extroverted nature.

How Lady Fortune had smiled on her the day she set foot on precious English soil! She gazed out the coach window at the dreary Welsh countryside, wishing the coach might somehow magically sprout wings and rush her home. The dark hinterlands of Her Grace's realm had never appealed to Merry, and she detested the annual sojourn through humble villages and squalid country shires.

She longed to be back at Whitehall, surrounded by adoring courtiers and her fellow maidens in service to the queen . . . to dance and laugh and while away the hours in the company of a wicked-tongued knave or an overbold swain. How she had missed such revelries when shut up in her brother-in-law's dour Falcon's Lair. Establishing some sort of order amid the chaos reigning in the dreary Welsh keep had kept her mind occupied for a few days, but Merry was easily bored, and challenges, once met, failed to keep her interest any longer.

She sighed and impatiently drummed her fingertips upon the padded armrest. She disliked travel in general, finding it tiresome and tedious, but there would be much required by way of travel as the wife of a border baron. The disadvantage, of course, was she would be far removed from her beloved Court, but mayhap after providing her lord husband with an heir and a spare, he would permit her to travel as a matron lady with Her Majesty's retinue. Failing that, Merry was determined to make Braidwood as famous as Whitehall in its own neck of the woods, and hence bring the gaiety and laughter she so loved home to roost in her own hall.

Her head gradually fell back against the cushioned seat, a dreamy half-smile touching her lips even though the coach subjected her to numerous jolts along the rutted road. She felt the weariness of travel descending over her like a tattered cloak, and closed her eyes for but a moment dreaming of Braidwood, her future home, and the eloquent and fashionable lord she would soon call her own.

Chapter Three

"Ho!"

A hoarse shout and excited whinny of horses roused Merry from her slumber with a start. With a cross exclamation she leaned forward to peer out the window but reeled backward as the coach suddenly lurched into a pell mell pace. Her right shoulder impacted the elegantly scrolled wood frame on the door. As she gasped with pain and outrage, more voices could be heard above the furious rattling of the coach's wheels and the thundering, splashing hooves.

Gripping the edge of the window, she braced herself long enough to push aside the swaying velvet curtains and take in the scene. What she saw made her pale. Four men rode low over their horses' necks, easily pacing the coach as it rumbled and shuddered over the rutted country road. They did not appear deterred by Jem's angry shouts, nor did their intent waver when the coach suddenly veered off onto a narrow path as Jem attempted to elude the pursuers.

Merry's wide-eyed gaze took in their pursuers. She was accustomed to sizing others up with a court-trained glance, and this motley bunch boded no good. Two appeared ordinary footpads, unwashed and unkempt, lean and hungry as wolves. Another was a veritable giant, roughly dressed out in woolen braies and dirty shirt, his shaggy yellow hair no cleaner than the rest of him. He almost dwarfed the stout pony he rode, great thighs clamped against his heaving mount's sides, a broad and roguish grin splitting his coarse features.

Merry shuddered and glanced to the last man. The fourth ruffian appeared a mere boy on closer inspection, a comely youth clad in black breeches that outlined somewhat gangly legs, and a cloak of matching black wool. A froth of white lace at his throat cast an incongruous light upon what otherwise appeared to be a simple highwayman, and Merry frowned. For a moment fear was supplanted by curiosity, and a burning desire to seize yon grinning knave and throttle him till his brain rattled in his skull.

Then she heard Jem swear emphatically, over the din and confusion.

''Milady, brace yourself—''

His warning barely reached her before Merry pitched violently forward, her momentum stopped only by the opposing seat. She slammed into the cushions and slid in a heap to the floor. Suddenly there came a terrible scream, a horse's shrill bugle of pain. The coach buckled on its wheels, spinning sideways down a small embankment, hurling Merry and the rest of its contents to one side, the same side it came to rest upon after it struck the muddied earth.

After the crash, there was a long spell of silence. Merry stirred, conscious throughout the events but too crumpled and filled with pain to care. She heard a murmur of male voices and decided she only imagined the concern in their tones. Her hand scrabbled weakly, desperately, around the upended coach, searching the door that had now become her resting place, looking for something, anything which she might raise in faint defense against the brigands who had set upon them. If only she had listened to her mother. Bryony Tanner had tried, time and again, to persuade her daughter to carry a little dagger in the Gaelic fashion of self-defense, but Merry abhorred weapons and had refused.

For 'twas certain she was part of the men's motives now. Waylaying and robbing fine coaches was but a pleasant pastime in some of the rougher outlying districts, and Merry knew how foolish she had been to venture forth with no more escort than her uncle's driver. Not only was it highly improper she was alone with Jem, but one retainer was scarcely adequate defense against footpads, scoundrels, and the like. Her fumbling fingers encountered the overturned satin box housing her jewelry collection, which she had not allowed Jem to pack atop the coach with the other baggage. The silken cord tying the box shut had broken loose, and Merry saw the glitter of semiprecious stones and gold strands flung about the coach from the corner of her eye. Mayhap the baubles could buy her and Jem a precious moment more of life, if not spare them altogether. Or . . . did she not have a brooch or two among the hoards? A brooch with a sharp pin . . .

"Christ's wounds!"

Someone swore roundly, the voice very near, and Merry's heart quickened its pace. She was afraid to move, lest the coach rock and betray the fact she was alive and relatively unhurt.

The male voice continued, sounding young, agitated. "I never expected the idiot to drive off the main road, Hugo."

Merry heard a rather distant grunt in response, and surmised it must be the blond giant whose evil delight in their mischief-making pursuit had been apparent.

"By all the bloody hounds of hell, what do we do now?"

Merry might have laughed had her stays not dug painfully in her ribs with each breath and was she not so outraged and pensive. The uncertainty in the youth's voice gave her pause, however, and faint cause for hope.

She thought she heard a nearby splash of horses' hooves through the thick mud. She heard a panicked shout as a pair of horses galloped off. She heard the younger man groan with what seemed either dread or resignation. For some reason she imagined him sitting forlornly on a tree stump, face buried in his hands.

"Of all the cutty luck!"

"Yet you do not seem surprised, Gil."

The second voice that spoke was deeper, and resonated with authority and a faint trace of wry humor. "Did you suppose I could not follow the wide swathe of destruction and rampant rumor you and stout Hugo left throughout hill and dale?"

"Nay." Merry pictured the youth's head hanging low. Certainly he sounded humble and contrite enough in the presence of . . . could it be his overlord?

"Fortunately your ill-chosen friends decided not to toy with my temper today. We'll talk later." The one in charge switched to a brusque tone which suggested he was not used to being gainsaid. Immediately orders were given. "Hugo, see to the driver. Check for broken bones before you move him, and for God's sake don't forget your own brutish strength."

Expecting a bellow or sneer of rage at the crisply worded command, Merry was surprised to hear a respectful chorus of mutters instead from the two remaining men.

"Aye, milord."

So a peer had come to her rescue. How apt. She almost relaxed, until she realized this man knew these fiends. If he associated with such lowlifes himself, he could be of equally notorious character.

She heard a sudden thump-thump, like a man stepping across the body of the upturned coach. Someone jiggled at the coach door directly above her, and she gasped. She prayed the lack of light might obscure her prone form, but she saw a hand reach through the window as the would-be intruder brushed the dangling curtains aside.

At the same moment, Merry's groping fingers encountered a smooth, cool, round object. The brooch. She closed her hand around it just as the door creaked open, then was flung wide.

Light filtered down through the coach, pinning her as mercilessly as the pair of eyes she sensed above her.

"Ochone!"

The passionate exclamation surprised Merry. It was tinged with a Scottish burr, like the ones she had heard at Court.

But the surprised remark did not take her off guard as much as the large hand suddenly thrust down at her. "Are you all right, milady?"

Merry gazed up into a pair of dark eyes, the rich brown of newly turned earth and just as heady to her senses. Her throat felt suddenly tight as she looked at the man regarding her with equal scrutiny.

He was dark as the youth, and quite as handsome, though in a much more rugged way. There was nothing even remotely effeminate about his aura, even though she glimpsed one bare, bronzed knee braced against the coach where he knelt in his red and black watch kilt.

Somehow Merry could not detest him, though her rancor at these strangers was strong as ever. She looked at the proffered hand, wanting very much to scorn it, but she wanted out of the coach far more. She hesitated, then placed her free hand in his. The other palm still gripped the brooch, hidden in the folds of her voluminous skirts.

He evidenced considerable strength as he drew Merry up to her feet, kneeling still upon the upturned coach, and then before she could even think to protest, he reached down, wrapped a strong hand about her small waist and easily lifted her the rest of the way. Taken further off guard, Merry's free arm flew around his neck for support. His cape was damp from rain beneath her fingertips, the aroma of wet wool mingling with the scent of leather, horseflesh, and the natural musk of a male. The gentlemen at Court preferred perfumes to nature's own scents, and Merry was unused to such a heady mixture.

Still cradling her in his arms as if she weighed no more than a downy thistle, he jumped lightly down from the coach and lowered Merry to her feet.

"Thank you, milord," she murmured, feeling at once both overwhelmingly grateful and oddly self-conscious. He was a big man, muscular yet lean, well over six feet and daunting even in a kilt. She doubted even the bravest jester would risk a mock ballad about this Scot's bonny knees!

He merely nodded at her thanks, attempting no pretense of a gallant bow. Merry wasn't sure whether she should feel slighted when she saw his gaze had already dismissed her and returned to the dark-haired youth, who was posed very much as she had envisioned, though slumped dejectedly against a tree trunk rather than sitting on a stump.

"I am only glad yon rogue's notion of a prank did not end in worse disaster."

"Prank, sirrah?"

Merry could not keep a sharp note from entering her tone as she glanced at the boy the Scottish lord had referred to. In turn, the younger man looked back at her with very sober, violet-blue eyes which seemed to hold a silent plea. She sensed he had used such beautiful eyes to advantage before with women, and she flicked her skirts with irritation.

"Faith, I find the notion of such a prank to be no less than criminal, given the nature of its ending." Merry nodded in the direction of the overturned coach, whose axle had clearly snapped in half. She could not quell a faint shudder at the sight of the horses lying tangled in their traces, one dead and two others twitching with various degrees of injury. The fourth had, miraculously, escaped both injury and harness and now grazed rather indolently alongside a rain-swollen creek.

"Horses can be replaced. I assure you the proper recompense shall be made."

Merry's resolve firmed at the Scotsman's cool response. "What of Jem, my driver?"

"He is shaken, but unhurt. A sprained ankle, bruised ribs, and such. He was thrown clear before the coach left the road."

Merry nodded, wondering why the man's pleasant burr left her cold. Perhaps 'twas because there was no emotion behind the formal words, just a bare civility which left her feeling as if she had been assessed and found lacking in some way.

For some reason she felt a sudden wicked desire to throw *him* off guard.

"I must thank you for your timely rescue, sir. I am Mistress Meredith Tanner."

She curtsied despite her disheveled appearance, and felt a twinge of triumph when his surprised if somewhat preoccupied gaze rested upon her once more.

"I am Ranald Lindsay." The words were uttered almost reluctantly, as if he disliked sharing even the briefest bit of detail about himself. As if to confirm her suspicions, he nodded promptly in the direction of the youth. "This would-be ruffian is my younger brother, Gilbert, and the other his companion, Hugo Sumner. The two who wisely fled I did not recognize."

Merry did not follow the red herring. "Lord Lindsay?" she pressed him, and was certain she detected a flash of irritation in his eyes this time.

"Aye."

Mentally Merry quickly reviewed what little she knew of the Lindsay clan. She knew they were Highlanders, a warlike race, and held the power of pit and gallows far removed from English influence. Indeed, far removed was this dark wolf from his Highland lair. She wondered what lured a reluctant Scot into distant Welsh territory, and knew the answer when she glanced at the forlorn-looking Gilbert Lindsay. She mused upon the likelihood that she had already met Ranald Lindsay's sire at Court; it seemed this noble stature and proud bearing were very familiar.

"Perhaps I have—"

"I doubt it." He cut her off so abruptly, Merry was both stunned and insulted. Her temper flared as her little hand clutched tight the brooch, and she struggled to remain both civil and calm.

"Milord Lindsay," she began again, but much more firmly, so he might realize she would not brook another interruption. "I was en route to Whitehall, where I serve the queen. This shocking occurrence has quite upset my plans. I was already in Her Grace's disfavor for lingering er long at my sister's home."

"Then mayhap you should have hastened back to London sooner, Mistress Tanner."

Merry could not restrain a little gasp at his words. How dare this . . . this Highland oaf twist the circumstances to somehow blame her for the mishap!

"I will have you know, the queen shall hear of this outrage," she said, not entirely bluffing but also looking to get a reaction of some sort from the steely, reserved man. "When Her Majesty considers your brother's punishment, I pray she is more kindly disposed than I."

She saw a flicker of something in the dark eyes. "I will deal with Gilbert, milady. Stay out of it."

"Indeed and I will not, milord. How am I to be assured he shall receive any chastisement at all? You mistake my nature if you think I shall let matters slide and trust you to deal with the aftermath."

This time, she did get a reaction. His jaw seemed to tighten and his dark eyes were hard as flint upon her flushed face. "I would advise you not to pursue matters further, Mistress Tanner. Especially where my family is concerned."

"I see. Then perhaps I should let you explain to my betrothed why I did not arrive as planned at Court, and you may deal with Sir Wickham's ire!"

Something shifted in those dark, dark eyes, something so fleeting Merry was almost certain she imagined it.

"Wickham . . . of the Carlisle Wickhams?"

Merry nodded curtly. If nothing else, perhaps this ill-tempered Scottish lout would be impressed by her betrothed's status and humbly beg her apology. She almost snorted then. Nay, not this one. He enjoyed his lofty superiority far too much.

To her surprise, Ranald Lindsay smiled, a slow and rather impressive smile that made her heartbeat quicken despite her anger. Faith, Merry thought, but he was a toothsome fellow when he smiled, when those dark eyes betrayed something besides impatience or indifference. She had no reason to suspect his smile was anything other than a sudden change of heart toward her plight.

"Of course, you must allow me to personally escort you to Sir Wickham's residence," he informed her, and ignored the startled glance of Gilbert Lindsay who was listening but a few paces away.

"If you please, milord, I should prefer to return to Court and placate Her Grace first," Merry replied, though she was touched by his offer, even grudging as it must be. Perhaps Ranald Lindsay was not such a coldly deliberate man as she had first assumed. To be certain, he could charm a lady when he wished, and she offered him a small smile by way of gratitude.

His gaze met hers, never wavering. Merry felt suddenly breathless, and raised her right hand to her throat without thinking.

"What have you there, Mistress Tanner?"

Lindsay curiously regarded the circular object in her palm, which Merry had assumed was her pennanular brooch. To her surprise she found she held the red-gold raven amulet of her Irish ancestors, which Kat had pressed her into taking before she departed Falcon's Lair. Merry had promised to wear it but had no intention of draping such a primitive, pagan object over her fine gowns, and she had thrust it rather unceremoniously into her jewelry box the moment the coach was underway. She would not hurt Kat's feelings for the world, but the piece was simply too unusual for her tastes. She opened her palm and Ranald Lindsay regarded the amulet with a slight frown, his gaze traveling from the fierce raven carved into the gold to Merry's gray-green eyes.

" 'Tis but an amusing family memento," she replied somewhat awkwardly, sensing his curiosity rising by the moment. She hastily closed her fist about the amulet, startled by a little ripple of electricity that seemed to dart up her arm, similar to the crackling undercurrent of the air before a storm. She gave a nervous little laugh. "I daresay milord Wickham shall be forced to vastly improve upon my jewelry stocks when I arrive at Braidwood."

"Indeed." Ranald Lindsay's voice was suddenly quiet, almost speculative. Merry sensed dark thoughts roiling in the man's head, and wondered what cause she had given him to disapprove of her now. Ah, no matter. Soon enough she would be setting her dainty slipper on the charming garden paths of Whitehall again, planning a sweet rendezvous with some besotted young swain. One last innocent flirtation before she became Lady Wickham of Braidwood Manor. She smiled a little to herself, for 'twas far too easy to envision the dashing Ranald Lindsay as her handsome suitor, and if he presumed to steal a kiss amidst the brilliant blossoms, why, she was not certain she would protest. Not at all.

Chapter Four

Ran gazed down into the upturned face of Meredith Tanner and felt his insides clench, as if someone had delivered a sudden blow to his middle. There was nothing but a soft admiring light in her gray-green eyes, while all he could think of was Wickham. The man's name rang through his skull with the certainty of a pounding anvil. Blair's beautiful face flashed before his mind's eye, her sparkling blue eyes beckoning him with laughter, with love. Yet the last memory of the face he must carry forever in his heart was one of her still and pale, a marble figure sketched upon a cold stone bier.

The emotion sweeping over him was more than anger, less than rage. Rather 'twas an icy determination which must make his gaze as keen as the predatory wolf's, but Mistress Tanner seemed not to notice.

To his surprise, she even reached out and laid a little hand lightly on his arm. Like his Blair, she was petite, but this was no sturdy Highland lass. Her skin was white as the linen shirt Ran wore, a delicate tracing of blue veins visible just below the surface. Hands that had never toiled a day in their life, a redhead's porcelain complexion doubtless thus preserved by aid of costly potions and frivolous parasols. Ran barely refrained from shaking off her refined touch, it disgusted him so. She was everything he despised, the purest representation of a lazy, worthless, pampered lot of Tudor lapdogs. The only ones who might compete for the title were the equally pathetic followers of the Stuarts. He strove to maintain a neutral expression amid her tinkling laughter. Something about this woman aroused an emotion in him so dark and primitive he was afraid he might wrap his big hands around her neck and simply squeeze if he did not keep a tight rein on his actions at all times.

"La, milord, you are too quiet by half," Meredith remarked as she peered up at him from those darkly fringed, gray-green eyes. Eyes like the watered silk she wore, changeable like a Highland loch, reflecting blue sky one moment, stormy clouds the next. "Although I am sorely pressed to reach Whitehall, even I can see the humor in the situation."

Ran forced a grudging smile to his lips. He felt like a hungry wolf trying to grin, expecting her certain and sudden fear. Her eyes gleamed with mirth and she seemed oblivious as ever to the dark undercurrents swirling beneath his surface. To distract them both, he returned his attentions to the amulet she gripped in her other hand.

"A most curious item you have there, Mistress Tanner," he said.

She hesitated for some reason. "Aye, I suppose 'tis. A family heirloom, you might say." She made no offer to display the objet d'art further, but rather closed her fingers about it as if trying to shield it from his gaze. "I fear my jewelry was scattered when the coach overturned."

Her attempt at changing the subject was obvious, but Ran let it pass. He nodded and turned toward the wrecked vehicle, quickly surmising it was not worth the effort of trying to upright it again. The coach was a casualty of Gil's mischief, though fortunately nothing else was. Had Mistress Tanner or her driver been killed, the day would have ended very soberly indeed.

Ran's gaze drifted back to his little brother. Thus far Gil had escaped confrontation, though his posture clearly showed he anticipated the lecture to come. Hugo was still off tending the coachman, and Ran took the opportunity for a word aside with his sibling. In fact, he strode right over and stood before the youth until Gilbert could no longer stare at the ground, sky, or upended coach in an effort to avoid Ran's piercing stare.

"Gil, what the hell provoked this rash act?" he demanded, keeping his voice low enough so Meredith Tanner could not overhear their exchange. He read defiance in the violet-blue eyes which finally met his and felt anger lick at him again. 'Twas not the sort of icy anger he felt toward the woman and what she represented, but rather outrage tinged with a bit of uncertainty.

Ran was never certain how to handle Gilbert. His confidence was undermined by the fact his little brother was so vastly different in nature and outlook than himself. Gil delighted in mischief, in laughter, in life itself. Scolding did little good because he was oft shattered by the slightest criticism. His mischievous nature bore no trace of malice, and Ran was unused to understanding much of anything save vengeance or his own quiet despair.

Gil shrugged at Ran's question, though even he was not foolish enough to push his big brother much further. "I just wanted to get out and see the world a bit."

"A bit? Is that what you call up and disappearing in the middle of the night on a foolish lark to the godforsaken wilds of Wales."

"Oh, Hugo and I didn't come directly south," Gilbert corrected him promptly. "We went roundabout, by way of Glasgow."

Ran's fists clenched at his sides, merely to prevent him from grabbing Gil and throttling him senseless. Which was worse, he wondered, a lad who lived in his head playing at the dangerous game of a dashing highwayman, or a feather-headed court bawd with neither the brains nor the simple instinct to realize she had contracted herself a matrimonial union with the deadliest snake this side of the border? He wasn't entirely sure which one deserved the harsher lecture. In any case, lectures were Darra's specialty, not his.

"However you came to be here, 'tis pointless," Ran curtly replied. Gilbert looked subdued, or at least momentarily contrite; a glance aside at Meredith Tanner revealed her looking on, at an obvious loss but appearing no less determined to see justice done.

The proper thing to do, the chivalrous course of action, would be to escort Mistress Tanner to London posthaste, or at least see her safely settled in a nearby inn whilst he or Gilbert or Hugo rode ahead with a message to the queen. 'Twas the ultimate irony, Ran mused, flicking an assessing gaze over the young woman's proud posture, handling Sir Jasper's betrothed with kid gloves whilst his own wife had been subject to such indignities. Sweet Jesu, he almost lost his fragile grip on sanity just thinking of it.

Blair's sweet face flashed before his mind's eye, her serenity mocking him. Or mayhap it was Mistress Tanner's cool, rain-colored eyes that touched a nerve as she regarded him with obvious impatience.

"I see I have little choice except to trust these mischief makers will be dealt with eventually," she said. "You should know, the coach is not mine nor Her Grace's. It belongs to my uncle, who will surely demand some sort of reparation."

"As I assured you is forthcoming," Ran bit out, the curt edge to his voice causing an auburn eyebrow to arch on her heart-shaped face. He sensed Gilbert's wince and added for his brother's benefit, "Ahh, I wonder how many of the neighbor's stables need mucking . . . and how many 'twill take to earn out such an elegant vehicle."

" 'Twas an accident!" Gil protested.

"Does that make the consequences any less?"

"Well, nobody was hurt, not really . . ." Gil cast an anxious glance in Hugo's direction, reassuring himself that the driver was up and about at least, leaning against his childhood companion in at least a semiconscious state.

The redhead gasped faintly. "Not hurt? Ohh, you wicked little knave—"

Ran's hard look quelled her outburst. "I shall deal with this matter, Mistress Tanner. Perhaps you should glance through the coach and retrieve whatever valuables you wish to take along."

Merry could hardly ignore the note of censure in Lindsay's voice and she bristled. How dare he rebuke her, when 'twas his own scurvy relative who had caused her undue trauma. She tossed her head and turned away, biting back a retort she knew would only cause those dark eyes to harden further and his already chilly manner to turn to ice. Faith, she had no notion what she had done to cause him any distress, other than challenge his authority in matters of discipline when 'twas already quite clear he had no intention of dealing with the young ruffians beyond a token scolding.

She glanced at the amulet clutched in her hand, wondering again what had possessed Kat to press it upon her at the last moment, then she shrugged and slipped the cord over her head. A practical enough girl, she would not risk losing a family heirloom. She gathered up her rumpled skirts with some measure of dignity and returned to the coach, regarding the wreckage with a mixture of trepidation and determination. The thick, slippery mud sucked at her already ruined slippers as she delicately picked her way through the glop, and sensing several amused gazes on her rigid back, she kept her head high. She would not be humiliated by a lot of crude Scots.

Merry reminded herself of her royal connections as she leaned over the coach's frame, silently seething at the predicament she was in. Not only would Her Majesty be furious, but Gilbert Lindsay's antics had cost her the first acquaintance of her fiancé. The next time she saw Sir Jasper Wickham, 'twould be at the altar. By then 'twould be too late to beg off, should she find him displeasing. Not that she would, for she had seen his likeness rendered in several miniatures and paintings, and he was rumored to be as gallant as he was fair. Merry had agreed to the arranged match with only the faintest of concerns.

Her parents would never force her to wed anyone; her mother especially carried some quaint beliefs about love and destiny, but Merry had been more sensibly raised at Court and knew contracted marriages, made for practical and political reasons, were both a necessity and oft turned out quite well.

Upon her union with Wickham, her parent's growing trading empire would be guaranteed a foothold in the border region, and yet another Tanner mark would be laid upon the land. Her little brothers and her own future sons would be assured of decent inheritances. Wickham himself gained a dowry that was quite considerable by now, no small boon given the amount of funds required to sustain a man at Court. Merry had heard he was as fond of little luxuries as she was, a man not averse to spending his last groat on an elegant, pinked and slashed suit or frivolous costume for a masquerade.

A glance back over her shoulder revealed the contrast between her noble fiancé and someone like Ranald Lindsay. Peer or not, the rugged Scot was hardly fit for Court, not because of his countrified wardrobe but rather his churlish manners. Lindsay was not the sort to make a gallant leg to any woman, much less whisper sweet compliments in her ear. Merry sensed any proposals of an intimate nature would be as blunt and curt as the man himself, and though she normally admired practicality, for some reason this realization irked her.

She was not used to any man dismissing her so lightly. Granted, she was not reckoned a beauty, but her charm and wit and position with the queen had always assured her a bevy of admirers. Lindsay seemed unimpressed by her status and thus far she had no opportunity to charm him—not that she wished to, Merry firmly assured herself. He was scarcely deserving of recognition, much less such an honor. She sniffed and turned her attentions to gathering up what few items had been thrown free and she could reach. There were several small cases containing personal effects and precious jewelry she was determined to retrieve now, and she decided the men could handle the larger of her luggage. Fortunately she had traveled lightly for her impromptu trip to Wales, else the half-dozen suitcases should have easily multiplied thrice over.

Looking at Jem, she saw the driver was clearly in no condition to lift luggage or anything else. He leaned against the brawny Hugo, blinking as if still somewhat disoriented in the wake of their wild ride. Merry easily stepped into a role of control, the same she had adopted when organizing the household at Falcon's Lair. Indeed, she felt most comfortable when delegating tasks to others.

She turned, skirts still held up out of the mud. She felt a perverse tingle of pleasure when she found Ranald Lindsay's gaze on her again, though no smile softened the corners of his mouth. His dark eyes were inscrutable, as if he sought some explanation for her actions in her appearance. She nodded shortly in acknowledgment. "I will recover what I can, milord, but stronger shoulders will be needed for the baggage."

"Aye." He broke their matched gazes by glancing at his younger brother. " 'Tis the first act of atonement you can make, Gilbert."

The youth sighed but nodded with resignation. "Where shall we put the luggage? It cannot all fit on three horses."

"If needs be, you can ferry it to Whitehall a piece at a time," Merry put in a trifle sharply. She ignored Gilbert Lindsay's pained look and tried not to decipher Ranald's glance. " 'Tis the least you can do to make amends, I vow."

She tore her gaze from Ranald's grim expression. Maybe 'twas best not to know what the brooding Scot thought. She picked a few small, scattered items out of the muck and slogged back to join the others. Already the sky had darkened again and the threat of more rain was imminent.

Ranald glanced at the roiling clouds above them. " 'Twould appear nature would hasten our decision."

"Decision?" Merry looked at him.

"Aye. Shelter is advisable, but the nearest town is some miles distant."

"Mayhap someone could ride on for help, and have a coach sent back for the others?"

Ranald regarded Merry as if she was a feather-headed female, and she bristled under his faintly amused air. "By the time they returned, 'twould be long dark and travel all but impossible. I will take your suggestion under advisory, Mistress Tanner, but I believe the wisest course would be for all of us to forge on together."

"To London, naturally."

Ranald did not reply, but he had already turned back to Gilbert. "Hugo's mount is already taxed to the limit with his bulk, so you shall ride double on Finegas with Mistress Tanner's man."

Merry was still chafing a bit, annoyed, when Ranald turned and went to fetch the big brown gelding he had hobbled to a young oak. The animal was as shaggy as his master, its coat still coarse from the Highland winter, one of the sturdy ponies bred for a rugged environs without consideration for beauty. Merry wrinkled her nose; she was used to her uncle's fine stables of horseflesh, and this beast was surely as ill-tempered as its owner. As if on cue, the gelding tossed his great ugly head, its eye rolling so the white showed, and she took a step backward as Ranald led it over before her.

"Mistress Tanner, I offer you the ease of the only conveyance available at present," he said, and Merry frowned for she was certain she detected a mocking note in his smooth speech.

She eyed the beast rather warily. "I am not so certain 'tis the wisest course, milord."

"Please." His invitation was kindly enough, but his manner never softened. "I assure you, Uar has never bitten without provocation."

Had another spoken those same words, Merry might have smiled, but she was unsure if Lindsay jested or not. "Methinks I would prefer to walk."

His dark eyebrow arched, but without another word he walked past her, leading the horse, and paused beside the coach only long enough to retrieve something from the depths of the upturned passenger's side. He turned and tossed something at her. Merry scarcely had time to react and the velvet cloak glanced off her skirts, but she snagged it at the last second before it ended up in the mud. She stared at him, in silent outrage.

''I believe you may need it, Mistress Tanner. And soon.'' Ranald nodded curtly at her before mounting his steed in one swift motion. He settled into place, his strong tanned legs lightly gripping the gelding's sides, his posture as one born to the saddle. He tugged the hardy animal's coarse mane, and it obeyed him on cue, wheeling in a half-circle and plodding off through the thick mud in the general direction of what passed for a road.

With shaking fingers, Merry tossed the cloak around her shoulders and drew the hood up over her head, already feeling the cooling gusts of the incoming storm fast on their heels. It started raining, fat drops glancing off the fine velvet. Mud was already oozing up around her fine slippers; she knew them to be ruined and decided in a fit of pique that Ranald Lindsay and his brat of a younger brother were wholly responsible. Never mind. She would be recompensed in the end, certainly, and if an apology must be won by the point of a blade, so be it.

With that comforting and rather delicious thought held firmly in place, she set off in the deep tracks left by Lindsay's mount, determined one ill-bred Scot would never have opportunity to tell others *this* English rose was not made of the hardiest stock.

Chapter Five

Bitter wind sliced through Merry, tearing at her cloak and skirts. The storm rushed down upon the straggling travelers like a dark wraith, howling and plucking at what courage remained. She clutched her hood beneath her chin with frozen fingers, squinting through the downpour at the figures ahead. Jem rode half slumped over Gilbert Lindsay's gray mare, the younger man steadying him from behind. Though not seriously injured, the driver had obviously taken a beating during the accident. Merry's gaze moved to Hugo, whose solid bulk dwarfed his little Highland pony, his legs nearly dragging the ground. Twice already Hugo had stopped his mount and gestured, almost pleading, for Merry to ride instead of him, but she set her jaw and shook her head.

Riding would merely give Ranald Lindsay something to jeer about later, and she sensed the brooding Highland laird would like nothing more than another reason to dislike her. Though she had yet to uncover the source of his antagonism, she sensed it as clearly as if he had called her a Tudor strumpet before the entire Court. One had only to feel those piercing dark eyes fix on their spine, to know how it felt to be disdained and despised.

Merry shivered, skirts swaying to a halt as she encountered another miniature lake in the road. Within moments of her pausing, the others vanished into the deepening mist which had rolled down from the Welsh hills with the oncoming twilight. She heard a murmur of voices and assumed she could catch up easily enough. A moment's rest, surely, was not amiss. Her legs ached, muscles tense from the cold and damp, and she eyed a nearby copse longingly.

Just a respite from the rain would be welcome, so she picked up her hoops again, and picked her way through the mire, having long ago decided 'twas best not to even think about how she must look after the events of this day. Wearily Merry ducked beneath some low-hanging branches, then eased herself into a small clearing where the tree cover lessened the rain to an occasional droplet. She pushed back her hood and shook out her hair, feeling the damp locks tumble free of what little remained of her coiffure. Mist curled about her, and had she not been so exhausted and miserable, she might have been frightened by the deepening silence of the darkened wood.

Instead, she leaned against a young alder, letting the tree serve for support. Certainly there was none other she could count upon. Were Sir Jasper here, Merry assured herself, he would have gallantly tossed his cloak in the mire as Raleigh had for the queen, thus preserving her delicate little slippers and her dignity in one fell swoop.

Whereas the laird of Lindsay abandoned a lady to her own devices. Merry sniffed at the unbidden reminder of her adverse circumstances, conveniently forgetting 'twas she who had refused the offer of a steed.

A dark figure stepped from the curtain of mist before her eyes, startling Merry. She was unaware of another presence there at all until he spoke.

"Mistress Tanner, are you unwell?"

Merry might have imagined concern in Lindsay's deep voice, but knew better. Her challenging gaze met his level one, and for a moment they simply regarded each other with a wary, mutual respect.

"Nay, sirrah. I but decided to avail myself of a break from the enforced march."

Merry spoke lightly, but her tone betrayed her pique. She no longer cared what Lindsay thought of her; indeed, she was eager to be quit of his company as well.

Something suspiciously close to a smile touched the corners of his mouth. Beautifully shaped lips, she noted almost resentfully, the lower one full and slightly reddened as if a bee had stung it and flew away. His dark hair glistened with rain, and even at a distance she caught the scent of him, hauntingly familiar now though they had only the briefest of acquaintances.

"I must needs remind the lady she had the option of riding."

Aye, trust him to toss that in her face! Merry stiffened, her gaze never leaving his. "I assume I delay your journey, milord?"

"Not at all. I have, in fact, taken the liberty of sending the others ahead. I fear your man is not doing well."

"Jem looked uncommonly pale," Merry agreed, frowning with concern.

"Precisely why I instructed Gilbert and Hugo to ride on and see him settled for the night in a village or inn. Warmth is what he needs now, warmth and rest and plenty of quiet."

She nodded. 'Twas difficult, nigh impossible, to ignore Ranald Lindsay looming over her, making her feel absurdly petite by comparison. Something about the man set her heart racing and yet raised an instinctive alarm, causing mixed feelings and confusing her senses. Perhaps 'twas the intimacy of the misty little clearing, the pressing of heavy air around them swirling her up in a maelstrom of emotion.

"We should forge on as well." Merry was dismayed at the sound of her own voice, breathless and a bit too rushed to pass for the cool mien she was renowned for at Court. She glimpsed a flash of something in Lindsay's dark eyes at her remark; was it amusement?

"I quite agree. Travel will only worsen with the dastardly Welsh weather, I fear."

"Surely Scotland cannot be any vast improvement," Merry replied with some asperity, and when he chuckled a little at her remark she was quite surprised.

"Have you ever been to Scotland, lass?"

"Lass?" Merry looked at him, unsure if he meant to insult her or not, but quite unwilling to be mocked. She shook her head. "Please do not call me thusly. Nay, I've no need nor desire to cross the border until this year."

"Until the betrothal with . . . what was your fine lord's name?"

"Sir Jasper Wickham." Merry did not attempt to conceal the annoyance in her tone this time, almost certain he was mocking her. Quite good at it, he was, too, she conceded with a silent annoyance. Those dark eyes gleamed with triumph, yet nothing but the smoothest of words escaped his lips.

"Ah, the esteemed Sir Wickham." Ranald nodded and managed to project an appropriately sincere air. She succumbed to the urge to bait him in turn and looked in the direction of a stirring dark shadow in the mists.

"Your ill-natured mount, I presume?"

He laughed shortly. "Aye, lass—ahh, milady. Resist though you may the notion of riding, at this late hour 'tis only sensible. Already the sun races us to the inn."

Merry knew he was right and clamped down the urge to mount a spirited, if token, resistance. She glanced at her muddied skirts, ruined slippers and sighed. She ached from head to toe; this miserable damp did nothing but accentuate her misery. Surely even an uncouth Scot was halfway bearable under such trying circumstances.

"Pray assist me then." Doing a passable imitation of Her Grace, Merry hiked her skirts and farthingale a bit and half stomped, half strode toward the tethered horse. It shied at her sudden emergence from the mist, but Lindsay was right there, soothing the nervous animal with a surprisingly gentle hand. Merry noticed his fingers were not blunt and thick like a peasant's, but long and tapered, like those of a musician. It contrasted with his roughshod nature, and for a moment she felt almost breathless again. A kilt-clad warrior with an artist's hands. Why did such a realization send little shudders through her?

Before she realized it, Ranald Lindsay had circled her waist with those remarkable hands and boosted her easily into the saddle. She was forced by necessity of the farthingale to ride sidesaddle, and the seat was not suited for such, but Merry was a passable horsewoman. Her Majesty and Uncle Kit would have stood for nothing less. Every Tanner born was a neck-or-nothing rider, and she smiled a little as she supposed Lindsay assumed her a helpless bit of fluff clinging terrified to a horse's mane.

A second later he joined Merry, lithely swinging into position behind her, strong thighs again gripping the gelding's sides, his hips seeming to meld against her backside even through layers of material. Against her will, Merry gasped and gripped the gelding's mane, and the instant she did so she sensed his amusement.

Ranald Lindsay laughed low, in a rich baritone which rolled through her like the thunder in the distance, and before she could debate the wisdom of riding with a wild Scot, he had touched his heels to the horse's ribs and they bolted into the mist.

As Uar lapsed into a canter over marshy ground, Ran steadied his passenger with one hand circling her waist. A tiny waist, he noted with an irritation he couldn't fully explain, feeling the smooth ridges of whalebone stays blocking any definition of the flesh beneath. Meredith Tanner was like a female caged in steel and silk, enticingly near, yet beyond all boundaries just the same. For a painful moment, he imagined 'twas Blair he held in his arms, her flaxen hair spilling over her shoulders and her sweet laughter rippling over them like the wind.

A deep shudder coursed through him, causing his arm to

tighten about Merry Tanner's waist, and she let out a little mewl of pain.

''Forgive me,'' Ran muttered, immediately removing himself from any deliberate contact with the woman, only praying she wasn't such a needle-wit as to slide off the saddle when they hit a rough spot. Grudgingly he conceded Merry Tanner appeared to have some grasp of riding, as evidenced by her natural posture. Her tension came not from Uar's unpredictable nature, he suspected, but the intimate contact necessitated by riding double with himself.

She was not alone in her discomfort. His loins betrayed his need, his hunger after months of denial and suppression. After Blair's death, he had not succumbed to any woman's wiles, though there were certainly a share of fair lasses upon his demesne. Ran's treacherous body reminded him he was not dead yet, though his heart had been burned and buried with his beloved wife and child. He set his jaw, feeling anger rise as his conscience warred with base physical needs.

How could he even look upon another woman, especially some court-bred tart who simpered about the magnificent rat she was to marry, a man spawned from the bowels of hell who had enticed Blair Lindsay to her untimely end. Wickham's fiancée. The realization set him to shaking, not with fear but rather a cold, deadly rage all too familiar over the past months.

How ironic life was. He had Wickham's woman in his arms, a frilly Tudor rose as worthless as the snake himself. How easy 'twould be to simply lift his big hands and wrap them about her slender neck. Ran considered this course only briefly; 'twas not in his nature to murder innocents, even a lass as vexing as this red-haired virago. Besides, Wickham would not be truly injured by such an act. Shocked, perhaps, and maybe a trifle disturbed even, but in his self-absorbed way, Sir Jasper would quickly forget and move on.

Nay, the means to wound Wickham lay not in futile acts of desperation, but in slow, measured humiliation. He was a man whose reputation depended much upon public opinion, and the best way to strike at his black heart was to wound his ego.

Ran's lips thinned in a calculating smile. He imagined he held a sword to Wickham's groin, and with one quick thrust he could render a *Sassenach* fiend forever impotent.

Merry was never aware when she nodded off, but what surprised her most was awaking with a jolt to find herself nestled intimately against Lord Lindsay. His muscular arm encircled her waist, and she leaned precariously to one side, her head cradled against his broad chest. She resisted a first impulse to jerk free, and instead inhaled slowly as her mind wildly sought any escape from looming humiliation. There didn't seem to be any.

It seemed they had traveled leagues already, and it had been dark for several hours. At least the rain had stopped, surrendering its hold on the heavens to a waxing moon bright with promise and a web of stars that tangled above them like a jeweled strand. Merry caught a whiff of saltwater and prayed 'twas Bristol Channel at least. Weariness gripped her like a stony hand, and she slumped back against Ranald despite all her resolve. His sturdy frame seemed to absorb the worst impact of Uar's jolting gait, cushioning the shock to her already bruised body.

His deep voice rumbled against her hair. "Almost there, Mistress Tanner."

Merry nodded, not trusting herself to speak. Something about his presence, the masculine tones reverberating through her, set her quivering with both anticipation and an unfamiliar trepidation. Never had she felt so wary of a man, but then Lindsay was no ordinary man.

"I confess I shall be glad to be quit of this roughshod beastie," Merry said, attempting a carefree little laugh she did not feel. "Remind me, milord, to recommend my uncle as a source of fine, smooth-gaited steeds."

"Only if you address me as Ranald henceforth, and dispense with all manner of title."

Merry twisted a bit in the saddle so she might look at him. By moonlight his features were darkly handsome, almost saturnine. She quelled an urge to shiver and instead injected mirth into her tone. "But y'are by rights a peer! 'Tis unseemly I should not acknowledge your status."

"More my bane." Something flashed in his eyes, though his gaze remained steadfast ahead, not meeting hers. "Better yet, keep it simple. Ran will even suffice for now."

Ranald . . . Ran . . . a name as harsh and unforgiving as the rugged mountains from whence this dark Scot issued, Merry thought. She conceded his request, though it did not rest easily with her courtly upbringing.

"Very well, Ranald . . . how much longer to the inn? I thought 'twas but a few hours?"

She peered ahead into the inky darkness, judging the emptiness of their surroundings by the lack of any light.

He did not answer for a moment. "I remember you blamed me for missing an encounter with your betrothed."

"Not you specifically, of course. Your little brother—bent on mischief, that reckless, would-be, incompetent Highway Jack."

He chuckled low. "An apt description of young Gil. You ken he meant no mischief?"

"Ken?" Merry glanced at him, the Scots dialect taking her by surprise. She sensed he worked hard to match her precise English, and by the way his hand balled under her rib cage, knew he was annoyed by the little slip.

"You know he meant no harm, Mistress Tanner. A cad's trick, to be sure, but Gil has not a malicious bone in his body, lass."

"Merry, please." It seemed only fair since he had invited her to indulge in similar familiarities, and she disliked the playful spin he put on "lass." "As for your brother, we shall see." She kept her tone cool and noncommittal, expecting a plea or demand she be soft on the wayward knave. None came.

Instead, they jogged on for several more miles in relative silence, until Merry remembered he had not answered her last question.

"The inn, milor— Ranald. How far?"

"We are not going to the inn."

"Nay?" Merry was surprised and no little disconcerted by this news. This time, she did wrench herself halfway round to stare at him. "Then where? Directly to Whitehall?"

"No."

His curt response did not bode well for her temper. "Wherever are you taking me?"

"The border."

"Border? You mean, north?"

Merry heard herself stammering like a little idiot, or worse yet, Penelope Rich, and flushed with frustration. Something about this man pushed her to the edge. Mayhap his refusal to deal with her directly. Whatever the source of this irritation, she was determined he would not get the best of her.

"Indeed, I note we've changed directions. The moon was rising in the opposite direction when we left the glen." Merry strove to remain calm, not easy considering she risked provoking a man who controlled not only the horse, but her very life at the moment.

"Aye. It occurred to me you risk the queen's certain wrath, Merry, for your tardiness, and also you have missed the one opportunity to meet your intended bridegroom before the ceremony. I but strive to set matters aright."

Merry frowned a little, not understanding where he led her. "Then where are we going?"

"I am taking you to your betrothed."

Surprised, Merry did not quite know how to respond. Licking her lips, she carefully replied, "I see . . . you curry Sir Wickham's favor, then."

"Curry his . . ." Ranald started laughing, then abruptly went still and serious again. "Nay. Not at all."

"I am certain he would welcome your chivalry, sir, but Her Grace is not inclined to be so generous."

"Precisely why I decided you should not be subjected to such an intense interrogation when the accident 'twas hardly your fault. If I returned you to Whitehall posthaste as you wish,

Her Majesty's ire has but one focus. Time, and distance, will soften her mood.''

Merry considered his words. 'Twas true, Elizabeth was renowned for her vile temper. Like the proverbial adder, she often struck, blindly and without any particular target. Merry knew the queen must be incensed already by her failure to appear at Whitehall by the appointed hour, and once her slippers set foot in the place, she would be fair game to royal wrath.

Merry shuddered. She had witnessed firsthand what damage Tudor temper might do, with the executions of Mary Queen of Scots and others. Her own father had narrowly escaped beheading on Tower Green. One did not toy with the fierce Tudor monarchs. Even a favorite such as Devereux might fall with the simple expiration of royal grace.

'' 'Tis a point of consideration, to be sure,'' she replied, aware of him awaiting her response. ''Yet how worse her wrath, upon discovering I avoided a lecture by fleeing north with a stranger? And a man at that? Faith, sirrah, you should know by now Her Grace does not tolerate any sort of scandal among the ranks of her ladies.''

''Naturally I have taken that into consideration,'' Ranald answered. ''The accident provides more than ample excuse for any erratic behavior. There are also three other witnesses, besides ourselves, who can attest the vehicle was damaged irreparably. Perhaps Her Majesty's position will soften when she hears your desire to meet your betrothed exceeded that of personal comfort.''

Despite her cross mood, Merry chuckled a little. If only Lindsay knew! She was accounted a spoiled chit in her own family, and a cheerful but exacting taskmistress at Court. Her tiring woman, Jane, oft remarked her mistress would not so much as set foot in the hall on the days the servants emptied the slop buckets. 'Twas true enough, Merry tended toward the fastidious end of the scale and preferred creature comforts to rough accommodations. Right now she wanted nothing more than to soak in a hot tub for hours, then sit curled up in her favorite chair before a blazing hearth whilst Jane brushed out her hair and rubbed it with a square of silk until it shone like crimson wine.

She sighed, realizing 'twas a bit late for arguing over which direction they were headed. Already they had traveled a goodly distance, and truth to tell she was more than a little curious about meeting Sir Jasper. 'Twould not bode well to turn up on her betrothed's doorstep bedraggled and exhausted, however, and Merry wracked her mind for the solution. Mayhap Falcon's Lair. Nay, she decided, Kat and her husband deserved their privacy after months of painful separation, and besides Merry had no desire to see her hard work all undone. Doubtless the moment she had left, the lackadaisical servants slipped into their cozy procrastination again.

"How far is your own residence from Braidwood, milord?" Merry asked, forgetting his request she not adopt a formal title of address.

The arm resting about her waist tightened a bit, as if in silent rebuke. "Not very far." She heard him inhale deeply, as if he might say something more. Yet the silence weighed like a hundred stone between them. She quietly, yet firmly, began again.

"Would you estimate within three days' ride?"

"Aye."

"Perhaps your lady wife would not find an unexpected guest too vexing?"

Merry sensed, rather than saw, tension rippling throughout his broad frame. For a moment, she half expected him to hurl her bodily from Uar's saddle. Though she did not understand the source of such a vehement reaction, she could hardly mistake it.

"I live alone at Auchmull, but for kinsmen and servants."

"Oh." Merry sought for the appropriate words, instinctively grasping the underlying message that she was not to pursue the matter any further. "I trust some of the retainers are female?"

"Enough to safeguard your reputation, aye." A hint of amusement colored his tone at last, and Merry relaxed a little. "I take it you would like to attend to some manner of . . . ahhh . . . restoration before you meet your future husband?"

"Precisely." Merry refused to be embarrassed over what might appear such a frivolous female notion. When Ranald laughed and agreed they might retire to Auchmull first, she felt instead a flush of triumph. For the first time since their paths had crossed, she and the Scottish wolf were seeing eye to eye.

Chapter Six

Ran gazed at the redheaded woman curled in his tartan, where she slept on the damp ground. Firelight flickered across her features, burnishing her hair to living fire and sculpting alabaster angles from her cheekbones. A stray wisp of fiery hair clung to one cheek, adding an oddly poignant reminder of a sleeping bairn. Ran looked away, before he might find himself regarding Merry Tanner as anything but the self-centered little *Sassenach* bitch she was. Hell, not only had she demanded his tartan, but she insisted he stay awake, tend the fire, and kept watch for brigands as well.

Not that he could sleep. Ran leaned back against the large boulder, his gaze drifting to the night sky instead. He remembered bits and pieces from his lessons as a lad at Edzell, and the mighty bull winked the red eye of Aldebaran at him as if confirming his memories. If only real life was as logical, as comforting as the old myths and legends. Ran had evolved into somewhat of a legend himself by now, and the stories of the fierce Wolf of Badanloch were ominous enough that Mistress Tanner should have run screaming into the wood whilst she had the chance. He chuckled softly at the thought, sparing a glance for the tousled-haired lass. At times she reminded him of an auburn-tressed elf, with her sharp little features and small frame. Her temper, however, was as fierce as any Highlander's, he suspected. He had yet to test it fully.

They were several days' ride yet from the border, and Auchmull. It amazed him still she had agreed so readily to the journey, but then 'twas obvious she was anxious to lay eyes upon her betrothed. No cost too high, no journey too far for the cause of true love, Ran thought bitterly. He felt his gaze drifting once more from the stars and found his attention focused on the sleeping woman. Wickham's woman. Sweet Jesu, here was his chance.

The idea had only flirted with him before, but Ran felt it solidifying by the moment. Meredith Tanner was completely dependent upon him for her survival. He had shared his water, the better portion of Hertha's Forfar Bridies, and now the warmth of a Highland tartan. Her reputation, if not her entire family's, rested in his hands. He could shame this lass, and Wickham by association. If a moment's conscience flared, Ran shrugged it aside. He had no personal quarrel with the Tanners. Mayhap a fine match would be lost, but in the end he would save this redheaded vixen untold years of agony.

Meredith Tanner was not displeasing to look upon. Not a ravishing beauty by any means, but fair enough and sweetly curved in all the right places. His gaze traveled downward, where her hips lay hidden beneath the colorful tartan. 'Twas hard to judge through a damned farthingale, but they seemed sleek enough for bed sport yet broad enough for bearing a man's bairns.

As if sensing his perusal, Merry's eyes suddenly snapped open. By moonlight her irises were silvery green, almost iridescent. She did not seem alarmed, but rather confused by her surroundings. She sat up awkwardly on one hip, blinking at Ran somewhat dazedly.

"How long did I sleep?" she asked.

"Several hours. 'Tis almost dawn." He gestured at the faint blush on the horizon. "Hungry?"

Merry nodded. "Parched, too." She ran a hand over her disheveled hair as if to magically restore her coiffure, but already the blazing locks had slipped to her waist and the ends defiantly curled there from the lingering humidity.

Ran rose and retrieved a soft leather water bag from Uar's saddle, returned and handed it to her without a word. She nodded gratefully, uncorking it without the faintest evidence of hesitation such as she'd displayed last night. She drank, while Ran watched the slim column of her throat. He wondered if any man had dared taste that rarefied ivory flesh before. He knew the queen demanded absolute loyalty from her ladies in waiting, with chastity as the ultimate end. He also knew of the Court's reputation for corrupting innocents. Into which category did Merry Tanner fall?

There was an obvious coquetry in her manner of speech, laughter, even something so minute as a slanted glance from those gray-green eyes. She had been carefully coached, or else emerged, into a state of womanly graces, complete with the talent to pout, rail, or cry at the drop of a pin. Ran detested such artifices. False emotions were worse even than the unholy rage which gripped him whenever he thought of his dead wife and child. At least his rage was honest. As keen and glittering as the blade he wished to drive through Wickham's black heart.

At the moment, however, Merry did not appear either coy or simpering. The delicate skin beneath her eyes was bruised from exhaustion and her cheeks hollowed with shadow. When she finished drinking, he fetched a makeshift meal to break their fast, handing two barley bannocks to her without a word. She nibbled cautiously at the dry bread between sips of water while Ran tended to Uar.

Merry finished the humble meal, rose and drew Lindsay's tartan closer about her shoulders, shivering in the humid morning air. A glance at her soiled skirts revealed they were damp as well, ruined beyond repair. How Jane would scold! Her tiring woman seemed to take personal pride in her lady's wardrobe, and became quite a termagant whenever her authority in such matters was usurped.

Merry's attentions moved from a quick study of the makeshift camp to Ranald Lindsay. His back faced her as he resaddled his mount. Even without his tartan, clad only in breeks and a bishop-sleeved white shirt, wavy dark hair spilling over his broad shoulders, he was ruggedly handsome. With a sudden burst of vanity, Merry wished she did not appear so rumpled and weary. She had never traveled well, even in the queen's retinue with the utmost comfort of a luxurious coach and frequent breaks. Lindsay must suppose her as fragile as the wildflowers Uar demolished with one wide swathe of his ugly head, as the horse greedily grazed a fresh patch of ground where his master led him.

'Twas too tempting to whimper about things he could not change, like the weather, but Merry vowed she would not give him the satisfaction of succumbing to female ploys. If she was to gain and keep the respect of such a stalwart man, she must call upon her own internal strength. Just as she was thus resolved, he turned suddenly and captured her in his dark gaze.

"Mistress Tanner?"

Ranald extended a large hand with those artist's fingers so she might mount Uar with his assistance. Merry felt the breath leave her in a silent rush, and without a word stepped forward and laid her smaller, paler hand in his. He glanced at the point where their flesh made contact as if he, too, was startled by an invisible tingle racing up his spine.

A moment later, she was safely settled in the saddle, her ruined skirts arranged as neatly as if she rode in a royal procession. Habit was a hard thing to break, though Merry sensed her riding companion's mixed amusement and chagrin. Why bother to act a lady when one presently resembled a London bawd?

"We shall cover ground more quickly, now the rain has fled." Ranald's remark did not require a response, but Merry offered one anyway.

" 'Tis fortunate, too, for I confess I am weary of the journey already."

"Or the company?"

She smiled a little at the touch of asperity in his tone. "Nay, Ranald, you have not given me any cause for grief. Indeed, but for the timeliness of your rescue, I daresay I might still be sprawled within that coach, while the gentle Welsh rain poured down upon me."

He laughed, a spontaneous and warm sound. It rumbled through his chest and hence Merry's by proximity, as by necessity she was pressed back against him to make room for her voluminous skirts. She liked his laugh, when 'twas not tinged by ugly sarcasm or scorn. Was this Lindsay not so dour-natured, she could see him winning hands and hearts at Court.

They rode for several hours, stopping only for brief rests and another barley bannock. At first it did not occur to Merry to wonder why Lindsay avoided the inns and villages scattered throughout the Welsh province, but when she spied a distant spiral of smoke and sighed longingly, it seemed he read her mind.

"A fire and hot food must seem very tempting right now, I am sure." He pronounced "very" more like "verra," another unconscious reversion to his Scots heritage.

"Oh, aye! You cannot imagine. I could soak for a week in a hot tub, and eat with both hands all the while."

Again a hint of humor in his chuckle. "If you ate so enthusiastically, you should never fit into such an elegant gown again."

"Formerly elegant." Merry frowned, touching the soiled fabric.

"Precisely the reason why I dare not expose you to public scrutiny, Merry. Certainly gossip travels quickly, even in these rural parts. Eventually word would reach the queen of your being seen in such a state of disarray, riding double with a barbarian and disheveled in a most alarming manner."

"I had not thought of that. S'truth, Her Grace would be enraged."

Merry decided 'twas most considerate of Lindsay to protect her reputation, despite her niggling suspicion he gained great amusement from regarding her as some sort of dim-witted little prude. She shuddered at the mental image of her walking into an inn full of strangers on Lord Lindsay's arm, her skirts torn and muddied, wearing the man's tartan for warmth and modesty.

Nay, 'twould never do. Word of a red-haired woman with the Scottish laird would reach the queen's ear eventually, and none of Merry's charms would serve to soften Her Majesty's opinion on the matter. She would be branded a strumpet, Lindsay's whore. Merry shivered, for to lose reputation at Court was a fate worse than death.

Her worst fears materialized later in the afternoon, when they encountered another party headed south on the narrow country road. Ranald cursed and yanked at Uar's reins the moment they heard the approaching hoofbeats, but 'twas too late to avoid the passerby. Rather than plunge guiltily into the underbrush, he drew his mount up and they waited tensely as the other man slowed his galloping gray to a prancing halt.

"Hail and well met!"

The fair-haired rider wore a fine woolen cloak trimmed with fur, over a jerkin and doublet of watchet-green, embroidered with gold. Merry instantly recognized those colors and the soft cap he wore. A royal messenger! The worst possible soul she might encounter under the circumstances.

She had no notion if Lord Lindsay knew the occupation of the fellow or not, but she dug an elbow into his ribs just the same, silently warning him. She dared not speak for fear her refined speech would betray her, and she was not about to attempt mimicking a peasant's accent.

She waited tensely while Ranald took stock of their situation, and when he spoke his utter calm amazed her. So did his sudden, rolling Scottish burr.

"Greetings, sir. We bid ye pleasant travels."

The messenger nodded, touching the rim of his cap as his curious gaze flickered over them both. A red-haired woman, wrapped in tartan. A big, burly Scot riding double with her on a shaggy Highlands pony. What could be more unremarkable? Nevertheless, he eyed the Scot's scabbard and the healthy-sized sword inside it with respect.

"Aye, a good day for journeying. Is the road passable after the rains?"

"Och, if ye stay off the Cambrian branch, where the coaches caused such great ruts." Merry suspected the real reason Ranald discouraged that road; her uncle's wrecked coach lay in grim splendor amidst the greenery, and a royal messenger would recognize the crest on the door.

The other man nodded at Lindsay's advice, but made no move to press on. He obviously was not in any hurry; doubtless returned from delivering a message or royal summons, and malingering on his way back. Merry shifted uneasily in the saddle when his gaze fell on the hem of her skirt, visible beneath the long tartan. She saw his eyes narrow slightly, as he recognized the quality even through the mud stains.

Sensing the change in atmosphere, Ran spoke quickly. "Och, mon, we must be pressing on . . . make the border before dark."

The other man's gaze had risen to study Merry's features by then. "Aye," he said, as if he aimed to memorize her face, just in case. Perhaps he did not recognize Mistress Tanner, but Ran sensed his curiosity and suspicion mounting by the minute. His right hand slipped down to the hilt of his claymore, hidden behind the mound of Merry's skirts, while the other still cradled her about the waist in intimate fashion. There was only one way he could think of for throwing the other man off guard, but it required the woman's cooperation.

When the queen's messenger made no move to press on, Ran moved his left hand and ran it lightly, caressingly, over Merry's form through the layers of tartan and silk. She gasped, loud enough for the other man to hear and yet did not betray her identity with some foolish remark. She knew as well as Ran, she had too much at stake.

The other man's eyebrow arched slightly, but as Ran hoped, a little smirk curved his lips. The old image of the lusty Highlander groping a comely lass did help serve his cause. Now, if only he could make Mistress Tanner squeal and squirm a bit . . .

"Canna blame a mon for wantin' to hurry home wi' his

blushing bride,'' Ran said, adding what he trusted came across as a suitably crude laugh. "Welsh mud dinna serve half so well as a pile of rushes in the stables. Aye, hinny?''

Ran pulled Merry back against him, wrapping his fingers in the flaming hair. He held her immobile while his lips crushed down on hers in a passable imitation of a rough, emphatic kiss. She was too shocked to struggle at first, and by the time she gathered her wits again, he had already released her to the coarse laughter of both men.

Merry's gasp this time was laced with outrage, and Ran knew there would be hell to pay later. Still, he enjoyed a fleeting moment of the woman's discomfiture, knowing she dared not react openly without betraying her identity. That did not stop the little witch from digging her elbow into his ribs again, a bit more emphatically than called for. Ran grunted with surprise, his ringing laughter cut short by the lancing pain in his side.

The queen's man chuckled, his suspicion abating. At least a wedding explained a fine gown on a mud-stained Highland lass. He touched the brim of his cap and his heels to his horse at the same time.

"Travel swiftly," he said, grinning at the flushed maiden as he passed. Maid no more, indeed, judging by her fine Highland blush. He envied the Scot his flame-haired prize, but not the trials he'd endure in taming her. One did not envy the doomed.

As the gray galloped off behind them, Merry twisted in the saddle and glared at Ran. "Cad! How dare you presume to manhandle me . . ."

"Would you have preferred the alternative?" Ran calmly rejoined. "The man was on the verge of challenging us. If I had been forced to defend us, the outcome would not have been pretty."

She angrily tossed her burnished curls. "Whatever can you mean?"

"I was ready to cut him down."

"A queen's messenger! Are you mad?" Her voice echoed in the little clearing, but when she glanced into Ranald's dark eyes she saw they were twinkling. "You . . . you are naught but a barbarian, sirrah," she sputtered.

Ran grinned a little and touched his heels to Uar's sides. "Aye, lass." He would not presume to argue with a *Sassenach* wench whose farthingale was tied in a knot.

Chapter Seven

The border was the daunting line drawn between English might and Scottish determination, and for centuries had seen all manner of bloodshed, strife, and treaties made and broken over tankards of heather ale. To cross in daylight was pure folly, unless one bore the protection of either Tudor or Stuart arms, and a brace of men besides. The border reivers were famous for their feistiness, as well as a genetic predisposition for a fight.

Merry knew much of this already from gossip at Court, yet she saw no alarm on Ranald's face as they made for the border. Indeed, he appeared almost bored as they navigated the many small streams and hillocks. Conversation had dwindled to inane subjects a long time ago, and Merry had given up trying to pry the barest civility from the man. 'Twas not that he was a dullard. On the contrary, she suspected he would keep her on her toes if a match of wit and wills ever came to pass. Alas, he did not seem so inclined.

For the longest time after his kiss, Merry's lips throbbed with a cadence no less steady than the horse's hooves. Such a brazen act was deserving of a slap, or perhaps a challenge to a duel. Certainly her father Slade would be outraged if he knew of Lindsay's boldness. Her Irish mother was even fiercer, but a secret romantic beneath her bluster. More than once she had hinted 'twould take a strong man to handle her flame-haired daughter. Merry suspected Bryony might even approve of the laird of Lindsay, which made her all the more determined to detest him.

In the beginning, she had given Ranald the benefit of the doubt, supposing his little brother an imp and Ranald serving as Gilbert Lindsay's long-suffering guardian. But that kiss . . . ohhh, that wicked, willful kiss! Merry seethed, remembering how he'd seized her hair by the nape of her neck to hold her fast, baring her vulnerable throat and shaming her before the queen's messenger. Worse, she had not struggled overmuch, too shocked at first. By the time she'd gathered her wits, the Scot had already released her, his hearty laughter making her cheeks burn like Greek fire.

'Twas only for show, Ranald later implied . . . but was it? Merry simply could not fathom the necessity of such a thorough, punishing kiss. Yet she avoided the issue when she failed to acknowledge her body's reaction. Her spine stiffened while her belly fluttered in anticipation, and a deep, sweet ache spread throughout her loins, culminating in a tingling she could not define.

Aye, she had played at love before, dallying with bold knaves in the queen's gardens and sneaking kisses in the halls. But never had a man so affected her as Ranald Lindsay did, with a single burning glance from those dark, dark eyes. She knew those eyes scoured the surrounding countryside now, ever alert though his relaxed posture did not betray any undue concern.

Merry had just decided he was possessed of some magical cloak of invisibility when a fearsome shout rang over the hills.

"Bellendaine! Bellendaine!"

Echoing answers, the lusty cheers of a number of men. Merry panicked when she saw a dozen kilt-clad warriors riding down upon them. These men were fierce, armed with pikestaffs and short swords. She glanced back at Lindsay, expecting to see fear or concern sketched across his saturnine features at last, but to her surprise his lips parted not in shock but mirth.

The slow grin spreading across his face transformed the brooding laird into a winsome dark knight for a moment, and Merry felt the familiar coil of tension in her belly. La, but the Earl of Crawford was comely! She had never seen him truly smile until this moment, and it seemed the years fell away, and she glimpsed a darker version of the mischievous Gilbert.

The band of Scots circled their ponies about Uar, several shaking their fists in their air. Merry realized 'twas all for a show of bravado when Lindsay laughed outright, his deep chuckle quelling the would-be marauders and obviously disappointing their leader.

A big, freckle-faced man with a wild mane of red hair grinned rawly at them from the back of a shaggy piebald.

"Dinna fash yersel drawin' a claymor, Lindsay," he said, his burr so thick Merry could hardly follow it. She shook her head as if she might shake off the entire lot of brigands, and the fellow roared with laughter.

"Guid on ye, Ranald loon! Plucked a bonnie bizzam from the feckless *Sassenach.*"

Merry had no notion what a "bizzam" might be, but she suspected 'twas hardly a compliment. She scowled at the rude fellow with the braying manners and it only made him laugh harder. His big frame bent like a willow as gales of laughter shook him.

"Now, Gord, why ever would you assume the worst of me?" Ranald's reply was laced with mirth as well, and his hand clamped Merry fast when she began fidgeting with agitation. She wanted to hurl some particularly colorful insults at the rough border reiver, yet she wasn't entirely sure they were out of danger yet. Perhaps Ranald merely laughed along with the other man to preserve their lives.

"An' the wud Wolf of Badanloch asks why." The raw-boned border lord chuckled, his pale-blue gaze raking over Merry as if she was a particularly tasty morsel. "Walie! A sorry day indeed when a mon canna dub an old friend a proper Lord Rakeshanks.''

"Aye, well, that title 'tis surely reserved for Gordon Scott,'' Ranald replied with a twinkle in his tone which surprised Merry. He sounded almost . . . whimsical. One did not describe this man in such terms. She was surely mistaken.

She waited for Ranald to introduce her, and when none was forthcoming, she realized he intended to keep her identity a secret as he had with the messenger. She should have been relieved, but a tic of annoyance touched her instead. As if she had anything to be ashamed of!

'Twas a Lindsay had wrecked her uncle's coach, and a Lindsay who swept her over the border to her betrothed without so much as a by-your-leave. Merry owed this bunch of Highland oafs nothing at all, except perhaps some small acknowledgment for the laird's consideration. In turn she was asked to endure endless miles over rough terrain, the near-silent company of a sullen and moody companion, and now the lusty perusal of a border reiver. 'Twas not to be borne!

She raised her chin a notch and stated calmly, "Greetings, Lord Scott. I am Mistress Meredith Tanner."

Her precise, refined English clearly rocked the border lout back on his heels, or in this case, his saddle. He looked from her to Ranald, his gaze demanding further explanation. A certain wariness supplanted his mirth at her statement.

Ranald's long fingers dug between her ribs. Merry flinched, realizing he was annoyed. He bade her be silent with his actions but she was tired of being mistaken for a trollop. She might be tousled and stained with mud, but she was still a lady beneath the grime. A virgin, for good measure.

"Mistress Tanner, eh?" Gordon Scott's thick brogue added more than a touch of sarcasm, but Merry did not waver under his fierce stare. Just as quickly then he seemed to dismiss her, turning his broad grin on Lindsay instead.

"Been a hairst or two since ye visited Goldielands," he drawled, wrapping one beefy fist around his leather pommel as he shifted his great bulk in place. "When was it last?"

"A year, at least." Something in Ranald's manner did not encourage further pursuit of the topic, but The Scott seemed oblivious.

"A'maist forever," he nodded, and for a moment the twinkle in his eyes dimmed. "Ochone! I heard about Blair—"

"Tell me of your kin," Ranald interrupted, and to Merry's surprise the topic of the mysterious Blair was neatly circumvented, while still she seethed at Lord Scott's rudeness. "How many arrows in your quiver now, Gord?"

"Three and Fiona bairned again," the big man said. He sounded proud, and for some reason Merry sensed a fleeting envy in Ranald. Nothing he said or did, just a woman's intuition which told her he should have very much liked to be in Gordon Scott's place at the moment.

"I take it your lady is well then?"

"Aye! Plump and feisty as a little cloker. Ye must come see! 'Tis but a hop to Goldielands as the bummie flies."

Without waiting for their reply, Gordon Scott wheeled his sturdy mount around, and his men followed without demur. Merry looked back to Ranald, and saw mingled longing and regret sketched in those dark eyes.

"D'you wish to go?"

"'T'would be rude to decline," he replied. He chuckled. "Besides, I've never known Gord to take no for an answer."

"Rudeness is something Lord Scott appears to grasp quite well."

She sniffed, letting him know there was no place less she wished to be than the stronghold of some rough-hewn border lord. If Sir Jasper should hear of her folly . . . Merry frowned, realizing her betrothed might well cry off altogether. Even rumor of her alone with Lord Lindsay, no matter how gallantly he behaved, would give rise to nasty speculation.

"Aye, Gord can be gruff, but he's a good man. I think you'll like his wife, Fiona," Ranald said as he urged Uar into a canter after the other horses.

"Will she not find my bedraggled appearance . . . unseemly?" Merry worried aloud.

To her surprise, he laughed.

"I see you've not yet made acquaintance with the infamous Scotts of Goldielands." He said no more, which left Merry's curiosity unsatisfied and her desire to secure Ranald Lindsay's confidence stronger than ever.

Goldielands, a famed border peel, stood above the Teviot a mile or so beyond Hawick. There was nothing especially remarkable about the square stone keep, and its reputation came not from its appearance but rather those who occupied it. At once Merry noted the swarm of redheaded children spilling from the ward to greet the riders, and realized with a hint of amusement that here, at least, her flaming locks would not stand out.

Once again, Ranald read her mind with uncanny accuracy. His fingers playfully snatched and wiggled a blazing curl before her nose. "Almost like coming home, eh, lass?"

The momentary, uncharacteristic playfulness ended with her terse reply. "Hardly." Merry freed her hair from his grasp with a sudden twist of her head, gazing off pensively for a moment toward the west. "We cannot be far from Braidwood now."

Ranald did not reply, but just then a stocky, freckle-faced boy with an unruly mop of orange hair hurried up to take charge of Uar. He was perhaps twelve or thirteen, and though he wore homespun, he appeared reasonably clean and well fed.

"Welcome, sir," the youth boomed out in a voice that was just beginning to turn, his mannerisms as rough-and-tumble as Lord Scott's, his gestures just as sweeping.

"Brodie lad, can it truly be?" Ranald did not sound as if he feigned shock. "Last I saw you, you were a shaggy pup at Gord's heels."

"Aye," Brodie laughed as he gave Uar's forehead a hardy scratch which the gelding appeared to love. "But even 'ta stalk of a cabbage grows up."

"A philosopher you'll be, Brodie Scott," Ranald predicted

as he swung down from the animal and lifted Merry down a moment later. "Lad, please meet Mistress Tanner. I am escorting her home after an unfortunate carriage accident."

Ranald's smooth words almost convinced Merry of the innocence of their sojourn. She smiled at the wide-eyed youth. "Pleased to meet you, Brodie."

The boy merely nodded, looking a bit overwhelmed. He quickly busied himself unsaddling Uar, all the while sneaking surreptitious glances at Ranald and Merry as they crossed the inner ward. The central grounds were bustling with livestock, children, and dogs as shaggy and unkempt as their young masters. Merry wrinkled her nose at the pungent if honest smells, but did not bother complaining. She knew Lindsay would dismiss any remark as that of a spoiled Tudor court-bred female, and mayhap he was right. She did not intend apologizing for her fastidious nature, and though her skirts were thoroughly soiled already, she raised them as she picked her way through the assorted mire and horse droppings in the yard.

Gordon Scott awaited them in the great hall, already sprawled back behind a trencher on the high seat. The narrow hall was functional but far neater than the ward, with thick Turkey carpets lining the walkway and a number of small, expertly woven tapestries lending accent of color here and there. As Merry's eyes adjusted to the relative gloom, she made out the rows of gleaming weaponry displayed above a huge hearth, rusted from the humidity but no less the fierce for it. Following her gaze, the border lord chuckled, seeming obliged then to offer a running commentary upon her surroundings.

"I find the gleades far more appealing when framed by *Sassenach* glaives," The Scott said, grinning as he indicated the brace of captured swords ringing the hearthstone. There was no safe comment Merry might make in response to this boast, but a glance at Ranald revealed he looked amused, too. Both men seemed to derive great pleasure from her discomfiture.

With mingled relief and curiosity Merry regarded another woman who entered the hall at the opportune moment. Tall, sturdily built, with dark-gold hair neatly dressed under a lace cap, she commanded instant attention. Her gown of deep blue matched her clear eyes, and although obviously *enceinte* she carried herself with pride, neither embarrassed at her condition nor feeling obliged to hide away when guests arrived. She nodded greeting at Merry and Lord Lindsay, a warm smile curving her lips.

"Och, Fiona me luve!" Scott exclaimed, waving her over as his ruddy face beamed. His thick arm shot out and curled around her waist, drawing her against his side. 'Twas apparent his adoration of the golden-haired woman went beyond mere lust when he reached up, drawing her head down to his for a moment and exchanging a passionate kiss.

Merry blushed a little, but Fiona Scott smiled through the kiss, straightening again so she might welcome their company more formally. "I bid you welcome to Goldielands," she said, her voice soft yet commanding. It bore none of the rough border accent of her lord, and indeed by the graceful executions of each movement she might have been raised at Court.

Merry glanced at Ranald and saw him regarding Goldieland's mistress as if an angel had suddenly appeared in a burst of golden flame. She was not certain why the admiring light in his eyes annoyed her; perhaps because he seemed to regard Merry with a critical air by comparison. Whatever the source of his emotion, 'twas clear he held Lady Scott in high esteem.

"How are you, Fi?" Ranald inquired when their gazes met, and the border lady smiled at him with warm recognition.

"Fat," she laughed, patting her rounded abdomen, the very portrait of domestic bliss and tranquility. But for the sparkle of mirth in her deep blue eyes, Fiona might have passed for a suitably demure matron. Despite the irritation Ranald's rapt attention engendered in her, and the shockingly intimate kiss the lady had exchanged with her lord in the hall, Merry decided she liked Gordon Scott's wife.

She liked Fiona even more when the woman turned on the crusty clan chief and thumped matter-of-factly upon his shoulder. "Gracious, Gord, where 'tis your hospitality. Have you offered our guests any ale or mead?"

The big man looked almost abashed at her rebuke. "Nay, luvey," he muttered like a recalcitrant child, and Merry found herself smiling at the scene.

"Fi brews the finest heather ale this side of Glasgow," Ranald put in for Merry's benefit, and overhearing this, their hostess laughed again.

"Aye, Ran, but you would say anything sweet to curry Mac-Dougall favor," Fiona replied with a saucy wink which quite surprised Merry. She was equally surprised The Scott did not lurch out of his seat and wrap his beefy hands around Lindsay's throat for bantering with his wife, but the rusty-haired lord looked replete. Fiona's presence alone seemed to calm him.

After introductions were completed, the lady of the keep summoned a silver tray bearing all manner of delicious treats, including caramel shorty and sweet iced cakes. Merry was ravenous after the tiring journey and meager fare thus far, and Fiona sensed this with her natural hostess instincts. She pressed Merry to try any number of the treats, then whispered instructions aside to a pair of young girls as to the evening menu.

"Of course you will stay the night," Fiona said when Ranald remarked they must be headed on, and when he tried to demur, the matter was settled with the simple arch of Lady Scott's golden brow. After initial pleasantries and a more formal introduction was completed in the hall, Fiona offered Merry opportunity to freshen up. She led her guest upstairs where a small, neatly kept bed chamber stood service for travelers.

"Please consider Goldielands your home whilst on the road, Mistress Tanner," Fiona graciously invited, and Merry smiled in response.

"Your hospitality is appreciated, milady," she replied, already eyeing the basin of fresh water with longing. "I feel obliged to explain I do not normally visit anyone in such a frightful state of dishevelment."

Fiona nodded. "I know, my dear. 'Twas evident from the way you carry yourself, you are gently bred. You need not fear

I will judge you harshly for the difficult circumstances which have befallen you.'' There was a kind light in Lady Scott's blue eyes, and Merry instinctively trusted her.

"Although,'' Fiona continued with a twinkle, "I cannot help but wonder how you came to make the acquaintance of a notorious hermit like the Wolf of Badanloch.''

"Lord Lindsay, you mean?'' Merry knew the answer already but needed time to seek a suitable reply. "Alack, he was kind enough to rescue me from the ruins of my coach after a disastrous encounter with bumbling highwaymen.'' She did not feel obliged to identify the footpads, although she was fairly certain Lady Scott would have gotten a rich chuckle out of it.

"Aye, Ran can be chivalrous when he chooses to be,'' Fiona said, and there was a troubled light in her eyes which prompted Merry to inquire after the lady's familiarity with Lindsay.

"Oh, I was a MacDougall lass before wedding my wild Gord,'' Fiona said with a little laugh. "MacDougall daughters traditionally foster with Lindsays. I was sent to Edzell by my eighth birthday, as I was of an age with Darra Lindsay, Ran's sister. There I learned the tasks of chatelaine and such alongside Darra, now Lady Deuchar. While being subjected to practical instruction, we girls also suffered the more creative pranks of Ran and his evil shadow.''

Merry smiled. '' 'Tis hard to imagine that one as lighthearted, milady.''

"Fiona, please. Fi, if you like. We do not stand on formalities at Goldielands.'' Then Fiona nodded at Merry's remark. "Aye, even in his younger days, Ran tended serious. Yet not so grave as he has become since Blair's death.''

"Blair? Another sister?''

"Nay. His lady wife. You did not know?''

Merry shook her head, surprised at the pang which pierced her and took her breath for a moment. So Lord Lindsay had been married. Questions swirled in her mind, yet pursuit of the topic would only lead to Lady Scott's curiosity and her own embarrassment. The man's past, or his current light o'loves, did not interest her in the slightest.

Chapter Eight

Evening repast at Goldielands tended toward the same general good-natured chaos as the keep itself, and the residents at table seemed content amidst screeching falcons and noisy children. Not only did the lord and lady sup in the great banqueting hall, but all those within the realm of the Scotts of Branxholm attended festivities on a regular basis at the border stronghold. Even a bard came from St. Mary's Loch, and by the deference with which even Lady Scott welcomed him, Merry supposed the sad-eyed man held some sort of sway over an audience.

Seòsamh Douglas was at first glance innocuous, being slight of build for a man, with a scraggly mane of brown hair and an unkempt appearance that lent itself to the need for a good scrubbing. Merry fought the urge to suggest the fellow occasionally wade into the loch from whence he came, although for a certainty the water would have made short work of the island harp he carried tucked beneath one arm like a precious child. He never set down the humble instrument, not even at table, but merely laid it across his lap while he availed himself of Scott hospitality.

Indeed, Merry admitted the fare might rival the Court's in terms of generosity. Fully five tables creaked with the offerings of the house as well as those items guests felt inclined to bring. Loaves of golden bread, wheels of sharp cheese, and an assortment of wines but served to whet the guests' appetites. There was salmon smoked to a tender flake, freshly caught trout, and eel cooked in a sweet wine sauce. Crisply roasted boar and a full haunch of red deer appeased heartier appetites, while ladies were invited to indulge in pear-glazed partridge and pigeon's eggs. No glass was left unfilled, no tankard remained dry for long. Ale and mead flowed as plentifully as the conversation around the long trencher tables in the banqueting hall.

At first, Merry felt self-conscious, even wearing the clean outfit Lady Scott insisted she borrow. The gown was of simple design compared to her court ensemble, but 'twas not peasant's garb by any means. The gently scooped bodice and fitted waist complemented Merry's figure. Surprisingly, the deep rose hue did not clash with her hair, nor did the wool scratch her delicate skin. Only the finest materials were used in Lady Scott's gowns, and though the hem had been tacked so Merry might wear the taller woman's garb, the gown otherwise appeared custom-made.

Lacking any proper jewelry, Merry decided to wear the red-gold raven amulet, sensing it would appeal to the earthy occupants of Goldielands. Whereas fine pearls might be wasted on swine, she did not mistake the covetous gleam in The Scott's eye when his gaze fell upon the heavy gold ornament. Aye, she mused, Lord Scott was a genuine rascal indeed, for he obviously knew it for the ancient and priceless thing 'twas.

Even Ranald seemed impressed when Merry descended to the hall, restored from their travels thanks to their hostess. Her hair was freshly washed, and shone like the ruby wine in the glass he held. Lady Scott had offered Merry use of her own maid servant's eldest daughter, and the clever Peigi had woven the auburn locks into a shimmering circle of braids about Merry's head. The natural crown added several inches to her petite frame, and she felt more confident when she met his gaze. Being restored to cleanliness helped her self-esteem as well.

"I take it you do not regret our stopping at Goldielands altogether," he remarked when Merry joined him for a bit before adjourning to the feast. She noticed his gaze, too, lingered for a moment on the raven amulet.

"Nay," she admitted. "I was only loath at first because I feared what sort of welcome a burly fellow like Lord Scott might have in mind."

Ranald chuckled a little. He, too, had taken the opportunity to bathe and exchange his shirt for another of identical style but a much whiter linen. Merry noted the stir his presence created among Goldielands' female residents; even the youngest serving girl with a timorous manner snuck admiring glances at the famed Wolf of Badanloch. While Merry had not been afforded the chance to ask Lady Scott where Ranald gained such an impressive reputation, she gathered 'twas not without cause as all the border reivers greeted him with due respect.

" 'Twill not harm your cause with the queen despite your present association with Braxholm Scotts," Ranald told her in a low voice before they parted company at table. "Fiona has an upstanding reputation among English and Scots alike. She attended both Courts before her children were born."

Merry nodded. "She is a kindly and resourceful hostess." She marveled that the woman endured such a cacophony and all manner of children and beasts underfoot, but then Fiona appeared equal to the task. She was quite half a head taller than her stocky laird, and never needed to raise her voice to be heard. Her quiet yet firm statements immediately yielded results.

As guests of honor, Merry and Lord Lindsay were seated near the head of the table, facing each other. To Merry's right, the visiting bard was accorded a spot of honor as well. Seòsamh nodded acknowledgment at Merry's polite greeting, but seemed disinclined to converse further. Which was just as well, for Merry was ravenous and much preferred sampling the rich fare to exchanging social pleasantries with an ill-groomed stranger.

The chair to her left, the only one yet unoccupied, remained empty until midway through the meal. Suddenly a silence fell over the hall, and Merry looked up from her partridge and saw an elderly woman carefully making her way down the stairs with Peigi's aid. Peigi steadied the white-haired crone, who was simply clad in black worsted with a dark-blue shawl pinned at her shoulder with a bell heath silver badge. While Merry and the others watched, Lady Scott rose from her own chair and greeted the late diner with visible surprise.

"Mother MacDougall, how good of you to join us."

Fiona's mother, mayhap, or her grandmother. Merry wondered at the relation, and at the others' rapt silence, for nobody spoke or ate another bite until the older woman was settled at table with all due pomp and circumstance.

Feeling the crone's keen gaze turn on her, Merry attempted a smile at her left-side neighbor. "Good eve, milady."

Piercing, pale-blue eyes sought Merry's so intently she almost gasped aloud. For a moment, she was too shocked to respond. No true lady stared thus at anyone. 'Twas not a hostile glare, but neither was it warm and inviting; it seemed to reach deep into one as if the crone read an open book.

Merry shivered. She felt suddenly vulnerable, especially when all attention in the hall focused on her and the old woman. From the corner of her eye she saw the bard shift slightly, as if leaning closer so he might listen in on any ensuing conversation.

"Tide, tide, whate'er betide, the Wolf be daein brawlie on his night ride."

The words muttered by Mother MacDougall seemed more a prophecy than any idle commentary upon the weather, and Merry tore her gaze from the crone's and noted the shocked faces about the table. For the first time, Lady Scott looked distressed, and clasped her hands together across her rounded abdomen as if in an unconscious protective gesture.

More interesting yet was Ranald Lindsay's expression; he might well have been slapped as the color rose in his face and his dark eyes flashed.

Used to averting disastrous encounters at Court, Merry spoke quickly to the old woman.

"I am Mistress Meredith Tanner, milady. I am honored indeed to enjoy the hospitality of Goldielands."

Fiona nodded slightly, gratefully, encouraging Merry's efforts, but the older woman merely looked at Merry as if to say, "I know who you are, lassie." She even might have been amused.

The next time she spoke, Mother MacDougall looked directly at Ranald Lindsay. "At Wolfen Den, if ye should be, A corby hert ye there may see."

Upon which Ranald rose from table, scraping back the heavy oak chair, and abruptly left the hall. Merry sensed his restrained fury, punctuated for emphasis with a few collective gasps around the table. A strained silence echoed his departure. Quickly Gordon Scott seized his quaich, and raising it high, shouted a toast to banish the somber atmosphere.

"Hout! Here's ta the Land o' the Bens, the Glens, an' the Heroes! Here's ta the heath, the hill, and the heather, The bonnet, the plaidie, the kilt and the feather! Here's ta the song that Auld Scotland can boast, May her name never die!—that's a Bordermon's toast."

"*Bellendaine! Bellendaine!*" roared his kinsmen, fellow Scotts and reivers all. Many a fist pounded the table so hard it trembled with threat of collapse, and during the melee Merry saw Lady Scott rise and slip away from the table, hurrying off in the same direction Ranald had gone.

"Hae ye nae sic wisdom ta impart us, Seòsamh?" The Scott bellowed down the trestle at the bard, whom Merry noticed did not drink with the others. The slight, bearded fellow nodded. He raised his tankard at last, and when the din had dropped to a passable level, offered quietly:

"There's meat and music here, as the fox said when he stole the bagpipes."

Gordon Scott grinned. "Och, and there's no much guile in the hert that's ay singing. Tune yer clarsach, laddy."

Seòsamh Douglas nodded and uprighted the island harp in

his lap, adjusting it minutely until it sat within the circle of his arms upon his thigh in the precise fashion he preferred. Softly his fingers strummed the strings, and the silvery sound rippled over the watching assembly. Several were heard to sigh in anticipation, or perhaps Gaelic anticipation of a mournful saga, but not Mother MacDougall. After blurting her second bit of nonsense, she subsided into a catatonic sort of silence, gaze affixed to her trencher as if her mind wandered the misty Highland hills.

Eventually Seòsamh opted for the comfort of another chair before the great hearth, and drew his audience with him. Merry seized opportunity to slip away as the others deserted the table one by one. Nobody noticed her exit during the exchange and she was able to ford the hall. She did not know why she felt the consuming need to follow Lord Lindsay and Lady Scott. Certainly it never occurred to her there was anything improper in their mutual absence. Nor did she intend eavesdropping, yet opportunity confronted her just the same.

She heard voices issuing from behind a door left ajar.

"—when she is clearly mad," she heard Ranald state in an ire-filled voice.

From Fiona Scott's softer tone, 'twas obvious she attempted soothing the bristling laird. "I do not think Beitris is even aware when the spells happen."

"Aye, and I suppose her eyes did not gleam when she spouted such clishmaclaver at my and Blair's wedding," Ranald said. His voice was cold, but Merry imagined his dark eyes flaming.

Fiona sighed. "Ochone. You cannot deny The Maclean prophecy was brought to bear."

"Aye, they are forever dubbed The Luckless Macleans now. Mother MacDougall doomed an entire clan with her fey prattling. Would you dub that harmless, Fiona?"

Merry heard another soft sigh, this one resigned. "She did not mean to vex you, I know, when she spoke of a wolf and a raven. Even in her younger days, she cried when she realized how her words upset others. In truth, The Sight 'tis not the cherished gift Seòsamh sings of in romantic ballads. 'Tis more a curse.''

''Aye. To me,'' Ranald stated flatly, and Merry winced for Lady Scott's sake. The Wolf of Badanloch snarled at anyone when wounded. A second later, Fiona's words sank in. Wolf and a raven? Mother MacDougall's mutterings had not made much of an impression upon Merry, but then the thick burr was hard to follow and she was distracted by the others when the verses had suddenly spouted from the woman's lips.

She touched the amulet at her breast, traced the indentation of the flying bird with some apprehension. It could easily be a coincidence. Else Mother MacDougall had spied the amulet and decided on a whim to discomfit the others with a sudden ''prophecy.'' 'Twas not incredible she might favor an occasional jest upon her impressionable kin. Merry thought of her own grandsire, The O'Neill, a great braying Irishman with a particularly wicked sense of humor.

To Brann O'Neill, she would always be ''Erin,'' though he knew quite well his flame-haired granddaughter preferred ''Merry.'' One of the reasons Merry did not care to visit Ireland, aside from the rough and tumble way her Irish relations behaved, was they reminded her of her own humble roots. 'Twas easy at Court to forget she was but the spawn of an Englishman without title, the youngest of four sons. Slade Tanner was wealthy now, but his fortune had amassed only with great effort and the devoted aid of his wife. Bryony O'Neill Tanner was the proverbial black-haired, blue-eyed Irish colleen with a courage matching any man's and a reckless nature she did not fail to exercise.

Merry had always been embarrassed by her mother. Oh, she adored Bryony, but in her opinion 'twas most unseemly for a mother of seven to flit about the high seas, wearing men's breeks and swearing like a sailor whenever she felt thus inclined. 'Twas an admitted relief her parents spent most of their time traveling, or in Ireland. They rarely visited Court anymore. In the while Merry had come to consider the queen her foster mother, albeit a stricter and more exacting taskmistress than Bryony Tanner had ever been.

Thus, Merry considered most Gaels possessed of a mischievous nature, and it did not seem unlikely Mother MacDougall enjoyed similar sport with her kin. Ranald Lindsay was simply too serious-natured to appreciate a good jest, besides which she knew his surname was of Norman derivation originally and hence he did not qualify as a genuine Scot in Merry's opinion.

"I regret the evening has brought unpleasant memories," Fiona was saying. "Truly, Ran, I never expected Beitris to join us at table. She rarely leaves her tower room anymore."

"I think the old witch takes peculiar delight in baiting me. No matter. I shall simply avoid her until the morrow. We shall be gone quickly enough."

"Ah, that is another matter I would speak of. Gordon said only you are escorting Mistress Tanner somewhere."

"Aye. Auchmull, and then to her intended."

"Why Auchmull at all?"

Fiona's question was followed by a moment of silence. "I suppose there is no true need now. She seems recovered from travel with your admirable assistance."

Fiona laughed, pleased by the compliment. "The lass has a fragile appearance, but I oft find such indication is misleading. Mistress Tanner is charming, is she not? A ready smile and a sweet laugh. I like both in a woman."

Merry did not hear a reply but imagined he shrugged.

Ran exited Goldielands' library some time after Fiona departed, first availing himself of a rich claret left upon a small sideboard. 'Twas well known the Scotts liked their libation, but even Gord's taste was not confined to border grog. The Scott had much of his stock imported from France, always in ready supply in case a Stuart or nobleman should wander through. Ran swirled the ruby liquid in the glass thoughtfully, reminded for a moment of Meredith Tanner's hair. A color as bold, as unapologetic as the Tudor chit herself. He wasn't certain why or how she'd captured his attention, other than the fact of her identity as Wickham's woman. He only knew some pattern was beginning to form in his thinking. Something he didn't particularly like.

He tossed back the claret, letting the piquant flavor burst in the back of his throat and distract him from further musings about a red-haired wench with rain-colored eyes. Tomorrow they would press on, and even Fiona assumed he would safely present Mistress Tanner to her frantic intended at Braidwood. Ran wasn't so sure. The concept of revenge, however fleeting, made the Wolf of Badanloch salivate with anticipation.

Chapter Nine

Merry resumed her place in the great hall just before Lady Scott and Lindsay returned from their private conference. She felt somewhat abashed over eavesdropping, even though 'twas commonplace at Court—indeed, even expected—and a clever spy was worth their weight in gold. Yet this incident had left her with a sour taste in her mouth. She was not proud of her actions, while at the same time felt she had a slightly clearer glimpse of the man she had ridden with across the desolate Welsh marches.

The pain, the anger evident in Ranald's voice when he'd spoken of his wedding gave Merry pause for thought. Mother MacDougall had obviously contributed in some fashion to an incident which Lord Lindsay could not, or would not, forget.

Forgiveness also was out of the question. Merry sensed the laird was a hard, proud man whose opinions, once formed, would never waver. She already suspected what Ranald thought of her. He cast her in the role of a shallow, flighty, vain female with little chance of redemption in his eyes. His cool civility indicated he tolerated her, but he would not stand for any defiance. Which only pricked Merry's pride all the more.

She was seated on a green velvet settle near the bard, her rose skirts spread about her in a shimmering circle, when Ranald reappeared. He leaned against the wall near the door, folding his arms and looking for all the world like his namesake, a brooding wolf with slitted eyes. Darkness shadowed the corner where he lingered, no product of the night but rather the aura of the man. The nape of Merry's neck prickled with anticipation, aware of the precise moment his narrowed gaze slid over her. She quelled the urge to shiver and instead leaned toward the fire. Meanwhile Seòsamh's rich baritone drifted across the hall, mesmerizing all in its path.

> "*. . . The blossoms that were blicht and bricht*
> *By her were black and blue,*
> *Scho gladit all the fowl of flicht*
> *That in the forest flew.*
> *Scho micht haif comfort king or knicht,*
> *That ever in countrie I knew,*
> *As wale and well of warldly wicht*
> *In womanly virtue.*

> *Her colour clear, her countenance,*
> *Her comely crystal een,*
> *Her portraiture of most plesance,*
> *All picture did prevene;*
> *Of every virtue to avance,*
> *When ladies praisit been,*
> *Richtest in my remembrance*
> *That rose in rootit green.*

> *This mild, meek, mansuet Mergrit,*
> *This pearl poleist most white,*
> *Dame Natouris dear dochter discreet,*
> *The diamond of delight,*
> *Never formit was to found on feet*
> *Ane figure more perfite,*

> *Nor none on mould that did her meet*
> *Micht mend her worth a mite.''*

As the words trailed off in a plaintive echo, and Seòsamh bowed his head over the clarsach, Merry absorbed the corresponding silence in the hall. For a long moment nothing was heard but the crackling and popping of the fire in the grate, and then she saw Lady Scott wipe at her eye. The poem the bard had rendered into such a lovely ballad was said to have been written by King James IV, dedicated to Margaret Drummond, the one woman he truly loved. She had been poisoned when it was feared he might marry her, and the substitution of Margaret Tudor for a bride had forever changed the course of history. Merry had heard the poem before, but hardly rendered in such dramatic fashion. She could not resist glancing at Ranald, and was disappointed, though hardly surprised, when she saw his countenance as stony as ever.

From the high seat beside his wife, The Scott scowled and tipped a flask to his lips. "Wailie! Canna we hear ye blether something asides the' gey-dowie ballants, Douglas?"

Seòsamh looked up and smiled faintly at the rusty-haired lord. "Perhaps a song of loyalty, and a border reiving ballad?"

"Aye!"

So they heard Kinmont Willie, then Jamie Telfer of the Fair Dodhead, which roused the male company again and shouting and stamping of feet soon replaced the gloomy mood. The old border ballad was a colorful account, and the harp was accompanied this time by the wail of a single bagpipe and a pounding drum.

> ". . . *"Revenge! Revenge!" auld Wat'gan cry;*
> *"Fye, lads, lay on them cruellie!*
> *We'll ne'er see Tiviotside again,*
> *Or Willie's death revenged shall be.''*
>
> *O mony a horse ran masterless,*
> *The splintered lances flew on hie;*

> *But or they want to the Kershope ford,*
> *The Scotts had gotten the victory ..."*

Merry saw the men's eyes shining by firelight, their breath almost collectively held as they leaned forward in anticipation of conclusion of the rousing tale. By comparison, Lady Scott and the other women present appeared resigned, and Merry knew why when the ballad ended in a lusty cheer and a call to arms.

"Bellendaine! Bellendaine!" cried the Scotts of Branxholm as if on cue, already a familiar refrain by now. When Gordon Scott laughed drunkenly and proposed a border raid that very night, he was met with cheers of approval and fierce accord. The Scott staggered to his feet, his lady wife supporting him without a word, though disapproval clearly shone in Fiona's blue eyes.

"Aye an' the Wolf of honor shall lead the border snool," Scott roared, baring his teeth in an impressive display.

"Mayhap Ran does not wish to join the reivers, dearheart," Fiona put in quietly.

Heads swiveled in Lord Lindsay's direction, and Ranald stepped from the shadows with a grin. 'Twas not, however, a grin of mirth nor even revelry, but rather one of grim resolve.

"On the contrary, Fi, I should relish the opportunity." Ranald's hand dropped to his side where the sword normally rested, but he had earlier removed his scabbard as a courtesy to his hosts. The gesture, however, was not lost on Merry, who shivered and averted her gaze. She did not wish any reminders of the true nature of this Lindsay, a warlike soul if ever one existed.

The Scott grinned back, pleased. "We'll bide awee," he said, motioning young Brodie over to refresh his drink. "Reivers shouldna be ruers."

"Tho' a drukken reiver makes fer a muckle gab," Brodie said in a teasing tone as he poured golden-brown heather ale into the tankard his uncle offered up.

"Haud yer gab, pup!" The Scott cried with mock outrage,

but then he reached out and thoroughly ruffled the boy's rusty mop. Brodie's hazel eyes twinkled with delight.

"Can I go, Uncle Gord?" he wheedled, drawing out the "o" in "go" so long that everyone listening chuckled. 'Twas obvious the youth was regarded with much affection in the clan.

"Na, ye wee nickum," Scott grumbled. "Now leave me be." As the pleading became more eloquent, he waved aside the youth like a bothersome fly, and at last Brodie returned to his spot beside the hearth, sulking there over the cup of watered wine his aunt Fiona permitted him.

While the men gathered round Gord Scott in anticipation of the night's adventure, Lady Scott invited Merry to the solar for quiet conversation and a late dessert of early berries and clotted cream. The room was cozily decorated in shades of gold and forest green, with delicate furniture imported from France and luxurious tapestries softening harsh stone walls. Fiona lit an assortment of candles in iron sconces, banishing the shadows. Shortly they heard the horses being saddled in the inner court, the coarse laughter and drunken boasts of the reivers preparing for departure. Fiona rose and went to the window, looking down upon the scene but briefly before she drew the green velvet curtains closed. Merry sensed the woman's distress and remarked, "It must be difficult, being a border wife."

"Aye." Fiona nodded, her demeanor sober as she returned and lowered her girth carefully into a deep chair fashioned for comfort. "The thought 'tis always there that one day Gord may not return. Goldielands would fall to the mercy of the strongest Scott, or mayhap a greedy English neighbor, and then my fate and the children's would be decided by a stranger."

"You are young yet, and very beautiful," Merry remarked. "Doubtless the new owner would wish to wed you, and secure the loyalty of your kinsmen as well."

Fiona appeared to shudder. "I see you are not unfamiliar with the practical Scots nature."

Merry laughed. "Scotland cannot lay sole claim to practicality, I fear," she said. " 'Tis much the same in England. Rich widows fetch a high price in the Tudor Court. More so if they are comely. A stubborn man can always be swayed by a pretty face."

"Certainly it must make the aftertaste more pleasant," Fiona agreed with a smile as she sipped at a chamomile drink she had poured for both women. Setting the cup and saucer aside, she invited, "Tell me of your betrothed, Mistress Tanner. What sort of man is he?"

"Meredith. Merry to my friends and family." When Fiona nodded and smiled in response, Merry sensed their green friendship quickly ripening. "I fear I know little of milord husband-to-be. He is said to be handsome, possessed of a well-turned leg, and accounted a good dancer."

Fiona chuckled. "The latter 'tis an important attribute in Tudor circles, I take it?"

"Oh, aye, to me it is. I adore dancing. I should be heartbroken if he did not permit frequent visits to Court after we wed, especially attendance at the masques Her Grace puts on. Already I have half a dozen costume notions I have not yet had opportunity to display.

"I am quite vexed I missed the spring masque planned at Greenwich. I was going as Diana, goddess of the Hunt. I had a marvelous outfit made, a jerkin of amber damask and trunk-hose of moss green with gold stripes. I had a jeweled quiver fashioned to sling over one shoulder. There was even a yew bow painted gold, and arrows with ruby tips."

"Sounds more like Cupid," Fiona remarked with a laugh, and Merry nodded, smiling impishly.

"Aye, I confess the mischievous thought did occur to me that I should target Wickham while wearing the garb, and reveal my identity while he was quite outraged."

"Wickham?" Fiona stared at her, the pleasant smile instantly replaced by a guarded look Merry did not understand.

"Aye, Sir Jasper Wickham. He is my betrothed."

"Oh, my God." Fiona's hands flew to her mouth, her blue

eyes huge. Shock rendered her nearly speechless, though Merry was unable to let it pass.

"What is amiss, Fiona?"

The golden-haired woman took several deep, ragged breaths and finally regained her composure. "Does ... Ran know this?"

Merry nodded, frowning a little. "Aye, I told him at once I was en route for a meeting at Whitehall with the man I am marrying." She tilted her head. "You seem uncommonly alarmed. Is there something about Wickham I should know?"

"I do not know what to tell you, Merry." Fiona shook her head in obvious distress. "I only know, Ran blames an Englishman named Wickham for his wife's death. His rage is evident whenever the man's name arises."

"He said nothing of it. There was no reaction when I mentioned Sir Jasper, none at all."

Fiona nodded, looking stricken. "That is what worries me. Ran's silence is even deadlier than his rage. 'Tis possible he has forgiven the man, I suppose, whatever trespasses he incurred, but far more likely he bides his time for ... some sort of opportunity."

"Such as?" Merry did not want to admit Fiona's words frightened her, but they did. She already knew dark undercurrents swirled beneath Lindsay's calm exterior, yet she did not know what lengths he might go to in order to gain satisfaction. Was it possible he intended using her in some manner? He might have killed her a dozen times over if 'twas personal harm he planned, so the plot, if there was one, was more subtle than either she or Fiona suspected.

"Auchmull," she whispered.

Fiona nodded emphatically. "You must not go there, under any circumstances. I shall appeal to Gord, insist you stay on with us until Wickham can be contacted. Hopefully Ran will suspect nothing, if I give him no cause for doubt. We have always been friends, more like brother and sister."

"If Lindsay did anything to me, he should reckon with the queen," Merry said a trifle shakily. The full impact of Fiona's words had yet to sink in. "Would he see Tudor wrath brought to bear upon the entire Lindsay clan?"

"For Blair's sake, aye." Fiona did not hesitate, and Merry felt a pang of emotion she did not intend examining too closely. "He adored Blair beyond this earth. Her shadow has never left his eyes since her death."

"How did she die?"

"I am not certain, exactly. There was an incident involving Wickham, I know. Something about Blair becoming lost, forced into accepting shelter at Wickham's keep. She became ill, I believe, and Wickham did not send for Ran. Not until 'twas too late. She died, and Ran holds the Englishman responsible."

" 'Tis a very thin tale," Merry said, frowning. "There must be much more to it."

"No doubt, there is. Ran does not talk much of the incident, nor do those of wise persuasion ask for detail. I advise you, Merry, against trifling with his temper. 'Tis slow to rise, but once established, there is no escaping unscathed. Growing up at Edzell, Darra and I both suffered his occasional blasts of cold rage. There was a time, for about three years, when I did not speak with Ran at all."

Merry set her jaw. "Yet you had reason for wishing reconciliation. I have none. I owe Ranald Lindsay nothing, neither fealty nor respect. He lost the latter when he did not tell me of his previous acquaintance with Wickham."

"Perhaps I am mistaken. Some months have passed since Blair's death, his anger may have eased by now."

"Nevertheless, I do not intend to be an unwitting pawn any longer. When he returns from reiving with his border cronies, he will deal with me in an honest fashion or by heavens he will learn firsthand of a Tanner temper, as well."

Merry was waiting in the great hall when the men returned in the wee hours of the early morn. Shouts and excited whinnies of horses heralded their arrival, and there was no doubt as to their success when the doors flew open and Lord Scott strode in. Swaggered, rather, his broad face gleaming with sweat and grinning with triumph, the docked tail of a calf swinging from his own red braids. Most of the men had peeled off on the way back, returning home to their own wives and warm hearths, so the number entering with the laird was considerably smaller than that which had left. The handful included Ranald.

Merry's eyes widened a bit at his appearance. His kilt was torn, revealing one bloodied knee when he walked. 'Twas obvious he favored his right leg now, and whatever happened was likely not innocuous, for his shirt was stained and smeared with dried blood. Someone had plaited his dark hair, which fell in straggling clumps over his broad shoulders, a victim of wind and rain, and he looked for all the world like a wild Highlander there to storm Goldielands. Yet there was a gleam in his dark eyes she did not recall before, a sketch of primal satisfaction. Something deep within her shivered, and courage almost deserted her.

Too late. The Scott noted her in the shadows, and seemed surprised. "Hout! What's this?"

Merry stepped forward, her head held high. She looked not at Scott, but Ranald Lindsay. " 'Twould appear there is dire need for some answers, sirrah." Never was she so aware of her own diminutive size as the bloodstained Wolf of Badanloch loomed over her, and their gazes met and locked. He must have read the icy glint of anger in her eyes, yet his only response was a faint shrug which mocked her confrontation.

"What is your claim against Wickham? I demand an answer, milord." Merry's voice shook a little, but she was pleased her body did not do likewise. The other men lapsed into stunned silence, a few drifting away to their beds, but Lindsay remained firmly planted before her and The Scott folded his brawny arms and observed their terse exchange with interest.

"My quarrel with Wickham does not concern you." Ranald's words were clipped, intending discouragement, but Merry was buying none of it.

"Then why did you feign ignorance whenever I mentioned

his name? This reeks of the ultimate deceit, and I would know why you lied.''

He spoke through gritted teeth. ''I did not lie, woman. I merely did not offer comment on a matter which warranted none.''

Lord Scott spoke a little drunkenly, breaking the strained silence which followed. ''Whaur is m' wife, lass?''

''Fiona wished to stay up, but she was weary. She says this babe has tired her more than the others.''

Gordon Scott nodded, looking concerned. After a muttered good night, he sought the comforts of his chamber and his fair Fiona. Soon only Ranald and Merry remained in the hall, as the weary reivers retired one by one.

''I take it the raid was successful.'' Merry cast a disparaging glance over her gore-stained adversary, and as if deliberately provoking her, Ranald drew his great claymore and minutely examined the blade. She shuddered at the action, as the evil weapon lay balanced across his big palms. Firelight gleamed off the cold steel, but Merry noted no blood there. Frowning in puzzlement, she looked at him and caught a glimpse of mockery in his eyes.

''You assumed the worst, I see.''

''I had no other indication. The blood—''

''Cattle. Calves too young to run, beasts too old to keep up are swiftly dispatched. 'Tis a messy business, aye, but Gord and his clansmen are most efficient.'' He returned the sword to its rest upon his hip, folding his arms as he considered her.

''Then . . .'' Merry licked her lips a little nervously, ''there was no battle?''

He cocked an eyebrow. ''D'you not suppose someone would be hammering at the gates if there had been?'' He gave a short laugh. ''*Sassenach* may not be bright, but Sweet Jesu, they are dogged.''

''A thief is a thief, and should be summarily dealt with,'' Merry angrily replied, stung by his reference to half her heritage. ''What you did was no better than Gilbert's foray into highway robbery, and I pray you hang for it!''

She tossed her head, whirling away. To her surprise, Ranald reached out and seized her left arm firmly, pinning her in place. Her outraged glare elicited only a stony stare in response, and to her further indignation he actually laughed. Faith, but she was beginning to loathe the rogue!

"Unhand me at once," she hissed.

"When I am ready." His dark gaze raked her almost contemptuously. "You wished to know about Jasper Wickham. Don't ask if you cannot handle the reply, woman."

She subsided in place, but her anger did not abate. "Very well. I am listening."

"Aye, you are quite right I had no intentions of telling you of my prior acquaintance with the man. First, there is no reason you should find interest in such discourse, because it does not concern you. Secondly, I knew you should refuse to accompany me anywhere if you knew the true depth of rancor between Wickham and me."

Merry nodded, but her attention remained on the steely grip Lindsay maintained on her. Just his touch made her quiver deep inside with some emotion she cared not to examine too closely. She felt his strength, the warmth of his fingers encircling her upper arm. Even through the soft wool sleeve his touch was as searing as the flames in the great hearth.

"You are quite right," she said a trifle breathlessly. "I should have refused your escort at once, for it appears you are every bit the Scots scoundrel your little brother is."

Something flashed in those dark eyes. "If you damme me for a knave, madame, then I may as well die a sated knave." Suddenly Ranald yanked her into his arms, pinning her firmly by the shoulders as he brought his lips hard upon hers. Merry gasped through the kiss, clutching his waist in a reflex she later despised. He threaded a big hand through her crown of hair, tugging Peigi's creation apart so the braids fell heavily to her hips. The twisting knot in her lower belly unfurled like a rope flung wild, and she moaned beneath the fierce assault of his hot, hungry mouth.

Then he was kissing her neck, ear, leaving a fevered trail

down her shivering flesh where he tugged aside the cloth draping her shoulder, and gently bit her shoulder blade. Merry's
eyes flew open, as the wince of pain was quickly soothed by
a swirl of his tongue which left her gasping. Madness, 'twas
sheer madness, yet his passionate assault did naught but heat
her blood and fire her senses until she, too, was rendered wild
with primitive emotion, a hammering need.

The exquisite sensations his touch evoked left her trembling,
but sanity warred with the base instincts of their powerful
attraction. The male scent of him, heady with the sweat of
exertion, the coppery tang of dried blood, brought her to her
senses. Her gaze focused on his stained shirt, she felt a corresponding shock sweep over her.

"Nay . . . !"

He silenced her protest with a final kiss, almost bordering
on savagery in its intensity. Then he set her roughly back, dark
eyes glittering with either satisfaction or icy triumph, perhaps
both.

"There. A taste of a true scoundrel, Mistress Tanner." His
mocking voice rang in the hall, or mayhap 'twas Merry's own
shame and despair which made it seem so.

"I despise you, sirrah! You are naught but the lowest cad
to e'er walk the earth."

"No doubt you are quite right." Ranald's cold glance was
dismissing as he turned away, his boot heel echoing with finality. He paused near the stairs and cast a final word at her. "You
wonder if I intend turning you over to Wickham on the morrow.
The answer is nay. You will be my guest at Auchmull until I
say otherwise."

"I will see you in hell first!" Merry cried after him.

"So be it, madame. So be it."

Chapter Ten

The night passed tensely for Merry, though she comforted herself with the knowledge Fiona would never permit Lindsay to remove her beyond Goldielands. Upon rising, she was pleased Peigi awaited her, the young girl anxious and willing to sculpt some new creation from Merry's wayward locks. She also brought another outfit Fiona had insisted their guest accept, a gown of fine green linen with a darker green velvet cape and cork-heeled shoes to match. Peigi dressed the auburn curls off Merry's forehead with a small lace cap on the back of her head. The heavy hair was secured with velvet ribbons matching the gown, a simple but fetching country look.

Certainly it never occurred to Merry she might endure any travel, so she wore her farthingale and joined the others early to break her fast. There were trenchers of thick, honeyed oatmeal called *drammach,* and flaky biscuits appeared when Gordon Scott called for "bakes." As the meal commenced and Fiona did not appear, Merry inquired after her hostess. The Scott frowned and wiped his mouth on his sleeve.

"She's warsling wi' a fever, lass," he said. "I sent fer Mother MacDougall last night, an' Fiona dree the garlic and May butter."

Merry felt a tingle of unease when she realized her champion, likely her only defender, was indisposed. As if her thoughts were as transparent as her expression, she saw Ranald nod slightly, as if satisfied there should be no further obstacle to his intentions. Merry felt tension settle over the meal and picked at her food, no longer hungry. Before Lord Scott departed again in anticipation of counting his new cattle, she asked if she might visit Fiona.

The border lord denied her request, though less gruffly than she supposed, pointing out his lady wife needed her rest and should be fine "on the morrow or so." The trouble was Merry would not be there, for as soon as their host departed for the pastures Ranald called for his horse to be saddled and she realized he was seizing opportunity by the horns.

Ran saw the daggers in Merry's eyes when she looked across the table at him. "I am not going anywhere with you, sirrah," she hissed as the lasses cleared the table, pretending not to listen in and lingering all the while.

"I do not recall asking your opinion," he curtly replied. "We have stayed our welcome and 'tis time to press on. You may have half an hour to assemble your things, no more."

At least the Tudor wench was bright enough to realize her options were nil. There were none she could appeal to, and after a few aborted attempts to locate Goldielands' lord, she flew upstairs and salvaged what was left of the time remaining. Merry reappeared in the great hall, defiant curls already escaping the confines of the severe hairstyle Peigi inflicted on her. By then she was shaking with indignation. She clutched a bundle in her arms, the remnants of her old gown. She regarded Ran as one might a slithering serpent.

He did not care. Her opinion of him was as inconsequential as Wickham's. His sole intent was to use this woman as a trump card and thus render Wickham somehow vulnerable. At least she appeared bright enough she grasped the concept herself. Meek she might never be, but biddable she was, and for now 'twas all that mattered.

While Brodie saddled Uar in the yard, Ran sought out their host. Gord was clearly worried about his wife, pacing the room where Fiona normally tended business matters in the mornings. First, Gord reminded Ran of his promise to foster Brodie for a year, and Ran agreed this was a good time for the lad to come. Gilbert was staying at Auchmull however long Darra would permit it, and the boys could take their lessons together.

Then the subject of Fiona rose. For being such a crusty soul, 'twas obvious the Scott was shaken by Fiona's sudden illness.

Gord gestured helplessly when Ran inquired after Fiona. "Wae worth! Ta crone canna find what's wrong. 'Tis afeared she'll lose the bairn."

Ran laid a hand on the laird's shoulder. "I'm sorry, Gord. Truly."

The other nodded, looking stricken and at a loss. "Mother Mac-Dougall said pr'haps a bad shock . . . Fi maunna be moved . . ."

Ran frowned at the mention of the old woman. He considered her a troublemaker. "I think a proper doctor should be sent for, Gord. Do not trust superstition to save your family."

"Spoken a'lik one who trusts none," replied the Scott, raking a big hand through his rusty mane. "Fi winna let me call any."

"That's because she is an overproud MacDougall." A ghost of a smile touched Ran's lips.

"Pride, och. Ye ken tha', too."

"Aye. At least let me send for a physic from Sterling, a man of some renown."

Gord nodded, his blue eyes moist with emotion. Without another word he clutched Ran quickly and fiercely, in a silent gesture of thanks, then hurried off to hover at his wife's bedside. Gazing after his old friend, Ran felt both sympathy and a faint pang of . . . was it envy? Surely not. The notion of being thrust into a position for caring for another person again, of being responsible, was sheer anathema to him. He had opened his heart to one woman, Blair Maclean, and there would never be another for him. On this, he was firmly resolved.

The journey to Auchmull seemed interminable. Merry was accounted a good rider, so though Lord Lindsay had offered her the services of Uar again, she was determined to exert some measure of defiance. Her pride would not let her appear weak before the enemy, and so she regally requested her own mount from the Goldielands stables.

Fortunately, the sorrel mare produced by Brodie Scott was docile and easy to manage. The boy referred to her as Ladybird. Still, trying to ride in a farthingale in an unfamiliar saddle proved no easy task. Ranald did not trust her with the reins, of course. Ladybird was secured and led, palfrey-style, behind his high-spirited gelding.

The early snows were far deeper in the Highlands than Merry had anticipated. As the three rode up out of the gentle border-lands where Goldielands was situated, the going got measurably rougher. Several times Ladybird plunged to her fetlocks in the snow and floundered for a few moments to regain her balance. The horses snorted great white clouds of steam as they slowly plowed through a narrow, high pass overlooking the side of wild Scotland she had never seen.

Glancing down over the steep cliff, Merry felt a familiar fear seize her in its grip. She remembered with sickening clarity the sensation of slipping, teetering on the edge, as she had walked a high stone wall at Raven's Hall that her twin had dared her to climb. Then the horrifying feeling when she realized her balance would not hold. Kat's grin had faded, too, as she reached out to steady her sister, too late. Eight-year-old Merry plunged over the wall, her cry silenced by the impact of hard ground. She had suffered a terror of heights ever since. She shivered now, cold despite the warm velvet cloak with its fur-lined hood that Fiona had given her. Merry would have given anything to have the other woman accompany her, if only as a companion in misery, but naturally 'twas impossible due to Fiona's present disposition as well as the fact she knew Lindsay would have flatly refused.

Blinking stray snowflakes from her eyelashes, Merry turned her attentions from the cliff to study the man riding ahead to her right. Ranald rode with a natural grace and style that might have seemed affected on any other man. She noted he looked utterly at ease in the saddle, as if he'd been born on a horse and took their long journey in stride. Yet, as ever, Merry sensed he was uncommonly alert. As if sensing her perusal, he glanced over his shoulder. But his eyes were completely unreadable, shadowed.

"How do you fare?" he asked her.

Merry wondered if it was concern or merely politeness that prompted his question. After all, he should appear hard-hearted indeed not to inquire after the welfare of a woman he had, in essence, kidnapped.

"I am tired, milord," Merry admitted. She was aware of him watching her closely as he nodded, and noticed for the first time the crest badge pinned to his black cloak. Like The Scott's, 'twas a silver strap-and-buckle style. Instead of a stag, however, the image of a swan rising from a coronet seemed a stark contrast to the spirited motto, Endure Fort. She wondered if the man was like the badge, a measure of both gentleness and strength. Thus far, she had only seen evidence of the latter.

Merry's grip on the saddle tightened as Brodie Scott's pony suddenly slipped and went down on its side with a crash. Luckily its rider was flung clear. As Ladybird came to a smooth halt beside Ranald's mount, Merry saw he did not hesitate. He leaped down from his saddle and assisted the injured youth to his feet.

"All right, lad?"

The boy nodded a bit shakily, dusting his cloak free of snow. "Thank ye, m'laird."

Merry knew Brodie must be of considerably lower social status, hardly one of Lindsay's Highland cousins. Yet Ranald treated the young man with the same concern one might expect from family. The morning sun cast relief onto Brodie's freckled features and thatch of orange hair. The bright color was almost comical, contrasting her own deeper shade of auburn. She remembered Ranald teasing her about being related to the red-headed Scott clan, and frowned.

"Is your horse injured?" Ranald asked the youth.

Brodie quickly retrieved his dun mare, which had since clambered back to her feet and was limping a little. He knelt and examined the animal's right foreleg with some expertise.

''Och, she's twisted it a bit, milaird. 'Twouldn't be wise to push her.''

Ranald nodded. ''Ride double with me, then. Have Duncan take a look at her the moment we reach Auchmull.''

''Aye,'' the boy said, already leading his dun over so she might be secured as Ladybird was. Then Ranald helped secure Brodie's injured mare to his saddle. Before he remounted, however, Ranald knelt and studied some tracks in the snow, scattered hoofprints Merry had not noticed until she saw him tracing the outlines with his long index finger. For some reason, he looked up at her. Merry almost flushed at the faint, accusatory look in his eyes. Or was it only a trick of the sun?

Nobody spoke. The horses shifted restively. Saddle leather creaked, harness jingled. The wind sighed across the rugged landscape, rippling the dried stalks of heather, stirring up little flurries of snow which swirled around the horses' legs. The end of Ranald's tartan snapped in the breeze. Merry's eyes remained locked with his as he slowly rose to his feet.

He made no move to brush off his breeches, but simply turned his back to her and vaulted smoothly up into the bay's saddle, where Brodie settled behind him. Uar snorted and pranced at the return of his master's hand. Ranald wheeled the horse about and set his heels firmly in place. The animal lapsed into a brisk pace, dragging the injured dun and Ladybird and her unwilling burden behind.

Every muscle in Merry's body screamed for reprieve by the time the riders forded the last creek and rode up a narrow ravine. The borderlands had gradually given way completely to a dense thicket of pine, mountain willow, and larch. They had been climbing in elevation for the final leg of the journey, and here and there early patches of snow testified to the Highland winter not so long away. Her fingers had nearly frozen as sunshine gave way to a cold Scottish drizzle. To her surprise, Ranald noted her predicament, and during one of their infrequent rests he rummaged in his saddlebags.

He tossed something at her. Startled, Merry caught the gloves and murmured a grudging thank-you as she pulled on the soft leather gloves. They were far too large, fashioned for Lindsay's longer fingers, but the warmth they provided was nothing short of delicious against the damp chill. She was aware of the intimacy of wearing a man's gloves. If Ranald was, he gave no indication. But it seemed he slowed the pace of their journey, perhaps in consideration of her weariness.

At last their destination loomed before her. The unwilling prisoner was too exhausted and saddle sore to fully appreciate the herd of red deer they startled as Uar cantered through the protected mountain pass, but Merry knew her first glimpse of Auchmull would be forever etched in her mind. She realized it the moment they broke free of the forest's gloom and a piercingly blue sky bowled above them, the color of lapis lazuli and just as pure but for a single golden eagle tracing lazy spirals against the sun.

Uar quickened his pace, anticipating food and shelter, and Merry's gaze fell upon the laird of Lindsay's keep at last. Against a backdrop of wind-scoured cliffs and rugged, emerald-green hills, a dark stone castle rose amidst ruins of older buildings. Just beyond Auchmull, Merry glimpsed a river sparkling like a deep blue thread of sapphire under the sun. The waters of the Esk formed a natural barrier in the south and west, while the remaining sides were guarded by two towers bristling with arrow-slits and crenellations. In an oddly softening touch, violets speckled the grassy knoll.

Merry knew Ranald awaited her reaction, and she didn't disappoint. " 'Tis beautiful," she said, albeit unwillingly, and though he said nothing in reply, she sensed he was pleased. Uar and the other horses shot forward in a sudden burst of speed, clattering noisily across a low stone bridge which marked the beginning of a narrow, winding trail up to Auchmull.

Merry was painfully conscious of her appearance after four days of hard travel, and sensed the perusal of Auchmull's occupants as they wound up toward the laird's home. Even after Lady Scott's hospitality, and the brief respite, she was worn from the journey.

She supposed she should cast off her borrowed raiment and enter the keep with the remnants of her English dignity intact, but 'twas cold yet in the bracing breeze and at least the velvet cloak served as a shield from the cutting wind.

She did not know what to expect by way of hospitality, nor did she know if Ranald had other mischievous relatives tucked away in the heathered woods, would-be rogues like young Gilbert who would take great delight in humiliating her however they might. She looked upon this new prison with trepidation, for prison 'twas and she made no mistake about it.

The tense silence between her and Ranald only deepened during the last leg of their journey from Goldielands, for no longer was this a pleasant jaunt, nor would Auchmull serve as a place for simply restoring her appearance. She was, in fact, the captive of a man whose conscience seemed as thin as autumn sunshine.

After his venture south to retrieve his wayward kinsman, Merry was surprised Ranald had let Gilbert and Hugo proceed on their own, spiriting the injured Jem only heaven knew where. ''The lads are in dire need of a lesson'' was all he said in response to the question she posed. She was hardly surprised when, upon reaching Auchmull, the stable master who hurried to greet them reported the boys had not returned.

Noticing Merry, the middle-aged man doffed his cap and held it to his chest. His awkward greeting betrayed his curiosity, but Ranald did not satisfy the man's questioning look.

''Aye, the lads will be along in a day or two, Duncan,'' he said. He swung down from Uar and swept Merry after him before she could think of a protest. Angrily she shrugged off his touch, cheeks burning as she recalled the passionate kiss of the previous night. He but sought to punish her, mock her naiveté, yet she could not deny her body had responded. 'Twas maddening, but this man appeared to wield some sort of magic over her she was powerless to fight.

Chapter Eleven

There would be no extra amenities because of who she was, Merry soon learned. If anything, the stares marking her progress into the outer ward of Castle Auchmull were hostile, suspicious, and full of hatred. English were the enemy, plain and simple, be they man or woman. Merry heard several low hisses from the onlookers and was surprised when Ranald turned a sharp, censuring gaze on the guilty parties.

The moment was shattered when the stable master spoke again. "M'laird, 'tis glad I am that yer back. There's been no end of trouble these past few days."

Ranald looked sharply at the man. "What happened, Duncan?"

The stable master's face was pinched with worry and outrage. "One of the horses is missin'. Starfire, it be. Young Dougal went to her stall to muck this mornin', and she be good as gone. 'Twere no sign of her breakin' free—"

Ranald swore under his breath as he turned and unceremoniously thrust Uar's reins into Brodie's hand.

"It must have been our uninvited guest again, Duncan. 'Twas apparently not enough that he tried to murder me in my sleep, but he must needs steal my best mare, too." He shot Merry a sidelong glance which she did not mistake for anything other than guilt by association.

He turned and motioned to another person across the courtyard. A pretty young girl with dangling flaxen braids, probably not more than fifteen or sixteen, came forward with obvious reluctance.

"Siany, show Mistress Tanner to the uninvited guest quarters."

"Aye, m'laird." The maidservant glanced curiously at Merry, then tucked her chin under and dashed across the yard. Merry had to hurry to keep up. She swallowed her indignation at the girl's lack of finesse, an obvious result of Lindsay's own laxity as a master.

She was admittedly curious, however, about the innards of the castle. Her first discovery was that Auchmull had a wonderfully acoustic main hall; an infant's screams echoed quite amazingly off the rafters from the depths of the servants' wing. Along the hall, she saw a few more retainers peering out from various spots, most openmouthed with either outrage or shock. The girl Siany was clearly displeased to be the one assigned to serve an Englishwoman. She deliberately hurried up the first set of stone steps and through a long hall, ignoring Merry's plea for mercy. Finally, after navigating an endless series of spiral steps and cold stone corridors, they arrived at a tiny chamber set well apart from the others. Merry realized with a pang of dismay and fury this was designed so on purpose. Here she could be easily watched and yet also removed from the main activity of the household. Here she would be nothing less than Lindsay's prisoner, in truth.

"Nay," she stated flatly.

The maidservant paused in the act of opening the door. She regarded Merry with awe and no little outrage herself.

"Nay," Merry repeated, " 'twill not do at all. 'Tis much too drafty. I cannot endure the cold."

Siany bit her lower lip, looking sulky. "I hae my orders, milady—"

"I realize that, but surely Lord Lindsay will understand when you explain the circumstances to him. I can wait here whilst you deliver the message. I've no desire to traipse up and down all those cursed stairs again."

The girl just stared at Merry, wide-eyed. She had pretty eyes, robin's-egg blue, with just a hint of green around the irises. Eyes Merry did not doubt she used to advantage whenever she wished to sway someone, particularly men.

"I . . . I dinna ken," Siany stammered at last. " 'Tis up to his lordship."

"Precisely," Merry coolly replied. 'Which is why I'm telling you to fetch Lord Lindsay up here; if nothing else, he should feel this drafty corner for himself." She glanced into the room, wrinkling her nose. "When was the last time anyone cleaned in here? The thirteenth century, mayhap?"

Siany didn't seem to notice the cobwebs draped from the rafters and billowing in the breeze, but Merry wasn't about to subject herself to such an ill-kept prison. The chamber was mean, and consisted of nothing more than a sagging mattress in a wooden frame and a broken old table leaned up against one wall. 'Twas an outrage, all right! If this was the way the Wolf of Badanloch treated his guests, then no wonder he had so many enemies.

"I see we're getting nowhere fast," Merry said briskly. "Please point out the way back downstairs."

Siany hesitated, as if she might actually refuse, and then reluctantly led Merry back down the halls and stairs, this time at a much slower pace, as if terrified of facing Ranald Lindsay.

He can't be such an ogre as all that, Merry thought, firmly setting her mind on accomplishing this one little goal. If she could get him to acknowledge her point about decent accommodations, then surely he would also consider being reasonable as well about keeping her here against her will. The matter of Wickham was obviously a sore one, but if they could just sit down like two civilized people, Merry was relatively sure he would be eventually swayed by her sincere speech. Of course, she'd have to avoid gazing into those dark eyes, or she knew she'd lose her nerve. There was something incredibly intense about the man's eyes, and she'd once heard a saying that the eyes were the windows of the soul. 'Twas certainly the case when it came to Ranald Lindsay.

"Good heavens," Merry gasped when they finally reached the main hall again. "I was beginning to fear I'd died and walked clear up to heaven and back again."

Siany looked stricken by the remark, but wisely said nothing. A little disgruntled, Merry decided that, like their master, the servants at Auchmull had no sense of humor. She sighed and brushed at her skirts, gazing about the great hall with a coolly critical air. At least Goldielands had projected some warmth and charm, whereas this place had none. The hearth was cold and dirty, as if a fire had not been lit for months. She wrinkled her nose, surveying the sparse furnishings with dismay. She knew the Lindsays were not a poor clan, and indeed Sir David Lindsay of the Mount had been renowned for his generosity.

Merry sent Siany after Lord Lindsay. Getting a response from the earl was quite another thing. She was tapping her foot impatiently by the time Ranald finally appeared; he looked as irritated as she herself felt.

"Thank you for coming so quickly, milord," she said with just the faintest trace of sarcasm.

Ranald in turn regarded her with no lost love. "I am given to understand there are some problems with your quarters, Mistress Tanner."

They were back to icy formalities. Their previous exchanges might never have taken place. Just as well. She could not bring herself to call him by his Christian name, in light of what he had done.

"'Tis mildly put. D'you honestly expect me to meekly assume residence in a filthy, rat-infested hole beneath some leaky rafters?"

The rats were a last-minute inspiration, Merry admitted, and she had no idea whether the rafters truly leaked or not, but it sounded so much better than just complaining about the filth.

After all, he could simply set Siany to cleaning the room or, heaven forbid, even order Merry to do it herself.

Ranald did neither. He simply frowned.

Encouraged, Merry continued briskly. "I am uncommonly susceptible to cold, milord. An ill hostage is scarcely a boon, rather a burden. I know you would not want the death of an innocent on your conscience." She added that for the benefit of the servants blatantly listening in on their conversation, and congratulated herself for winning the strike.

"D'you intend," he said, looking at her incredulously, "for me to be at your constant beck and call? Think you I have nothing better to do than listen to some *Sassenach* caterwauling from dusk 'til dawn?"

Merry stared at him for a second, dumbstruck. She blinked once or twice and felt herself slowly turning scarlet with fury.

"I beg your pardon, sirrah. I did not ask to be brought here; nor do I recall asking any special favors from you. However, I will be treated like a human being. If you cannot find a decent room for me in this crumbling heap of yours, then kindly send someone to muck out a stall in the stables. At least 'twould be warm and dry; I fancy the horses are kept well enough here!"

To Merry's further outrage, Ranald threw back his head and laughed. She watched the tanned column of his throat producing those low, ironic chuckles, and her hands clenched at her sides as she valiantly resisted the urge to hurl herself across the hall and throttle him. She quenched any further attraction to an obvious madman.

"That's more like it," he finally said when his laughter subsided. "Show the good folk of Auchmull just what a spoiled little bitch Tudor wenches truly are! Your superior airs have been the talk of this place since your arrival, m'dear; I'm so glad you didn't disappoint. For a time, I was beginning to wonder if your spirit was possibly broken, for you were refreshingly silent on the last leg journey here."

"You . . . you cur," Merry gasped, every inch of her frame trembling with fury.

"Aye, we mustn't forget your fiancé's favorite word for

Lindsays. Curs. Don't look so surprised. Of course I know every vile name and oath your betrothed has hurled in my direction over the past years. I could hardly miss hearing details; Highlanders tend to be very clannish, you see.''

Merry flushed and clutched her skirts in her fists. ''Faith, I can't believe you'd treat a woman so abysmally. I thought Highlanders professed to uphold some sort of chivalry . . . or at least moral decency,'' she added.

Ranald's eyes darkened to the color of thunderclouds. ''What would your kind know of morals?'' he coldly inquired.

Angrily she tossed her head, and the hood of her cloak fell back. She caught him watching the fiery rippling of her hair as it tumbled down her back.

''I only asked for the barest consideration you'd give anyone, Lord Lindsay. I realize I am not welcome here; I understand you have no intention of listening to my side of the story concerning Sir Jasper Wickham. Regardless of your feelings toward my betrothed, I have done you and your kin no harm. I should not suffer the consequences of your ill temper. If you will not provide me decent quarters here, then pray release me altogether.'' Genuine emotion thickened Merry's voice as she spoke.

Something flickered in Ranald's eyes. Not quite sympathy. Grudging admiration? Merry sensed some hidden emotion there. Yet his expression was, as always, impenetrable to her searching eyes, his heart immune to her pleas.

''Your point is well taken. In my haste to serve justice, perhaps another has been inadvertently crushed under my heel.''

Merry could have sworn the Wolf of Badanloch's gaze softened ever so slightly as it traveled up her rigid form. Ranald took a deep breath and spoke so softly she had to strain to make out the words.

''I bear you no personal malice. Yet you have the misfortune of being Wickham's woman, and I have a score of vengeance to settle with the Sassenach. The most I can offer is a chamber on the main floor, nearer the kitchens. 'Tis the warmest place in Auchmull. Aye, my ancestral seat is old and decrepit and I do not apologize for it. That's the most I can do.''

Merry lowered her gaze and blinked fiercely once or twice. She would not cry. She must not let the Wolf win! Nevertheless, she felt a single tear fall and leave its warm track down her left cheek. She simply nodded, too choked up to speak.

Ranald sighed, seeming more irritated than moved by her tears. With a curt wave of his hand, a pair of servants suddenly emerged from the shadows.

''Hertha. Ready Mistress Tanner's new quarters. Cleary, please assure the room is secure at all times.''

The two retainers, an elderly woman and young strapping man, each gave respective curtsies and bows.

''Aye, m'laird.''

Ranald then briskly disbursed the remainder of his staff to their various duties. As all the others moved off, he proffered Merry an eloquent if stiff little bow of his own.

''Mistress Tanner, I must request your presence this evening in the dining hall. There are some matters demanding my attention which require your cooperation. I trust you will not find them too taxing.''

Merry regarded him warily. Yet she knew she dared not refuse, for he held all the cards and they both knew it. She sought for any excuse to decline what would surely prove another unpleasant clash of wills.

''I fear I haven't any other clothes,'' she said at last. ''Just this gown Fiona lent me, and 'tis soiled from travel now, too.''

Ranald digested this information for a moment. ''Your personal possessions should arrive in a few days, along with Gilbert and Hugo. Until then, I'll set one of the maids to perusing the old wardrobes. Surely there is something suitable.''

''Thank you,'' she murmured reluctantly.

He nodded and turned to go.

''Wait, please.'' Merry noticed the way he stiffened warily at the mere sound of her voice. She spoke quietly in case anyone else was listening in. ''I know how easy 'twould have been for you to humiliate me completely in front of your staff, milord.

I'm sure in your eyes I deserve as much. Yet you didn't. And
. . . that is a sort of chivalry in itself, I suppose.''

"Do not presume to label my actions as anything other than
what they are,'' came the Wolf of Badanloch's frigid reply.
"Good day.''

Chapter Twelve

Merry could not find fault with the next chamber summarily produced for her inspection. 'Twas small, but more than adequate for one. The simple stone room had been enhanced by a few colorful wool tapestries on the walls, depicting various scenes of hunts and revelries. These not only added relief to her otherwise stark quarters, but helped to cut down on the drafts.

As Ranald had promised, 'twas far warmer there near the kitchens, and by the time afternoon fell, Merry had already made quite a little cozy nest for herself. She was surprised and touched when the woman Hertha, the maidservant who had originally readied the room, also went to the trouble to secure a hand-carved rocking chair from some mysterious source. This was then generously padded with sheep's wool, one of the main products of Highland farmers. This particular wool, Hertha informed Merry proudly, was the softest of the lot from Argyllshire.

"Ye remind me of m'middle daughter, Alyce, God rest her sweet soul," Hertha said as she looked at Merry. "Och, I swear I can see yer like in her. All that lovely red hair."

Merry was a little taken aback by the woman's friendliness, after her previous encounter with the younger maid. It proved even more puzzling when during their conversation when Hertha admitted to being Siany's grandmother.

The woman, who looked to be about sixty, clucked her tongue and shook her head at the mention of the girl. Merry could see the strong resemblance when Hertha frowned.

"Oh, milady, ye canna imagine the trouble tha' lass hae given me! Why, ever since Siany sprouted curves, all the Devil's own handiwork has broken loose 'round here!"

Merry smiled. The trials and tribulations of young womanhood were not restricted to Court, after all.

"She's popular with the boys, then?"

Hertha sighed with exasperation as she spread a heavy eiderdown quilt over the single bed frame where Merry would sleep.

"Aye. 'Tain't jest that, milady. I canna understand why the wench has no notion of weddin', proper-like. Says she dinna intend to marry, ever!" Hertha was obviously distraught by the possibility of her granddaughter never marrying. She lowered her voice as if confessing a particularly heinous secret. "Siany be almost sixteen, ye ken. What mon will hae an dried-up old apple like her in another year or two?"

Merry laughed. "Oh, Hertha, I am older still! And Milord Wickham was willing to accept my hand." She added carefully, "Mayhap your granddaughter just hasn't met the right one yet. Maybe she's waiting for love."

Hertha snorted at that. "Love? What use is love, miss? Does it feed the wee ones when 'tis frightful cold outside, or bring in the kindling from yon wood? Nay. Like I tell the foolish wench, ye may as well wed wi' a rich laddy as a poor." Something in Hertha's blue eyes sparkled with a memory then. Her work-roughened hands whitened as she smoothed the quilt down with firm, brisk strokes.

"Ochone, love." She sniffed, shook her head as if predicting dire calamity. "Nothin' good has ever come of that fancy notion, mark me words, milady."

Merry smiled. "I think you and I shall get on grandly, Hertha.

I, too, am of a much more practical bent." Perching on the neatly made bed to rest, she gazed up at the maid and said, "But surely you've loved someone in your lifetime, Hertha. What of Siany's grandfather?"

The woman looked startled. She glanced at Merry and then hastily lowered her eyes.

"Dinna ask me, miss," she whispered, sounding stricken. "I be a foolish trull then, all of Siany's age. I would nae listen to my folks, who 'trothed me to a right young farmer. I ran away, I did, and the rest 'twere dark history. Many's the time I've wept, milady, thinkin' of what I could hae had these two score and eight, a life o' ease and luxury compared to the hovel I kept until Lady Lindsay took me in."

Merry was not so much stunned by the story as she was the realization of Hertha's true age. Only forty-eight! Yet she looked like she could be Siany's great-grandmother. The Highlands were not merciful on people, she realized. Most of the servants she had seen thus far looked crabbed and worn, particularly the women, yet the odds were that they were no older than Hertha. She shuddered, imagining herself resigned to such a dismal fate.

Never would she willingly exchange the bright gaiety of Court for the prison of dark stone she found herself in now. By fortune's hand, at least Sir Jasper was wealthy. He would not subject his wife to the horrors of a crumbling keep, nor ban her from courtly merriment. She wondered then how much the servants at Auchmull knew of Ranald's intentions. Very cautiously, she inquired:

"D'you know aught of my betrothed, Hertha?"

Again the retainer looked startled, almost guilty. Then she lowered her voice, her faded blue eyes wide with dismay, and whispered, " 'Tis true, miss? Yer 'trothed wi' Wickham?"

"Aye. What have you heard about it, Hertha?"

"Nae more than most, miss. Least, I'm nae one for the gossip," Hertha added a bit defensively. "Tale is, ye'd agreed to wed wi' the Englishman, but young Ran dinna intend allowing it." Hertha glanced at Merry, as if measuring her reaction. "Och, caused quite a ruckus, miss, here at Auchmull, when ye arrived and the word spread like wildfire. That the Wolf of Badanloch seized Wickham's lass raised both fears and cheers."

Merry nodded. "Most sympathizing with Lindsay's cause, I imagine."

"Aye, miss. Fer we've all watched him wither away, in spirit, since Lady Blair's death." Hertha shook her head, clearly distraught but unable or unwilling to say more.

"Why does Lord Lindsay believe Wickham is responsible for his wife's death?" Merry gently prompted.

Hertha shook her head. "I was nae here myself when Lady Blair died, miss. I was visitin' m' eldest daughter, Meg, who wed a fisherman o'er at Oban."

"What happened?" Merry asked, still trying to comprehend what all this might mean and how it affected her own future. "To Blair, I mean." She understood how grief might unhinge a mind. Her own sister, Kat, had suffered memory loss when her first husband died. No telling what such a shock had done to Lord Lindsay. No wonder he seemed so set upon vengeance, with a single-minded disregard for others.

Hertha sighed and shook her head. "I'm nae sure, lass. The details are slim at best. I only ken Lady Blair traveled to Braidwood, or was waylaid there by a storm. She sickened whilst under Wickham's care, and he dinna send word to Auchmull. Nae until 'twas too late."

"Aye, Lady Scott told me the same tale. Yet this is motive enough for such cold-blooded revenge on Lord Lindsay's part?"

" 'Tis more, I'll warrant. The feud involves Blair's family, the Luckless Macleans."

"Why luckless, Hertha?"

"Because they lost their lands through dishonor. Their embittered chief sought alliance wi' the *Sassenach* to regain what measure he might. Lie down 'wi dogs, get up 'wi fleas, miss. Ran canna e'er forgie them betraying their Highlander blood.

"M'own husband was a Maclean, lass, descended from a

Macdonald vassal o'er on Mull." Hertha explained how she had been married to the man for only ten years before his heart failed.

Hertha shuddered and dropped her voice to a confidential whisper. "An' that be the vagaries o' love, lass. A starvin' wider and three hungry bairns. Dinna hae to tell ye how I cringed whenever I looked at what one feckless night had wrought. Thank heavens for Lady Lindsay; she heard of m'plight and sent for me an' the queans to come to Edzell. At last 'twas food on the table. We ne'er went hungry after that."

"How did you come to be here at Auchmull?"

"Och, after her ladyship died, m'lasses were already wed. Alyce died in childbed five winters ago. I raised Siany as m'own, and we came to Auchmull. Lord Ranald was kind enough to take us under his wing as his mum had done. He's a good master, is Ran. Treats us like kin, ne'er separates the families, like so many high n' mighty lords these days."

Hertha suddenly shivered. "Unlike Black Cullen, Lady Blair's brother. That one bears the mark of the Devil, I vow."

Merry was not interested in Blair's family. She wanted to hear more about the woman herself.

"Tell me, Hertha, how was it with the feud and all that Lord Lindsay and Blair were . . . that is, ever became . . . er—"

"Handfasted, miss." The retainer looked eager to be of help in the matter. "Two-and-twenty, Ran was then. Blair was ripe fer weddin' as well, being just fifteen. The tale was, they met at the Highland Games. Ran could nae take his eyes off her, so the story goes. The Scottish champion Black Cullen was there to compete in the caber toss, and as fortune would hae it, the two men drew and came up against one another. Ran won and Cullen Maclean ne'er forgot, or forgave. Public humiliation, 'twas. But as for love 'wi Lady Blair, best ask the master himself. He can tell the story better, milady. That is, if he's a mind to."

"I doubt he wishes any dealings with me at all."

Hertha nodded, but said soothingly, "I understand, lass. 'Tis hard sometimes to look at the past."

Or forget the future, Merry added silently. What man or devil would she be facing in the dining hall tonight? How could she deflect Lindsay's anger when she knew nothing of the story.

"God's nightshirt!" Merry swore aloud. Hertha looked at her, startled.

Merry laughed when she realized what she'd blurted out in her frustration. " 'Tis one of my mother's favorite oaths," she said.

Hertha looked delighted. "Why, yer halfway to a Highlander yerself now, lass."

"Do ye like it, miss?"

" 'Tis—different," Merry said honestly, gazing at herself in the wavy pier glass as Hertha adjusted the many pleats and folds of the plaid skirt. A long length of wool was thrown over her shoulder like a sash; Hertha called it a *feileadh mor*. The shirt beneath was a bright saffron. Merry had thought the color would clash with her vivid hair, but the silk was just the right shade of yellow to bring out deep golden highlights in her hair.

Hertha was right. When a *kersey* was added for full effect, she looked every inch a Highlander. The maidservant had found the gown, she said, in one of Auchmull's guest chambers. The previous owner, who was doubtless a wealthy lass, Hertha explained, would surely not miss one gown among so many. Merry suspected the clothing must have belonged to Lady Blair, but was merely grateful she was clean again.

She could have wept with gratitude when Hertha had badgered a couple of sturdy boys into lugging in a wooden tub, and then helped Merry to wash her hair. It had proven no easy task, but at last the waist-length locks were dry and gleaming with rich highlights. Merry had declined Hertha's offer to curl her hair, not sure what particular torture that might entail. She also thought Ranald might look more kindly on her if she looked very young and innocent.

Merry took a deep, steadying breath as she turned away from

the mirror. "Hertha, I'm beginning to fear this isn't such a good idea."

"Yer nae pleased wi' the clothing?"

"Nay, 'tis just that—"

A scratching sound came at the chamber door. Hertha hurried to answer it, apparently having assumed the position as Merry's tiring woman without any undue conversation between them. 'Twas just as well, Merry decided, since she hadn't the faintest notion of how to go about doing anything around here, and she felt helpless as a babe herself in the maid's capable hands.

Hertha spoke softly with someone at the door and returned a moment later.

"Lord Ranald has requested yer presence at the high table, milady. We finished here nae a moment too soon!" The white-haired retainer looked pleased with her handiwork. "Och, ye look right bonny, ye do. He'll nae recognize ye wi'out all the dust and grime."

"I pray so," Merry murmured, seized with a pure and utter panic.

Perhaps she could try to escape. Definitely out of the question, Merry realized, having eyed the surly Highlanders in the ward. She would have to stumble through this interrogation as best she could, and pretend she knew what Ranald was talking about—assuming, that is, he had anything to say to her other than making a few ugly accusations without any basis in truth.

Merry hadn't known Blair Lindsay, so she couldn't offer any comment upon the woman's death. Neither could she feign total immunity to Ranald Lindsay. 'Twas a nightmare of a situation, one that was giving her progressively worse nerves as the dinner hour drew nigh.

By then the sun had dropped from sight and the torches lining Auchmull's halls cast smoky relief onto the winding halls and corridors Hertha led Merry through. The retainer quietly pointed out several places along the way—a library, chapel, and the huge pantry beyond the kitchens. Most of the bedchambers were on the second level and up, Hertha explained, including the women's solar which had been used when Lady Blair had been alive.

Merry also learned from Hertha that Ranald's parents had both died relatively young. There had been some sort of riding accident which had taken the fourth earl's life, and Lady Lindsay had succumbed to a fever a few years before that. Besides Darra and Gilbert, there had also been a set of twins, boy and a girl, who had died of something Hertha called "white throat." Ranald was heir to Edzell, Auchmull, and Invermark now, unless something happened to him and Gilbert both, and then their nearest male kin, Lady Deuchar's sons, would inherit.

The worst fact was, Hertha explained, the Macleans were allied with Lord Deuchar. Which meant Ran still dealt with Blair's family, who were quick and cruel to hold him responsible for her death. Hertha shuddered again at the mention of Black Cullen. Her voice dropped to a whisper that echoed eerily in the narrow hall.

"He's a devil, that one, lass. Ye'll see what I mean if ye ever lay eyes on Lady Blair's brother. Different as night and day, those two, and they fight like hawk n' hound, too. 'Tis said Black Cullen wants t'see the last Lindsay fall. That way he'll hae a clear path to Auchmull, and Edzell, too. Beggin' yer pardon, milady."

Merry wasn't listening anyway. They had reached the great hall which served as a combination drawing, dining, and breakfast room. From the peaked ceiling dangled an iron chandelier, ablaze with white candles. A long wooden table occupied the center of the hall, and was generously decked with a variety of colorful dishes. At the far end of the hall, a minstrel's gallery jutted out above the shadowed recesses of the room, but 'twas empty. Only one man occupied the chamber, and he moved to smoothly intercept Merry as she entered.

The Wolf of Badanloch looked almost civilized this eve. His dark hair blended invisibly with the brown velvet doublet and breeches he wore, and the only mark of his Highland heritage was the silver badge Merry had seen before. This time, 'twas pinned in the center of a goffered frill. She caught a glimpse of a cream silk waistcoat beneath his unbuttoned coat, and soft ruffles fell over his hand as he extended it to her.

"Mistress Tanner."

His tone brooked no disobedience, yet Merry could not have denied him had she wished to. Something inexplicable drew her to this man, her nemesis, and she moved forward with a rustle of skirts as Hertha discreetly withdrew from the room. Merry heard the soft thud of a door behind her. She was alone with the Wolf.

"You look much restored" was all Ranald said. He did not compliment her on her appearance, as Hertha had hoped.

Merry felt a small, annoying pang of disappointment. "What an interesting room," she said instead, letting Ranald walk her as far as the table and then quickly freeing her hand from his. She had not missed the fact that her palms were moist and his were not. She wondered if he mocked her when he suddenly produced a lace-edged cloth from the pocket of his jerkin and handed it to her without a word. She twisted it nervously in her hands as she listened to him.

"Auchmull was originally built in the twelfth century, but not fortified until over a hundred years later, by means of the largest stone tower you saw outside. In my grandfather's time, 'twas again rebuilt. You stand in the most recent addition, though of course it cannot compare to Whitehall or Richmond Palace."

Merry thought she detected a note of bitterness in his voice. "It has great character," she said, struggling to be polite. He flashed her a faint smile.

"I'm gratified you find it acceptable by Tudor standards. Shall we dine?"

Merry let the jibe pass and agreed that they should. She was relieved when they were seated at opposite ends of the table, and servants reappeared, in order to serve the various dishes. Merry could not identify most of the food. She tried to surreptitiously sniff at each portion with the pretense of dropping the kerchief, but the ruse was spoiled when one of the servants quickly leaped forward to restore the kerchief to her lap. She smiled and nodded, though she was in actuality annoyed.

Merry was afraid of trying any strange dishes, in case she should become ill. She was used to depending on the queen's taster and she knew only too well how Ranald felt about her. She was Wickham's representative, for better or worse. She considered refusing to eat, but this would surely anger Ranald more. At Goldielands, she had only had a simple porridge to break her fast, and Hertha had filched her a couple of apples and a wedge of hard cheese from the kitchen earlier in the day. But this dish before her was positively swimming in creams and sauces, and her stomach roiled dangerously as she stared down at her plate.

"Mistress Tanner?" Coming from the other end of the table, Ranald's voice had a distinct edge, though he managed to sound solicitous enough before the servants. "Is there something amiss?"

She shook her head and pushed at what appeared to be mutton with the single spoon she had been given. Aware he was watching her, she finally took a tiny, cautious bite. It wasn't too bad, just very overcooked and salty. She smiled weakly down the table at her host.

"Delicious," she mumbled.

"Do you think so? I've never particularly cared for haggis myself, but then I suppose Sassenach have a more refined palate from birth."

"Haggis?"

"Sheep's pluck: Cook mixes heart, liver and entrails with oatmeal and beef suet," Ranald answered offhandedly as he helped himself to a crisp rack of beef from a silver platter held by a servant.

Merry gagged discreetly into the kerchief, and then quickly reached for a goblet of what she assumed was water. She was wrong. After gulping the vinegary drink halfway down, she found herself coughing and gasping for air.

Ranald was the first one to the rescue. He materialized behind Merry and slapped the flat of his palm hard between her shoulder blades. She wheezed and clutched the edge of the table to keep from ending up face-first in the haggis. Her back throbbed from the impact of his hand.

"Water," she gasped.

A fingersnap sent the servants running. One eventually returned with a pewter goblet which Ranald shoved into Merry's hand.

"Here. Drink this down and you'll feel better."

Merry did. The water was brackish and odd-tasting, but at least it obliterated the vinegary residue. She looked at Ranald accusingly.

"Blaand 'tis an acquired taste," he said, referring to the vinegary malt she had gulped unthinkingly.

"Like Scotland, apparently."

He smiled faintly at her insult. "I've never known Highland-ers to have a weak constitution, lass," he said softly. Merry was aware of the fact the other servants had not returned; the last one had slipped discreetly away at his signal. Ranald remained behind her chair, resting his hands on the backrest, just inches away from her hair. She could almost feel the Wolf's warm breath on her neck.

"Aye, well, I much prefer England. Living at a civilized Court."

Ranald chuckled. "Do you know, Merry," he suddenly said, as casually as if he were discussing the weather, "I've never seen a woman with hair the exact color of yours. 'Tis like live flames. Fire plays in it . . . like so."

She gasped very softly. His use of her Christian name sur-prised her as much as the fingers running slowly, leisurely, through the silken strands, as if he were an appraiser admiring the reflection of candlelight on her gleaming auburn tresses. Then he bunched the soft hair in one hand and raised it above her head, pinning it in place as he bent to place a kiss on the exquisitely sensitive nape of her neck.

Merry's eyes closed as she felt his lips trailing across her skin. He punctuated each tiny kiss with a word.

"Damme you, woman . . ."

She tingled all over, her own fingers clutching the table for support. Light and fleeting as butterfly wings, Ranald's kisses intoxicated Merry like a heady wine. She could no more fight him than she could herself, and a small, choked sob escaped her own lips as he sensuously nuzzled her right ear.

"I wonder how a dark wolf and bright flame would dance together," Ranald mused, and his grip in her hair tightened as if in unspoken threat. He was warning her not to answer, Merry knew, and she could do no more than give a little shake of her head, at which he abruptly released her and stepped back.

"Nay," he growled under his breath. She rose from her chair, turned and saw Ranald raking a hand through his hair. His dark eyes flamed with rage, directed more at himself than her.

"I must seem nothing more than a coarse barbarian to you." He gave a self-deprecating little laugh. "I can hardly compete with seasoned courtiers like Wickham, after all. You must forgive my lapse of sanity. 'Twill not happen again, I assure you."

Merry's heart was still pounding furiously. Stung by his words, she faced him. She wanted to give him the tongue-lashing he so deserved, and opened her mouth to do just that. She never had a chance.

"Spare me your pretty little speeches. Your mock outrage. Admit what I did was no bolder than the knaves who discreetly grab and paw you at Court."

He was gazing contemptuously at her. Heat rushed to her cheeks. The worst thing was, 'twas true enough. He obviously did not believe she was a virgin, but rather one of the Court bawds who coyly solicited men for favors and rewarded them however she might.

"I am an engaged woman, sirrah," she shakily replied. Anger heated her voice, made her quiver where she stood. "How dare you imply I lift my skirts for any cad!"

"Yours are not the eyes of a devoted fiancée. They gleam far too brightly after my attentions."

Merry was livid. So furious her voice was nothing more than

a raspy whisper. "How rich. My kidnapper sits in judgment of me! You don't know me at all, sir. That much 'tis obvious."

"Surely you cannot deny everyone 'tis shaped by their experiences. The sheltered yet tawdry life at Court you lead has made you what you are."

"Aye, then mayhap your mistrusting, antagonistic nature is derived from the harshness of your surroundings, Lord Lindsay." She glanced pointedly at the cold hearth, then back to him.

Ranald stiffened at her words. "You need not tell me my home is a travesty. I know it well enough. Wickham is a far better catch. I grant the enemy that much even now." He was silent a moment, and she saw a pulse beating furiously in his neck. The silver badge flashed at his throat. Merry saw banked fires in his eyes. A cold fire . . . one of rage.

"There is nothing I can say." Merry lifted her hands in a gesture of frustration.

"Say anything more, madame, and I'll throttle you myself." The Wolf's voice was smooth as a blade, thrusting invisibly between her ribs. "You are my prisoner, not my guest. I'll not forget it again. Neither shall you. From now on, you'll take meals in your room. I wish to see and hear nothing of you, unless I request it. Is it understood?"

Merry looked at him. Her throat ached with all the unspoken words, apologies, excuses; they were not hers to make. He would not hear them anyway, coming from her. Wickham's woman, he'd dubbed her. To Ranald Lindsay, she was the shrewd Court vixen who rucked up her skirts for any passing buck. She felt powerless against his rage; the legacy of hate his wife's death had left was so daunting, how could she ever expect fair treatment or impartial regard in this man's eyes?

Finally she broke the daunting silence. "I believe you said— there was something you wanted to see me about."

Ranald gazed at her incredulously. Merry held her breath, wondering what he'd seen, what kind of monster he made her out to be in his own mind.

"Aye." He gave a low bark of laughter at the reminder. "I

intend to send a missive to Wickham on the morrow. I will dictate it, you may soften it in your own sweet fashion to your fiancé. I presume you can cipher?''

''Of course.'' While not many women of the time were well educated, Merry was proud of her neat hand.

He nodded curtly. ''Wickham enjoys controlling others, making others dance like puppets on his strings. But this time he shall not have the satisfaction. This time, I am in control.''

Merry felt the ice of his words. What kind of hell had Sir Jasper supposedly put this man through? And why?

Ranald's glittering eyes gave no answers. At this moment, she knew she could beg for answers and he would not even give her the satisfaction of a response. With the posture of one who has been defeated and knows it, Merry quickly turned and left the hall, before she said something she would later regret.

Chapter Thirteen

Merry greeted the new day considerably refreshed. She had slept long and hard, over twelve hours, and such a sweet, unbroken sleep was the greatest gift she had received since arriving at Auchmull.

Hertha met her with a breakfast tray in bed. "There's stove tatties and porridge, and pirr ta whet yer appetite, lass."

Merry gamely tackled the strange offerings, though with a marked reservation after the meal of the previous night. She discovered she didn't mind the porridge, though it was somewhat bland, and the tatties were too salty by half. The drink, however, had a rich flavor with a sweet aftertaste that kept her returning for more. She remarked upon its appeal to Hertha.

"Aye, Lady Blair favored it also." Hertha gave a sad, drawn-out sigh. "It seemed to quell the sickness a bit, 'wi the bairn and all."

"She was *enceinte?*"

"Aye, lass. We thought the poor thing too delicate to survive a hard travail wi' a large bairn anyway, but ne'er found out. Such a weep and a wail as ye never heard, lass, as when Lady Blair and the Lindsay heir was lost. Nae that 'tis the only tragedy hereabouts. Nell Downie and her mon, Fergus, had been tryin' to hae a bairn for years. She lost her little one last week, and Fergus died at Badanloch.'' Hertha shook her head sorrowfully. '' 'Tis God's will, I reckon.''

Merry suffered a pang, this time one of conscience. Ranald had lost not only his wife, but his child, too. Despite her anger and outrage at his actions, she could grasp his motivation. He blamed Wickham for all his misfortune, and, logical or not, he intended to see the revenge through.

She shivered. Caught in the middle as she was, she might very well be destroyed by either or both of two powerful men. Anything was a welcome distraction now.

''I'd like to meet this Nell,'' she said impulsively. ''Is't possible?''

Hertha looked surprised. ''Why, o' course. She'll be honored, that's for sure.'' She hesitated then, remembering Lord Ranald and his rules. But he had merely specified Mistress Tanner never leave Auchmull. As far as Hertha knew, there was no law against socializing *within* the keep walls.

''Tell ye what,'' she said to Merry. ''After ye've finished yer breakfast here, I'll take ye up to Nell's room.''

''She lives here in the castle?''

''Aye, just for a while. What wi' her losin' the bairn, and the fearful winter coming on, Lord Ranald insisted she stay here until she's well enough to return to her own cottage. Fergus rode wi' Ran, ye ken, so he was nae always there to look after Nell. Though he was a good mon, was Fergus Downie.''

''Hertha,'' she asked, ''Has there been any word how Lady Scott fares?''

The maid nodded. ''Word came from Goldielands late last night. The illness has subsided, and the physic is at her side. Time shall tell if her bairn survives.''

''I shall pray for her. Send a message even, if Lord Lindsay would permit it.''

''He canna say na, lass.'' Hertha smiled her crooked little smile. ''Lady Scott is verra dear to all the Lindsays, and Brodie said she took a shine to ye whilst ye were there.''

"Aye, I liked her, too."

After breakfast, Hertha kept her promise and took Merry to the south tower, where Nell Downie was recuperating from her own tragic misfortune. Having rather expected a huge, slovenly woman with pendulous breasts, Merry was admittedly startled by the petite, pixielike lady whose pretty brown eyes affixed with some apprehension upon her unexpected visitors.

Nell looked about twenty, but then again, Merry was beginning not to judge age by appearance. Madame Downie was clearly surprised that an Englishwoman took such an interest in meeting her, and her greeting was hesitant but warm.

" 'Tis an honor, miss," Nell said in a soft voice. She was still abed, her glossy brown curls tumbling down around her shoulders. Though small-framed, she appeared sturdy and capable, and Merry unconsciously relaxed. She also sensed, somehow, that this young woman would be as fierce as a tiger where children were concerned.

Feeling a sudden tug on her own heartstrings, Merry said, "I'm sorry for your recent losses, Nell."

The young woman's eyes widened, and for a moment Merry thought she might cry, but then Nell gave a brave sniffle and choked out, "Yer so kind, miss. I canna hardly picture ye as a *Sassenach* lady."

"Aye, our Nell here would nae believe me at first when I told her ye dinna sprout horns from yer flaming hair," Hertha put in merrily.

Merry laughed. "Methinks Lord Lindsay might disagree with you there." Hands on her hips, Merry gazed around the small chamber, cold and dismal as her own before she and Hertha had put it to rights. Already her mind tidied and swept and restored the room so the patient might rest more comfortably.

She had a sudden idea. She knew Hertha would cooperate, for the tiring woman had approved of her fastidious nature more than once. With a smile tugging at her lips, Merry vowed to enlist the aid of Hertha and the good women of Auchmull in rendering these ramshackle quarters more livable. 'Twas unconscionable that a young woman suffering childbed trauma and an old woman with aching joints should be subjected to such a cold, cheerless place. Thus resolved, Merry began planning her first tasks as Auchmull's makeshift chatelaine, for nothing buoyed her spirits more than assuming control of disaster and magically transforming chaos into order.

Two days later, Ran returned from riding over his demesne in a foul mood. The message had been delivered to Wickham as planned, but as yet no response issued from the great border peel. He had expected at least a cry of outrage, one he hoped to hear echoing across the Grampians for miles distant. Nothing.

He knew Sir Jasper for the calculating, cold-hearted bastard he was. But surely even a puffed-up Sassenach lordling would not be immune to a lady's call of distress. Especially when she was his fiancée, chosen for her courtly connections and favor in the queen's eye. To occupy himself while awaiting Wickham's response, Ran rode out and checked on the welfare of his tenants and kinsmen, as he did each autumn after Mabon and the harvesting, assuring they had enough stores for the long winter ahead. Rain started during his last leg, an icy drizzle which quickly soaked his woolen breccan and turned to snow within the last mile. A wet snow he knew would not stick, but a daunting reminder of the hard dark days to come.

Responsibility weighed heavily upon Ran's mind, a legacy from the last Earl of Crawford who had drummed the notion into his son's head from birth. Ran had been carefully groomed for his role as clan chief, and personal preferences were inconsequential to his sire. Normally he did not mind the duties associated with his lot in life; after all, it had led to his union with Blair, but in the past months Ran began to question his position. Over a hundred depended on him for food, shelter, and protection. Lindsays and all their related septs were fiercely loyal to the core, but Ran was starting to resent, however churlishly, their almost childlike devotion. He was a loner by nature, not a leader, though his reiving days were legendary, and word that the Wolf of Badanloch had joined the Scotts for a border foray brought a sparkle to his kinsmen's eyes and much comment this day wherever he went.

Ran knew they prayed the Wolf had returned so all might be right with the world. In his heart, he knew it could never be. Nothing would be the same without Blair. His hands tightened in Uar's coarse mane and he blinked back a mist of emotion, resolved not to succumb again. Sobs shook his big frame for one dark night after she died, as if an angry god rattled him in a knotted fist, but since then he had turned grief into hard, cold resolve and nothing, nobody, would ford his defenses again. On this much, he was determined.

Riding through the wet snow, up the muddied path toward Auchmull, Ran gazed bleakly at his legacy and the keep he called home. Sweet Jesu, had ever a castle seemed so empty, devoid of light or warmth, Blair's laughter forever gone, only the shuffle of feet and murmuring servants lending any sign of life. He had never thought he might despise Auchmull as he did his daunting childhood home, Edzell, but at this moment he desired nothing more than to wheel Uar about and disappear into the cloak of night.

He pressed on, however, meeting Brodie in the yard, who took charge of Uar at once and informed him of Gilbert and Hugo's return. Ran nodded and swung down from his tired steed, groping for energy he did not find. He knew all that awaited was a cold hearth and an empty trencher, for he thought it nonsense a meal should await a man who came and went like the wind.

Wearily he trudged up the steps and into the hall, where he stopped short and blinked stray snowflakes from his lashes. Surely he was imagining things now. He heard a low murmur of voices coming from the great hall, a clink of glass and . . . laughter. A woman's laughter. Not husky like Blair's, but silvery, tinkling, like a little fairy's mischievous chuckle. He unfastened his soaked breccan and tossed it onto a wooden peg, beginning a slow burn even as the laughter subsided into a contented drone of conversation. He recognized Gilbert's voice and frowned. Whatever was going on, Ran intended it would stop at once.

He burst into the hall without fanfare and the abrupt, guilty silence confirmed his suspicions. Gilbert was lounging upon the low couch before the hearth, which blazed as brightly as Ran's temper. His little brother looked quite at ease, too, falling band undone and carelessly draped about his neck, dark hair mussed and violet-blue eyes glinting with high spirits. Ran's narrowed gaze traveled down to Hugo, where the blond giant sprawled on the rug before the hearth, toasting his huge, dirty bare feet as casually as if he attended a country fair.

'Twas Merry Tanner who captured the brunt of his attentions, though, draped as she was across a burgundy velvet chair, one leg slung in very unladylike posture across the arm of the chair, a golden slipper dangling from her toes. She was wearing some outrageous courtly frippery, a lavish gown of pale-gold silk trimmed with ivory lace and seed pearls, whose skirts were so voluminous she appeared to be a redheaded doll propped in the chair.

At Ran's entrance her laughter trailed off, and she struggled to sit upright, but dissolved into soft gale of giggles when she was unable to effect a graceful recovery. Ran noted the nearly empty glass of claret clasped in her little hand, and his frowning gaze traveled from his prisoner back to Gilbert, then swiftly crossed the shockingly clean, orderly great hall.

"Ran. Welcome home!"

Ran ignored Gil's cheerful greeting. "I presume your mission was accomplished to my satisfaction?" His deadly cold voice echoed in the hall as he looked at Gilbert. The young knave stopped grinning and sprang up like a puppet at his brother's inquiry. He shifted a little nervously under Ran's regard but maintained his jaunty air.

"Aye, Mistress Tanner's man will recover nicely. We saw him to an inn, left him in the care of a couple who promised to see him home. I left my own purse for their troubles."

" 'Twas the least you could do, I should think." Ran offered no compliment when none was warranted. His gaze raked Gil up and down. "You do not appear much the worse for wear, despite your lengthy journey."

"We've been back a whole day. You were out riding the hinterlands, Hertha said." Gil sounded a trifle defensive, and Ran's ire raised a notch further when he saw the boy sneak a glance at Merry, as if seeking her support or reassurance.

She had set the liquor aside and appeared considerably sobered, through her gray-green eyes were bright from spirits or with spirit and her overall air was defiant. She righted herself in the chair and smoothed her skirts, returning Ran's cool regard. "Indeed. Welcome home, milord."

"Home? Not as I recollect it." Ran's retort encompassed the merrily crackling hearth, the jewel-toned rugs he had not seen for months, which had been relegated to storage after Blair's death. He felt as if an army of emotion invaded his home, the contented demeanor of the others only mocking his private despair. How dare any woman, and Wickham's at that, assume proprietary rights over Auchmull, how brazen of the Sassenach wench to move items about and clean and rearrange to her heart's content, as if she owned the place! Ran stared daggers at Merry, but she raised her chin a notch and their silent battle of wills raged beneath the already tense undercurrents in the hall.

"Mistress Tanner has been amusing us with tales of a masque at Greenwich this eve," Gil put in quickly to ease the awkwardness, his grin raffish as ever. "I declare, I should very much like to visit Glorianna's Court one day."

"One does not step unwitting into an adder's nest, Gil," Ran replied, still looking at Merry. " 'Tis the first lesson in life I thought I had taught you."

Merry bristled at his remark. "Methinks judging the worth of somebody of whom one has no personal knowledge rather high-handed, Lord Lindsay."

Her cool use of his title informed Ran she was in a high dudgeon, but he no longer cared. At this point he wanted her out of his life, her meddling ways relegated to the court where she belonged.

"I see you are quick to take advantage of even the slightest lapse in rules, Mistress Merry,'' Ran said as he glanced over the unfamiliar hall.

"Christ's wounds!" Gilbert suddenly exploded. "This place was a sty! You cannot deny the change is for the better, Ran, and I, for one, have no complaint." The younger man flung himself back on the couch, hands linked over his middle as he glared at Ran with a sulky countenance.

" 'Tis not the place of a prisoner to rearrange furniture, Gil. I hold you responsible for letting matters get out of hand. I told you Mistress Tanner was to keep to her room until negotiations have been finished."

"What negotiations?" Gil hurled back. His defiance touched a nerve in Ran and suddenly he resolved to clear the room.

"That's enough. You and Hugo are dismissed for the night. Don't trifle with my temper any more than you already have. And as for you, Mistress Tanner—"

"Aye?" Merry faced Ran with equal aplomb, rising from the chair and folding her arms across a décolletage he noticed was far too daring for every day wear. Had she attempted a curtsey, he was willing to wager her breasts would tumble out in all their silken ivory glory.

Ran flushed a bit at the thought, feeling overheated. He was used to the hall being cold and dank, and the warmth permeating his bones now, while welcome, was most disconcerting. So were the emotions this redheaded woman roused in his chest, her clear eyes transmitting both a silent challenge and a plea he found strangely compelling. Exciting, even. He did not understand his attraction to a woman so unlike Blair, his beloved wife. None could compare to his flaxen-haired, sweet-natured lass and he was determined none should ever try. He tore his gaze from Merry with some effort.

" 'Tis over late," he muttered. "We shall speak on such matters another time. For now, 'tis enough you understand when boundaries have been crossed."

"Aye, milord. I understand quite well." Merry's voice was frosty as she spun on her heel and vacated the hall, leaving only the scent of damask roses in her wake.

Chapter Fourteen

Late the next evening, just before the crimson sun slid down behind the dark-gray clouds marching over Auchmull, a rider arrived at the gates.

Hertha found Merry gazing out at the thickening clouds from the single, narrow window in her room. "Och, 'tis surely the messenger from Braidwood. Lord Ranald is away."

Jolted from her reverie, Merry turned from the window. "I'd like to meet the rider in the yard," she said. "Mayhap he has word of how Jem is doing."

"I'll stay and finish mending this hem, lass. Ye go on ahead."

Tossing Hertha a quick nod of thanks, Merry grabbed up a cloak, gathered up her cumbersome skirts, and hurried out the door. It never occurred to her to think she might be breaking Ranald's rules. Even after the previous night's incident, she was determined she would make the best of her lot. She'd been cooped up too long without benefit of fresh air or stimulating company, and was anxious for news about her fate.

Nevertheless, she couldn't forget the chilly reception she'd received from Auchmull's inhabitants upon her first appearance, and she paused to self-consciously tug up the hood of her cloak about her face. In the twilight, her features and distinctive red hair were reduced to shadowy nothingness. She completed her journey without incident.

The inner ward was bustling with activity as Auchmull kinsmen were busy unloading a wagon piled high with kegs of heather ale. Merry heard a little grumbling as she passed by the workers, most of it directed at her.

"I thought she was supposed to be our prisoner, nae our bleedin' royal guest!"

"Did ye see the gown she wore at sup? Whoosh! How many falderals does the *Sassenach* wench have, I wonder?"

"Enough to snare poor Ran, nae doubt," one fellow snickered under his breath as he swung down the last barrel with no little ease, and it slammed to the ground at his feet.

Merry overheard a few more muttered remarks about the fickle hearts of females as the men rolled off the barrels. She stared after them a moment, troubled by what she'd heard. There was no lost love for her in any of their voices. Why their opinions should matter at all was just as disconcerting as the contents of their speech.

Merry saw the lone rider had dismounted and was tending his steed. Duncan and Brodie had gone with Ranald after dinner on a mission to purchase a horse to replace the stolen one, and though Gilbert was supposed to be guarding her, he and Hugo had imbibed a bit much with the meal and lolled about the hall, slumped laughing over a half-finished chess game.

Merry approached the messenger, supposing he was bewildered why he was not hailed with eager questions. The other men had admitted him after a cursory inspection and gone about their business tending the ale. With the fading light silhouetting the man's figure against the horizon, Merry couldn't make out much more than the fact he seemed very cold or tired. His shoulders were hunched up around his ears, and a long cloak was tightly wrapped about his body, a hood shadowing his features. His hands appeared strong, however, as he juggled the reins about. He was gazing straight ahead, and Merry approached from the side.

"Excuse me," she said quietly. "I was wondering if you might carry word from Braidwood."

The man started, his head swinging around sharply at the sound of her voice. She made out a narrow, sharp-featured face belonging to a youngish man with a curl of brown hair dangling over his brow. He was not uncommonly large but appeared sturdy.

"Mistress Tanner?" he inquired almost warily, studying her closely.

"Aye."

"My name is Cullen Maclean."

"Cullen!" she exclaimed as a wave of shock and disbelief rolled over her mind, threatening to overshadow her composure. Blair Lindsay's brother. The dreaded "Black Cullen" Hertha had warned her about. His blue eyes narrowed in warning.

"Hush, gel," he said, and glanced around them almost furtively. "There's others who'll overhear ye. And if ye wish to leave Auchmull alive, 'tis wise ye listen to me. I bear word from Sir Wickham."

Merry realized with a sense of mounting hope he must be part and parcel of some rescue attempt. He could help her. It seemed ironic she should be forced to turn to Lindsay's brother-in-law for aid, but she did not question her good fortune.

Lowering her voice, she said rapidly, "La, you won't believe what's happened to me. 'Tis all so incredible. But of course, you must know. You're here, aren't you?"

He gave her a level look with uncanny blue eyes. "Dinna say The Wolf has nae earned his reputation," he growled under his breath. "Like Blair, ye seek to find a conscience where there is none. Ye women hae to go and meddle wi' things ye know nothin' about."

Merry had a sudden pang of fear. Perhaps he was right. Maybe the last shred of humanity she sought in Ranald's dark eyes was simply not there. Now Cullen Maclean appeared to be her best chance for rescue, and Merry was desperate for an explanation.

"You're right," she blurted. " 'Twas wrong of me to foolishly trust Lindsay. I thought him Providence at first, after the coach accident. It seemed coincidental when he appeared at my rescue—''

''Nae so coincidental now, eh?'' Cullen said, and she thought he might be laughing at her with those cool blue eyes.

''Nay,'' Merry replied softly, stepping forward so she could see his face more clearly beneath the hood. ''What has Sir Jasper to say of these appalling matters?''

''He is livid,'' Blair's brother tersely responded. ''He will have Lindsay's head for this. A grave insult hae been dealt the house of Wickham, and as Macleans are vassal to Sir Jasper we shall stand wi' him against the Wolf o' Badanloch.''

Merry was gravely silent a moment. ''How did it happen, Cullen? How did your sister die?''

He didn't immediately answer her. Instead, his keen gaze moved across the yard, where he spied several men hurrying out from the keep.

''Yer lord and master has noted yer absence, lass,'' Cullen told her. '' 'Pears he dinna trust ye.''

''Lord Lindsay is not my lord or master,'' Merry replied sharply, but as she spun about, she saw Gilbert Lindsay dashing down the steps, clothing rumpled, raking a hand through his dark hair, a frantic expression on his face. He had been ordered to watch over her, and Ranald had trusted him to the task.

''Ran's a clever one,'' Cullen mused in a low voice, ''but he canna watch us all at once.'' He shook his head and a faint smile sketched his lips. ''Och, what a coil this be.''

''I had nothing to do with any of this,'' Merry said defensively, realizing with a sinking sense of despair that Gilbert's frantic search about the yard would soon unearth them both. Gil had not drawn attention to her missing status since he obviously did not wish Ran to know of his failings, but he was now striding in their general direction. Soon she would lose her only chance for answers.

''Cullen!'' she pleaded softly, extending an entreating hand to the messenger. The other man merely shook his head, indicating the time for conversation had ended the moment Gilbert

Lindsay had spied their exchange. Seconds later, Gilbert joined them. He took in Merry's high color and recognized the visitor at once. His violet-blue eyes flashed.

"I can imagine what brings you to Auchmull," he greeted Cullen shortly. "You'd best get on the road again before Ran returns."

"Please," Merry blurted, stepping between the two wary young men. "There must be a way to settle matters peaceably, without further conflict."

Gilbert set his jaw. He clearly didn't like the sound of such a notion.

"If you're planning an escape, Merry, you may as well realize there is no use," he told her. "Ran has Auchmull well guarded by day and night, and our clansmen don't ask questions when they find something amiss. Ran's orders are that you shall not leave, and his wishes shall be met whatever the cost."

Merry sighed. She pulled the cloak closer about her form, shivering as she felt Cullen Maclean's sharp gaze scouring her face a bit too closely for comfort. She cleared her throat and spoke briskly.

"Please give me a little credit, Gilbert. I know better than to try to escape. I simply don't wish to see conflict further heightened over me."

"Then you will avoid the company of this one, Merry." To her surprise, Gilbert's gaze was level and cold on Cullen. He almost reminded her of a younger version of Ranald then.

Drawing himself up proudly, Black Cullen gazed contemptuously back at the young man. Something very close to hatred burned in his blue eyes.

"Yer skeevin' leader killed nigh ten innocents," he rasped, "and we will nae soon forget it! Those Macleans who lived will carry the memories of Badanloch in our hearts and minds forever, and live each day with a fresh curse on our lips for all Lindsay curs and their treachery!"

Gilbert looked pale but proud as he stared back at Blair's brother.

"Y' know Ran cannot be responsible for what happened,"

he replied in a shaking voice. " 'Twas a terrible miscarriage of justice, aye, but twisted circumstances led to that outcome and you may rest assured a full investigation has been started in the name of the king.''

"The king! Pah!" Cullen spat, and Merry was shocked by his vehemence, and the murderous rage which briefly lit his eyes. They flared bright blue for just a second, and she could see the proud young man matched Ranald's temper for sheer ferocity.

"Darra has Queen Anne's ear," Gilbert said. "If anyone discovers the truth, 'twill be Lady Deuchar."

Cullen sneered. "Doubtless Her Majesty will find in favor o' the Lindsays who dance on the strings of the new Kirk. We canna expect a fair hearing from thievin' Jacobites." He pressed his lips tightly together for a second, as if gathering his composure. Then he said, almost humbly, " 'Tis a long ride back to Braidwood. A storm lurks on the horizon. I feel it in me bones. Canna let yer own shirttail relative hae the shelter of yon livery fer one night?''

Gilbert looked displeased by the request, but before he could even answer, fat white flakes began to drift lazily down from the sky, a few catching in the thick tangle of his eyelashes. He blinked them aside with a sigh.

"All right," he said in a low voice as tension throbbed between the two men. "You may sleep in the stables with your horse. Hugo will watch over you. If there is any trouble, any at all, you will reckon with Ran personally when he returns."

Cullen bobbed his head in what Merry thought was a mock gesture. He did not speak to her again of Wickham or any other matter, and with mounting despair she allowed herself to be drawn away by Gilbert. His hand gripped her arm by the elbow, and she shook herself free of his grasp as soon as possible.

"Oh, Gil!" she exclaimed somewhat crossly. "I meant what I said. I have no intention of trying to escape. D'you think I would trust Cullen Maclean if I did? I have only his word he serves Sir Jasper, and the truth of the matter is far from clear."

"I think you had best not meddle at all, Merry," Gilbert

replied, leading the way back to the keep with a considerably sobered air. They entered the castle, and he led her directly to her room. He obviously intended to return her to the status of prisoner. Her disappearance had shaken him up, and their former comaraderie seemed to have vanished.

Merry felt a mounting panic at the thought of entering the small stone chamber again. What if Gilbert told Ranald of her actions, and Lindsay locked her in tonight? She had the feeling his dark eyes could read her mind somehow. They bored into her as if silently challenging her to attempt an escape. Something in his gaze had told her he was expecting that very thing.

How could she bear to let Cullen Maclean leave Auchmull without giving her any answers? At least ask him to take a message to Wickham for her, reassuring Sir Jasper of her good health and relatively strong spirits. Her heart raced with anticipation and desperation as Gilbert bade her good night and left the chamber. She would find a way to meet with Cullen before morning came. She must!

Not long after, darkness fell and the full onslaught of the first Highland storm hit Auchmull. From her room, Merry could hear the high, thin whine of the wind whistling through the cracks in the stone walls. The sound made her nervous. She set Hertha to the task of helping her move the tapestries about, to try and cut down on the drafts, and also occupy both of them while her mind wildly churned for ideas on how to escape the confines of the keep.

She only needed an hour, at the most. Under the cover of the storm, mayhap none would notice her slipping out to the stables, especially if she wore a dark cloak. Merry had quickly inspected the contents of her belongings from the coach after Gilbert and Hugo brought them to her. She had hoped for something useful amid the frippery, but her gowns were as frivolous as any notion she might escape.

There was also a brief message from Wickham which had been passed on from Gilbert once it had been determined to contain no seditious information. The note simply stated Sir Jasper would be arriving soon at Auchmull for negotiations with Ranald Lindsay. He was, of course, hoping to have Merry removed from such horrendous circumstances at earliest opportunity.

Merry felt a shiver course through her body as she read the terse note. She must trust Ranald had no treachery planned. She prayed he had no intention of trying to kill Sir Jasper. She feared less for herself than for the involvement of so many innocents.

It dawned on Merry with a distinct sense of dismay, that Sir Jasper and his men might be similarly inclined to attempt an overthrow of the seat at Auchmull. 'Twould be a nice plum, and offer the Englishman direct control over the fractious Highlanders. Wickham had the money, and the favor, of the queen. Why he had not bothered to attack Auchmull before still bothered Merry. He had the manpower, and surely an excuse if he so chose.

These thoughts and others were nearly driving her mad. She paced half the night away, while Hertha alternately soothed and watched her mistress with grave concern.

Eventually Merry stopped fussing with the tapestries and tried to concentrate on a sampler Hertha had brought her to pass the time. She was so nervous she kept poking her fingers, and in a fit of frustration, she finally hurled the cloth across the room. After helping Merry change into a nightrail, Hertha mentioned she needed to visit Nell, check on the young woman's progress, and retire herself for the evening. With a mixed sense of relief and resignation, Merry agreed the tiring woman might go.

Merry realized as she watched Hertha depart that this offered the perfect opportunity to effect a quick escape to the stables. With the maid gone, nobody would miss her for a little while. The moment the door shut behind Hertha, she threw off her lethargic air, put on her slippers and proceeded to dig through her belongings until she had unearthed a full-length cape of dark wool. Swiftly Merry pulled it over her nightrail. She drew the hood close about her face, covering her auburn hair. Only the pale oval of her face remained, and this she kept carefully shielded as she cracked open the door to her chamber and peered both ways up and down the hall.

The storm had driven everyone indoors, so the greatest danger lay in escaping the keep. She heard the lazy banter of men engaged in a dicing game somewhere off to her right and knew she dared not risk trying to leave by means of the main door. She remembered Hertha mentioning there was a back exit through the kitchen. Stealthily Merry slipped out into the hall, keeping her back flush to the wall, and inched to her left until the laughter and rattle of dice had faded to a muffled, indistinct noise. She smelled the kitchen long before she saw it. Someone was baking bread, even at this late hour. Merry sniffed longingly and felt her mouth begin to water.

Her soft-soled slippers made no noise as she crept up to the oak door left wide open to the hall. She heard desultory feminine chatter and peeked in, watching as a pair of young serving girls poured up mugs of stout ale for the clansmen in the hall. One was Siany, Hertha's granddaughter.

"Lord Ranald's in a terrible black mood, he is," she was telling the other servant, a brown-haired girl with plump, pink cheeks. " 'Tis all the fault of that red-haired beldam."

"She's nae beautiful, but she's verra striking," replied the other, and with a little start Merry realized they were talking about her.

"She's naught but a *Sassenach* strumpet, Ellen," Siany said frankly. "Ye canna tell me any differently. The way she looks at Lord Ranald is nothin' short of shameful. Law, ye should hae seen her! Gawking at him like a empty-headed little goose. Men be such fools."

"I dinna like it when ye talk about others that way, Siany," Ellen said uneasily.

"Why not?" responded the other a trifle belligerently. "Ye know 'tis true. Anyhow, Ellie, ye've no knowledge of men."

"Neither hae ye!" cried little Ellen, stung.

From her vantage point, Merry saw a strange light enter

Siany's blue eyes, and a smug half-smile curved the girl's lips. It unsettled her for some reason, and she remembered Hertha's despair that her granddaughter would ever wed.

The moment was shattered as the two girls picked up their respective trays, each loaded with brimming tankards, and departed the kitchen through another door. Merry waited a moment more until she was sure they wouldn't return, and then inched into the kitchen, keeping to the shadows. Her ears still burned from Siany's words. She was mortified by what she had heard. Was her unwilling interest in Ranald truly so obvious? Or had jealousy colored the girl's words?

She impatiently shook aside her worries by reminding herself that there were more important things to be done this night. As she moved past the great stacks of baked scones, however, she couldn't resist snatching a couple and stuffing them into the pockets of her cloak. Cullen might be hungry. Doubtless, Gilbert's grudging hospitality had not included food.

She was nearly to the door when she heard a whinny of horses in the yard, a murmur of men's voices. The Wolf was back! Heart pounding, Merry froze in place, her wide eyes fixed on the door, realizing with a jolt of pure emotion she had nowhere to hide.

Merry saw him before he noticed her. Ranald walked with a weary gait, broad shoulders still hunched from the cold, snow melting in his dark hair, and an air of resignation about him. Off guard as he was in those few moments, she caught a glimpse of the vulnerable man behind the fierce facade, the laird Blair Maclean had loved with her flawless devotion.

Feeling tension thicken in the air as she watched him from the shadows, Merry was surprised to discover 'twas not fear but fascination which rooted her in place. Something about this quiet, cold, remote man compelled her to reach out. At Court, she was renowned for making others laugh with her sparkling wit, easing uncomfortable situations and even placating the queen. Surely if Elizabeth Tudor could be charmed into eating from Meredith Tanner's proverbial hand, so, too, could the mighty Wolf of Badanloch. She pushed the cowl back over her hair.

"Milord."

Merry spoke softly from the shadows, startling him. Ranald pivoted and his dark gaze focused on her with surprise, but before the anger might mount, she stepped forward beneath the light of a sconce and made no attempt to disguise the fact she was there.

"I trust your mission was successfully accomplished," she said brightly.

He stared at her a moment, obviously confused and searching for an explanation not only for her appearance but her straight-forward manner. There was little logic in the notion of a woman trying to escape who had stepped out and addressed him so openly. Yet his scrutiny took in her cloak and he appeared suspicious nonetheless.

Merry bit back an irreverent chuckle. 'Twould not do, not at all, if she burst into gales of laughter at his wariness. For the first time since they met, she sensed she had the upper hand. Or perhaps it was the sight of her trim ankles beneath the nightrail which disconcerted Ranald so, a thought most amusing since he feigned the air of such a calloused man.

" 'Tis past midnight. Why are you roaming about? Where is Gilbert? Hertha?"

The questions he tossed at her in short succession were clearly intended to take her off guard, but Merry did not flinch. She met the Wolf's onyx stare with enough aplomb to make Uncle Kit proud. She doubted even a seasoned courtier like Bess's favorite "Fox" would have been so bold as to turn an attempted escape into a social situation, while garbed in such an intimate fashion.

Swallowing a smile, Merry said, "I fear I was hungry, Lord Lindsay. Opportunity knocked and I did not question it." She pulled one of the still-warm scones from her pockets, glad now she had the foresight to snitch them in passing. Ranald looked from the scone to her sheepish expression, and she could have sworn a faint smile curved his lips for a moment.

"I take it you do not find haggis filling, after all."

"Oh, 'twas not sheep's pluck tonight, but rather fried herrings and some curious kind of boiled mutton with mushy vegetables."

"Hotch-potch?" Ranald laughed shortly, and Merry felt the echo of his laughter curl through her as warmly as a sip of Hugo's bracing poitìn.

"Aye, I think Hertha dubbed it thus." Merry wrinkled her nose. "I regret I must be honest, but I am beginning to doubt I shall ever acquire a taste for Highland fare."

Expecting a stinging response, she was surprised when Ranald nodded. "It takes a body time to adjust to unfamiliar customs, lass." His gaze met and locked with hers, as he idly brushed stray snowflakes from his hair. Merry resisted the urge to reach out and run her fingers over those damp dark locks gleaming beneath the torchlight. She caught the scent of him again, familiar now as her own, male and leather and the sweet pungent tinge of horseflesh and snow.

She saw Ranald looking at her form where the cloak parted over her breasts, and a flash of heat rose between them. She knew he felt it, too, by the way he suddenly inhaled. In the narrow hall where they stood so close together, each rasping breath scraped against stone, and the smoky air was intense, taut with emotion. She wondered if he experienced the same reckless thrill and had her answer when his hands suddenly came down on her shoulders, drawing her closer.

"*Yince*," the Highland Wolf rasped, translating in a softer vein, "Once . . ." and then his mouth descended on hers, not with the fierceness she had come to expect but a shattering gentleness that shook her to the core. Merry swayed and clutched his shoulders, head thrown back, shivering with forbidden pleasure as his lips blazed a path from her gasping mouth down over her bared throat, pausing there where Ranald tasted her with luxuriant slowness, skimming her pale flesh and leaving a faint blush in his wake.

She trembled in his embrace, knowing in her heart it could never be, 'twas utter madness, yet her emotions swirled like the storm and suddenly she was like a snow raven, caught up in the tumultuous wind. Ranald, too, seemed shaken by the depth of their mutual passion. She saw the flash of emotion in his eyes before he walked her back a step against the wall, pinning her between cold stone and wet wool, devouring her mouth with a leisurely hunger which made Merry whimper deep in her throat.

She gasped when his hand slipped beneath her cloak and gently, yet urgently, kneaded her breast. She arched into his fingers, driven to surrender with neither rhyme nor reason to the one man who was her mortal enemy. Her captor. A fierce Highland laird accused of brutal murders, a man known as the Wolf of Badanloch.

Suddenly Ranald froze in place, his dark eyes clearing as he broke off the passionate kiss and gazed at Merry in equal shock. Or perhaps shock was too kind a word, for the disgruntled expression he wore as he reeled away from her was like a knife thrust between her ribs.

"Damme!" he swore, thrusting a hand through his tangled hair, the expletive hardly encompassing the roiling emotions or terrible guilt seizing them both like a vise. They stared at each other as if seeking answers, or rather pleading for them, and silence descended like a brutal hawk as the scone crumbled and fell from Merry's numb fingers.

Ran could not asleep. Hours later, after leaving Merry at her chamber, he sat slumped in a deeply cushioned chair in his study, absently nursing a warm brandy while the snow beat silently and furiously against the leaded windowpanes.

Night haunted him. It always had. From the time he was a lad and his fey mother had restlessly wandered the halls of Edzell after dark, he had never slept much, nor very well. The annoying habit had also inadvertently saved his life more than once. He had not been sleeping when a killer had slipped past the guards and entered his bedchamber a month ago. He'd glimpsed the wavering shadow of a man on the stone wall, and rolled aside just as the dagger came down viciously to bury itself in the bolster where his head had lain just a moment before.

His assailant sprinted away before Ran could even gain his feet. He'd shouted for his men, and there was an immediate search of the entire castle, but too late to find even a hair attesting to the presence of the stealthy assassin. Ran was far more furious than afraid.

Death had never particularly frightened him, but the thought of Wickham ordering someone else to do his dirty work made his blood run cold. None other had motive, except perhaps a Maclean or two, and they were sniveling cowards, the lot of them.

The only doubts he had now concerned Merry Tanner. Ran had to admit the woman daunted him. Assuming the task of chatelaine at Auchmull had infuriated him, but he grudgingly admired her pluck. He could not deny she had a winsome air, and others obviously agreed, for Hertha and Gilbert and Hugo all hurried to her bidding now. Others were coming 'round, too, including those who had cursed loudest when she came. Merry Tanner had a way of giving orders that left one feeling almost grateful for the task. Truly, she was a whirlwind to be reckoned with.

Not that it wasn't in the vixen to scheme like a master, he was sure. Yet Merry was nothing if not proud. He had decided to let her be where matters in the household were concerned. He couldn't quite imagine her instructing some lowly servant to kill him, not when she'd so dearly love to do the deed herself. In her eyes, and those of her family, he surely deserved it, though.

Ran cursed under his breath and finished his brandy in one gulp. He set the snifter aside and resumed thumbing through Auchmull's accounts, aware of the numbers dancing meaninglessly before his eyes. Usually he enjoyed handling his own ledgers. It made up for not having a family, in a small way.

He kept himself so busy with overseeing his lands he didn't have too much time to think about Merry, or how she might feel in his bed, her *Sassenah* skin warm and silken to the touch . . .

Abruptly he slammed the ledger shut. Jesu, he was a fool. The woman didn't want him. He didn't want her. Their kisses were mistakes, whatever drew them together so inexplicably was simply prompted by desperation or convenience. She'd marry Wickham in the end, if Ran didn't kill the scoundrel first. His lips curved in a bitter smile at the memory of Blair. The Highland Games. Ah, had it really been less than two years ago? It seemed nigh a lifetime behind him now.

He remembered how fetching Blair had looked in purple heather plaid, her flaxen hair a riotous tangle about her shoulders, blue eyes sparkling like the waters of Badanloch. He recalled how she'd shown off her new little dirk, which she kept cleverly hidden up one sleeve. She'd informed all the lads there that they'd better not try anything, because if Black Cullen didn't gut them, she would!

The Games had been a gesture of truce between the clans for many years. Fighting was forbidden, and there was a strict code of honor, but Ran cared less about any of it when Blair pulled him aside one evening to show him her prized weapon. They had met on and off in secret for several months by then, and though they had kissed and exchanged small tokens of love, naught had been said of a future between them. Too much bad blood yet raged between Lindsays and Macleans.

There was a mischievous glint in her eye as Blair drew him behind a stand of oak and hawthorn trees, and presented the little dagger for his inspection.

"Do ye think I'm well protected now from the likes of lusty men?" she'd saucily inquired in her soft Highland burr.

Ran had spared the dagger a contemptuous glance and then flashed her a grin. "That would not stop a fly, sweetheart." Unbidden, he reached out and drew her into his arms. Blair gasped and began to mock-struggle.

"Ssh, lovey, we don't want to call the troops," Ran chuckled, and brought his lips down on hers. A moment later, he felt the sharp point of the little dagger digging into his neck. With a muttered oath, he let her go.

"Ye'll nae take such liberties with me again, Ranald Lindsay," Blair hissed, eyes narrowing to gleaming slits of sky blue. " 'Tis a ring I'll hae or a tumble ye'll nae get!"

He laughed at her spunk. "I think you'd run away with me this night, if I asked it, hinny."

The dagger dropped to her side. "What!" she cried, and her denial was too swift, too hot. It proved his words true.

"Blair, I know the Macleans intend you for the Chief of Clan Donald, and though I'm an earl, I'm not half as rich as he. But we both know your heart belongs to the Wolf."

Ran's gaze on her was warm and knowing. He recalled her broken cry as she flew into his arms and nestled there like a little white dove.

"Ranald! Nay! Never think that of me, that I could wed another," she whispered, and he was moved by the tears in her eyes. She dropped the dagger in the grass and surrendered to him. There was something else in her eyes, as if love and utter despair had mingled to turn them a piercing, shadowed blue. He was troubled by her obvious agony, but Blair didn't speak for a long moment. She simply laid her head upon his chest.

"I canna cry off the wedding wi' Macdonald," she murmured thickly into his velvet doublet, "but please know 'tis for the best . . . for both of us."

"Do you crave eternal misery, Blair?" he demanded roughly, hauling her back from him by a silken hank of her hair. "Because I don't! Not a night goes by that I don't dream of you, hinny. Of you in my arms, my bed, my life . . ."

"Oh, Ran!" Her sudden, heartrending sob shattered his anger like fragile glass. He grabbed Blair fiercely, protectively, in his arms. She raised her face to his, her loch-blue eyes glittering with tears. This time, she did not deny his kisses . . . or his claim on her heart . . .

Ran shook himself free of the haunting memory with a start.

His fist came down on his desk with a crash, the pen flew from his grip. Blair had wed him and paid the price. He had, in essence, killed the thing he loved most in life. The mighty Wolf of Badanloch buried his face in his hands, and wept like a bairn.

Chapter Fifteen

Over three feet of snow fell during the night. A pristine, glittering sheet of white covered everything. All of Auchmull was slow to rouse the next morning. It felt good to lay abed, Merry thought, stretching contentedly beneath the heavy blankets. Usually the hustle and bustle in the halls awoke her long before dawn. This time the servants were content to sleep in, too. Of course, she had nigh exhausted them with her lists of chores over the past few days. She chuckled a little, for though they all complained, none could deny the castle was beginning to resemble something more than a mews.

Eventually Merry straggled from bed, and Hertha offered to help her to dress in one of the practical woolen gowns Ran's sister had left behind.

"Come wi' me, lass," Hertha said, holding up Merry's cloak. "Ye look like ye need a breath of fresh air."

"What about Lord Lindsay?"

The elderly woman sniffed. "What, indeed. He's nae got the right to keep ye all penned up like a milch cow!"

Merry giggled. "Oh, Hertha, I'm supposed to be a prisoner.

You will make his lordship ever so angry if you persist in treating me like an honored guest.''

''I've benefit of age and wisdom,'' Hertha replied. ''I changed Lord Ranald's nappies nae so long ago. Both of ye can humor an old woman now.''

As the two women shared a conspiratorial grin, Merry realized they had become friends, even as different as they were. She was grateful for Hertha's cheerful presence. It made it easier to ignore the furtive, hostile looks tossed at her from any Lindsay kin. Although they had decreased of late. Most of the women and children were inside today, barricaded away from the cold and snow. Merry buried her chilled hands deep into the pockets of her cloak and discovered the remaining scone she had snitched from the kitchen the night before. She gave half to Hertha after making the woman promise she wouldn't tell. On the contrary, Hertha seemed delighted by Merry's boldness. They happily munched the scone together, watching the activity in the yard.

While they were outside, a sudden uproar in the gatehouse brought more men running. There were muffled shouts and words exchanged between the gatehouse guards and the men on the other side of Auchmull's great gate, but no words were readily discernible. The women exchanged concerned looks when they realized somebody was running to get Lord Lindsay. But there was no time to slip back into the keep before Ranald arrived, clad in his red watch kilt and tartan.

Barely glancing at Merry, he brushed by the two women and went to consult with his men across the yard. He looked mightily displeased about something, muscular arms folded across his chest, but eventually he nodded, and the huge gate was slowly drawn upward on oiled hinges, shuddering and groaning with the weight of the snow.

A group of perhaps twenty-five men were ranged behind the gate, and their horses snorted great clouds of steam. They rode slowly forward once the gate had cleared the wall, and Merry heard Hertha release an inadvertent gasp.

" 'Tis Wickham! Oh, lass, no wonder Lord Ranald looks so fearful angry.''

Hertha's voice was barely above a whisper, but nonetheless Merry looked to see if the man under discussion had possibly overheard. She tensed with expectation as the leader of the band nudged his fine gray mare forward. She was surprised by her first glimpse of Sir Jasper. The sight of a rigid fellow with fussily coifed blond curls and a neatly trimmed beard did not compare favorably with the miniature in her possession.

Wickham's cloak was swept back to reveal a canary-yellow doublet and beribboned breeches of bright red velvet. Merry saw his riding boots had matching red heels. He rode with one hand held out at an affected angle, the other gripping the reins with pale, thin fingers. He looked about as dangerous as a monk.

Merry might have chuckled were she not so nervous, and appalled by this telling portrait of a man she had imagined as hale, handsome, and hearty. Wickham's horse looked ready to expire from the journey. A glance aside showed Hertha was not amused, either.

"Oh, miss. He's a devil, that one. Dinna let his foppish ways deceive ye!"

As if sensing their perusal, Sir Jasper drew his laboring horse to a halt and eyed the two women across the yard. His pursed little mouth resembled a rosebud from a distance, but Hertha shivered and clutched Merry's arm.

"He's seen ye, lass! Och, those beady little eyes o' his dinna miss a thing . . .''

For such a gaudy fashion plate, Sir Jasper had a surprisingly strong voice.

"Well met, Milord Lindsay," he said as the unsmiling laird of Auchmull stepped forward to meet him. "I've come so we might settle things peaceably, eh? Man to man.''

Ranald nodded curtly. "Your men may wait in the ward. I see you followed my decree of no weapons.''

"But of course," Sir Jasper responded, arching an elegantly plucked brow. "We are not barbarians, Lindsay." The slight emphasis upon the "we" seemed to imply otherwise in the case of Highlanders, and Merry overheard a low murmur among the watching clansmen. A sweep of her gaze over the assembled throng revealed eyes bright with emotion, jaws clenched with mute rage. Clearly Wickham was despised among these quarters. She saw Sir Jasper's cool gray gaze skimming the crowd, alighting on her where she stood slightly apart from the rest with Hertha.

He nodded short recognition, but addressed Ranald instead. " 'Tis true then. The brave Wolf of Badanloch captured himself a pretty little English partridge." Sir Jasper laughed, and a few of his men turned and leered across the yard at Merry as a squire hurried to take his mount.

"Are you here for business or socializing" came Ranald's cool reply, delivered in a voice so low Merry almost didn't hear it. "If you wish to have your fiancée restored to your side, then I suggest we begin negotiations as soon as possible."

Wickham shrugged and dismounted from his horse with the aid of his squire. He fastidiously brushed at his clothing, and for some reason airs which might have seemed elegant at court appeared ludicrous here. Dismissing the squire, Sir Jasper turned his attentions on Merry.

"Mistress Tanner, I regret our first meeting must be under such unfortunate circumstances," he said, bowing over her hand, ignoring Ranald's challenging stare. As he rose, Sir Jasper's cool gray eyes raked slowly up and down Merry's trembling body. She felt stripped and exposed beneath his gaze. Her hands clutched in defensive fists at her sides. It suddenly became hard to breathe. She was so infuriated by his casual appraisal she didn't realize for a moment Lord Lindsay had joined her on the steps. Taking her arm, in light but possessive grip, Ranald said to Wickham, "There will be plenty of opportunity for you to socialize with the lady when she is your wife. I suggest you concentrate upon meeting my demands if you wish to depart Auchmull with your Tudor prize."

The words were delivered in a mock civil, yet firm voice. Sir Jasper's eyes narrowed thoughtfully. Then abruptly he laughed, and strode past them where he stood at the entrance to the keep.

" 'Tis a pity you do not possess the legendary Lindsay good humor, milord," Wickham said. "Under other circumstances, perhaps we could be allies."

Ranald's dark gaze smoldered where it rested upon the other man. "I find such a notion utterly abhorrent."

Sir Jasper looked taken aback. He stroked his pointed beard thoughtfully, gray eyes glinting, but Merry noticed he did not provoke the Wolf of Badanloch further.

Chapter Sixteen

"My compliments, milord. You set a fine table," Sir Jasper said, and followed up his statement with an exaggerated yawn behind one gloved hand. He didn't seem to notice the dangerous gleam in Ranald's eye, but pushed back his chair, signifying he was finished. As if on cue, a serving girl moved forward from the shadows, her blond hair like a glistening mantle about her shoulders. Wickham glanced up with interest. The wench was a comely thing, young the way he liked them, with pretty blue eyes and a saucy swing to her hips.

"More ale, sir?" She bent over to fill his tankard, and Wickham ogled her swelling bosom with appreciation.

"Siany! 'Twill be all for the evening," Ranald said sharply, dismissing the girl. Sir Jasper smiled with faint amusement as he took a long draught of ale, then yanked a lace kerchief from his sleeve and dabbed a cloth to his lips.

"Aye," he mused, stalking Siany like a predator with his narrowed gaze until she had left the hall, "you set a fine table, indeed, Lindsay."

"You've not come to sample the bread nor the wenches," Ran said bluntly. "Supposedly you wish to free Mistress Tanner from my dastardly clutches.'' He leaned forward, folding his arms across the table as he met Wickham's gaze levelly.

An expansive smile crossed Jasper Wickham's face. For dinner, he had donned an elaborately embroidered blue velvet jerkin, the laces of which fastened over a puce-green satin waistcoat. Yards of frilly white lace had been sewn up into a huge ruff that rose so high it appeared he had no neck. His fingers winked with costly jewels as he waved his hands about.

"Now then, a little civil conversation is hardly out of hand," he rebuked Ran. He clucked his tongue disapprovingly. "Our families used to socialize, y'know. Your ancestors and mine were united in more than one cause over the centuries."

"I cannot account for past foolishness on the part of my relatives."

Sir Jasper smiled thinly. "I believe by tradition I still invite the Lindsays for Twelfth Night at Braidwood each year. Your mother was not so ungrateful while she lived. Lady Lindsay sent a costly gift, at least."

Ranald scowled down the length of the table at his English nemesis. In turn, Sir Jasper noted with considerable irritation that the young earl had not so much as gained an ounce of fat over the past months. Nor had Lindsay wasted away from grief. The Wolf was still lean and strong and dangerous looking, his darkness accentuated tonight by the stark black watch belted plaid he wore. Ranald's dark eyes gleamed with a deadly light. Not without reason had Sir Jasper insisted upon a food taster, though the memory of Lindsay's mocking sneer at his request still burned in his gullet.

Sir Jasper considered Ranald Lindsay little more than a glorified savage, a Highland rogue who plundered and pillaged from some archaic sense of tradition rather than any true need. Certainly the Earl of Crawford did not need to go reiving with lawless scoundrels, and though the laird's illegal activities had abruptly stopped after the death of his wife, Sir Jasper knew 'twould only be a matter of time before The Wolf hunted again beneath the moon.

He also knew Lindsay bore a personal grudge against him

over Blair, as did half the Highlands. Sir Jasper's reputation as a hard taskmaster did not lend him popularity among the lower classes, and many enjoyed seeing the Wolf of Badanloch snapping at his heels. Sir Jasper had returned the favor by spurring on the story of the killings at Badanloch. Clearly 'twas a topic Lindsay wished to forget, and for that very reason he raised it now.

"You've heard of the legend of Badanloch, I presume?" Sir Jasper inquired. "A most amusing bard passed by Braidwood on his way south, and regaled us there with the knotty tale."

Ranald asked in a deceptively soft voice, "How much did you pay him, Wickham?"

Sir Jasper frowned. He did not like the way this upstart laird kept turning the tables on him. With an airy shrug, he said, "Well, what's one less Maclean anyhow? You've had that lot raking at your back for nigh two hundred years. Don't tell me you're sorry to hear of Suttie Maclean's passing, either!"

"I never bore Blair's father any ill will."

Sir Jasper shrugged eloquently. " 'Tis odd, but it seems Cullen Maclean does not seem to believe it."

"I care not one bawbee what opinion Black Cullen holds of me."

"Nor are you apparently swayed by the lovely little prize you have in your possession."

Ranald stiffened slightly at the reference to Merry, but his expression remained shuttered. He realized the other man was pressing the issue of Badanloch. He wanted to know why.

"There was a traitor," he said, his voice still low and seemingly calm. "Someone intercepted my truce-bearing messenger. Fergus never reached Maclean's camp. When he did not return, I assumed I had Suttie's answer. Later Fergus's body was found floating in the loch. Of course, you would know nothing of this, I presume."

Something flashed in Sir Jasper's eyes, eyes too cold to be considered the window to his soul. He visibly restrained his temper as he fumbled for the linen napkin in his lap. He pressed it hard against his mouth for a moment, leaving a stain from berries he had eaten.

"I have known true insult from you, Lindsay," he said, hurling the napkin aside. "You must know I don't meddle in common clan frays, being far more inclined to gentlemanly pursuits at Court."

"Such as rape?"

Sir Jasper stiffened and wouldn't meet Ranald's eye. Bastard! He knew the laird referred to a specific incident which had occurred at the Stuart Court two years ago. Sir Jasper could admit now he'd had a wee bit much to drink, and he'd roughly taken his pleasure with one of the castle wenches. How was he supposed to have known she was only twelve? The little bitch had been teasing him unmercifully.

At least the king hadn't needed any explanations. He'd forced Wickham to give the girl a generous dower, then probably bundled her off to her relatives near Morvern. There must not have been a child, for Sir Jasper had heard not another word about it. He was sure Lindsay would be badgering him to support the little slut and her bastard otherwise. He felt the disgust emanating from Ranald's eyes now, just like a killing frost.

"Come now, Lindsay, we are men of the world," Sir Jasper finally said, stroking his beard as was his habit. "Don't begrudge me a little harmless pleasure."

Ranald replied through gritted teeth. "You killed her, you Sassenach bastard," he snarled. "Little Rosaleen Duncan died birthing you a son. Only I suppose you did not ever bother to find out."

"A son, hmm?" Sir Jasper appeared mildly interested. "You're sure 'tis mine? She was a cheeky little thing, as I recall."

"She was a virgin, damme you!"

Sir Jasper stared at the younger man with mild reproof. By Jesu, Lindsay believed it! He began to laugh. Lindsay must have been hot for the wench himself, and resentful he hadn't gotten under her skirts. Sir Jasper was not about to accept blame for a slut's behavior. He'd been dubbed as cunning as a fox and a slippery as an eel by one of his contemporaries at court, and he was hardly going to sit back and let Lindsay spout moralistic slop at him.

Plastering a bland smile to his face to hide the devious workings within, he merely said, "You've always been chivalrous when it comes to the ladies, Lindsay."

Ranald looked momentarily startled. Then he laughed, a little bitterly, remembering himself how Merry recently accused him of being anything but.

Sir Jasper sighed. "God's bones, man! I'll do my duty by the brat. Where is the newest Wickham?"

"Dead." Ranald spoke flatly. His dark eyes scoured his nemesis with withering contempt. "The bairn died, as well. Lady Deuchar saw to their burial at Edzell."

Wickham appeared disappointed. "I wouldn't have minded another son. I look after all my issue. Braidwood could use another Wickham or two, even under the bar sinister."

"You could have used a bit of restraint far more," Ranald growled. He rose from the table, disgusted by Wickham's presence and nonchalant attitude. He knew Sir Jasper ill-treated the serving women at his high seat at Braidwood, which made the fact of Blair's death there all the more appalling.

Ranald remembered how he'd found little Rosaleen curled up in a ball in a corner of a room at Falklands Castle, bruised, her thin legs covered with blood. He had sent for Darra, and together they had bundled the poor child up and hurried her home to Edzell. Within a few months, the consequences of Wickham's lust became obvious. Perhaps 'twould have been more merciful if she had died at Court, rather than in torturous childbirth later.

Ranald felt a quiver of white-hot emotion ripple through his frame, remembering how he had lost Blair, as well. He doubted he would ever know the full circumstances of his wife's death at Braidwood, for Wickham was not forthcoming with details. The man seemed to enjoy taunting him with feigned ignorance and mock regrets. He could hurl himself across the table now, and crush Wickham's scrawny neck in his hands, but then he would never know what had happened to Blair. He burned to hear the details of her final moments, whether she had spoken of him, her last words, if any.

Wickham obviously knew this. His cocky demeanor spoke volumes. Both realized though the Wolf of Badanloch longed to slay Sir Jasper outright, Ranald would have to answer to both the Stuart and Tudor monarchs. All the Lindsays stood to suffer if Ran's rash temper overcame logic. Kidnaping the man's fiancée was bad enough, outright murder might even deprive Gilbert of the right to inherit should Ran swing for the crime.

Loathing curled Ran's lip as he stared at the man now occupying the chair at the end of his dining hall. How he longed to turn the trestle table over, denying Wickham even the meanest hospitality. Still, he was bitterly aware of the other's very real power. Sir Jasper had the ear of the king, and he used his position ruthlessly. Ranald was surprised, however, when he heard King James and the court no longer visited Braidwood on their annual sojourn. Was their monarch finally beginning to get a true glimpse of the viper he so recklessly cradled to his own breast?

The matter was obviously on Wickham's mind, too, for he suddenly frowned.

"Milord, pray let's not be unreasonable," he said cajolingly. "We both know you have something I want very much, and 'twould appear I also hold the key to some satisfaction on your part. We have but to agree on the niggling little details, *n'est-ce-pas?*"

Ran nodded curtly. "I agree. Keep to the business at hand. You wish Mistress Tanner safely returned, while I ask two things: return of my family lands, and answers."

"Answers?" Sir Jasper sat back and steepled his thin, pale fingers under his chin, gazing at his adversary with that feigned innocence Ran found so infuriating.

"Aye. I want to know every last detail concerning Blair's death."

Wickham sighed heavily. "Milord, you have a mighty enough task ahead of you, if you are to reclaim the lands near Glenesk forfeited to the Macleans after Badanloch. Why torture yourself with visions of a woman you will never see again?"

Each word, cold and logical, was like a stabbing pain in Ran's heart. Wickham dangled Blair's last moments before him like a juicy haunch, watching the Wolf salivate, pacing back and forth with frustration. 'Twas a game between them, Ran knew, an old game, but 'twas beginning to wear dangerously thin.

"Let her go, Lindsay," Wickham said, his voice gentle, and oh so reasonable. He leaned forward and folded his arms across the table, gazing at Ran almost pityingly. "Your lady is gone, to a better place. All that remains is you and me, and in her memory you owe peace a chance."

"Do I?" Ran rose abruptly, kicking back his chair. He was pleased to see Wickham jump. He glared down the length of the table, wondering if Sir Jasper sensed how close he was to death at that very moment.

The other man regarded him warily, then rose to his feet. "I see there is nothing more to be gained by my presence here," he said stiffly. "If we cannot come to terms, then I may as well depart now."

Ran met his bluff coolly. "Aye, you might at that."

While the two men were squaring off in Auchmull's great hall, Merry took her meal in the privacy of her chamber. She was restless, nervous with anticipation. She finished her dinner, having not tasted a bite, and set the tray with the dishes aside to fitfully pace the room. She was quickly becoming claustrophobic in the small stone chamber, and more than ever she longed to fling open the window, if only to admit gusts of wind and sheeting snow. But the bolt had rusted shut on the lead pane, and after tugging at it uselessly for a while, Merry gave up and simply pressed her face to the glass, trying to catch a glimpse of any activity in the yard.

Auchmull was eerily quiet, for so many beneath the roof. Even Sir Jasper's boisterous guardsmen had finally subsided to quietly drinking and gambling in the hall. Merry knew Cullen Maclean had not left yet, for the pass was temporarily blocked by snow. It might be many days before it was clear again, since 'twas not true winter yet, though they all hoped for a gradual thaw. Hertha had explained a sudden thaw could raise the loch to a dangerous level, and cause flooding if the dirt levies broke.

Merry felt like beating her forehead against the glass. Would she never escape this place? The only thing she didn't want to escape was the man. Ranald. She inhaled suddenly at the mere thought of him. Sweet Jesu, what a traitor she was, mooning over a man who was her intended's worst enemy! She was a traitor to Sir Jasper, the queen, her own family and moral fabric. But having met Sir Jasper, feeling nothing but instant repulsion despite his fine attire and fussy manners, Merry realized her life had altered its course. She couldn't change her feelings, nor stop the anticipation racing through her blood at the very thought of Ran.

Her hands tightened on the windowsill, and already she felt the invisible ominous weight of Wickham's wedding ring on her finger. She longed to yank it off, even symbolically, and cast it into the loch. How long could she keep up this pretense of being a loyal betrothed? She felt nothing for the man she had agreed to marry, and soon she would be forced to share a stranger's bed. She shuddered, biting a knuckle to keep from crying aloud with pure frustration. Her feelings meant naught, since Ranald could never return them. All his love was reserved still for his dead wife.

Merry drew in a ragged breath when she saw a dark figure suddenly emerge from the stables and stumble through the snow, clutching something to his chest. Cullen? She squinted to make out any details, but all she could tell for sure was that it was a man. He fell to his knees in the snow, wobbling drunkenly for a second. Merry assumed he was intoxicated until she saw the dark stain spreading between the fingers clutched to his chest. Blood!

She didn't think. She turned and ran instead, unbolting and flinging open her chamber door, grateful at least Ranald didn't lock her in at night like a disobedient child. She flew down the hall, hoping Ranald was still there even at this late hour. He was. He and Sir Jasper had finished their supper, and appeared to be warily enduring each other's company over cups of hot mulled wine.

Merry rushed past a pair of startled men-at-arms, and into the hall before anyone could stop her. She halted at Ranald's side.

"A man!" she gasped out, pointing toward the stables. "Out in the snow . . . he looks injured."

Ranald brushed past her. Merry was suddenly aware of being left alone with Sir Jasper. He was staring at her like a hungry dog. She was wearing a gown of soft blue silk, embroidered with silver thread, the low neckline shirred with delicate French lace. Auburn plaits were wound around her head now, secured with pearl pins and silk ribbons Hertha had filched from the former Lady Lindsay's collection.

Sir Jasper smiled ingratiatingly. "Good evening, my dear." He leered at her in the courtly fashion to which she was accustomed, but it seemed suddenly vulgar when compared to Ranald's frank, forthright appreciation of a woman's form.

"I regret you were unable to join us for the repast. I do so love feasting upon a fine spread."

His cool gaze raked over her, the simple words carrying a wealth of disgusting connotations. Merry shuddered and started to turn away, unable to think of even a civil response. Suddenly a hand closed about her arm. Long, thin fingers dug into her flesh.

"Not so fast," Sir Jasper said, his faint smile not matching the grim intensity of his gaze. "I have one question for you, Mistress Merry. Has the Wolf touched you?"

Merry gasped at his audacity. "Certainly not!"

The memories of her intense kisses with Ran caused her to flush, but she let Wickham assume 'twas maidenly modesty which colored her pink. He seemed pleased by her sudden confusion, and nodded as if satisfied she was still a virgin.

"I asked Lord Lindsay if you could share our sup, but he said you were under the weather. I see now 'twas a falsehood, but I cannot blame you for wanting to avoid the man. He is little more than a coarse barbarian, a Highlander most foul."

"He has behaved quite honorably toward me." Merry spoke through gritted teeth, wondering why Wickham's criticism was as painful as it was infuriating.

To her outrage, Sir Jasper held her hands fast with one of his own, reached out and rudely groped her breasts with the other.

"You've lovely tits, m'dear," he remarked offhandedly. "A bit smaller than I prefer, but aye, they'll do. They'll do."

On pure reflex, Merry yanked a hand free and slapped him. She had disciplined more than one randy knave at Court with such blunt technique, and his status as her betrothed gained him no leverage with her heart. For all his intensity, Ranald Lindsay did not offend half as much as this leering, puffed-up peer who would treat her like some common bawd.

Sir Jasper swore, cradling his burning cheek. He stared at her in mingled shock and indignation but made no further move to molest her. Merry took a deep breath and seized opportunity to escape his company, nearly barreling into Ranald as he came striding back into the hall.

"One of my men is hurt—" he began, coming to an abrupt halt and looking from one to the other of them with marked suspicion.

"Do not imply 'twas one of mine who did it, milord," Sir Jasper growled, his pride preventing him from commenting on the obvious; his reddened cheek made it plain enough. "Strict instructions were given that peace would reign until matters here were resolved."

"Which apparently is moot at this point," Ran replied.

"Indeed. There is nothing more to be said." Sir Jasper swept up his high-crowned beaver hat from a nearby table and tugged it down over his brow.

To his fury, Ranald merely shrugged. The concern written in Lord Lindsay's eyes was not for Sir Jasper or the notion of a lost truce, but for the injured man they had found aside.

"Duncan's been stabbed," he said grimly, turning to observe Merry's high color.

"Your stable master?" she exclaimed. "Why would anybody want to hurt him?"

Ranald shook his head. "I've no idea. But I intend to find out."

"Is there anything I can do?"

He hesitated, studying her curiously for a second. "Nell may appreciate an extra set of hands. Hertha is tending another lass whose time is upon her."

"Here now, Lindsay," Sir Jasper put in imperiously, "Mistress Tanner is not some drudge to be ordered about your household."

"Nor am I some blowzy bawd to be mauled beneath the stairs!"

Merry's furious retort rocked both men back on their heels. Glaring at her, Wickham said, "I regret discovering your conduct is as outrageous as the hue of your hair, m'dear. A pity, for I had assumed you a gently bred lady who would do the House of Wickham proud. When 'tis far more apparent you prefer the company of uncouth rogues to that of your own betrothed."

She glared right back at Sir Jasper. Why had she not noticed before how pasty his skin was, how narrow his face. The miniature clearly flattered him. "When a Highlander is more chivalrous than an Englishman, Sweet Jesu save womankind."

Without another word, she resumed her march for the door. She thought, though she could not swear, Ranald chuckled beneath his breath. "Nell's tending to Duncan now," he called after her. "The men carried him upstairs."

Merry nodded and hurried out. In Nell's chamber, Lindsay clansmen had already lain the old man on the bed, and were huddled near the doorway, watching. Merry pushed through the knot of bodies, aware of a surly mutter when she did so.

"The *Sassenach* taupie will like as kill him," one of them grunted. "Mind ye watch her, Nell."

Nell Downie was dressed and standing in the center of the room. She appeared fully recovered from her own recent travail, and she turned on the men like a little hurricane.

"Shut yer maw, Will Campbell! Move back and gie me some air. There's work to be done here, and I intend to see 'tis done."

"I'm here to help." Merry spoke firmly.

Nell faced her. To Merry's surprise, the young woman's dark eyes softened and she smiled. "Bless ye, milady. Do ye ken anything about nursing wounded men?"

Merry laughed a little. "More than I do about placating angry Scots." She saw a few of the men smile grudgingly, and the tension in the room eased a bit.

Nell nodded. "Dinna fret, milady. Ye'll do fine. Now, let's see about Duncan."

Together the two women approached the bed, where the old man lay breathing shallowly. The wound in his chest seemed almost minor. Still Merry winced at the sight of it, the blood staining his leather jerkin. Nell didn't seem to mind. She knelt right down on the soiled coverlet and examined the injury.

" 'Tis deep, but clean," she said with some satisfaction. "Looks like a single knife thrust to me. Milady, I'm going to gie ye some lamb's wool to staunch the flow of blood. Can ye hold it fast while I make a poultice?"

Merry nodded. In truth, she'd no experience in tending patients of any sort, and had a deathly fear of illness herself. Whenever the ague or pox swept through Court, she was the first to escape to Ambergate, Uncle Kit's country home. She felt a little woozy at the sight and coppery smell of blood. But when Nell handed her several thick pads of wool, she pressed firmly where she was told, and held the makeshift bandages in place until they were soaked clear through to her palms. Nell ordered one of the men to help, and he rushed forward to hand more wool to Merry as she needed it. She worked methodically, trying to keep the pressure firm and steady, and though the blood seemed as if 'twould never stop, she was gradually aware that it was slowing a little. Poor Duncan had finally lost consciousness, although perhaps that was for the best.

A shadow fell over the bed while Merry was working. She glanced up at Ranald, but for once was too intent on something else to pay him much heed.

"Here," he said quietly. "Let me, lass."

He nudged her out of the way, and Merry fell back, her arms bloodied up to the elbows. She watched as he continued applying pressure and changing the woolen bandages until Nell took over again, and though it had only been an hour or so, it had seemed like a lifetime to Merry. Exhausted, she slumped down in a chair while Ranald and Nell continued to work. The wound was clean, as Nell had observed, but Duncan was elderly, and had lost a great deal of blood.

Merry saw the old man's lips turn blue just a moment before Nell spoke into the taut silence of the room.

"I'm sorry, m'laird."

Ranald made an anguished sound and stepped back from the bed, his eyes dark with grief. Merry longed to go to him, sensing this Duncan had been very special to him. Yet she dared not. She simply gazed on, silently and helplessly, as Ranald turned and stalked out of the room.

Chapter Seventeen

Ran did not waste any time. He immediately ordered a search of the entire keep, top to bottom, as well as every outbuilding within his demesne. Even as he did so, he was bitterly aware of the slim odds in catching Duncan's killer.

He burned with frustration, knowing Duncan must have seen his attacker, and yet could not tell them anything now. Any final words from the old man must have been muttered before Ran entered the room, which meant only Merry or Nell had heard them. He bitterly wondered if Merry would feel the same triumph as Wickham from withholding that information. Then he remembered his first reaction, how he'd first felt, watching Merry working so feverishly to save Duncan's life. She'd been covered with blood, the sleeves of her fine gown ruined, but she'd never flinched once, never hesitated in her frantic attempt to save Duncan's life. Auchmull's stable master was a stranger to her, yet her unflinching service in a crisis was not something Ran could easily set aside. She had great pluck, for a court-bred *Sassenach* lady.

Ran relegated the enigma of Merry to the back of his mind while he organized a search party to ride out a short distance in the snow in an attempt to track Duncan's killer. Though the main gate had been closed, a single man would have found it easy enough to climb and vault over the barricade, especially under cover of darkness. Ran was also aware of a number of ancient, underground tunnels beneath Auchmull which his ancestors had used to access the outside world during sieges. Most of these he had ordered destroyed or sealed off, realizing they presented an equal danger for present-day invasion, but he suspected there were still a handful in existence that he did not know about. Ofttimes, servants were better informed than their masters. He set several of the staff to searching the keep for secret passages. Even though the attack had occurred in the stables, the murderer might find it convenient to slip inside the castle and hide in the labyrinth below until the search was over.

It occurred to Ran that Duncan's killer, like the man who tried to snuff out his own life, was remarkably well informed about Auchmull's layout. He considered for a moment the possibility of one of his own people being disloyal. Such troubles had not plagued the clan before the incident at Badanloch. The logical assumption was that the Macleans or Wickham were somehow connected to it all. Cullen had come here and addressed Ran with his customary insolence, not missing a chance to remark upon Blair's death and imply Ran was wholly responsible.

Ran remembered the emotions which swept over him when he had found a jeweled dirk stuck in his own pillow. Incredulous disbelief, outrage, and later a cold, icy fury had gripped Ran like a northern wind, shattered what little faith he had left in humanity. That the woman he had loved beyond anything on earth was gone . . . the pain of that realization would live with him forever, without Cullen's reminders. The thought, however fleeting, that one of his own . . . a Lindsay . . . should betray the clan was beyond comprehension.

There were no answers to be found in emotions run rampant, Ran realized. He wanted to lash out at someone for Duncan's death, strike back, wound another as he had been wounded. Merry was the logical outlet. An injured wolf turning on the one who cornered it. Remembering the genuine anguish in her beautiful gray-green eyes when Nell Downie had quietly announced Duncan's death, Ranald found he could not direct the rage festering in his heart and soul at Merry. It simply trickled away, like water dribbling through a bairn's cupped hands; no matter how hard he tried, 'twas impossible to keep hold of it. As the Earl of Crawford prepared to ride out with his men, seeking the killer, he found himself hoping with every ounce of his being that Merry's was the first face he saw when he returned.

As the hours passed, and the fruitless search continued, Dearg shifted restlessly under his control, pawing the ground whenever he relaxed his guard. Few except Duncan knew the blood bay was the Spawn of the horse who had killed his father. Even Ranald himself didn't know what he had hoped to prove by taming and mastering Dearg, except it gave him a feeling of control over his life. Control he had been lacking ever since Blair's death.

He felt a fresh pang of loss when they returned and he glanced over at the stables, now bristling with his men-at-arms searching every stall and haystack. He expected Duncan to come out blustering into the yard at any second, so possessive and protective had the old man been of "his" livery and all the Auchmull mounts. Ranald's hand gripped the leather pommel and he swung himself down, his knuckles white with tension. Dearg snorted and pranced a little, sensing his master's dark mood.

Brodie Scott stepped forward to take charge of his steed, the lad's freckled face scoured with seriousness. He filled Duncan's duties in his absence but would never fill the void, and he knew it. His gaze soberly met Ran's.

"Lord and Lady Deuchar just arrived; Lady Darra an' Mistress Merry crack thegither from the go."

Ran felt a sudden headache coming on, The last thing he

needed was his sister meddling in events now, but his message to Edzell must have stirred the nest.

"By Jesu, lad, we might as well hold Yule tidings now, everyone's here." Ran chuckled grimly, glancing up as a man strode out of the darkness to join him. 'Twas his brother-in-law, Kinross Deuchar, Ran's second cousin on his father's side. Ross had ridden in on the distinctive pure white mare Brodie now led off with Dearg. The animal was Ross's own pride and joy, much as Uar was Ranald's.

Though distant cousins, the two men looked nothing alike. Kinross's coloring was fair, and he usually wore his pale hair loose, though he was known to don a wig on occasion at court. He was clad in mulberry velvet with a matching cloak. His face was thin, his nose a trifle long, and he rather reminded Ran of a ferret. A kindly disposed ferret, though for some reason, Ran had been never felt entirely comfortable with Ross. Perhaps because Lord Deuchar was another one for court politics, and he himself was not particularly impressed with titles.

Nevertheless, it could not be denied Ross was an excellent husband and father. He had never ill-treated Darra, and both Jesu and Ran knew his high-spirited nature would drive even a priest to drink. 'Twas Ran's good fortune Kinross had taken a brief hiatus from her duties, and could stay on at Auchmull for a time. He would put the man's expertise to use now.

"Ross," he said, nodding shortly in acknowledgment. "I hear you've a man who's a passable tracker. Can you lead another foray in the morn?"

"Certainly. Thank you for sending word to Edzell, by the way. I see Wickham is here. Does he intend to aid us in the search for Duncan's killer?"

Ran smiled wryly. "Nay. He's never been partial to horses, nor they to him. I've set him and his men to searching the castle sewers."

Ross's eyes widened, and then he gave a chortle of laughter. "Truly, you're not an enemy to have, Ran! I hear rumor Wickham pushed the border with his betrothed, as well."

"And has pink cheek trophy to show for it," Ranald said,

though not without a faint chuckle. "I doubt he'll try to fondle her again."

"Is she truly as ornery as I hear tale?"

Ran's smile broadened. "Och, even more so."

"Then you'd best steal the bonny lass from Wickham while you can, Ran. She'd throw strong lads for the House of Lindsay."

A tic of annoyance tugged Ran's mouth into a scowl. Usually he appreciated Ross's wicked sense of humor, but not today. "I'm not interested. Neither is she."

"How do you know? Have you bothered to ask her?"

Ranald frowned and pivoted on his heel toward the keep, effectively ending their conversation. Kinross just grinned after his brother-in-law. He knew full well what was on Ran's mind. The vibrant redhead obviously rattled the Wolf's infamous icy control.

Chapter Eighteen

Unaware Ranald and his men had returned, Merry continued her polite conversation with Lady Deuchar in Auchmull's northern tower room. She and Ranald's sister had hit it off at once; each quickly recognized a kindred spirit and a fellow source of fascinating courtly gossip. They had been chattering for the better part of an hour, and already Darra insisted they converse with Christian names, rather than titles. Merry did not demur. It had been so long since she had visited with another woman who had similar interests; her own twin, Kat, was as different from her as night from day.

Darra told her all the latest Stuart gossip. It seemed King James had recently published a treatise called "Basilikon Doron," the follow-up to the year's previous dry "Trew Law of Free Monarchies." In this, he again expressed his opinion that rebellion against a king was unlawful and blasphemous. Darra's eyes twinkled when she added his timing was poor as ever; the greater nobility were even less amused by James's demand that guests at courtly receptions were asked to bring their own food. While he waited on his tentative inheritance, tied to Tudor courtstrings, James had lapsed into a sullen, wary, withdrawn monarch. Queen Anne could, on occasion, be both bright and witty, but her Danish heritage made her an outsider and she had never been fully embraced by the Stuart assembly. Public approval, however, had bounded upward upon the birth of Prince Henry, now five, and the Court collectively held their breath awaiting the next heir apparent. Elizabeth Tudor was no longer young; a reign of over forty years was a rare thing. If James intended to hold on to the whole of Scotland and England in the wake of her encroaching death, he needed more sons, and quickly.

Yet the proposed union of the countries after so many years of strife was exciting. At best, Scotland and England had been cautious allies, and Merry warmed to the thought of being able to visit both courts without criticism. Now she had made the acquaintance of Lady Deuchar, who obviously held influence with the Stuarts, her position was all the more secure. The only detail marring the picture was Sir Jasper Wickham. Suddenly the thought of the cold, fishy-pale Englishman introducing her as his wife was not a pleasant one. Her heart beat much faster when she envisioned Ranald in his stead, imagined the envious stares and whispers of the other ladies as a rugged, brooding Scot clad in kilt and breccan escorted her before the throne.

She shivered and Darra paused and regarded her curiously. "Is something amiss, Merry?"

"Nay." Merry took a sip of the mulled cider from the mug she cradled in her hands. "I was just wondering if the men had found the culprit yet."

"I doubt they will. Duncan's killer was long gone by the time they bothered to search."

Merry nodded, troubled. " 'Tis late, m'dear," Darra offered kindly, "and I have kept you up . You look weary, perhaps a good rest would restore your spirits."

Merry shook her head and set the cider aside on a small table. "Faith, I can't. I have to see Lord Lindsay. I have to tell him . . ." She hesitated. She didn't know what she planned saying to Ranald. That she was sorry? That she felt bad because she hadn't helped Duncan in time? Did he even want to see her face again? What if he blamed her for the old man's death?

Darra sensed her upset. "There's naught you can do tonight, Merry," she said soothingly, "except get some rest. Poor Duncan is beyond help."

"I know. But Ranald—Lord Lindsay—seemed so fond of him."

"Oh, aye. As a lad, Ran nearly lived in the stables, learning about horses from the best. Duncan was like a father to Ran after Father's death." She sighed. " 'Twill be too quiet around the stables now."

"Who will take Duncan's place?"

"Grady, perhaps, or if Brodie Scott stays on, I think he would be very good with the animals."

Merry nodded agreement. "I met Lady Fiona at Goldielands. She mentioned you fondly."

Darra laughed. "Aye, dear Fi . . . I still chuckle over our mischievous days, long past. I confess I miss her terribly. She was a feckless child, but everyone adored her. I was sorry to hear of her recent travail, though I received word she did not lose the babe."

"I am glad." Merry was silent a moment, running her fingers over the vivid plaid pattern of the blanket draped across her lap. Red and black, Lindsay colors. She wondered if she should feel like a traitor wearing it. She wondered, too, why she didn't.

"Darra," she asked softly, "who do you think killed Duncan? And why?"

Ran's sister frowned a little. Even so, the dark-haired woman was attractive, her half-mourning a flattering hue of deepest plum, trimmed with black lace. Her cork-heeled shoes tapped an absent rhythm on the braided wool rug, her expression was thoughtful.

"I'm not sure," she said at last. "But whoever 'twas, I believe it to be a deliberately calculated strike at Ran. Or an attempt to provoke another flare-up like the incident at Badanloch."

"Tell me more about that, please. I want to understand

everything, but my head gets so muddled from trying to figure it all out. There appears to be bad blood between Macleans and Lindsays.''

''Aye. It goes way back, Merry, beyond Ran and Blair. Centuries ago, one of our ancestors, William de Lindsay, was Baron of Luffness and Laird of Crawford. His eye fell upon a likely lass, Caitlin Maclean, whom he resolved to make his own. She was betrothed to another . . .'' It seemed Darra paused here, perhaps a bit awkwardly. ''Anyhow, the Gallant Laird, for that 'tis what he was called, charmed Caitlin into betraying her family's choice, and great with his child, she appeared at the wedding feast. Her family forced her to heel, William was killed, and the bad blood and lost love spawned from that dark day seem to have spiraled down through the years, Macleans and Lindsays have been dancing around one another, ever since.''

Darra sighed. ''I do not need to tell you, perhaps, Ran's choice of wife was unsettling to the lot of us, for not only was Blair a Maclean, the enemy, but I personally found her sly and deceitful.''

''Deceitful?''

Merry looked at Darra, surprised. She detected a crisp tone beneath the soft, refined speech of her Scottish contemporary.

''Lord Lindsay appears to hold her . . . above reproach.''

Darra nodded. ''In Ran's eyes, she was, and still is, above reproach, a flawless little Maclean angel.''

Merry nodded ruefully. ''Aye, that much 'tis obvious.'' She clasped her hands before her, silent for a moment as she pondered the comparison. Nay, she would never be the sweet, circumspect, demure woman Ranald obviously preferred; after all, she was certain his beloved Blair would never have slapped Sir Jasper, but rather blushed and stammered in confusion, feigning ignorance about the man's crude intentions. Yet Darra apparently did not see the same Blair as Lord Lindsay, and Merry found this most interesting.

''I confess I am most curious. In what way was Lady Lindsay deceitful, Darra?''

"I caught her several times lying to Ranald about seeing certain people who were accounted Lindsay enemies, most notably Cullen after the troubles at Badanloch."

"But he is her brother. I do not find that unseemly."

Darra nodded, her expression as inscrutable for a moment as Ran's. "Perhaps. Yet when she wed my brother, she took the Lindsay title. She failed or perhaps did not wish to realize divided loyalties are dangerous . . . to us all."

Merry looked at Darra, nodding thoughtfully in turn. "Troubled times, aye, and the wanton destruction that so oft accompanies it."

She then indicated the tower room where they were sitting. "Lady Blair's retreat?" Merry asked, though 'twas obvious enough from the fine tapestries and delicately woven shawl draped over the back of Darra's chair. Merry had not moved anything out of respect, and memory of Ranald's reaction to her tidying the great hall still stung. He had reacted so harshly when she intended nothing more than a general restoration of order. And warmth. How cold the hall had been, how drafty the corners without even a blazing hearth to combat the encroaching winter.

"Aye, Ran had Rose Tower added as a wedding gift to Blair. Her favorite flowers were roses."

"Mine as well." Merry's gaze swept over the small, yet cozy tower room with its muted feminine decoration and coloring, and she could not help but wish, for a moment, 'twas hers. She knew, instinctively, Sir Jasper would never build anything like this for his lady wife. As soon as the thought crossed her mind, a movement in the doorway caught her attention. She glanced over, eyes widening as Ran's figure loomed there.

Darra heard her swift intake of breath and pivoted also in her chair, dark brows winging upward. "Ran. Did you find the criminal yet?"

He shook his head, gaze lingering on Merry as he advanced, with seeming hesitation, into the Rose Tower. Merry realized he had probably not been there for months, which explained the air of neglect and layers of dust coating everything when she first discovered the place in her restless roaming. A few hours of studious cleaning made it livable again, but she was glad now she had not moved anything. Ran seemed to be searching for something, and she assumed it must be another reason to find fault with her.

She swallowed when his dark gaze refocused on her. "There were no clues at all?"

"None. The culprit seems to have vanished into thin air. Which means, 'twas someone here . . . someone still here . . ."

"Aye, I tend to agree," Darra put in. "But don't jump to conclusions, Ran. Right now, there is nothing to be done but try and divert further trouble. 'Twould not hurt if we address the issue of Gilbert as well."

Ranald glanced at his sister with obvious exasperation. He looked weary and dispirited. "I am glad you and Ross came, but I don't have time to deal with petty family matters at present. Gil acted very foolishly, aye, and I shall hold him fully accountable for his actions, once this matter with Wickham is settled."

Darra looked pointedly at Merry, then back at Ran. "So you men would sentence an innocent to suffer whilst you feud over equally petty matters."

"Petty!" he exploded. His eyes flashed with pure emotion, reminding Merry the Wolf was always there, lurking behind even a seemingly exhausted facade. The fangs were quickly bared when the issue of Wickham or his dead wife were raised. She wondered if this proud man could ever, would ever, trust or love again. His big frame even trembled a little as he faced down Lady Deuchar, reminding Merry even the greatest mountain might shake from a tiny earthquake.

"Need I remind you, Dar, Sir Jasper is responsible for Blair's death? However indirectly, he contributed to it by failing to summon me or someone from Auchmull when she was ill."

"Aye, but why ever was she at Braidwood in the first place?" Darra retorted, in what was obviously an old and familiar argument by now. "That has never been explained to my satisfaction, and you certainly cannot swallow that tale about her hunting for herbs and getting lost. I know you for a brighter man than that.''

Ranald glared at his sister. ''The subject is closed. You are a meddler, Dar.''

Darra in turn regarded him with equal frustration. ''And you are an infuriating, obstinate man with no regard for others.'' She gestured at Merry, then rose and angrily gathered her skirts about her. ''The fact you hold this young woman hostage tests even my filial affection for you, Ran. Do not sever the little good grace you still possess with me by ruining Gilbert's future, too.''

Ranald stared at his sister in smoldering fury, and for a moment Merry wished she might sink into the cushions of the furniture and become invisible. She had never noticed how truly alarming a large, muscular male might appear in such small quarters. For a moment, the two Lindsays regarded each other with matched defiance, then the petite Darra tossed her head and made for the door, brushing past her much larger sibling without another word but with admirable aplomb.

After Lady Deuchar disappeared, Merry expected Ranald to turn his aggravation on her. Instead, he sighed, and raked a hand through his hair.

''Dar is right,'' he said. ''Whatever the outcome with Wickham, your reputation is quite likely ruined. I am sorry.''

'' 'Tis too late now, milord. Perhaps you should have considered that before you kidnapped me.''

''Aye.'' He looked at her, as if wanting to say something more, and the strained silence beat at them both like the snow against the leaded panes.

After a moment he sighed again. ''None wish more than me that Wickham had not forced my hand. This entire situation has left a bad taste in my mouth, lass, of that you may be sure.''

Merry smiled a little. ''Lass. I will never forget the first time you called me that.''

''Oh, aye. Highly offended, you were.'' Ranald chuckled a

little at the memory, too. ''A proper English lady cannot be accounted a mere lass, 'twould seem.''

''I am sure there are worse words, mayhap a few quite apt for a woman who dares to defy her captor.'' Her amused gaze met his, and for a second they both smiled at each other.

''I cannot complain, Mistress Tanner. You have been an exemplary prisoner.''

''Why, thank you, milord,'' she responded in kind, and rose from the chair to execute a little mock curtsey. The tartan throw tumbled from her lap, and they both bent to retrieve it at the same time. Their gazes locked when their faces were but inches apart, and Merry trembled a little as the Wolf's warm breath came upon her cheek.

Slowly, very slowly, his hand reached out and cupped her chin. They straightened together, his grip firm but gentle there, and when fully upright, he leaned forward and kissed her. Exquisitely tender was the kiss, yet she sensed the barely restrained passion behind it, and his tongue flicked against her lips with increasing fervor as her arms slid up around Ranald's neck, drawing him closer.

He shuddered. She felt the angles of his male body even through the layers of her skirts, edging her backward, scalding her emotions and making her shiver with anticipation. Suddenly the backs of her knees bumped the low couch; a second later she was descending as he cradled her in his arms.

Feverishly his mouth devoured hers, as his weight came to rest upon her, but he bore the brunt of it upon his arms and she was too caught up in the moment to care. Sweet, hot, wild emotions tumbled over Merry as she clutched Ranald's shoulders and met his kiss with her own newly unleashed passion. She sensed his desire, his frustration mingling with the shame of what they did, for it matched her own. Two lonely souls willing to risk all for a single moment of blazing bliss.

She trembled as the drawn-out kiss ended, and Ran looked into her eyes. The expression there was one she would never forget, both a silent plea and simple gratitude, and her soft little sigh answered the unspoken question. Merry let her head fall back against the cushions, and he dipped his own and nuzzled the proffered neck with a restrained yet eager passion, trailing fiery kisses from the delicate line of her jaw down her throat, until his lips came to rest upon the swell of her breasts. He swirled the tip of his tongue on silken flesh. Merry gasped, arching upward, and she felt the hard edge of his arousal pressing against her.

She quivered as Ran's hand slid up beneath her skirts, traveled slowly up her thigh, tracing lazy spirals upon her skin while the other cupped the back of her head and drew her mouth to his again. She surrendered without a qualm to the ardent caresses of this man she could not deny, who engendered such feelings in her as she had never felt before, everything from fury to delight and passion, to the most exquisitely tender emotions she had ever felt for another.

Gently he released her head against the cushions, and his free hand traveled down to the laces of her bodice, where his fingers caught and drew upon the silken ribbon with dramatic slowness. Merry felt herself shaking as he tugged open the bodice, peeled aside the frill of lace and bared her breasts to his worshiping gaze.

She had always fretted that part of her was too small, but there was nothing but the softest admiration in the Wolf's dark eyes before his head dipped and he laved her there with a warm tongue. Merry gasped as his lips circled, seized and drew upon a little pink nipple. She arched again, this time the hand upon her thigh traveled higher and sought the secret of her woman's mont, already dewed from the passion of their embrace and the sweet emotions tumbling in her breast.

His fingers stroked her softly there, while Merry whimpered a little entreaty without words. The tightness in her belly seemed a bane destined to shatter her very being, and she surrendered to his caresses without shame, trusting her gentle captor as she had never trusted another. He teased the pearl of her femininity with the tip of his finger, while his lips drew upon the taut berry of her nipple. With a little whimper, Merry arched yet again. He slid the tormenting finger deep into her welcoming warmth, and then she felt nothing at all but sweet, wild waves of desire.

Ran moaned as well, his mouth sliding against hers, hot and tasting faintly of drambuie. His tongue met and fenced with hers in a delicious dance, each of them quivering and taut as a quarrel ready to fly from a crossbow. If ever Merry had felt something so right, 'twas the sweet rapture she found in the arms of the Wolf of Badanloch. Forbidden and delightful.

She shifted against him, her yielding clear in both action and silence, and when the hungry kiss finally ended, Ran gazed into her eyes for a long moment, and then something shuddered through him. He abruptly ceased tormenting her with passionate caresses, and instead removed his wandering hand and smoothed down her skirts. She looked at him, silently questioning, but he merely shook his head.

How deep ran the grief in the Wolf of Badanloch, and Merry's heart ached when Ran drew a ragged breath and laid his head upon her, shaking with emotion. She knew he thought of Blair then, of betraying his beloved wife's memory with another woman in the Rose Tower.

All she could do, and did, was clutch his head to her breast and run her fingers through the dark waves of his hair, over and over, soothingly, while his shoulders shook and a silent maelstrom swirled about the keep, without and within.

Chapter Nineteen

Merry sat curled up in a chair before the blazing hearth in Auchmull's great hall, trying to occupy herself with finishing the embroidery on a wall hanging depicting a tower with battlements under the Crown of Scotland. Her English contemporaries would no doubt consider such work treasonous, but then those little goose-brains were not enduring the same circumstances as she, and, furthermore, Merry no longer cared what anyone thought of her actions. Especially since she had watched Sir Jasper and his men ride off the previous eve, her emotions a mixture of relief and dismay. So in the end, Sir Jasper had abandoned her to her fate, a fate come about only because of his own actions. Courage was only a title in the Wickham tradition, and Merry was admittedly embittered.

She had no notion what might happen now, save the fact her reputation was certainly destroyed and she could never return to Court. Her family would not reject her, she knew, but the notion of returning to Ireland and suffering the mingled pity and outrage of the entire O'Neill clan was not a pleasant one. She supposed Uncle Kit and Aunt Isobel would permit her to live at Ambergate for a time, and she did have a dower house property in Kent, though she assumed 'twas nearly uninhabitable after so many years of neglect.

Without a sterling reputation, a woman could not hope to secure a good marriage. At most, Merry might be accepted by one of the O'Neill vassals or lesser men in Ireland who did not know of her disgrace. Or a man with title but no funds whom her father could pay to ease the burden of the shame she brought. She shuddered at the thought, stabbing her needle through the fine silk and leaving a slightly larger hole than was wise. She looked at the flawless rows of stitches preceding her own and sighed. Naturally, Blair Lindsay had been an exquisite seamstress, too. Was there nothing the little paragon of virtue had not accomplished to perfection?

Merry heard footsteps and glanced up, still frowning over her work. Gilbert Lindsay laughed at her dour expression.

"I take it you are not fond of the gentler arts?" the young man inquired as he vaulted neatly over the couch facing her and landed there with a thud. Merry could not suppress a laugh, especially when he wiggled his eyebrows at her.

"You are a knave, Gil," she rebuked him playfully, then bit off the length of dangling silk thread and tied it. "I wonder I ever agreed to introduce you at Court."

"Because y'know the fair maidens will swoon, and you are anxious to impress upon Her Grace as well," he countered with a twinkle.

Merry laughed. "Indeed, and I should be accounted very foolish if I rested the remnants of my reputation upon your roguish character. La, Gil, but you are a wicked one who would surely add to the great heap of guilt upon my shoulders in light of circumstances here."

"Guilt! How now, when you cannot be held accountable for Ran's actions!" he cried. " 'Twould be cruel indeed of Gloriana to blame you for such trespasses." He flushed. "Besides, I was the cad who decided a bit of adventure was worth the risk, and unwittingly dragged you into the tangled plot we now occupy."

"True enough, but think you the queen will care as to the cause of a ruined reputation? Nay, Gil, the mere fact of its existence will coax her outrage to the fore. I shall be banned from Court within the week, mark my words. Doubtless a missive from Sir Jasper is already flying south, as the man washes his hands of me forever.''

''I am not so certain that is anything to grieve over, Merry.''

''Aye.'' She set the embroidery aside with a sigh. ''Certainly I cannot feign grief over losing someone I hardly knew. But the upset it brings my family, that is what troubles me. By now they must know of my situation and are doubtless both outraged and appalled.''

Gil nodded, looking thoughtful. It seemed he had grown up a great deal in just the fortnight of their acquaintance, and Merry enjoyed his lively company. Often they played chess or strolled the long gallery with its portraits of great ancestors long gone, and when he and Hugo were not joined hip-to-hip, she saw a different side of Gil altogether. With his boyhood friend he was rash, noisy, reckless. Away from him Gil could be quite civil, even gallant. He simply had inherited a stronger dose than usual of spirit in his Lindsay blood.

''Where is Hugo today?'' Merry asked, for normally Gil went nowhere without his brawny companion.

''He rode to meet a messenger from Falkland. The king is sending a dispatch in the matter of Macleans and Lindsays.''

''Lord Lindsay did not permit you to go along?''

Gilbert scowled. ''Nay, he said 'twas too dangerous for a Lindsay heir. Darra even wanted me to return to Edzell with her and Ross. They are all mollycoddling me and I don't care for it.''

Merry smiled a little. ''You are the youngest, 'tis understandable. I doted on and hovered about my baby brothers just the same.''

He tilted his head, considering her. ''I should think you would make a fierce and overprotective elder sister.''

''They complain of nothing else.'' Merry chuckled, adding, ''Except, perhaps, bossy as well.''

Her words were punctuated by the sudden entrance of a familiar figure into the hall. Black Cullen smirked a little at

Merry's surprise when she looked up. He clutched his soft cap to his chest, snow flecking his black and green, white striped Maclean tartan. "Ye wouldna happen to be lookin' for me, lass?"

Gilbert, too, tensed at the familiar voice. "So you did not return to Badanloch, after all. You were to leave with Hugo and the rest."

Maclean stood before them in the center of the great hall, surrounded by several trestle tables still piled high with the remnants of the men's meals. Except for Merry and Gilbert and a handful of servants and a few guards, Auchmull was mostly empty. Ranald and the others had ridden out in search of Duncan's killer and fresh game, and Merry felt suddenly vulnerable. She glanced over in time to see Gilbert's eyes narrow, and knew his thoughts matched her own. Black Cullen meant trouble, in any guise.

"I wasna quite ready ta go. By the by, ye look lovely, lass." He eyed her somber attire with dismay. "But is it mournin' yer wearin' now?"

"Aye. I mourn for a man who was senselessly struck down, by an animal," Merry replied sharply as she rose to face him. "I'm sure you realize as much, sirrah."

Cullen looked uncomfortable, exactly as she'd hoped. " 'Twas sorry I was to hear about Duncan, truly I was. But I canna do anythin' about it, now can I?"

"Methinks you can, but you won't." Merry dismissed any forthcoming excuses with her curt reply. "I know of this age-old, ridiculous feud, and I believe an innocent has paid for it with his life. Needlessly."

"Dinna meddle in matters ye canna understand, lass."

"I shall meddle where I please, when it concerns my life. 'Tis what led to the outrages I have suffered of late." She regarded him levelly. "Whatever mischief you plan in Lord Lindsay's absence, I do not doubt you'll account for it later."

"In Blair's memory, even Ranald dinna deny me access to Auchmull," Cullen replied. "Is that nae true, Gilly lad?"

" 'Tis Gilbert." The younger man's violet-blue gaze rested

icily upon Cullen a moment before he glanced at Merry. "I reluctantly concede Ran has permitted this weasel to slip in and out as he pleases in dubious honor of their relationship by marriage. Yet I would not be overly distraught should a Lindsay dirk find his belly one of these days."

Merry looked from one to the other, the crackling hostility between the two a palpable thing. Several apt remarks came to mind, yet she bit back any retort which might serve to provoke a scene further.

Cullen chuckled, undaunted. "So hae ye seen what the Wolf and his lair's made of yet, lass? What do ye think of yer ruthless captor? He let Sir Jasper leave empty-handed rather than settle what ye dub a foolish feud."

"Wickham left of his own device. There is nothing going on here can't be resolved. And once Duncan's murder is solved, I intend to address the issue of this petty feud as well. Too many have hurt for too long."

"Noble aspirations, but ye canna expect sympathy from one of the wee folk caught in the middle." Cullen, too, suddenly sobered. "If ye interfere wi' ancient feuds, lass, dinna expect to emerge unscathed."

"I should think I have already paid a hefty penalty."

He looked at her long a moment, then sighed and nodded. "Aye, lass."

Gilbert had risen and meandered to the window. He spoke into the strained silence. "The riders have returned . . ."

A moment later, they heard the hoofbeats in the court, and Merry met Cullen's gaze one more time. "Mayhap they've found the killer."

He regarded her coolly. "They might at that."

"Nay, Ran looks thunderous." Gilbert put in. "It did not go well."

"Och, I was afeared of that," Cullen said. "Save yer breath, lass. Fate hae already been set into motion, and none can stop it now."

"What is that supposed to mean?" she demanded.

He hesitated. "Ye read too much into m'words."

"Do I? You have knowledge of Duncan's killer, don't you?"

"Nay."

"What's going on here?" a deep voice demanded from the entrance to the great hall. Merry spun around and felt the blood rush to her head in her anger and frustration. Ranald stood there, scowling darkly at both her and Cullen, obviously leaping to rather wild conclusions of his own.

"I was just . . . that is, Cullen . . ." Merry began, waving her hand in a feeble attempt to explain. She was still flustered by Cullen's evasiveness.

Ranald's eyes were like black ice. "Go on."

"Mistress Tanner was but askin' m'humble opinion on her attire," Cullen said, a bit too smoothly to be believed. "Lasses and their gewgaws, ye ken."

Gilbert shot them both a glance, but said nothing.

"Nay, I don't understand, but I'm glad you're here anyway, Cullen. You were sleeping in the stables the night Duncan was stabbed. Did you see or hear anything?"

Cullen shifted a little under Ranald's cold stare. Merry wondered if Hertha was right, if Blair's brother might be responsible for the betrayal at Badanloch which led to the deaths stoking the old clan feud. But surely even Black Cullen would not be so bold as to murder an innocent old man, then linger about and strut through the keep as he pleased. He must know Ran disliked him; none could be so dense as to not sense the waves of hostility emanating from the Wolf.

"Nay, Ran, I dinna hear a thing. I sleep verra deeply. Blair always said me snore could wake the dead."

Ranald did not look amused, either by Cullen's poor attempt at humor or the reference to his wife. "Too bad your snores cannot wake poor Duncan, too. Somebody apparently has little respect for life around here. There's no excuse for slaughtering an innocent old man."

Merry saw Ranald's garb was damp, his dark-brown hair glistening from remnants of wet snow. Yet something else besides the search for Duncan's killer made him taut with anger now, and she met his gaze with a wariness that was becoming all too familiar.

"What happened?" she asked.

"His Majesty has forwarded a missive from your Virgin Queen."

Merry was startled by the venom in his voice. She stared at Ran blankly a moment, unable to grasp what this might mean. The Lindsay holdings at Badanloch had been forfeited to Macleans after the treachery there, and her first thought was perhaps the king had reconsidered his punishment. But nay, 'twas nothing so benign, and besides Ran should have been grinning rather than glowering if that was the case.

" 'Twould seem your regal Gloriana has hit upon the perfect solution to your predicament, Merry." Ran reached inside his damp breccan and withdrew a parchment, which he thrust unceremoniously at his younger brother. "Go ahead, Gil, read it aloud for everyone's enlightenment. We must not let Darra's fine tutors go to waste." He folded his arms and stood there like a fierce sentinel, expressionless.

Hesitantly Gil pulled the string and unrolled the parchment, licking dry lips as a pall of anticipation settled over the hall.

To His Royal Majesty James VI of Scotland and the Earl of Crawford Ranald Lindsay "For His Majesties' Service:"

In the matter of Mistress Meredith Tanner you are hereby ordered that the presence and honor of such maid shall be preserved at all cost and hence Lord Lindsay is hereby commanded to amend with the Tudor Crown by and with such actions as mend reputation with the decree of sanctified and holy union prescribed in the Church.

Gilbert paused and drew a deep breath, no less shaky than Merry's own. Her head whirled as the words pounded against her temples:

Such matters attend to Her Majesty's noble kin His Majesty James VI of Scotland, to have special care that the Wolf and his actions do upon no account escape due merit. This union to be sealed in the Church by the proper Authority and necessary witnesses, to wit: and you are to secure all the avenues, that Lord Lindsay does not elude justice. This you are to put into execution by Martinmas, and by that time, or very shortly after it, Lord and Lady Lindsay commanded herein to appear before Her Majesty Elizabeth Tudor I of England. This is by the queen's special command, for the good will of both countries. See that this be put into execution without feud or favor, else the Earl of Crawford shall forfeit his title and adjoining lands herein. Expecting His Majesty will not fail in the fulfilling hereof as he loves his country, I subscribe these orders with my hand,

Sir Robert Cecil, Minister to the Crown Whitehall,
1 November. 1599

The hall was deathly silent as Gilbert finished reading the royal decree. Even Merry could not summon a gasp, for the shock roiling throughout her now went far deeper than such mere expressions could attest. 'Twas a royal command . . . to wed the Wolf of Badanloch.

Chapter Twenty

Merry slowly sank back down into her chair, gazing at Ran in a helpless sort of appeal for answers he could not provide. He was not angry with her, but was unable to keep the terseness from his voice when he spoke.

"Aye, Merry," he said, his dark glare pinning the parchment Gilbert held. "King James had no choice but to agree to his royal kin's decree. He tastes a Tudor inheritance all too keenly now. Gloriana could ask him to crawl to Kindrogan on his knees and he'd do it without the bat of a lash. The seat of Lindsay is forfeit unless you and I wed before Martinmas."

"But . . . 'tis utter madness," Merry said at last, very faintly, still stunned by the news and obviously uncertain how to react. Ran nodded curtly at her words.

"The prospect is an unpleasant one, to be certain." She stayed silent, and a moment later he heaved a weary sigh and changed the subject. " 'Tis snowing like a blizzard in Hades again. We lost the trail of Duncan's killer on the other side of the pass. More clues are unlikely to surface before spring."

After a moment of tense silence, Cullen cleared his throat. "With yer permission, Ran?"

Ranald looked at him again, and was pleased to see the other man fidget a bit under his cool regard. "Aye, 'tis over late. Get some sleep. But in the morning, speak with Rob Byers. He's in charge of the search. You get some rest, too, Gil. I believe Darra is expecting a report from the tutor on your progress tomorrow. 'Twould not do to disappoint."

The younger man frowned, setting the parchment on a nearby table when Ran made no move to take it back. "Books are the last thing on my mind right now."

"Well, I suggest you renew interest in them right quick. I for one do not wish to be the one who informs Lady Deuchar you have abandoned your studies. 'Twas part of the agreement with her and Ross so you might be allowed to stay on at Auchmull."

"I know." Gilbert heaved an exaggerated sigh but was bright enough to realize Ran wished to speak to Merry alone. He nodded at them both, trailed Cullen out of the hall.

Left alone with Ran, Merry raised her gaze from the clasped hands in her lap and met his regard with a distinct challenge in her eyes. She couldn't resist tossing a barb at him.

" 'Twould appear the queen's sentence is one worse than death. Or is it the gown that displeases you this time? Mayhap my hair?"

"I'm sorry, lass. You don't deserve a scowl, to be certain." Ran sighed and ran a hand through his own hair, exasperated. "None of this is your fault. Except perhaps for a fleeting moment of poor judgment when you chose to travel without proper escort."

"Aye," she snapped back, " 'tis of a certainty ample excuse for the fate that befell me, sirrah. A folly I shall pay for with a lifetime of regrets."

He turned away. Not in rage this time, but hurt. He couldn't let her see how her words pained him. He wasn't entirely sure why they did himself.

"We could appeal to Her Majesty. Beg her mercy. Mayhap by now her pique of temper has passed and she is in a more reasonable frame of mind."

"D'you truly believe that, Merry?" He slowly pivoted and faced her again. Her beautiful gray-green eyes were filled with emotion, but of what sort, he could not guess and dared not try. "Besides, what alternative do you face? Banishment from Court, disgrace among your peers. Humiliation is what I intended for Wickham, not you."

"Be as that may, the cards have been turned," she whispered. "My fate may not be fair, but 'tis final."

"I'm sorry, lass. I never expected Wickham to abandon you to it. I thought he would rush to your side, assume responsibility like a man, and that I might even restore Lindsay lands by regaining title to Badanloch."

"Perhaps a reasonable man of conscience would have. Sir Jasper displays neither trait."

Ran chuckled a little at her matter-of-fact remark. "Aye, is that not the truth. Regardless, I regret my hasty decision, Merry. You should not be forced to suffer for it."

He watched her carefully. He longed to know what she was thinking, what depth of dismay she felt upon hearing the royal decree. Jesu knew he deserved to be loathed, yet somehow the notion of Merry Tanner hating him did not rest easy with his conscience. He heaved a sigh. "What shall we do, lass?"

She looked at him expressionlessly. "It does not appear we have much choice in the matter, does it?"

"There is always a choice. A Lindsay defying a royal decree would not be a first."

Despite her upset, Merry smiled a little. "Aye, I imagine not."

Ran crossed over to the sideboard, availed himself of a spiced wine Hertha had placed there. He offered her a glass as well but she shook her head, and he drank in silence, occasionally glancing at Merry over the rim. She picked up her embroidery again and he thought the wall hanging looked vaguely familiar. Then he saw the whole picture when she spread it on her lap, the tower with its battlements, the words she was embroidering in gold thread. "Virtue mine honour." The Maclean motto.

A jagged bolt of emotion coursed through him. He had never

seen something of Blair's clutched in Merry's hands before now. His first impulse was to yank the embroidery from her hands, berate her for daring to touch his wife's things. Yet the unfinished hanging had tormented him these past months, reminding him of ends hanging loose, of things left unsaid. What troubled Ran the most was not being there when Blair died, not being able to tell her he loved her one last time. 'Twould haunt him forever.

Yet Merry was finishing what Blair had begun. The significance of this slowly sank in as Ran watched her little hand plying the needle with swift, if not calm, accuracy.

For a moment, 'twas easy to imagine himself sitting before a cozy hearth, enjoying a glass of spiced wine and visiting idly with his wife while she worked on such homey tasks. Suddenly the prospect of being thus disposed was not so unpleasant.

He took a deep breath. "Merry," he began, and her auburn head rose, firelight glinting off the burnished curls. "I am not unwilling to obey Her Majesty's decree."

She regarded him, head tilted a bit, questioning. "Certainly you do not wish Gilbert to lose his inheritance, or the Lindsays their lands. 'Tis quite understandable."

"Nay, quite apart from all that, I simply do not find the prospect of wedding you . . . distasteful."

Her eyes widened. She appeared stunned, then even a trifle embarrassed. She played with the threads in her lap. "Not dismayed by the thought of being shackled to a . . . what did you call me once, a spoiled little *Sassenach* bitch?" she murmured.

Ran nodded. "Aye, I was angry then. Lashing out. I have never had opportunity to tell you, I admire your courage and resourcefulness in the face of darkened odds."

"Thank you."

He understood her cautious reply quite well. She had no reason to trust anything he said after the events of the past days. He sighed. "Tell me, Merry, what you plan to do. If I released you today, where would you go?"

"England, I suppose."

"After defying the queen's order, you would appear at her

Court?'' He shook his head. ''I think 'twould be the height of foolishness, to toy with Her Majesty's temper. Especially in view of the goings-on with Essex in Ireland. She is sorely vexed and lashing out left and right.''

''Well, my uncle Kit would not turn me away, I am certain. He has an estate there outside of London.''

''Where he, too, would cross the queen and pay the price in the end. You do not seem to grasp the serious nature of this decree. To punish me and placate Wickham, Elizabeth Tudor is willing to sacrifice you to the Wolf of Badanloch.''

Merry drew a shaky little breath. ''Aye, 'twould appear so.''

''She must know of my reputation from Wickham, yet she does not hesitate to offer you up to an uncouth Scot in the name of the Crown. A noble sacrifice for your country.''

Ran could not keep the bitter note from his voice. Merry looked at him, and he was surprised to see a tender light in her gray-green eyes for the first time he could recall.

''If Her Grace thought so little of me in the end, mayhap I am well quit of Court,'' she said. ''I was Elizabeth Tudor's goddaughter, my family and me served her loyally for years. If my sole purpose is to be a pawn, then perhaps my own loyalty was misplaced.''

Ran arched an eyebrow. ''What are you saying, lass?''

She straightened proudly. ''I am saying . . . I suppose . . . I should not be wholly averse to the role of Lady Lindsay, either.''

Their gazes met, and Ran nodded slightly. ''If that is the case, I must speak frankly with you. I do not deny I find you attractive as a woman . . .'' He trailed off, noting her faint blush at his words. ''However, lest there be any misunderstanding, I must stress that I loved my late wife . . . beyond anything . . .''

Merry nodded, eyes shadowed with some emotion he could not read, but she did not interrupt as he forced out the words in a sudden rush.

''There will never be another who can replace Blair . . . and I could never let any woman ever assume so . . . all I can offer is a hearth and home, and my respect. Perhaps the respect of a title is enough, to some, but I wished there to be no mistake about it. I can care for you, Merry, and already feel a tender regard of sorts, a responsibility, if you would, both for your plight and to see things put right, but beyond that . . . I am sorry.''

She nodded again. ''A loveless match is what I would have had with Wickham, at any rate.''

He was relieved by her practicality. ''Aye. Marriages of convenience are both sensible and sane, contrasted with the reckless and tragic results of . . . love.'' He remembered what he had risked, and lost, in loving Blair, and felt suddenly weary.

Merry set the embroidery aside and rose. Her skirts unfurled about her ankles, and the ebony silk contrasted with the fairness of her skin. Ran was touched by the fact she wore mourning in Duncan's honor, when she had not even known the stable master. There was a sweet nature behind this redhead's fiery temper; he caught glimpses of it now and again.

She went to him, and in a surprising gesture, stood up on tiptoe and kissed his cheek. ''A truce then, milord, if you think we can begin again.''

He smiled. ''Aye. At least one truce in my life would be very welcome.''

Merry laughed softly.

''By the by, lass, I already responded to the queen's order. I informed both her and King James we would honor the royal command and wed by Martinmas.''

''What!'' she exclaimed, taking a step backward. Her eyes were wide with shock.

''I knew, in the end, you had little choice. And in light of the events in the Rose Tower the other day . . .''

Merry flushed as deep a rose as Blair's flowers, and he chuckled low. ''Let me finish, Merry. I knew then the physical attraction was enough to sustain that portion of a marriage . . . for us both. 'Tis important to have a meeting of the bodies as well as minds. To set your mind at ease, know any issue we have will be acknowledged and inherit accordingly.'' His sweeping gesture encompassed the keep. ''Auchmull is but a portion of my inheritance, lass. I would as lief give it to Gilbert, and the greater Edzell to our firstborn lad. There is also Invermark, though it has weathered the feuds and fierce winters less successfully than the others. If there are no sons, any daughter may hold title and lands by right of primogeniture. I would petition King James to honor her claim.''

"You would truly do that for her?'' Merry whispered faintly.

There was a long silence. ''Nay. I would do it for Lady Lindsay.'' When her wide-eyed gaze met his, Ran added quietly, '' 'Tis the least I can do after all that has happened. I cannot bear the thought of you hating me, Merry.''

His words shattered her last reserve. She opened her arms to him. Ran's eyes burned into hers, fierce with longing, fiercer yet with pride. He didn't move. She realized then he would not come to her. 'Twas entirely up to her, this first move.

Merry stepped closer, raising her hand to tentatively touch his jaw. "Thank you,'' she said again, softly.

With a single swift movement, Ran drew her into the circle of his arms. Merry laid her head against his chest, and he gently stroked her back with ever-widening circular motions, like ripples in a lake. She trembled as if she might cry. For she realized as he already knew, they could be lovers, but never in love.

"Why?'' she whispered, mostly to herself.

"My heart was lost to Blair Maclean and I never found it again, lass. It does not mean we cannot live comfortably as man and wife, for already I bear affection for you. We can raise bairns, even, and be content ... as happy as possible without the complications of love, which may in fact be preferable.''

She brushed her cheek against the soft wool as she tilted her head to look up at him. "Y'are certain this is what you wish to do? Wed an impertinent *Sassenach* wench?''

"Aye, lass. You? Can you endure the reputation of the murderous Wolf of Badanloch?''

She gave a shaky little laugh and removed herself from the circle of his arms. "Yea. Anyway, it doesn't matter now. I've little choice.''

Ran was silent a moment, searching her eyes as if he could possibly find answers there. Maybe he only wished he could. "Aye," he said simply.

His gaze dropped to the gleaming red-gold amulet resting just below her ivory throat, and he traced the outline of the raven thoughtfully.

"D'you remember Mother MacDougall's words at Goldie-lands?"

Merry frowned a little. "Not precisely. Something about a wolf's den?"

" 'At Wolfen Den, if ye should be, A corby hert you there may see.' " Hert . . . heart. A corby is a raven, lass."

Merry's eyes widened.

"Beitris MacDougall is the seventh child of a seventh child. I never doubted she had the Sight, I simply did not care for the evidence of it or her timing. She foresaw the tragedy of Blair's death and announced it at our wedding feast. At least this would seem a less ominous prediction. Except I cannot accept your heart, lass. Keep it safe, here . . ." His fingers trailed down, coming to rest upon the sweet curve of her upper bosom. "We will both be the better for it."

"Will we?" she asked softly.

He had no answer for that. Neither did she.

Chapter Twenty-One

"Yer all packed, lass. Cleary carried out the last trunk a few minutes ago."

"Thank you, Hertha." Merry studied herself in the mirror. She looked unusually pale today, especially for a bride, though perhaps it was the stark unrelieved black of the combination of her mourning and traveling attire. She had donned four quilted petticoats under her wool gown, and sturdy leather half-boots. A Lindsay *feileadh mor* completed the ensemble. Her hair was neatly braided and tucked up under the hood of a fox-trimmed cloak. She wasn't cold, though she was likely to be by the time they reached Edzell, where the ceremony would take place with the requisite witnesses in residence.

She finally turned from the mirror, and her gaze swept one last time over the chamber which had become a sort of haven for her. It looked almost bereft, without all her clothing strung across the bed and chairs. The cradle Ran had carved sat empty in the corner. She had discovered it beneath a quilt in the Rose Tower, and had it removed so he would not be reminded whenever he went there. A lump formed in her throat, looking at it. What dreams had died with the death of innocence, how raw the mighty Wolf's emotions after months had passed.

"I bundled Nellie up, every last inch," Hertha put in, softly so as not to startle Merry. She seemed to sense her mistress was preoccupied. "She's waitin' in the wagon with the bairn."

Merry nodded. Another tragedy, the loss of a young girl to childbed fever, had emptied another household but filled Nell's arms. She was standing wetnurse to the orphan and already cleaved fiercely to the tiny human being. Merry was only glad if something good could come of disaster, 'twas for someone deserving as Nell.

It had been suggested by Ran himself that Nell accompany Merry as her tiring woman for this journey. Hertha was getting too old to travel comfortably, especially in winter, and he thought Edzell would be a better place for the young woman and babe in the end. Nell would stay at Edzell in Lady Deuchar's household until the child was weaned.

Merry let her gaze sweep over the room one more time, then turned to Hertha. "I'm ready." The next time she entered Auchmull, it would be as Lady Lindsay.

In the inner ward, a wagon waited. It had stopped snowing, but it was a cold, gray, blustery day with a distinct bite to the wind. This time Merry would ride with Nell and her trunks in the wagon. Four horses had been hitched up in order to pull the heavy conveyance through the snow. She glanced about, but Ran was nowhere to be seen. 'Twas Brodie who helped her up into the seat.

"There's extra blankets ahind tha' seat," the red-haired squire told them. He moved away to see to his master's horse as Hertha came forward to say good-bye.

To Merry's surprise, there were tears in the woman's eyes. "God bless ye, lass," she said quietly, reaching up to squeeze Merry's hand. "I'll ne'er forget yer kindness ta me."

"I'll miss you, Hertha. Nobody else can do my hair the way you do."

"Och, 'tis nothin'." Hertha drew back her hand and openly

wiped at her eyes. "Take good care of her, Nellie lass, or ye'll answer to me."

Nell Downie laughed. She was rosy-checked and her brown eyes sparkled. She was excited about the upcoming journey, since she'd never left the vicinity of Auchmull in her life.

"Dinna fret, Hertha. I intend to take verra good care of both these little ladies." Nell juggled the baby wrapped securely in her arms. "Dinna ye ken I do hair, too?"

"Nae half so well as me," Hertha shot back, but there was a twinkle in her eye as she stepped back. "Godspeed, lassies!"

"Good-bye, Hertha." Merry forced herself to sound as cheerful as she could manage. If she didn't smile, she was afraid she would burst into tears.

Merry spied Siany, Hertha's granddaughter, standing a little ways off in the distance. She, too, was watching the crowd of men and horses preparing to depart; an impressive, fully armed escort would ride alongside the wagon. The girl was not paying attention to Merry and her grandmother's exchange, but peering at someone else across the yard, her mouth curved in that annoying little half-smile.

Merry turned slightly and glanced through the milling crowd. She was curious and somewhat disturbed by Siany's behavior ever since she had arrived at Auchmull. She couldn't make out the exact target of Siany's interest, but she did narrow it down to one small group of men who had just come striding out of the keep. Among them were Cullen Maclean, Ran, Gilbert, and Hugo. When Merry looked again for the girl, she had vanished into the crowd.

She forgot about the odd incident as the men approached the wagon. She noted Ran's brisk stride, his no-nonsense demeanor. He wore dark wool riding trews beneath his red-and-black breccan, and a leather doublet was visible through the open cloak. The Lindsay badge was nowhere to be seen. Merry wondered why. Then she glimpsed the gleaming broadsword strapped to his waist. Her indrawn breath caught Nell's attention.

" 'Tis a claymore," Nell said, as if she read Merry's mind,

or more likely, the dismay in her expression. "The two-handed Highlander sword. The men even name their weapons, milady. Scathach belonged to Lord Ran's grandsire, and was named for the legendary woman warrior who once ran a battle school on the Isle of Shadow."

"I know about claymores. But why is he wearing it on his wedding day?"

Though he doubtless overheard the women's anxious whispers, Ran didn't stop to speak with Merry, but passed directly by the wagon to meet Brodie, who was holding his stallion's reins. The animal's coat glistened bloodred under the stormy sky, and Merry shivered as Ran vaulted up into the saddle in one smooth movement. The sword clanked against his muscular thigh as he mounted Dearg. There was something ominous hovering in the air today. Even the horses were restive, and the men likewise.

A few of the clansmen appeared to be staying behind. Nell informed Merry in a low voice they would be in charge of Auchmull until Ran's return. Though no trouble was expected during his absence, Ran was taking no chances with Wickham or war-mongering Macleans. Meanwhile, Cullen departed to his own mount, and the uneasy moment was relieved with a bit of humor when the gelding laid back its ears and bared impressive teeth. Cullen promptly cuffed the animal across the nose, drawing blood, and then hollered for Brodie to hold the animal fast while he swung up into the saddle.

"Please tell me he's not going to Edzell, too," Merry whispered to Nell.

"Nay. I hear he is headed back to Glenesk, but he'll ride partway wi' us to take advantage of Lord Ranald's protection." Nell made a wry face. "Black Cullen is nae one to look a gift horse in the mouth, ye ken."

Merry chuckled at the familiar expression, especially as Cullen was now struggling to stay aboard the gelding, which was crow-hopping around the yard.

"Worthless spawn o' a *Sassenach* nag!" Black Cullen shouted, and a moment later his tartan bonnet flew off, landing in the fresh mud resulting from melted snow. Nell clapped a hand to her mouth to stop the gales of giggles, and Merry stared in amazement at the spectacle. A ripple of low laughter went through the ranks of mounted men, even Ran, but when Cullen finally got control of his fractious steed and raised a mottled purple face to glare at the onlookers, a deathly silence fell over the yard.

Ran broke the spell by waving a hand to the guard in the gatehouse. The wooden barricade began to slowly rise, pulleys squealing noisily and straining to lift the gate and its heavy accumulation of half-melted snow.

Brodie returned to the wagon and took the reins in hand. 'Twas a tight squeeze with three in the seat. Nell sat in the middle, discreetly nursing the baby beneath her cloak. Merry braced herself on a wooden post as the wagon suddenly lurched and began to move forward. They made a wide arc in the yard, coming about in time to occupy the middle portion of the departing crowd. The vanguard, led by Ran and his men, had beaten down the snow enough to make it relatively easy going for the wagon. Once outside the walls, the front riders fanned out in a half-circle. Cullen rode behind, and Merry glanced over her shoulder when she felt the icy sensation of eyes boring into her back.

Cullen rode directly behind the wagon. He had crushed his soiled hat down low over his head, and glared at Merry from beneath the brim as if to blame her for the incident in the yard. She felt only a cool contempt for the man now. His failure to exhibit any true remorse over Duncan's death, as well as his deliberate attempt to cause mischief at Auchmull ever since he arrived, had not endeared him to her. She wondered if her marriage to Ran might not cool the relation between the two men even further.

Fortunately, they soon parted ways with Black Cullen. Once they were safely through the pass, he branched off in a westerly direction, while the other travelers continued southeast.

Journey by wagon was no less exhausting than a coach, Merry soon found. They bumped and jostled roughly over hidden obstacles in the snow; the wagon shuddered and squirreled in the slushy remnants of the storm. The four big-hearted horses strained in the harness, gamely stumbling through the mess, but even they were rapidly becoming exhausted. Merry herself was freezing.

Shortly after they left Auchmull, the gray sky had begun to churn and darken, but the storm did not hit until they were too far to turn around. A bitter wind sprang up from the east, snow flurries gusted around the weary travelers. Ice crystals blasted their eyes and cheeks, and Merry huddled close to Nell, trying to share meager body warmth. At least the baby, christened Ashet after her deceased mother, was warm. She slumbered contentedly between the two women on the seat, wrapped in a profusion of warm blankets and both of their cloaks.

When Ran dropped back to check on their progress, Brodie shouted over the whistling wind, "We'll hae to rest the horses soon, m'laird! They canna take it much longer, ridin' into the storm."

Ran nodded, and Merry saw his expression was set and grim beneath the shadows of the winging storm clouds. She marveled he seemed unaffected by the cold, for he rode without hat or hood, and his cloak flapped open against the wind, soon liberally dusted with snow like his hair.

They halted in a sheltered copse of pine and spruce and larch, and Brodie sighed with relief as he climbed down to check on the horses. Here the storm was held somewhat at bay by the windbreak the trees provided. Merry glanced around the little clearing, clutching her hood around her chilled face, and for a moment she almost forgot her discomfort. The scene might have been plucked right from a Hilliard miniature.

Snow-flocked trees ringed the rolling hills, and the land sloped gently downward to meet with the plains of Forfarshire. They traveled beside a small stream, frozen in time by the winter temperatures. The snow was unblemished for miles in every direction, at least until Ran and his men dismounted and began to move about.

A short time later, the winter sun slipped out from behind

a cloud. Rays of sunshine streamed down, briefly turning the frozen stream to a glittering rainbow of colors. It seemed to shift and move, as if the icy waters suddenly had a life of their own.

"Look at the stream," Merry said to Nell.

"Aye. 'Tis a lovely little burn." Nell shivered. "Och, mayhap the kelpies live here. 'Tis said they favor such places."

"Kelpies?"

Nell regarded her with amazement. "Dinna tell me ye haven't heard tale of them, even in England. Why, lass, surely ye must hae heard the stories as a bairn, about the water spirits."

Merry shook her head. "Nay."

Nell frowned and lowered her voice, as if fearing the mere mention of the kelpies would summon them to her side. " 'Tis said they take the form of horses, and lure good Christian folk to their deaths. The most famous of all 'tis the Each Uisge, a steed who tricks mortals into riding it, and then races 'wi them into the loch and eats all but their liver."

Merry couldn't resist a small chuckle. "Maybe Black Cullen's horse is a kelpie."

"Milady, dinna laugh! 'Tis verra serious." The other woman glanced about a little fearfully, and her hand lowered to rest protectively upon the sleeping Ashet. "They hunger for the wee ones most of all. The power of innocence is great, milady. They feed on it and become ever stronger."

Nell's words were a bit too ominous to be believed, but Merry remembered how she'd shrugged off Mother MacDougall's prophecy. *Dinna mess wi' things ye canna understand,* she'd overheard Hertha telling one of the kitchen maids at Auchmull. She shivered, suddenly wishing Ran and the others would hurry up.

Brodie detached the horses from the wagon and led them down to the stream. With the handle of his knife, he broke the ice in several places so the animals could drink. Ran assumed a watch at the crest of a nearby hill, hunkered down on his heels, alertly scanning the peaceful valley for any sign of trouble. Merry saw him leap to his feet a split second before a hoarse cry rent the air.

"Buadhaich!"

Nell clutched at Merry's arm. "God preserve us. 'Tis a Highlander war cry!"

They heard Ran's claymore slide from its sheath with a furious hiss that sliced the morning air. He ran down the hill, his deep voice momentarily drowning out the shouts of the invaders.

"Gil! The women!"

Gilbert leaped up from where he was resting on a fallen log, grabbed two of the horses by their bridles and hurried through the snow back to the wagon. "Get out of there. Now!" he shouted at the two women. Merry and Nell moved to obey, each of them simultaneously reaching for Ashet. Merry won. She snatched the baby to her breast just as Gilbert reached up for her. He swung her down, then sent her stumbling in the direction of one of the horses.

Gilbert lifted Nell down from the wagon and immediately thrust her up again on the bare back of the other horse. When he saw Merry hadn't yet mounted, unsure of how to ride without a saddle, he made an impatient noise and then hurried back to help her. He heaved her up onto the horse's back just as the clang of steel began to echo in the glen.

Gilbert swung up lithely behind Merry, digging his heels hard into the animal's sides. The mare bolted into a brisk gallop, while Merry clutched Ashet with one hand and the horse's coarse mane with the other. Nell's horse obediently followed, both mounts weaving rapidly through the close trees.

Merry risked one glance backward, just as the plaid-covered figures of the enemy came boiling over the hills.

"Told him never trust a snake," she heard Gilbert mutter, and then their horse veered sharply, directed by a subtle change in pressure from his knees. Merry realized he was an expert rider, and had no need of bit or bridle. Just like Ran, Gilbert Lindsay had yet to meet a horse he could not master. He drove the plunging steed through the snowdrifts, away from the dangers of battle. Nell's mount was close behind, the woman weeping with dismay at the circumstances.

"Hist!" Gilbert ordered her over his shoulder. "Do you want them to follow us?"

Nell fell silent then, though sobs still shook her slight frame. Finally Gil judged it safe to slow their wild flight, and drew the horse to a halt in the midst of a protective bracken patch. He swung down from the steaming animal, extending his arms to Merry. When her feet touched the ground, she nearly crumpled from exhaustion. Holding the baby was all that prevented her from doing so.

Nell wasn't in much better shape. She immediately hurried to Merry's side, tear tracks frozen on her cheeks.

"The bairn?" she cried.

"She's fine, Nell. It never even woke her up." Merry peeled back the edge of the blanket and smiled down at the slumbering baby, whose tuft of pale hair peeked above the heather-colored blankets.

Nell gasped. "Brodie! He was fetchin' us water, down at the stream."

"He's with the others," Gilbert put in. "Sit down and be quiet, Nell. Any undue noise will bring naught but trouble down on our heads."

Nell shot a surprised glance at him, and Merry, too, was rather bemused by the brisk, no-nonsense edge to his manner. Usually Gil was the clown, the proverbial jester who kept things light. Never had she seen him more serious.

Merry drew Nell aside, and the two women sank down, exhausted, in the snow. There they could only wait, frozen with cold and dread. Luckily the storm had passed on. The shrill cries of battle and the ringing clash of swords and shields eventually faded into the distance, with the coming of twilight. After hobbling the horses, Gil couldn't resist sneaking back to see what had happened. 'Twas obvious he was itching to join his clansmen, and mayhap a little resentful to be the one assigned to protect the women.

After he was gone, Nell burst into quiet sobs again.

"I canna bear the waiting," she cried. "I hae a right awful feeling about this, milady!"

Merry quickly sought to distract her. "Why would anyone attack a peaceful band of travelers?"

"Och, several reasons, milady. First, 'tis sure to be some variety of Maclean. They've been stealin' Lindsay cattle for years. We're nae far from Badanloch here. Likely we just stumbled on top of them this time. They're a pack of lazy curs, they are, and would, as lief steal as hunt for themselves."

"They're probably hungry," Merry said. " 'Tis been an early, hard winter."

"Dinna make excuses for those traitors," Nell sniffed sharply. Then remembering who her mistress was, and where they were going, she apologized. "I think Black Cullen also believes yer usurping Lady Blair's position, milady. When ye wed Lord Ranald, she will no longer be Lady Lindsay. His rights to trespass on Lindsay lands and Ran's tolerance will end. He kens this and wants to strike first. Mayhap this was just a warning."

A short time later, Brodie appeared to fetch them, his freckled face split wide with a lopsided grin. "They've a'run!" he cried to the women. "Turned tail and ran back to their hidey-hole, like the puir bit craturs they are!"

Nell rose with the baby clutched in her arms. "Grady?"

He shrugged. "I dinna ken, Nell. I only saw Lord Ran. Law, but the mon can fight! Fierce as a badger and twice as fast." Brodie was bursting with pride at the rout.

"Can we go back?" Merry asked anxiously. Though Brodie's words had assured her Ran was all right, she wanted to see as much for herself.

"Aye. I suppose the horses hae rested enough now. Up ye go, milady. Hold tight."

They rode back at a more sedate pace, though Nell could hardly restrain herself from kicking her mount for more speed. The first thing the women saw as they rode into the little glen were the fallen clansmen. Though twice as many unfamiliar tartans dotted the field, Nell only had eyes for a man at the far end. She gave a sharp little cry.

"Nell!" Merry cried, and at the sound of her voice, Ran appeared and caught the fainting woman as she fell. He lowered Nell gently to the snow, baby still cradled safely in her arms. Even when she swooned, Nell never lost her grip on the child. Ran straightened and looked up at Merry. His breccan was drenched with blood, and she gasped softly, wondering if he was injured. Yet there was a fierce, hot glow in his dark eyes that told her otherwise. 'Twas a stranger's blood. For a moment, Merry saw the ghost of an ancient Highland warrior in him. Then she blinked, and the illusion vanished.

"What of Nell's brother—Grady?" she whispered.

Ran shook his head. "He's seriously hurt, lass." Merry closed her eyes in momentary anguish for poor Nell, but when she opened them again, he was gone.

Chapter Twenty-Two

Three of the attackers had lost their lives in the brief and violent skirmish, and a handful of men were wounded on both sides. The dead were buried there, though the frozen ground proved extremely hard to dig. Ran promised the others the bodies would be retrieved later for proper burial. He would give no more fodder to those who would accuse the Wolf of being a savage. He decided to press on to Edzell, since they were crossing the plains of Forfarshire and the threat of another storm was imminent. The space in the rear of the wagon was now needed to carry the wounded men, however, and Merry's trunk was left behind.

Though she quickly regained consciousness, Nell had yet to speak or even weep. She seemed numbly unaware of the goings-on around her, and sat silent and huddled beside her mistress. Even Ashet could not rouse Nell from her dark little world, though she methodically put the hungry baby to her breast and nursed her as usual. Grady lay unmoving in the rear of the wagon, seriously weakened from loss of blood. A tourniquet placed around the injury had saved the leg where he had taken a deep blow, almost to the bone, but without better facilities and competent tending, the odds were slim. Growing slimmer by the hour.

Merry was gravely worried about Nell. It seemed the closer they got to Edzell, the further the woman retreated into herself. She had lost her young husband, her baby, and now stood to lose her only living kin, her brother Grady. Soon she would be a mere shell of the vibrant young lady she had been. She saw Ran watching Nell with concern, too. His dark gaze was inscrutable, but she sensed his sympathy as he rode by.

The remainder of the journey was accomplished in relative silence. Whatever anticipation existed in light of the ceremony to come had fled with the disaster of the attack. Merry feared what might result from the skirmish. Accusations, a midnight ride for revenge, another clash, yet more tinder added to the already blazing fires of age-old resentment. It hardly seemed a positive omen on her wedding day.

Soon she was able to channel her attentions to the mighty castle rising before them, where the plains of Forfarshire ended at the base of the Grampian Mountains. Solemn, imposing Edzell was enormous in comparison with Auchmull. The castle was built around a quadrangle, the central keep consisting of two vaulted stories, the main tower decorated with double rows of corbels arranged in checkerboard fashion below the parapets.

They were met by a party of men from Lord Deuchar's ranks, who promptly took charge of the injured in the wagon and led the travelers' animals to shelter. Merry joined Ran on Dearg for the last leg, his grip on her waist both possessive and reassuring. She felt a true Highland lady as they clattered through the entrance on the spirited steed.

Hertha had said it rivaled Dunnottar in extent, and had no peer in the region. Merry decided this was well believable. As the party entered the inner ward, she noted the large garden on the south end, overhung with great trees now flocked with snow. The walls there were exquisitely decorated, divided into panels with recesses for flowers cut out checkerwise. Above those were stars pierced with loopholes for defensive purposes. A tier higher, there were recesses containing marble busts, and spaced between these were elegant bas-reliefs. As the horse she rode plodded past the garden, Merry saw the bas-reliefs represented the Celestial Deities, the Sciences, and the Virtues. There was also a summer house and a bath house attached to the rear of the wall.

Even a devotee of the Tudor court could not fail to be impressed by Edzell or the welcome which ensued. While their mounts and servants were properly attended, Ran and Merry were led inside the keep. Two guards flanked the front of the castle, armed with Lochaber axes and shields, forming a guard of honor.

When they entered, Lord and Lady Deuchar were waiting to receive them. Darra greeted them with her customary flair, garbed in deep blue velvet and cloth-of-silver and wearing an heirloom set of sapphires. Kinross looked no less elegant in his scarlet breeches and velvet doublet paned with gold, his red leather jerkin hung heavy with gold ornaments. The couple knew of the attack on the travelers as a messenger had been sent ahead, and so their mien was sober now, but nonetheless the welcome was genuine.

Darra hugged Merry, and whispered a word of reassurance. "I am so glad you are safe. I also wished to say, you are doing the right thing, dear."

"I hope so." Merry nodded and glanced around the great hall. The entrance resembled that of a cathedral, for it soared to the roof. The staircase ascending from it was richly carved and decorated. An oak-paneled gallery led them to the main hall, where the ceiling was ornamented with carved moldings and tracery, the walls lined with open bookcase housing a rare collection. The room was furnished with rich green silk damasks, ottomans and inlaid tables. A chimney dominated one end of the hall, stained-glass windows lit up the room from the west. Suits of armor, shields, halberds, and two-handed swords were arranged around the walls along with jewel-toned tapestries and paintings.

Merry had seen other castles and baronial manor houses that could not rival Edzell. Clearly the definition of barbaric

Scotland was limited by one's traveling experience. Darra sensed her amazement and laughed softly.

"Aye, charming is it not? For a little castle, of course."

Lady Deuchar slipped her arm through Merry's and led her about as if they were old friends, even sisters. 'Twas impossible not to warm to Ran's spirited sister. Meanwhile Kinross removed with Ran to the adjoining drawing room for a glass of port, and to discuss unpleasantries like battle out of the women's presence.

"Since your family cannot attend the nuptials, I shall serve as your present kin, with your permission," Darra said as she led Merry to an elegant chair and offered her sherry. "I understand your trunk was left behind. I would be honored to offer use of my own wardrobe."

"Thank you, Darra. 'Tis most kind. However, as this is but a marriage of expediency, such trivial details are quite unnecessary."

"Oh, you are so wrong, m'dear! This will be a treasured memory for your children, too, someday, and should be recounted with pride."

Merry flushed at the mention of children. She looked at Ran's sister almost shyly. "Why are you accepting me so readily into the family? A stranger, an Englishwoman?"

"A charming young woman who will do the House of Lindsay proud." Darra smiled at her. "I get feelings about certain people, Merry. I tend to trust my intuition. The moment I met you, I decided there was no contest between you and the former Lady Lindsay. Oh, Ran may not agree, but you are twice the lady Blair Maclean ever was."

"Simply because of the feud?"

Darra shook her head. "Nay. Blair was . . . sly. There is no other word which describes her quite so well. Ran was blind to it, as men often are, but he wore those blinders willingly during their courtship and marriage. In time, I pray he will wake up and realize he is better off with a sweet *Sassenach* for a wife than a sly Highland hussy."

Merry took a fortifying sip of sherry, let it warm her insides.

She was still shaken from the attack. Not only did it seem a dark omen, but merriment hardly seemed appropriate in light of three deaths. Ever-practical Darra pointed out that the wedding would be a welcome distraction from talk of war. 'Twould occupy the more hotheaded clansmen until the first rush of anger passed and reason set in.

Ran and Lord Deuchar soon finished their conversation and rejoined the women. 'Twas agreed the matter of the vows should be handled promptly, both to satisfy the queen's decree and free the men to attend the less pleasant chore of recovering the dead and reporting Maclean conduct to King James. Not that the Scottish monarch would react; indeed, he tended to turn a deaf ear to the clan feuds and squabbles of Highlanders, unless they personally crossed him.

Thus, it came to pass on Martinmas, November 11, Ranald Cameron Lindsay and Erin Meredith Tanner were wed with benefit of witness in the small family chapel at Edzell by Father Pettigrew. There were not many guests, on such short notice, but the important ones were there. Gilbert Lindsay beamed with satisfaction, for he adored Merry despite her tendency to lecture; besides which she was a marvelous card player, something even Hugo did not aspire to.

Nell, wearing her best Sunday gown of blue brocade, held the bride's bouquet during the ceremony. Grady was still unconscious, but Lord Deuchar's personal physic had come to Edzell and allowed there was a better chance than previously believed. Nell's spirits had risen accordingly. During the ceremony, she felt eyes resting on her and glanced over to find Hugo Sumner studying her closely. She blushed, the blond giant flushed, but after that their eyes met more often than usual. For the first time since Fergus's death, the comely young widow had noticed a man.

Wearing a gown of candlelight-colored silk borrowed from Lady Deuchar, delicately embroidered with tiny seed pearls and ivory lace, Merry made a beautiful bride. 'Twas not a proper wedding gown, so the dress was plain, without a train or veil, but Merry felt every inch a bride as she joined Ran before the altar. She was terribly nervous, and could hardly manage to repeat the complicated Latin phrases Father Petti-grew spoke, but at last the words were done, and Ran slipped a heavy signet ring onto her ring finger. As he did so, a signal was made and the great bell of St. Lawrence rang seven times, for it rang at the birth, marriage, or death of a lord or lady of Lindsay.

Everyone adjourned to Edzell's banqueting hall for the wedding feast. Families living at the castle were naturally invited, as well as Lindsays and their septs from the surrounding countryside. They were dazzled by the glitter of gold and silver plate, immense gold candelabra in the corners of the hall, and gold sconces placed along six tables groaning with all manner of delicacies. There were numerous kinds of meat—roe, chicken, mutton, beef, pheasant, and grouse. There was freshly caught salmon, pike, perch, and eels, even oysters in buckets of ice brought from the coast. A dozen or so varieties of cheese were offered, as well as rare fruits like oranges and persimmons, and Lord and Lady Burnett of Crathes Castle had even brought a giant marzipan cake.

For refreshment there was ale, table beer, red and white wine, malmsey, hippocras and, aqua vitae. Spirits flowed like a never-ending waterfall, and even children partook in a limited fashion, though Darra kept a watchful eye on the proceedings, especially since her own young sons, fair-haired Pierce and darkly handsome Thierry, who favored his mother, were among the first in line.

After the feast, the traditional bounty was bestowed upon the demesne by the generous "Kitchen of Angus." Each day, after the family dinner, the parish poor gathered in the courtyard, lining the stone benches in fair weather or foul, outside the entrance door. Here they were served meat and bread from the hands of the lady or daughters of the proud house of Edzell. This time, Merry was invited to dispense the remnants alongside Lady Deuchar, and the two women sent the assembled throng home, arms filled with bounty from the union of the Wolf and the *Sassenach* Flame.

Inside the hall, three pipers played songs, including "Gillie Callum" and the "Reel of Tullichan," while a set of dancers performed upon a raised dais, lit by the glare of the torches. A winsome lad called Fash Sinclair leaped and spun with great agility, a Highland sword dance, to the "Ballad of Sauchieburn," his feet flying so fast it seemed they must strike sparks.

During the revelries, Merry looked at her lord husband whenever she could feasibly do so without appearing to stare. Never had she seen Ran looking so handsome as he did on this, their wedding day. For the first time he seemed to be smiling without effort, and in his dress Highland of velvet and tartan, bonnet sporting a heron's plume, he appeared every inch a chief.

Ran cut a striking figure in the crowd. When their eyes met once, separated by a sea of well-wishers, Merry read the admiration and silent promise in his dark gaze. She blushed, prompting a chorus of giggles from the young women surrounding her. It seemed the Wolf was not shy about letting everyone know he anticipated full consummation of the vows.

As the hour grew late, and the well-wishers straggled off into the night, Darra tactfully suggested Merry might wish to retire, and after farewells to the others were completed, led her to the Stirling Tower, to a room where Mary Queen of Scots had once stayed during a council at Edzell.

Decorated in golden damask and frosty pale velvet, the room was an exquisite concoction boasting a large hearth, already crackling a welcome, and a large suite of furniture. The bed was an enormous canopy carved of finest satin-wood, with gilt ornaments along the moldings. The corners were twisted pillars, entwined with wreaths of the Rose, Thistle, and Shamrock, and marquises' coronets. The canopy hangings were rich white satin, lined with peach-blossom silk, trimmed with gold bullion fringe and tassels. The counterpane was of the same material, as were the bolsters and pillows, with sheets of finest lawn and snowy blankets of cassimere trimmed with white satin.

Darra lit several sconces in the room, and stayed to visit awhile, sensing Merry's uneasiness at being in a strange household, especially on her nuptial night. Merry did not request

Nell's or another tiring woman's services. In deference to Merry's sensitivity, Darra had not permitted the usual shivaree, wherein the rowdy clansmen bore the bridegroom up to his wife, and unmercifully teased the new couple about their prescribed duties. Instead, she offered Merry a silken nightrail the hue of a newly blossomed rose, palest pink, a bridal gift. After a murmured reassurance and a warm hug, Darra left the new bride to herself.

Merry exhaled shakily as the door closed behind Darra, hugging herself before the hearth. She supposed the correct thing to do would be to put on the nightgown, slip into the bed and huddle there, waiting, but she preferred the freedom of pacing. She knew what would happen, for her mother Bryony was nothing if not practical and blunt with her daughters, but it did not mean she was not nervous. She wondered how different it might have been if she awaited Sir Jasper instead. Right now, she felt everything from sweet anticipation to trepidation, but she knew as Wickham's wife she would have also felt distaste.

'Twas very late before the merriment finally drew to a close below, but since Lady Deuchar had long retired, the newlyweds were not to be spared the Scottish version of a shivaree after all. Ran's kinsmen had done their best to get him roaring drunk. After waving aside all but a sip of the best Scotch, the groom laughingly informed his would-be tavern mongers that he had had enough. At this, the menfolk moaned and groaned in good-natured dismay, but did their best to dishevel Ran quite thoroughly before he was sent stumbling up the stairs at the head of a wave of eager onlookers.

As yet unaware of the boisterous crowd surging up the steps, Merry sat before the mirror brushing out her hair, wavy from the plaits Nell had sculpted from her locks. The routine of the gilt-backed brush was reassuring, and the auburn waves fairly crackled with electricity. The air was heavy with promise of another storm,

On the bed was the flowing silk nightgown of palest shell pink, but Merry had stalled the inevitable by requesting a bath.

A large tub of steaming water awaited the new bride's pleasure. She still wore her makeshift wedding gown.

When the shouting and laughing drew near, Nell's cry from the hall warned her of what was to come. Merry leaped up from the satin bench before the mirror, and rushed to bolt the door. She was a second too late. The sea of rowdy men carried Ran right on through, and to her outrage Merry saw her groom was missing his breccan and bonnet. Even his kilt was askew. Seeing her dismay, Ran quickly gained control of the situation, pausing only to grab Nell by the elbow and hurl her into the hall to block the incoming tide, then slamming and bolting the door home himself.

Outside the men howled and pounded their disappointment upon the door, but the sturdy bolt held fast, and after a few more minutes of merry catcalls and suspicious noises, the hall at last quieted and Ran turned to face his bride.

Merry's gray-green eyes were wide and she looked like a young girl with her flaming hair tangled about her hips. He decided she had never seemed more beautiful to him, except perhaps today in the chapel, as she took his name and signed the document binding them as man and wife, Lord and Lady Lindsay. A ray of sunlight had streamed down from the chapel window, catching her hair and picking out golden highlights in the fiery locks.

"We're alone now," Ran said, realizing that his bride's discomfort probably had much to do with the fact she was fully dressed and he was not. Glancing down at his shirt where all the buttons had been ripped off but one, he slanted her a rueful grin. "Lindsays tend to be a wee bit enthusiastic at weddings, lass."

"So I see," Merry replied with a nervous little laugh. "I . . . I'm sorry, I'm afraid I wasn't ready yet . . ."

"Take as much time as you need, Merry. But if 'tis assistance you need, I'll be your lady's maid," Ran offered softly. When her eyes widened further, he added, "Don't worry, lass. I'll go very slow."

With that, he stripped off the remnants of his fine lawn shirt, tossing the shredded material in a heap on the floor. His shoes and stockings swiftly joined the pile. Wearing only his red watch kilt, Ran gently turned Merry around, unfastening the rows of tiny buttons with impressive speed and skill.

Her breath caught in her throat. "I see you're no stranger to undressing women," she whispered.

"I never claimed to be a saint," he responded quietly, but sensing her tension, paused and placed a single kiss at the nape of her neck where he had swept her long hair aside. "Would you prefer a green lad, Merry? Or Jasper Wickham, mayhap?"

She shuddered a little. "Nay."

Ran tasted the skin trembling beneath his lips. "Like ivory silk," he whispered, and when her gown slid free in a heap to the floor, he turned her to face him and devoured her mouth with a leisurely fire which left her gasping.

By contrast Ran's calloused hands felt like rough wool against her flesh, and Merry quivered with a mixture of apprehension and aching delight when he caught her fiercely to him. She felt her bare breasts glide sensuously against his broad chest and shivered at the feeling of his hand entangled in her hair. He arched her back like a bow, feathering little kisses up and down the column of her throat

"Sweet flame," he murmured against her flesh. "I wonder how brightly you'll burn for me this night . . ."

His other hand slid down to her most intimate area, and Merry gasped softly with surprise. His fingers found, parted her womanly cleft, gently teasing the hidden jewel nestled within until she moaned with rising desire.

"No need to be so shy, sweetheart." Ran chuckled a little. "They will not hear us way up here."

His finger began to teasingly flick the seat of her pleasure until Merry whimpered with need. She moaned with rising passion, and he paused only long enough to strip off his restraining kilt, sweep her up into his arms and carry her to the bed.

"My bath!" she faintly protested, but only once, for as Ran lowered her to the heather-scented, cool linen sheets, he silenced her with a heady kiss and his shadow fell over her like a bird of prey.

"I'll take you swimming in a lovely little burn sometime, m'lass," he huskily replied, shoving the unneeded nightgown aside and sealing his vow by raining a hundred little kisses over her breasts and belly. Merry's head fell back against the snowy pillows, her body framed by the living flames of her hair. With a low groan of pure delight, Ran lowered his masculine frame into the sweetly feminine cradle of her hips, branding her with lips which were fierce, eager and hard.

Then he backed off and captured the globe of a satiny breast in one hand, leisurely laving the dusky nipple with his tongue, waiting until she arched against him to press his advantage home. As Merry writhed beneath his expert touch, he gently shifted his position to bring his rigid manhood in contact with her woman's mont.

"Do you want me, Merry?" Ran whispered, and when her eyelashes fluttered open, he found himself gazing into rain-colored eyes swirling with emotion.

She nodded restlessly, clutched in the grip of a raging fever of a different sort. Her voice was low and husky. "Love me, milord, please . . ."

As if he could not! With a groan of pure bliss, he inched home, wrenching a cry of wonder and discomfort from Merry as she gripped his shoulders and felt him bearing slowly, slowly down. Her last defense fell away with a little cry, smothered by his hungry mouth, then he showered a bevy of kisses over her throat and face.

At last! At last! Fleeting pain gave way to silken waves of pleasure as he moved against her, hips moving in little circles while she moaned. If all was lost, Merry knew she would have this sweet, torrid moment forever, the precious feeling of Ran clutched to her heart, the memory of the passionate love song they shared this night. As Ran moved against her, strong and solid and warm, she felt the reassuring essence of his maleness surrounding her like a velvet cloak, completely within and without, carrying her to an unknown peak high above all others, where they alone would rule.

On her own wedding night, Merry finally learned the precious secret that had bonded men and women for centuries, the inexplicable pull of two separate and yet perfectly matched souls, straining together against the stars.

Chapter Twenty-Three

By morning, when the candles in the room had all melted to sodden lumps and the bathwater had cooled to a tepid degree, Ran drew Merry from the rumpled sheets to the tub.

"I'll scrub your back, lass," he offered, helping her step into the high metal tub, flicking admiring glances over her body. Merry was a little sore from her new husband's ardent attentions, but her skin was flushed and her eyes bright as she sank down to her hips in the water.

"Ooh! 'Tis cold."

"Not for long." She glanced back in surprise as Ran suddenly joined her in the tub, settling down close behind her and raising the water another good foot. With him he brought a round cake of hard soap and lathered it fiercely in his palms before he brought them down against her back.

The heady scent of lavender soon filled the air. Nell had left a wicker basket of scented soaps as a wedding gift. Ran's hands glided over Merry's back, arms, and sides, then slipped beneath the water to playfully nudge the cake of soap between her legs.

"Shall I finish your toilette, Lady Lindsay?" Ran breathed suggestively in her ear, and Merry laughed softly, then purred like a kitten while he soaped her thighs and buttocks with an air that was anything but impersonal.

Finally he finished, and she took her turn with the soap, turning about in the tub as best she could and covering Ran in the rich lather until he reeked of lavender. Wrinkling his nose, he said, "I think I prefer the stench of good, honest Scotch."

Merry playfully splashed some water against his chest. "Take your pick, you Highland brute."

In lightning reply, Ran seized her by both wrists and gently, slowly, drew her into his arms. The water was icy now, but the warmth of their bodies was enough. Merry shivered for an entirely different reason, and when his mouth claimed hers with swiftly rising passion, she succumbed to the fresh tide of desire washing over them both.

Then, over his shoulder, she spied a pink light spreading across the leaded windowpane. Tearing her lips free of his, Merry squeaked, " 'Tis nigh dawn already!"

"Aye, so 'tis." Lazily Ran rose and stepped from the tub, grabbing a couple of soft cloths to blot both himself and his lady wife dry. Still damp and shivering afterward, Merry dove back into the bed and pulled the cool linen sheet and counterpane up to her chin. From the middle of the floor Ran stood watching her, amused.

"Best get used to wandering about without any clothes, milady," he teased her. "I intend to keep ye in a constant state of déshabille for the next month or so."

She gave him a mock scowl. "Only a month?"

"Just till I'm sure I've safely planted our first son in your sweet little belly," he replied, hurrying to join her in the bed and yanking the covers back over them both.

His words caused a peculiar sensation to flutter through Merry's stomach. "D'you want a lot of children, Ran?"

"Aye, lass. Lots and lots," he assured her distractedly, nuzzling her neck and breasts until Merry pushed him away and demanded, "Exactly how many? Two? Four? Six?"

"Eight or so should do nicely," he murmured, nipping playfully at her earlobe.

"Eight!" she squealed in genuine shock.

"All right," Ran sighed, then added agreeably, "Ten, madam, but not a single bairn more. Even an earl doesn't boast bottomless coffers."

Merry scowled at him. "I'll have you know I'm not a broodmare, sirrah."

"Nay," he agreed pleasantly, "you are my wife. Whom I have promised to care for and in turn she has agreed to fulfill her duties. And I crave a couple of bairns from your loins, Merry. A son to carry on my name, and a wee lassie to spoil. Is it too much to ask?"

Merry gave him her answer by snuggling contentedly in the circle of his arms. "Are you happy, Ran?"

"At this moment, never more so," he confirmed quietly. "Ah, lass, never more so."

By midmorning the newlyweds finally managed to straggle from their nuptial bed and get dressed. Some of the wedding company had stayed overnight at Edzell, and Lord and Lady Deuchar had pressing duties as host and hostess.

While Ran slipped out to find a fresh set of clothes, Merry summoned Nell, and with the maid's help donned a gown of burnt-orange silk edged with black braid. Nell used a pair of hot tongs to curl Merry's hair up from her forehead so she could wear a fashionable shadow, or headdress, that matched the gown. 'Twas a small lace cap of black lace trimmed with orange silk, often worn by married women in the country.

"Ye look grand, milady," Nell declared with approval when she was finished. "Exactly as the Countess of Crawford should!"

Merry laughed a little self-consciously. " 'Tis hard to believe I'm a married woman, Nell. Much less to Ranald Lindsay, the Wolf of Badanloch."

"But yer content, milady. I see it in yer eyes."

Merry didn't deny it. "Yea," she said softly. "I think things may work out very well."

At that moment there came a rat-a-tat at the door, and Nell admitted another maid with a sleepy Ashet cradled in her arms.

"I apologize, milady," the maid said, "but this wee girlie is needin' her mam right quick."

"Of course! Bring her in," Merry said, smiling as Nell moved eagerly forward to take the little girl into her arms. She waited while Nell fed the baby, and 'twas that charming domestic scene that Ran happened upon when he returned to the chamber freshly shaved and dressed.

Seeing his beautiful new wife cooing over a bairn, a fleeting emotion of quiet pain and calm resignation coursed through him. Memories of Blair joined with guilt and he had to force himself to stay, when his first instinct was to turn and rush out of the room. Merry was not to blame for his emotions, nor the conflict raging with his heart, but he could not stop the tide of resentment as he watched her dandling the babe in her arms. Damme, it should be Blair here with him, and it should be their wee one, the precious Lindsay who had died in the cradle of his wife's belly.

Merry noticed Ran's eyes darkening and wondered what prompted the sudden change in mood, but she had no chance to ask. He curtly informed her 'twas time to return to Auchmull, and suggested she and Nell finish packing. Having expected to stay on a few days at least, after such a harrowing journey, Merry gazed at him nonplussed, but he simply spun on his heel and left.

A short time later, Merry and Nell joined the others in the great hall. "Are you ready?" Ran asked the two women. He seemed distracted, and Merry felt a distance between them that had not been there last night.

Nell nodded. "All set, m'laird. Will ye require m'further services at Auchmull one day?"

Merry saw the hope in the young woman's eyes. "Of course you must come see us, Nell. I should like you to come along whenever we visit Court. This new countess needs help just getting dressed."

"Oh, I figured ye'd keep fancier company when ye went to

court wi' Lord Lindsay,'' Nell said, but she looked delighted at the news. ''Then wi' yer permission I'll ride a bit o'way in the wagon to get some fresh air and say good-bye. I can walk back; the exercise 'twill do me good.''

Ran agreed, with the condition Nell accept an escort on the way back. It seemed Hugo was quick to volunteer, and Merry noted Nell's faint blush at the blond giant's obvious interest. Hugo was several years older than Gilbert, and his enormous size made him seem even more mature. He was daunting in appearance, but Merry had discovered he had a winsome, rather dry sense of humor. She was pleased by the notion of him and Nell together, especially since little Ashet deserved a father as well as a mother.

Darra and her husband were sorry to see them go so soon, but since the whole intent was to satisfy a royal decree, and Auchmull was relatively vulnerable with the majority of the clansmen away, they did not argue overmuch. Merry thanked Lady Deuchar, and the two women parted ways with hugs of genuine emotion. Darra said she was certain she could wrangle an invitation for the new Lady Lindsay at the Stuart Court, and Merry laughed at the intrinsic scheming of the mind behind the pretty face and sparkling dark eyes.

''Aye, mayhap I shall test my wit and wile on Scottish soil,'' Merry chuckled as she hugged Lady Deuchar one last time. ''But methinks I owe a quick explanation to my English kin first, as they will likely hear of my fate before I return and will be sorely vexed at me.''

''I cannot think they would be vexed at the notion of a title, even a Scottish earldom exceeds Wickham's influence,'' Darra replied with a twinkle. ''True enough, though, they must be worried about you, Merry. I would be happy to write a message of explanation if you think 'twould be helpful in any way.''

''No explanation needed,'' Ran put in, having overheard and stepping close to the two women. ''And I fear no excuse would suffice for wedding the Wolf of Badanloch.''

''Her Majesty's orders are rarely questioned by those in my

family," Merry said. "With the exception, mayhap, of my rather unconventional mother."

Ran shot her a quizzical glance, and Merry laughed. "Some day you must meet the reigning matriarch of the respective O'Neill and Tanner clans, milord. Until then, suffice it to say Bryony Tanner is renowned for standing toe to toe with Elizabeth Tudor, even on English soil."

"To be certain, I must discuss strategy with the lass sometime," he agreed, and Merry's mirth did not abate in the slightest. She imagined Ran calling her feisty mother "lass," while she stood back and watched the fireworks. Clearly the mighty Wolf had no idea what he asked for when he teased a fierce, proud Irish Raven.

Reminded of the amulet, Merry's hand rose and sought the precious article, which she had worn for her wedding but removed that evening while awaiting Ran. Without the familiar weight of it about her neck, she felt truly exposed now. She had grown used to the heavy jewelry and it brought a strange sort of comfort when she was able to run her fingers over the embedded bird in the gold.

Farewells concluded, the party departed for Auchmull. As they rode up the final steep, treacherous path, the castle rose like a dark behemoth from the plains behind them. Looking back, Stirling Tower and its solid outline was somehow frightening, sketched against an angry sky. Black clouds roiled above the keep; another winter storm nipped at their heels, like a dark omen of sorts. Merry saw Ran's mouth tighten as he surveyed the castle from a distance. Was he remembering a day not so long ago that he had wed another, and in essence led her to her grave?

Merry wanted to reach out and trace his frown, wiping all misery and guilt away with it, replacing darker emotions with the wonder and joy of a new love. Yet she sensed he held her at arm's length emotionally despite the sweet passion of their wedding night, and more than a twinge of pain resulted from this realization. Her gaze sculpted the Wolf of Badanloch almost hungrily, wishing Ran would glance over and smile or nod, just a simple acknowledgment of her presence, but she saw his attention was focused on the receding castle.

Lord Deuchar had supplied a brace of his own men for additional escort, so the odds of another attack were slim. Still Merry sensed Ran's preoccupation. She forced herself to look to the future instead, for as long as there was a chance Ran might come to love her, she would cling to it with all the tenacity of an English rose transplanted in harsh Scottish soil.

Chapter Twenty-Four

Auchmull was exactly as Merry remembered. Being Lady Lindsay did not change her perception of her new home as she thought it might. The brittle, sparkling backdrop of a Highland winter made it even more beautiful to behold, however. A brisk breeze greeted the riders as she and Ran cantered their horses ahead of the main party. Snow showered upon them from the blue-green pines as the wind stirred their heavy boughs. They rode up out of the valley, saw the castle framed by a glittering expanse of white, gray stone sketched against a deep blue sky.

"Home!" Ran called out to her, his handsome face splitting into a wide relaxed grin for the first time in Merry's memory, and Merry echoed his enthusiasm by touching her crop to her mount's flanks and racing him up the hill.

Mare and stallion thundered neck and neck across the low stone bridge and toward the great gate. Ran signaled the guards in the gatehouse and the barrier lifted even as the horses galloped up the incline. Merry slowed and held her mare back, not sure she had timed it right, but the gate had barely cleared when Ran raced on through, bent low over Dearg's neck.

Laughing, he drew the steaming animal to a halt in the yard, and waited for Merry as the remainder of his staff came pouring from the keep, calling out their congratulations. Ran's laughter died when he recognized the fat roan being tended by one of the stable hands, and he immediately demanded to know what Wickham was doing at Auchmull.

Those questioned exchanged uneasy glances. "We dinna ken, m'laird. He simply showed up."

"Sir Jasper requested shelter from the storm and right of hospitality, sir. We could nae turn him away."

Ran swore and swung down from his saddle just as Merry cantered into the yard on Orlaith, which name meant "golden lady" in Gaelic. The fine animal was a wedding gift from Lord and Lady Deuchar, one even her horse-mad Uncle Kit would approve. Orlaith was a creamy golden mare with a dark mane and tail. The horse had a smooth gait and a soft mouth, and seemed to anticipate Merry's every command.

"You should have waited for me!" she cried out in mock outrage, still laughing and winded from the hard run. But Ran did not smile back, and after one of the boys had helped her dismount, she hurried to her husband's side.

"What's wrong?"

"Wickham is back. You'll stay safely out of sight until I've dealt with him."

"I'm the Countess of Crawford now," Merry reminded him. "My place is at your side. He can do nothing to hurt me."

Ran gave her a fleeting smile before he turned and strode up the stairs to the keep. Waiting just long enough to assure the others arrived safely, and the animals were properly tended, Merry hurried up the steps after him and found Ran already confronting Wickham in the great hall.

Sir Jasper lifted a glass of claret in a mock salute to Merry. "My word, 'tis the beautiful English rose of Auchmull," he exclaimed, ignoring Ran's demand for answers and leering at Merry instead. "Did you keep her for your mistress after all, milord?"

"Not a mistress, but my wife," Ran coldly responded, and he lent the words an emphasis even Wickham could not ignore.

Wickham pursed his thin lips and looked Merry up and down, disparagingly. "You look tousled, madam," he drawled. " 'Twould appear association with ne'er-do-wells is wearing off."

Revolted as ever by the sight of this fussy peer wearing pink satin breeches and a fashionably loud burgundy doublet, Merry let her icy silence speak for itself and went to join Ran on the other side of the room.

"What are you doing here, Wickham?" Ran demanded again. " 'Twas agreed you would remove to Braidwood when we could not reach agreement on ransom."

"Aye, true enough. And I see that little matter has been conveniently settled just in time to save your neck and the girl's reputation." Sir Jasper smirked. At Ran's dark scowl, he added somewhat hastily, "Alack, I am not here to fence further words with you, milord. Nor debate pointless issues. Besides, intrigue has grown a trifle stale at Braidwood of late. Not to mention the wenches." He sniggered, and Merry glanced at Ran just in time to see her husband's eyes darken dangerously.

"You are not welcome here, Wickham," he said flatly. "Count your blessings I am willing to let you leave unscathed, in light of recent events. Someone struck a foolish blow the other day, one which I fear they will pay for over a very long, arduous Highland winter."

Wickham nodded. " 'Tis about that little matter I've come. I heard about the attack, and I assure you, I knew naught of any plans to waylay the wedding party en route to Edzell. I was most distressed to hear of it."

"Aye, I am sure you were."

If Sir Jasper detected the sarcasm, and only a deaf man would not, he did not respond to it. "Naturally I realize this will only fuel suspicion and bad blood between the clans. Braidwood therefore is also threatened, however indirectly."

Something short of a smile curved Ran's lips. "So you have come to beg mercy of the Wolf."

"Not exactly, milord. My defenses are more than adequate to sustain the household through even a winter-long siege. Nay,

I know of your enmity toward me, and respect it, and thus what I seek is opportunity to make amends.''

Merry glanced from Wickham's face to Ran's set expression, and felt a little shiver of dismay she could not explain. Wickham's insincerity seemed patently obvious to her, and she was certain Ran did not believe it, either, yet the uneasiness persisted.

''I must ask what the point is in continuing a feud over issues long dead and buried.''

''Dead and buried? Like my wife.''

Merry flinched. Ran did not even refer to Blair as his ''former'' wife. 'Twas as if she, Merry, did not even exist for him. Mayhap she did not. Mayhap she never would.

Sir Jasper sighed. ''There is nothing I can do, Lindsay, to bring Blair back for you. God's bones, man, I would if I could. 'Twas the height of misfortune that the previous Lady Lindsay expired at Braidwood, an incidental point for which you seemed determined to blame me, yet there is naught I can do but protest my innocence. Again and again, and if I may dare remark upon it, 'tis growing quite tiresome at this juncture.''

''As is the sight of your face at Auchmull,'' Ran bluntly replied. ''The audacity of the English never fails to amaze me. Not only do you boldly swagger into enemy terrain, but you avail yourself of a man's finest claret without a simple by-your-leave. You must be very confident of the king's affections, Wickham, else you are a madman in pink satin, and I am not so certain which is the lesser of the two evils.''

Sir Jasper stared at his rugged Scots rival a moment, then shrugged. ''I assume you have no intentions of meeting me halfway in a truce to benefit both sides.''

''I did not begin the war, Wickham. 'Twas lit the moment you sent word to me that my wife was dead. She ailed for hours, well over a day by a servant's telling, before you bothered to summon aid. All I have ever asked of you is why. Why Blair was allowed to die under such ignoble circumstances in your household. What her last moments were like, other than a haze of pain and doubtless terror, coupled with the hurt that I was not there as I always vowed to be."

Sir Jasper's pale eyes narrowed a fraction. "You imply I would be so cruel as to let a lady die alone, much less the wife of a man, albeit a rival, I admire and respect. Would I risk all-out war over such an issue? I think not. Call me a madman if you like, but I am not the one who clings to memories as desperately as a drowning man might a passing gull, which just happens to be flitting above the water."

Merry slipped away from Ran's side, knowing he was not even aware of her presence anymore. She might as well be a piece of furniture in the room; indeed, a chair at least should receive due attention if 'twas one Saint Blair had sat in. She could not quell the rush of bitterness. She was Lady Lindsay now, and Ran had vowed to respect and honor and keep her safe, enough to satisfy many women, yet she wanted the one thing he could not offer her. Love.

Whatever love existed in the great Highland laird was gone, wasted upon the dusty bones of a woman who could hardly appreciate it now. Merry was ashamed of her own calloused reasoning, but 'twas true enough. Blair Lindsay would never again walk the halls of Auchmull, and for this Merry must suffer mayhap her entire married life, for wont of love.

She could not help but resent, nay loathe, the golden-haired woman whose portrait hung above the hearth, smiling benignly upon the proceedings today as if holding lofty court above mere mortals. How could one compete with a saint? Especially a saint who held Ranald Lindsay's heart as firmly now as she had in life.

She blinked back tears of emotion, not the least of which was pure frustration. The beginning of their marriage, despite the odd circumstances of its coming about, had been encouraging enough. Their bridal night was a memory to make her both blush and smile. Yet someone like Wickham need only surface to remind Ran of what he had lost, and suddenly his whole life, his new wife, were inconsequential. Aye, she was bitter. How could she not be?

* * *

Ran did not notice Merry's quiet departure for a time, intent as he was upon Wickham's smug visage. The man seemed to take peculiar delight in baiting him, yet withholding the very details he so needed in order to have closure in the matter of Blair. The only reason Wickham dared such cockiness was he knew Ran would not risk forfeiture of more lands or Gil's inheritance. The loss of Badanloch was blow enough, for the lands had been in the family for centuries, ever since Sir David Lindsay of Glenesk was hailed Champion of Scotland in 1390 for besting the English champion in an epic joust on London Bridge.

King Robert II, then failing in his favorite castle of Dundonald, west of Kilmarnock, had bestowed Badanloch upon this honorable Knight of the Thistle before he died. Sir David returned to a hero's welcome and a generous portion of fine lands near the Dee. A later descendant, the fifth Earl of Crawford, another David Lindsay, was created Duke of Montrose in 1488. Such was the first instance of a dukedom being conferred on a Scotsman not of the Royal Family. The dukedom ended with his death in 1495, but the lands remained in Lindsay possession until the fateful day when Ran's messenger did not return, and he had put six Macleans to the sword for theft, rape, and mayhem upon his lands.

Justice from the Wolf had been harsh but swift. Ran did not believe in torture. It brought no honor to a warrior's hand or house. He did not execute the sentences himself, but in holding with tradition, the Lindsays' hereditary doomster, in this case Will Durie, was summoned from Edzell to see to the grisly task. Not until Fergus failed to return did he realize he had been baited and trapped. Blair's canny old father, Suttie Maclean, had been willing to sacrifice six of his own in order to obtain Badanloch. His outraged demand for reparation was already en route to the king before the bodies of his clansmen were cold.

King James, having wearied long ago of the petty feuds and

squabbles among the Highlanders, sitting with empty coffers and fretting over his own overdue inheritance, was not kindly disposed toward the Wolf of Badanloch on that particular day Without batting an eyelash, he gave over Badanloch to the Macleans to buy silence, for what once a king had given, another could take away. Since that dark day, Ran had been forced to endure the sight of Maclean green upon his lands, a bitter reminder of treachery and the oft dear price of honor.

Cullen had always claimed he knew nothing of his father's deceit, but now it appeared the son had indeed not fallen far from the rotten tree his father had been. Before Badanloch, Ran had enjoyed a spirited rivalry with Blair's brother, and more than once they had gone roaming and reiving together over the Border. In Scots tradition, *Sassenach* cattle were always fair game. So, too, were an enemy clan's, though an uneasy truce held for a time between Lindsays and Macleans after the union of the two houses. He and Black Cullen had shared laughter, bannocks, and even a buxom tavern wench or two before he married Blair.

Thus came his first encounter with Wickham as well, through Blair's family. The Macleans spoke of their English overlord with grudging respect, and Ran had been curious to meet the man who could hold such a rowdy clan in check. His title gave him access to Braidwood without invitation, and he used the excuse of a hunting excursion to visit whilst near the Border. Sir Jasper offered his hospitality with a certain wariness, understandable given Ran's daunting reputation and rugged appearance.

They circled each other then much as now, like two male grouse with ruffs high and feathers pricked, taking measure of the other with a wary respect. Ran had since lost all respect for Wickham; the last of it trickled away when the weasel abandoned Merry to her fate, even though he could never have brought himself to hurt a woman, much less an innocent.

Now Wickham dared call him a drowning man, clinging to anything he could . . . well, mayhap 'twas not so inaccurate, for certainly he clung to Blair's memory with the ferocity of one who has known true love and mourns its loss to his bones. But he would not be mocked for it. He scowled at Sir Jasper, arms folded across his broad chest, and was pleased to see the other man reconsider his tactics.

"I simply do not see the benefit in continuation of enmity among our households," Wickham said smoothly. "Although you did, in essence, whisk my betrothed from right beneath my nose, I suppose I bear you no grudge as you did the honorable thing and gave her your name in the end."

Ran stared at the man incredulously, then laughed. "By Jesu, that is rich! You failed to provide Merry proper escort from England, and expressed not even the slightest relief she was not killed or captured by true highwaymen. Nor did you evidence genuine concern when you first came here, ostensibly to retrieve her from the clutches of a brutal Scot laird. Nay, Wickham, you were only too eager to wash your hands of a woman whose reputation might be called into question after association with the notorious Wolf of Badanloch."

Sir Jasper sniffed. "You are sorely mistaken, but I cannot expect you to view me in a favorable light after all that has transpired."

"That, Wickham, is the first sensible thing you have said since setting foot on Lindsay soil."

The Englishman bristled, but set down his claret and swept up his high-crowned beaver hat. "I had hoped with the turn of recent events, you might be more amenable to a truce as a gesture of goodwill, if nothing else. Especially in an attempt to avert further disaster in the wake of the attack on your traveling party. There is naught I can do but extend my hand and await your good humor."

"You could call in your Maclean dogs, too, I suspect, but will not. For as long as I wrestle with Macleans and the nasty issues that accompany the green and black, I cannot trouble you with questions about Blair's death."

"I have nothing to hide, Lindsay. God willing you'll come to see that one day and we can both get on with our lives."

Ran noticed Merry's absence. Only the faintest trace of her

damask rose perfume lingered in the hall, almost haunting in its sweet simplicity. Blair had loved roses, too, but her scent of choice was heather. 'Twas odd, yet for a fleeting moment it seemed the Tudor rose supplanted the Scottish heather. Ran shook off the notion, and Wickham's company soon after. Nothing would change at Auchmull, not his taste for friends or distaste for enemies, nor would his devotion to his late wife waver just because a new Lady Lindsay graced his sheets.

Chapter Twenty-Five

Merry was nothing if not practical, and the first thing she vowed to do was restore her household to a state befitting the Earl and Countess of Crawford. Besides, concentrating upon mundane domestic affairs helped her deal with the inherited pain of her new position. She itched to dispose of many incidental items belonging to the late Lady Lindsay but knew 'twould be unwise to test her husband's temper so early in their relationship. She contented herself with a thorough scrubbing of Auchmull, fore to aft, great hearth to turret, and tumbled into bed exhausted after the labors of the day. She worked as hard as any of the staff, if not more diligently, letting the castle serve as an outlet for her frustrations and building loneliness

Ran was gone much of the time in the following weeks, concerned with matters in the demesne and quelling the threat of Lindsay retaliation. His kinsmen firmly believed Macleans were responsible for the attack on the wedding party, though the dead had never been identified and in the end were given anonymous but sanctified burial in a small plot at Auchmull. One of the slain's resemblance to the chieftain of a small Maclean sept, the Padons, led to the speculation they were mercenaries hired by their more powerful relatives to harry Lindsays in the hope of provoking another flare-up of the age-old feud.

Certainly the colors they wore were false, and Ran noted someone had gone to great lengths to throw him off track. Wickham was the obvious choice, but he no longer trusted Black Cullen, either, and perhaps Blair's brother had gone to such lengths in order to obtain more lands. Macleans were nothing if not opportunists. Ran's ancestors had learned this the hard way, and it seemed the family would pay forever for the passing lusts of William de Lindsay.

Merry anticipated Christmas at Edzell, and plans went forth to join Lord and Lady Deuchar and their family, but the night before they were to depart for the Grampians, trouble brewed in the outer regions of the realm. Despite the fierce Highland winter, and the difficulty of reiving in the snow, several dozen royal cattle turned up missing with strong evidence of being stolen. 'Twas Hugo who was sent to escort them to Edzell, and he first brought word from Lord Deuchar, for the animals in question had been turned out into the Grampians for forage.

Ran and Merry were together, sharing a quiet moment in the great hall before the crackling hearth. Merry was idly picking out notes on an old clarsach she had found in the dusty recesses of Auchmull, and cradled the island harp in her lap. At Court she had been Mistress of the Music, responsible for tending Her Majesty's song books and occasionally the virginals as well. She had a good ear for music, although she had never formally trained. Her soft, lilting refrain of "Draw On, Sweet Night" drew an admiring glance from Ran, bent over his accounts at a nearby desk, and she basked in his fleeting approval like the sun. He was always kind to her, but she longed for the passionate, far too rare moments they shared.

The sudden interruption of Hugo Sumner shattered the pleasant scene like ice upon the loch. Hertha presented the blond giant along with a tray of cakes and sweet malmsey wine, but realizing only something serious would have rousted Hugo from a warm hearth and the company of Nell Downie, Ran waved away the refreshment.

"I take it the pass it still navigable?" he asked the weary, cold Hugo.

Hugo swept off his bonnet, brushing the snow from its brim as he clutched it to his massive chest. He was breathing rapidly, having ridden hard through inclement weather to reach Auchmull.

"Aye, m'laird. But I've also come wi' urgent news from Lord Deuchar. Some of the king's cattle were discovered missing, and there's rumor renegade Macleans took them, and are drumming up support for their actions. Just now they've captured some unwary travelers and are demanding a heavy ransom for their safe return. 'Tis said they hae none other than the Master of the Stair himself in their filthy paws."

"Sir Ian Coates?" Ran looked dismayed. "They've kidnapped one of the king's own cabinet?"

Hugo nodded, looking more grave than ever Merry had seen him. " 'Tis a dire situation, m'laird, and word comes from Holyrood that King James is furious. He wants ye to try and negotiate wi' the pond scum since Lindsays are his most powerful allies in this region. If that fails, he hae promised to issue Letters of Fire and Sword so ye may dispense with the thieves. But 'twill be no easy task. 'Tis said they're led by a canny fellow claiming to be a descendant o' Robert the Bruce."

"What can they want with Coates?" Ran wondered. "Simple ransom? Any of a dozen others would have done, including myself."

"They claim Coates promised them sustenance through the winter, rations in exchange for fealty to the king, and harsh dealings 'wi their neighboring clan. That Coates failed to deliver on the promise and they've a right ta collect on it."

"Idiots," Ran muttered as he tossed down the ink pen, raked a hand through his dark hair. " 'Tis some skewered notion of justice they pursue. And of all times. Aye, no doubt we have another sept of rabid Macleans on our hands. Pity they cannot be dealt with just as expediently as Badanloch."

Merry started at Ran's words, for she had some inkling how tortured he had been by the events of Badanloch, yet his harsh Highland nature surfaced when he was weary or exasperated. She longed to go to him now, slip a comforting arm around his waist and lean her head upon his chest, but Hugo's presence and the uncertainty of Ran's reaction kept her still. Instead, she tried to read the expression on Ran's face. Resolve? Anger? He sensed her regard and met her gaze for moment, nodding slightly as if to reassure her he was all right.

"I'll assemble a party of men to ride out at once," he said reluctantly to Hugo. "Any ideas where the rebels are hiding?"

"In the forest near Badanloch," Hugo replied, glancing from Ran, then with a belated nod at Merry, "Lord Deuchar is sending men from Edzell, too, and they should be here by nightfall."

Ran nodded wearily. "We can ride out first thing in the morn, then. 'Tis too dangerous to blunder about in the dark, in the snow besides." He rose from the desk, moved over and put an arm around Merry's shoulders, gently squeezing. "I'm sorry, Merry. It appears Christmas revelries must wait. I must leave again for a time. God willing 'twill not take long to run these foolish renegades to ground."

"I hope not," Merry said, trying to ignore the sudden leap of her heart at his embrace, however distant and distracted, and the irrational pang of fear that he would not return.

Early Christmas Eve, Hertha and her mistress watched the men ride out, Ran leading the party of Highlanders, while Gilbert Lindsay brought up the rear.

Merry fought the urge to run out into the courtyard, cling to Ran's leg and plead with him not to go. She sensed terrible danger looming in the dark forests near Badanloch, even though she had never been there, and shivered even as the last horse trotted through the gate and was gone.

Hertha sought to comfort her. "They'll be back by nightfall, milady."

"I pray you are right, Hertha." Merry smiled absently when the woman brought her a warm, richly embroidered shawl and draped it round her shoulders. "Thank you. I can't seem to get warm today; 'tis like the winter has settled in my bones."

Hertha nodded. She patted her young mistress's shoulder comfortingly and recited, " 'To talk o' the weather's the folly o' men, For when rain's on the hill, there'll be sun in the glen.' "

Merry chuckled softly and snuggled into the shawl. "I am sure 'tis true enough, but only in fickle Scotland! So much snow already, whilst I doubt the first rime of frost has settled on Ambergate yet." She grew wistful, thinking of her uncle's charming estate outside London, where she had spent many an hour growing up. At this hour the family would likely be gathered round the table to break their Christmas fast: rusty-haired Uncle Kit, plain but radiant Aunt Isobel, and the two younger sons yet at home.

Sir Christopher Tanner had once spent most of his waking hours at Court, amusing the queen, but with the passage of years and the mellowing of "dear Bess," as he called her among the family, Merry's uncle now enjoyed a more leisurely pace. Besides, the earl of Essex, Robert Devereux, Cecil's rival and a decided coxcomb, demanded the queen's exclusive attentions more and more. He had recently been sent to Ireland to subdue the fierce earl of Tyrone, Hugh O'Neill, a relative not too many times removed on Merry's mother's side. Merry knew her grandfather openly supported Tyrone, and her mother perhaps more discreetly but just as definitely. Tyrone's revolt four years prior had inflicted a major blow on English forces.

The queen's position in Ireland had long been tenuous. Not enough money was had to enforce complete subjugation, many of the English plantations had failed, riots and uprisings of the great Irish families threatened what little order yet remained. Consequently, Ireland, or any association with it, was a sore spot with Her Grace. Merry never sought to remind anyone of her heritage and had been left in peace for much of her service. Only the vainglorious Essex, prone to petty little cruelties as he was, remarked once when Merry entered a banqueting hall that he thought Irish lasses were supposed to be uncommonly fair, and he should throttle the little leprechaun who told him such lies.

The remark stung. Sensitive about her looks, Merry had nonetheless raised her chin and pretended she did not hear the nasty comment. Essex could be cattier than other women. He knew the Tanners stood in a favorable light with the queen and begrudged any others a moment of basking in royal approval. He was half Elizabeth's age but flattered the graying queen outrageously, dancing attendance upon her as if he was a besotted swain whose heart he wore on his sleeve. Elizabeth let him. Certainly she was shrewd enough to realize 'twas but a political gambit on Essex's part, but she patted him fondly on the cheek and called him her "sweet liddes." When she wearied of his pouts and tantrums, she sent him to Ireland to deal with the tiresome rebellion and allotted herself time to concentrate upon the more pressing matters of state. Financial strain upon the Crown, poor harvests, and a growing Puritan movement were beginning to take their toll on the aging queen. Meanwhile, the war with Spain dragged on, freshly fired by evidence they were financing Tyrone's rebellion.

Such turmoil was the daily gist at Court, but Merry missed it. One never knew what to expect when caught up in the swirling maelstrom of ambition, spies, and political backstabbing. Very few moments were dull, though certainly they could be trying. Once she had nearly lost her life when a French madman had sought revenge against her family. He seduced her with his charms and within weeks had a blade to her ribs, a moment Merry did not care to remember, for the sour taste of impending death was a taste one did not soon forget. She wondered what Ran would have done if she had been his wife then. Torn Adrien Lovelle limb from limb, or merely summoned the Lindsay doomster to execute the sentence of doom. Of a certainty, she knew he would not have stood idly by.

Christmas at Court and Ambergate. What a gay, festive time 'twould be. She contrasted Auchmull's empty, gloomy halls and tried not to let her spirits sink. Instead, she roused the staff into helping her decorate with whatever she could find. The red watch Lindsay tartan made a seasonal wall hanging in a pinch. Merry considered her options, then took a deep breath and plunged on. The best display was above the great hearth. So be it. Soon the gathered, tucked, and beribboned tartan completely covered the space above the mantel, and Blair Lindsay's portrait as well. Meanwhile, Merry had sent Siany and the other girls out to find a sprig or two of holly or juniper. They returned with rosy cheeks and aprons full of pine cones, laurel, and yew as well.

Earlier in the season, berries had been picked and preserved, and now the cranberries, crowberries, and red whortleberries were called upon to lend a festive touch to the scene. Some were strung with needle and thread, others crushed and cooked in pies and jellies. Merry sent some of the older boys out to hunt for a suitable Yule log, since apparently there was nothing left of the old one or the season had never been celebrated thusly at Auchmull. She was determined things would change. If nothing else, she would live up to her name and add a little bit of mirth and drama to Lindsay legend.

Hertha remembered an old wassail recipe of mulled ale, curdled cream, roasted apples, eggs, cloves, ginger, nutmeg, and sugar. It was served in a huge silver bowl, bearing the Lindsay crest. Merry invited all the staff and those within reasonable distance to partake, and for a time the great hall rang with the laughter of children and the chatter of women left to tend their hearths while the men hunted down the Christmas reivers. For the first time since her arrival, Merry felt truly welcome. Her generosity and respect for the old traditions swung their opinions.

The children clamored for a manger scene of the Baby Jesus, and Merry agreed 'twas appropriate with the eve full upon them. So while the women hastily sewed cloth poppets, she sent Hertha to retrieve the carved cradle from her former room. Merry shared an adjoining bedchamber with Ran now, as befitted her station. Hertha expressed some reservation about using the cradle, but Merry saw no point to it gathering dust when it could be used in an appropriately touching scene of faith.

Garlands of ivy and winter moss soon covered the little cradle, and Merry added a gilt ribbon to the backboard. One of the little girls came shyly forward to place the cloth Baby Jesus there, and, with heads bowed, the new Lady Lindsay led those gathered in prayer. Auchmull had a small family chapel, but there had never been a resident priest and the great hall was necessary to accommodate everyone. With the great Yule log merrily blazing and the wassail toasts running round the room, the old keep took on a homey atmosphere. Merry only wished Ran might be present to witness the magical transformation of his home.

Soon the hour grew late, and most began to drift off to their own hearths, however humble they might be by comparison. Merry dispensed four pennies Scots to each of the departing children, earning fierce hugs and sticky kisses, and smiles from their doting mothers. She took one more satisfied look around the softly glowing, colorful hall before she retired, and then Hertha accompanied her upstairs.

Before Hertha readied her mistress for bed, there came a loud pounding at the bedchamber door. Hertha jumped. She reached for the heavy iron ring that served as a doorknob, but before the woman's hand could close home, the door flew back against the wall with a mighty crash. With a squeak, Heartha fled into the shadows as a familiar figure burst in on them.

Merry whirled around, surprised to see Ran. His face was mottled with anger and his dark hair disheveled from the wind. Her gaze took in his muddy boots and the limp gilt ribbon clutched in one hand. He had returned from an obviously trying excursion, and appeared ready to dish out a very unpleasant lesson in turn.

His voice was like a whipcrack in the room. ''Leave us. Hertha.''

Glancing worriedly at Merry, Heartha nodded and left the bedchamber, and Ran slammed it shut behind the woman with a negligent bang. A pulse visibly throbbed in his temple, just above his left eye. A faint smile touched his lips as he took in Merry's wary posture.

"I take it the hunt 'twas not successful?"

"You assume correctly. The villains are canny. However, I would wager even they are not as cruel as some I might know."

"Cruel?" Merry's voice quavered as she glimpsed the pain behind the anger in his eyes. Sweet Jesu, what had she done?

"You know perfectly well what I mean, madam." He crumpled the ribbon in his big fist, hurled it at her. It glanced off her skirts and she gazed at it helplessly a moment. "Don't look so innocent, m' dear. Or is there ample reason to feign ignorance?"

"Please, do not do this," Merry whispered, bending to pick up the crushed ribbon. No matter what she did, she could not smooth the tattered edges. The parallel struck her with the force of a slap. Never had she been more aware of her vulnerability as a woman. Ran was not unusually large for a man, but more than strong enough to beat her if he chose. She fought the urge to cringe, sensing somehow that would only provoke a worse scene.

"I can explain—" she began.

He interrupted her with a head shake. "It never occurred to me you would stoop to something like this," he said, his glance falling on the ribbon clutched in her white fingers. Then his gaze rose to accusingly pin Merry's. "Where the devil did you find that thing?" he asked bluntly.

She knew he meant the cradle. Stumbling over the words, she told him the truth. As well as her reasoning behind its use. He clearly didn't care to hear it. His fists clutched at his sides, his knuckles were white.

"And covering Blair's portrait, as well? I suppose it amused you, to think of my pain? Some small recompense for what happened to you, no doubt."

His hoarse remark startled her. Merry looked into those blazing dark eyes, saw the intense suffering written there. Her insides twisted, she felt sick.

"Nay, I never intended—" she stammered.

"Jesu, madam, what a cold-blooded *Sassenach* bitch you are! My first Christmas, without Blair . . . the bairn we would have had by now . . ." Furiously Ranald came at her in sudden long strides, driving Merry flush up against the wall. She was trapped. His hand flew up, and he encircled her throat with his long fingers.

"The way I feel right now, I could cheerfully strangle you," he muttered, and she saw the suspicious glitter of tears in his eyes just before his mouth came down, hard, with perfect accuracy, against her lips. He never released his grip on her neck, even tightened it slightly when he felt her begin to struggle. Gasping for air, Merry opened her mouth against his and felt his tongue immediately thrust home, claiming a brash victory as it fenced her own aside.

Traitorous tingles raced up and down her body, and her hands clutched Ran's damp breccan as he leaned fully into her, letting her feel the hard edge of his arousal even through the layers of her skirts. His other hand slowly slid down the curve of her right cheek, continuing on until she felt his warm fingers slipping into the low bodice of her gown.

With bold, unerring accuracy, he found a nipple and teased it to button hardness, absorbing Merry's whimper with his fierce kiss, letting her feel the full measure of his passion and pain. Finally, he tore his mouth from hers and buried it against the hollow of her neck, painting her flesh with a feverish intensity which left her gasping for air. She feared she would die either way; if he dared continued, or if he dared stop.

Ran shuddered against her, his hand slipping from her throat. "Damme you, Merry. You've bewitched me," he whispered raggedly, staring at her as if demanding an explanation.

" 'Twasn't intentional, I assure you."

Ran ignored her shaky reply. "I've marked you," he mused quietly, leaning back a little to study the marks left by his fingers. "Your skin is so damn fair." Then he lowered his head and began to gently kiss the rosy imprints, one by one.

Merry gasped and arched, her head lolling back, cushioned by the velvety tapestry covering the stone wall.

"Nay," she said, vainly pushing against his chest.

"Aye," he countered fiercely. "Aye!"

In a sudden fury of agony, he tore at the fastenings of Merry's gown, peeling back the burgundy velvet bodice to expose a richly patterned red silk lining, and the creamy expanse of her breasts. He shoved the wide sleeves halfway down her arms, effectively imprisoning her for further exquisite torture at his leisure. He captured a rosy nipple between his teeth. It puckered proudly, and Merry cried out softly as Ran's mouth wrought forbidden pleasure from her body. He nipped, then soothed the throbbing peak, tracing delicate spirals and fanciful designs with his tongue. A moment later, she felt him nuzzling her other breast, and his dark, silky hair tumbled over her skin as he worried the second nipple to a turgid, aching peak of passion. Then she felt his hand slip between her legs, pressing the velvet folds of her gown hard against her woman's point.

"Tell me you don't want me," he whispered in her ear, gently and harshly, all at the same time. Merry sobbed once, unable to deny it. She pushed up hard against his hand, a silent plea of sorts, and in that precise moment his hand yanked free. She bit back the urge to scream a furious denial. Ran, on the other hand, seemed to regain control quickly. She soon realized with a crushing blow, he had never lost it. He looked at her so closely she saw golden motes sparkling in his dark eyes.

"God's teeth," he said, stepping back to observe her flushed and trembling figure trapped against the wall. "You're even willing to act like a court strumpet when you think it will avert the consequences of your actions."

Merry yanked up the sleeves of her gown, trembling with anger and hurt. Her mind still whirled with the aftereffects of his angry lovemaking, and her fingers shook violently as she struggled to refasten the clasps. Impatiently Ran batted her hands aside and finished the job.

"Don't spare a single tear on me, milady wife," he said, glancing into her damp eyes. " 'Twon't work, and furthermore it lessens what little respect for you I have left. I will not deny my body wants you as much as ever, but 'twill be easily enough restrained. You made a conscious choice to disrespect Blair and our child, and now you'll live up to the consequences, like it or nay.''

Flustered and feeling humiliated, Merry turned away to finish securing her bodice and smooth her skirts. She could feel Ran's gaze boring into her back. She sought for the right words, but nothing came. When she finally worked up the courage to speak at all, 'twas just in time to hear his footsteps striding briskly from the room.

Chapter Twenty-Six

"Fearful angry he was, lass. I canna ever recall seein' Lord Ran like that before."

Merry, curled up in a window seat with a copy of Sir David Lindsay's *The Dreme* balanced across her knees, merely nodded at her maid's words. Heartha had been babbling about the incident for most of the day. She was still too upset herself to either concentrate upon the poetic visions of Ran's ancestor or continue any converse upon the matter of the man himself.

" 'Tis sorry I am I didna stay, lass. Why, he looked somethin' right fierce, he did, like one of the old Pict warriors! I was terrible a'feared for ye. What could I do?"

What, indeed? Merry wondered. Would anything have stopped Ran short of a claymore? She almost smiled at the thought, imagining the look on his face if she had whipped a wicked-looking blade from behind her skirts. 'Tis what her feisty sister Kat surely would have done in similar straits. She could fence on a par with men, and Merry had always envied her twin such skill and cool aplomb.

Her smiled waned as she remembered Ran's expression when he had glimpsed the cradle. He thought she deliberately sought to hurt him, and nothing she said would mend the chasm yawning between them now. Merry realized Hertha was watching her when the maid soberly remarked, "Ochone, lass, I do hate to see yer sweet spirits so low."

" 'Tis all right, Hertha," Merry said wearily. " 'Tis over now, and 'twould appear I'm none the worse for wear."

Except inside, Merry added silently. She would never forget the terrifying, yet thrilling proximity of Ran as he'd leaned into her, pinning her between his hard body and an even harder wall. How had Blair truly felt about the dangerously handsome Wolf of Badanloch? Had she quivered and whimpered at his touch, like Merry did? Had her stomach clenched into hard little knots whenever she felt his lips playing over her skin, his calloused hands caressing her body?

Sweet Jesu, Merry thought with a mental groan, tossing her book aside on a table. *I've got to stop going round and round in my mind. Ran doesn't love me, his heart died with Blair. Marriage with Wickham would have been purely practical, why could this not work comfortably as well?*

Because I love him. The realization, so simple and yet so poignant, caused her throat to tighten with emotion. *Why do you feel this way about him?* her conscience argued. *You know he's the enemy. You know nothing can come of it. You know you want to go back home.*

Home. England. The frivolous gaiety of Court, Christmas revelries at Nonsuch. Merry longed for the carefree days when she dangled her heart on her sleeve for the courtiers to vie over, and laughingly watched them compete for her favors. Harmless flirtations a man like Ranald Lindsay would never understand, nor forgive. Whilst he did not question his previous wife's appearance at Braidwood, he was quick to condemn Merry for the lifestyle she had led. She was still thinking about this, considerably sobered, when Hertha answered a summons at the door.

Hertha returned, looking a little concerned. " 'Tis Himself summoning again," she whispered to her mistress. "Shall I tell him yer abed?"

Merry shook her head and quickly rose from her indolent position, smoothing out her sapphire-blue silk gown. She wore dark colors still in respect for Duncan and the melancholy side of the holiday, but she had no intention of standing there meekly and taking any more insults, if that was what Lord Lindsay intended. Merry unconsciously tidied her hair as she moved toward the door. Ran himself was not there. 'Twas a young lad who regarded her for a moment with twinkling eyes before his gaze respectfully lowered.

"Follow me, milady," he murmured, turning and leading her down the hall to the chamber comprising Ran's study. Merry waited tensely while the boy scratched at the door, then opened it and stepped aside for her to enter. 'Twas immediately closed behind her. She faced her husband from the other side of a massive mahogany desk.

Ran glanced up at her with an unreadable expression in his eyes. "Sit down, Merry," he ordered.

She sat. Her hands clenched in her lap as she glanced around Ran's study. The room was lit only by a single lamp, placed well out of reach across the wide expanse of the chamber. 'Twas evening outside, and therefore the narrow, leaded windows offered little light. Though 'twas poorly lit, she could make out Ran easily enough. He was frowning a little as if preoccupied. She swallowed, wondering how she might have offended him yet again while she had kept to her bedchamber all day. 'Twas the most dour, loneliest Christmas she could recall, and even the tender goose and spiced apple tart Hertha brought her had not lifted her spirits.

"I suppose you wonder why I summoned you here at this hour. Suffice it to say, a missive has arrived from London."

Merry looked at Ran quizzically, waiting.

" 'Tis a dispatch from your English kin. Gord was kind enough to forward it to me, as the messenger was apparently waylaid at the Border." He unfolded several limp, travel-worn papers from a packet on his desk. He tossed them almost negligently at her. Merry caught the papers and he nodded she should read them, as he obviously already had.

Ran added the weather had delayed the messenger both ways, but 'twas obvious enough from the outset that Uncle Kit had received word of her marriage from Cecil at Court.

"*Dear little flame,*" Sir Christopher Tanner had written in his fine hand, dated over a fortnight ago,

> *How we rejoiced to hear you were safe, after many long days and nights of worry. Your sister especially was inconsolable, and I dispatched word to Falcon's Lair as soon as I heard the news. We all feared her distress might injure her health and that of the future heir of Falcon's Lair. I, too, must confess shock and no little concern over this turn of events. though certainly a title like Lindsay's is nothing to shrug aside. Your father aspired to make a good match with your permission and the queen's aid, and this came about with Wickham's offer earlier in the year.*
>
> *Your parents are even now returning from Ireland after receiving word of your marriage to Lord Lindsay. Despite the dangers of crossing the Channel in winter, they wish to join us at Ambergate for Twelfth Night festivities. I would as lief you and Lord Lindsay came, too, if only to unite the family for a little while and mend whatever bridges might have been damaged in the events of the past weeks. As long as you are safe, I have no serious quarrel with your lord husband.*
>
> *God keep you safe until next we speak, little flame.*

The letter was signed, informally, "Uncle Kit," and he had pressed his signet there to confirm he was the true writer. The ink was smeared in spots from rain or snow, but Merry had learned to decipher the worst of courtly handwriting long ago. Kit's was flawless by comparison to most. She knew, however, her uncle's somewhat stiff style was unnatural and prompted by the knowledge Ran would be reading the letter before his wife. Therefore, nothing of an intimate or familial nature was asked or shared. Not without reason had Sir Christopher survived the intrigues of court for nigh two score.

She looked up from the letter to find Ran regarding her somewhat coolly.

" 'I sense your uncle is a trifle displeased with my actions, Merry. Certainly I cannot blame him. He rightfully fears a madman has wed into the family." Ran laughed without humor. "I do not doubt my reputation has preceded me, even to Gloriana's Court."

Something in Ran's manner frightened Merry. She sensed nothing of the tender side she had glimpsed now and again, only cold resolve. She glanced down at the letter again, suddenly unable to make out a single word of the ornate script. The elaborately looped and scrolled letters danced before her tired eyes.

"Is this all you wished to speak with me about?" she asked, making move as if to rise.

He stilled her with a single look. "Nay. There is matter of your uncle's invitation."

"I never presumed you would consider it."

"A gesture of goodwill would not be amiss, given Sir Christopher's status at Court."

Merry flinched at Ran's cold-blooded remark. So she was to be a political pawn, maneuvered for the favor of her family and thus the queen. What a kindly husband might have dispensed as a Christmas gift, the Wolf of Badanloch tossed at her like a cup of icy water from the loch. She could not even bring herself to smile at the prospect of seeing Ambergate and her parents.

"Naturally I cannot spare the time to attend such frivolous affairs during a serious embroilment with reivers of the king's cattle. I have decided Gilbert may serve as your escort. He wished to see Court and all he has missed in dreary isolation here; therefore I deem this the most practical and expedient solution." A bitter note twisted Ran's words, and Merry sensed he held her responsible for Gil's mental defection to the colorful Tudor Court. 'Twas natural for a young man as light of heart as Gil was to long for the company of pretty girls and grand parties, but Ran seemed to regard his little brother's wishes as some sort of betrayal.

"I have enough men to see you safely to the Border. Gord and Fi have offered their hospitality and guaranteed safe passage through their lands. Once in England, Gilbert and Hugo should be able to handle things easily enough. Mayhap a message can be sent to your kin and they can retrieve you in the style to which you are accustomed."

Merry regarded him levelly, as if she did not even hear the insult. "As you wish, milord." She knew her reversion to icy dignity would needle Ran, and she saw his eyes narrow a fraction. "However, there is someone I should miss dearly . . ."

He waited, though she was certain she only imagined the slight tensing of his shoulders.

"I promised Nell if I ever went to Court, I should take her as my tiring-woman. She is still nursing the babe, but I do not mind little ones. Besides, 'twill give her opportunity to get to know Hugo better away from the prying eyes and ears of others."

"What the devil does Hugo have to do with anything?" Ran demanded with obvious exasperation, and Merry arched an eyebrow. He did not even notice the budding of love when 'twas right beneath his nose.

"May I take Nell along?" she pressed him.

"Aye. Take the chit and the brat and whatever else you deem necessary for amusement, madam." His dark gaze raked her almost contemptuously as she turned to go. Pausing at the doorway, Merry turned and found him still watching her. She smiled, sweetly, and executed a neat little curtsey.

"Thank you, milord husband."

He did not answer her. He looked away.

Chapter Twenty-Seven

"Do ye need me any more here, milady? If nae, I'll go up to yer room and finish the packing of yer trunk."

Merry nodded her dismissal. "Go ahead, Nell. I think I'll stay here." After the maid departed, Merry turned and surveyed the great hall one last time. The decorations were long gone, Blair's portrait restored to its full dignity. She tried not to let her hurt pride and anger consume her. Yet, since the incident on Christmas Eve, she had felt the compelling need to answer the question Darra had posed. What was Blair doing at Braidwood at all?

Lady Deuchar had mentioned Blair's slyness. Ran's first wife had also been a Maclean by birth, and Highland loyalties ran deep. Merry suspected a few of the answers might be found at Braidwood, but she was not foolish enough to approach Wickham's domain. After all, the luckless Lady Blair had met her end there. Her curiosity and Ran's bitterness must remain unresolved. With a little sigh, she gathered up her skirts and started up the stairs.

"Merry!" Gil's hearty greeting stopped her; she turned and smiled at the cheerful young man. "When are we away to Court?"

"Just as soon as I have changed to my traveling attire and Nell has finished packing." Merry laughed at his obvious enthusiasm. "I take it the horses and wagon are ready?"

Gil nodded vigorously. "Long so. I was up at dawn, prodding Hugo and the others." He hesitated, his violet-blue gaze reflecting concern. "Ran left last night, I hear."

"Aye. Word came the thieves and missing cattle were spotted in Drumtochty Forest. He was out the door by the time the messenger finished speaking." Merry did not attempt to disguise the wry note in her voice. If she had expected anything in the way of a tender farewell, she was doomed to disappointment. She could hardly mistake this unexpected boon as anything other than Ran seizing an opportunity to get rid of her for a while. He need not fear she would not return, however, as the dual monarchy had made Merry's position quite clear. Marriage to the Wolf, or eternal disgrace. Even her doting uncle would not be so foolish as to try and hide her from the queen's wrath.

"I know you are taking Nell, but have you considered another lady's maid?" Gilbert asked. "It seems to me a countess should have at least two tiring-women, and Nell has the baby to look after, as well."

"Nay, I had not thought upon it. Hertha is too elderly for travel now."

"What about Siany, her granddaughter?"

Merry was surprised and a bit disconcerted by the suggestion. She had never taken to Siany, though certainly the girl completed her tasks as needed. Perhaps she was unable to forget the unkind words she had overheard in the kitchens. Gil regarded her hopefully, and Merry could find no real excuse to demur.

"I suppose she could help Nell with Ashet," she said.

Gil nodded. "My thought exactly. Siany could tend the bairn whilst Nell sees to milady's needs." His manner was engaging, his smile so charming Merry could not remain unconvinced. She chuckled. "All right, Gil. If Hertha grants permission,

Siany may accompany us. I trust you to look after the girl like a sister.''

Too late she glimpsed the roguish twinkle in his eye. '' 'Twould be my honor, Merry.''

"Gil! You're far too young to entertain the notion of any mischief . . .''

He only laughed at her alarm and darted off again, leaving Merry ruefully shaking her head, wondering what she had gotten herself into.

The travelers reached Goldielands by nightfall of the second day, though 'twas a hard ride which left everyone exhausted. Bumping along in a wagon, forced to clamber up and down several times so the mired vehicle might be tugged or pushed free again, Merry and her maid servants were on the verge of exhaustion. Thus far, Siany had proved more than capable with the baby, and Nell seemed relieved for the extra help. Merry decided she would give the girl benefit of the doubt, and Gil seemed especially pleased by the company of someone near his own age.

The Scotts met them on the road with their usual boisterous welcome. Besides the five armed Lindsay escorts, Brodie Scott was driving the wagon, and his freckled face lit in a huge smile when he saw his kin. At the castle, Lady Fiona greeted them at the entrance with heather ale and oat cakes, and laughingly suggested Siany wait till the morrow and then be the first to enter, for 'twas considered good fortune if a stranger made first footing over the threshold after Hogmanay. The Scots version of New Year's Eve was rife with merriment and mischief, and Goldielands fairly hummed with excitement.

While Nell tended her lady's things and Siany put Ashet down for a nap in the guest chamber, Merry joined her hostess and the others. Fiona was visibly ripening with her lord husband's seed, glowing with health and happiness in her crimson velvet gown. Merry secretly envied the other woman her tranquility, and her growing family. She doubted with the present

rift between her and Ran, she would be a mother at all. She
was Lady Lindsay in title only, though Fiona seemed pleased
by the news.

"I understand the circumstances leading to this were anything but pleasant, but I confess I am glad you are my neighbor," she said, hugging Merry gently. "When summer comes,
we must visit more often. By then I will be delivered of my
own wee burden and can travel more easily. Perhaps I shall
visit Edzell and Darra, too. I do miss the old days, and 'tis
easy to dwell upon pleasantries from the past as one ages."

"Ages!" Merry exclaimed. You're but a maid in the first
blush of youth, it seems to me."

Fiona laughed. " 'Tis kind of you, m'dear, but Gord and I
have been wed nigh a decade. I fear the bloom left this Scottish
rose long ago." She settled beside Merry on a comfortable
divan where they might visit in confidence whilst the men drank
and blustered across the hall. Looking at Merry with keen blue
eyes, Fiona asked, "Are you happy, lass?"

"Happy . . ." Merry did not know how to answer the question
honestly. "I am pleased I can see my family again, and partake
of Twelfth Night revelries one last time."

"I meant with Ran. Is he kind to you, at least?"

Merry nodded, searching for the right words. "He has never
given me cause to fear for my life." She folded her hands in
her lap so she was not tempted to trace any faint marks left on
her neck. Fortunately her lace ruff obscured her throat. She
knew Fiona was not fooled by her evasive reply, however.

Fiona sighed. " 'Tis Blair, isn't it? The ghost of the woman
haunts Auchmull still."

"Aye, and Ranald Lindsay, too."

The other woman reached out, squeezed Merry's hand. "I'm
sorry, lass. I wish there was something I could do or say to set
matters aright. All I can say is, patience has been known to
work miracles."

Merry smiled a little. "Unfortunately, I am not Job."

"Nay, you are someone altogether different. Someone who
loves Ran unconditionally."

Merry's smile froze. She stared at Fiona in helpless denial. The golden-haired lady nodded emphatically.

"Aye, Merry, 'tis clear as the waters of Alemoor. Please, do not be ashamed of it. Love 'tis a marvelous, healing potion, and I believe if anything can save Ran, therein lies the hope."

"I wish I could believe that, too. I fear he hates me now." Merry told the tale of the cradle. Fiona listened gravely.

"In my opinion he reacted overmuch, but then Blair has not been gone a year. His emotions are raw yet. The best thing you could do for Ran, for each other, is have a child of your own as quickly as possible."

Merry blushed. " 'Twill prove difficult, I vow. He has not touched me since . . . well, for a long time. Now I will be in England for at least a fortnight, or longer if the winter worsens."

Fiona's blue eyes twinkled. "Perhaps Ran cannot attend Twelfth Night, but after the thieves are caught, who is to say you cannot send your lord husband an urgent if rather vague message from London?"

Looking at Fiona incredulously a moment, Merry laughed a little and shook her head. "He would be furious if he knew I summoned him there under false pretenses. Darra said he detests all manner of courtly affairs."

"Just the thing he needs to roust him from his gloomy exile," Fiona countered firmly. "Now, lass, I want you to relax and enjoy Hogmanay in infamous Scott style. Shall we join the revelries?"

On New Year's morning, since 'twas considered lucky, the unmarried girls in the household vied for the honor of being first to draw water from the well. The girl who did would be the first to marry that year. Lots were cast, and to Siany's delight, she won, though the other lasses grumbled 'twas not fair a visitor was permitted to partake of a Goldielands tradition. Lady Fiona settled the dispute with her customary tact, and Siany pulled up the first bucket. The household utensils were then washed in the water to bring plenty during the year, and a few more buckets drawn and given to the milch cattle to increase their yield.

Merry thought the customs a bit peculiar and quaint, but she could not deny she had found Hogmanay almost as fun as Twelfth Night. The Scots celebrated it with even more gusto than Christmas, and everyone had stayed up late singing, drinking, and carousing in the hall. She was tired but replete from the fine food and company, and even after the spectacle of the New Year's well was over and the others returned inside, she lingered a moment in the courtyard to gather her thoughts.

Merry did not even sense another presence until someone spoke behind her. She turned and stiffened at the sight of the familiar, crabbed figure. She had done her best to avoid Mother MacDougall altogether, but now she found herself alone with the crone. 'Twould be rude to beat a hasty retreat, though Merry very much wanted to.

She returned the elderly woman's greeting cautiously. " 'Tis a fair day for full winter, aye?''

Beitris nodded, and pointed at a patch of pale green poking through the snow. ''Gin the gress should grow in Janiveer, it'll be the worst for't a' the year.''

Merry shivered and buried her hands deeper in the pockets of her cloak. ''The weather, you mean?''

The woman did not answer, but her gaze roamed upward. Merry traced it and saw several large black birds huddled on the bare limbs of a nearby ancient oak. She felt a tic of unease and began to inch away from Mother MacDougall's presence. As soon as Merry moved, the birds burst into flight, winging overheard, and Merry saw they were three ravens. Her faint gasp was obscured by Mother MacDougall's wry recitation:

> One bodes wedding, two's a birth,
> Three's a grief, four's a death.

As the last word drifted away on the wind, a fourth bird screamed and flapped from the tree, streaking through the ice-blue sky to join its companions. Merry had not noticed it before, for 'twas pure white, and blended against the snowy backdrop. It flew so quickly, dipping and swirling like a frosty dream against the winter sun, she could hardly follow it. Yet it appeared to be a raven also. How could this be?

She glanced, startled, at Beitris as the ravens disappeared on the other side of the courtyard wall. The old woman nodded, her eyes gleaming almost feverishly bright.

"Snow raven," Beitris muttered, wringing raw hands covered with chilblains. " 'Tis a sign, a sign."

"There is no such creature. 'Twas a young goose, I vow." Merry spoke quickly, whirled and hurried off before the old woman could argue.

Despite the pleasantry of Lady Fiona's company, Merry was glad to be pressing on. The border was so close now, she could almost smell the fresh English air. The guards Ran had sent saw them safely to Goldielands, then returned to Auchmull to assist their lord in his relentless duty for the king. It seemed ironic Ran should serve the very monarch who confiscated his lands in a fit of pique, but he obviously had hopes such service might soften King James in future.

When they reached Newcastle Upon Tyne, word was dispatched to Ambergate while several rooms at an inn were secured for Merry and her companions. It took several days more before the Tanner coach arrived, but Merry was glad for the time to rest. When she heard the coach was there, she hurried out. The coach was new but driven by a very familiar personage.

"Jem!" Never had she felt so glad to see a retainer before. She even hugged the flustered man when he climbed down to see to her trunk.

"Mistress Merry, 'tis gladdened I am to see you right fine," Jem said.

"Oh, and likewise, Jem. Tell me, have you suffered many ill effects from the accident?"

He shook his head. "Few enough. Tough ol' English noggin,

this is.'' He tapped his head, grinning almost sheepishly, and Merry laughed.

''I am relieved to hear it.'' Just then, Gil stepped from the inn, and as the two men's gazes met, she stiffened in preparation for the worst. To her surprise, the grin never left Jem's lips, but widened perceptibly when he recognized the former highwayman.

''Well met, Master Gilbert,'' he said.

Gil chuckled and joined them, slapping the driver heartily on the back. ''How are you, Jem? I see you did not fare too poorly despite my best efforts to the contrary.''

Jem's faded blue eyes twinkled. ''I count it among the greatest of adventures, Master Gilbert. The young'uns clamor to hear the tale, o'er and o'er.''

Merry shook her head in amazement. ''Why, Gil's shenanigans might have handily killed us both, Jem!''

''Now, there's a word straight from your mum's Irish lips,'' Jem said. ''Shenanigans.''

''Marry, I fear y'are right. Have Mother and Father reached Ambergate yet?''

The manservant nodded. ''Just yesterday, blown in early by a foul nor'wester. But none can tame the seas like those two, miss . . . er, milady.''

Jem seemed a bit embarrassed about her new status. Merry smiled, realizing how awkward it must look to others. She had wed her kidnapper and in doing so both flouted Wickham and obeyed the queen. She had also secured the status of a countess, albeit a Scottish one.

''Come into the inn for a moment, relax and partake of some refreshment,'' she invited Jem. ''I must rouse my tiring-women anyhow, and ready the babe for travel.''

''Baby, milady?'' Jem gawked at her in obvious confusion.

Merry laughed. ''Not mine, Jem. It belongs to my maid, Nell.''

''Lud, in all the excitement, I forgot. Lady Trelane had a son on Christmas Day!''

''Dear Kat! How is she?'' Many times Merry had thought

about, wondered, and worried over her headstrong twin. Though Kat was happily wed to Morgan Trelane, and now the mother of a little lordling as well, Merry still tended to fuss and hover in mother-hen fashion even from afar. She felt a brief, yet deep pang of envy. She knew Morgan and Kat were in love. Now they had a son to prove it, too.

"Fit and feisty as ever, Sir Christopher says, but he would not even consider the notion of her traveling so far after the birth. Lord Trelane agreed to keep his family home."

"Aye, though I wager Morgan must needs sit on her for the effort," Merry said with a rueful headshake. She drew Jem into the inn, and while Gil saw the manservant happily settled with a mug of nut-brown ale, she returned to her room and finished packing for the last leg of the journey. Little Ashet was fast asleep from her last feeding, and did not stir as Nell placed her in the slinglike cloth carrier she wore in order to keep her hands free. Siany was gazing dreamily out the window, an affectation she had adopted of late which did not speak well of her serving potential.

Merry caught the girl's attention with a brisk remark, and hoped she mistook the flash of resentment in Siany's eyes as she turned. During the rest of the journey, Merry saw Siany had indeed returned to the sullen, grudging air she wore at Auchmull like a dark cloak. Merry regretted giving in to Gil's wheedling. She had enough to worry about with the upcoming audience before the queen. Whatever she might expect of Bess, outrage was sure to be among the lesser evils.

Chapter Twenty-Eight

Merry appeared immune to the stares and whispers marking her progress through St. James's Palace on her uncle's arm. By onlookers' accounts, she remained cool and unruffled, head held high and blazing hair coiffed in the latest fashion, little curls across her forehead and the remainder captured in a net of seed pearls and glittering braid. Her gown was a rich golden brocade, sleeves slashed and inset with alternating panes of watered green silk and crimson velvet, the full train embroidered with a fetching rose and thistle design. Lady Lindsay obviously refused to be humbled by her circumstances or the reputation of her daunting Scots lord, and the majority of the courtiers parted in her wave like so many dumbstruck sheep.

Inside, Merry quivered with uncertainty and no little trepidation, wondering how she would be received by Her Majesty after all that had transpired. Uncle Kit had encouraged her bold and direct appearance at Court, pointing out that while Elizabeth Tudor had a vile temper, she also had a deep respect for those who did not fear her. Merry had been kidnapped through no fault of her own, though her mother had certainly scolded her enough about the foolish manner in which she had set out across Wales with no proper escort. Surely even Her Grace could not blame Merry for the events that transpired, and in the end she had wed Ran as ordered, preserving her family's reputation and, to a lesser extent, her own.

The glittering throng of courtiers and whispering ladies seemed a sea, restlessly ebbing and flowing around her, and for a moment Merry's courage faltered. Something had changed. Not in the others, but her. Why did their laughing eyes and furious whispering seem suddenly immature? Not very long ago, she had huddled there with the other maids-of-honor, giggling and scrutinizing every passing knave or lady. Now she was the one subjected to passing critiques, and 'twas not so pleasant. She was glad she had followed her uncle's advice and dipped into her dower portion for a new court wardrobe. Whatever they might speculate about her morals, it could not be denied the Countess of Crawford had presented herself in the very latest fashion. Had Essex been here, she was certain the knave would have cocked an eyebrow, but nodded a bit in admiration.

Sensing her hesitation, Sir Christopher squeezed her arm reassuringly. "I will be right here to support you, m'dear."

Merry cast him a grateful smile. Despite his age, and the glint of silver in his once-flaming hair, her uncle Kit still commanded great presence and respect. He was garbed in a forest-green velvet doublet and breeches, the latter slashed and inset with gold silk. He wore a jerkin of buff leather, a multilayered ruff with tasseled ties, and several heavy gold chains and a medallion bearing the Tanner crest. Over the years, he had maintained his good graces with the queen and hence occupied a coveted position among the ranks of the courtiers.

The days preceding Twelfth Night were progressively more festive and lavish, each feast grander than the previous one, the entertainment more ribald and the costumes more shocking. 'Twas yet a week to go, but already the court dazzled the eye with sight and sound. The tawdry elegance of the participants contrasted the stark formality of the banqueting hall itself; regal silk banners bearing the Tudor green and gold clashed with the

frivolous Twelfth Night decorations and favors scattered about
the tables, or clutched in ladies' hands. At one end of the hall,
musicians played a somber rendition of "Angelus ad Virgi-
nem," while a madrigal in the contrasting corner sang a slightly
bawdy version of "Fair Phyllis I Saw."

Merry's gaze was drawn past the entertainers toward the
grand throne at the end of the corridor. Her Majesty was in
attendance with her bevy of young suitors, vying and swooping
about like so many gaudy butterflies about a wilting rose. 'Twas
a ludicrous sight, for Elizabeth Tudor was no maid, and had
ruled now for forty-one years. Her aquiline features were
sharply accented, her fair skin withered, her once-fine auburn
hair concealed by wigs. Still the young men gushed compliments and sickeningly sweet sonnets, knelt and kissed her pale
hands. 'Twas a sight both sad and grimly comical.

Merry's courage almost faltered, fearing Her Grace would
somehow sense her thoughts, yet even in her waning days she
conceded her queen was a majestic woman. Tonight Elizabeth
Tudor was clad in taffeta of silver and white trimmed with
gold, her dress open in front to display a stomacher of embroidered tawny velvet. Her ruff was higher yet than Merry recalled
the previous fashion, and her throat was encircled by pearls
and rubies besides. Creamy pearls also dangled like small pears
across her forehead, and she cradled a fan in her lap, marvel-
ously crafted of white feathers set in a handle of gold, garnished
on one side with fine emeralds, diamonds, and rubies, and
carved with a white bear and pearls, a lion rampant with a
white muzzled bear at his feet. Merry recognized the beautiful
fan. 'Twas a lavish gift from the Earl of Leicester, Robert
Dudley, dead nigh a decade now. Elizabeth's former favorite
had been presumptuous enough to place his own coat of arms
upon his queen's gift, but Merry remembered seeing the gor-
geous fan over the years, and whenever the queen picked it up,
she assumed a wistful and melancholy air.

Merry did not know whether this boded ill for her or not,
so when Kit presented her and she reached the base of the

throne, she merely sank into a deep, graceful obeisance with her gaze lowered.

"Meredith Lady Lindsay, Countess of Crawford," the Clerk of the Seal announced unnecessarily.

"Indeed, Windebank." Elizabeth nodded a trifle irritably, though whether from the obvious identity of the supplicant or vexation with the same, 'twas not clear. "I see marriage to a hardy Scot suits y'well enough" was her first gruff comment as she thrust out her hand at Merry.

Merry kissed the cool, thin fingers before she rose, her head still inclined slightly. "Aye, Your Grace."

To her surprise, the queen laughed. Not the tinkling tones of her early reign, but the husky chuckle of a weary woman. "We confess we have missed you, sweet cinnamon."

The affectionate nickname eased the tension in Merry somewhat. "As I have missed Court, Your Majesty, and especially your magnificent presence."

"Pfft," replied Elizabeth, waving a beringed hand dismissingly, but her keen gray eyes gleamed for a moment. She glanced then to Kit, looking almost girlish. "La, m'fox, I trow 'tis been a pace too long since y'have graced my hall."

"All of a fortnight, Your Grace," Kit gallantly replied as he bent over his monarch's hand in turn and pressed his lips to her ivory skin. Elizabeth's face bore the mark of time and worry, but her hands remained curiously young by contrast. She never missed a chance to show them off, and tonight her fingers gleamed with a pear-shaped diamond, an irregular smoky pearl, a golden beryl, and an exquisite piece of jade cut in the shape of a delicate rose.

Elizabeth patted Kit's face as he rose. "Dear Fox," she sighed, fondness softening her expression, "y'bring me consolation in the darkest hours. 'Tis well you've brought the wayward Mistress Merry home to roost; Jesu preserve any lessons she has learned."

Kit laughed at the queen's tart remark. "Aye, Your Majesty." He winked aside at Merry, who realized by then she had escaped true wrath. Elizabeth was irritated, but feeling indulgent. She slowly released her pent-up breath, just as the queen gestured to a tufted stool near her feet. A reluctant Mountjoy rose and vacated the spot of honor, and soon Merry was comfortably ensconced in the court's bosom as if she had never left. Seeing she still maintained Elizabeth's favor, the others were quick to follow suit, the courtiers vying to bring her choice bits from the feast and the other ladies slipping up here and there to gush over her gown or jewels.

Merry was not fooled by their cloying compliments, but she offered equally insincere smiles or nods in turn, wondering how she had ever endured such pretense for so long. She was not the only one speculating upon the changes in herself.

Elizabeth Tudor watched her newest lady of the Court with interest over the new few days. In but a few short months Merry had evolved from a vain, silly chit to a young woman with considerable poise and a sincere dignity. This appealed to the aged queen. She had grown weary of her maids-of-honors' childish tantrums and pouts, and preferred the company of older ladies. Merry was yet young in years, but considerably grown in maturity. As Lady Lindsay, a married woman, she could be granted further benefit of sleeping in the queen's chamber. This privilege was offered on Merry's second night back at Court.

Alas, while Merry was delighted to find her herself restored in favor, she chafed a bit she could not be at Ambergate more often. Her visits were fleeting, and she resented every moment lost with the family she had missed. Never had she felt more secure than when she first returned and her father Slade swept her up in a tight hug, her mother Bryony leaning in to kiss her cheek. Merry's five younger brothers skitted round, clamoring for attention, too, until she laughingly sent Siany to retrieve the little bags of sugarolly she had brought from Goldielands. With the boys occupied, she was able to visit awhile with her parents.

Bryony could not seem to tear her gaze from her second daughter. Nor the raven amulet gleaming at the base of Merry's throat. "You've changed, colleen," she said a little huskily. "I cannot put my finger on it, but you have."

Merry nodded at the observation of her attractive, dark-haired mother. As usual, Bryony was wearing the mannish garb she preferred when sailing, but such humble attire no longer shocked or outraged her court-raised daughter. "Aye, Mother. I think I have grown up a bit."

"It suits you, sweeting," Slade Tanner interjected, punctuating his words with another squeeze of the arm still looped behind Merry's shoulder. "I confess I was relieved to hear you did not wed Wickham, after all. I met him during negotiations and did not particularly fancy the man."

"*You* did not fancy him?" Bryony laughed at her husband. "He was a pompous *Sassenach* arse, and a lech besides. Imagine, ogling a woman of my age!"

"Well, I cannot find fault with the man for that," Slade said, flashing a rakish grin. Merry literally saw the love reflected between the two, so intense 'twas. Growing up, her parents' unabashed affection and passionate embraces in public had embarrassed her greatly, but now she found herself smiling and feeling as wistful as the queen.

Sensing her daughter's distraction, Bryony inquired, "What of Lindsay, Merry? Will we approve of the Scots rogue?"

"Aye, I fain as much. He is overproud and heavy-handed and incredibly thick-headed at times."

Bryony laughed at her daughter's dry retort. "A true Celt, then." She glanced amused at Slade. " 'Twould appear I've inherited a fierce Highlander for a son-in-law, rather than a *Sassenach* fop and wastrel. Again, I must thank my wise old ancestors and the amulet for their protection and timely intervention."

Slade shook his red-gold head, smiling. "Faith, don't tell me you still believe in such quaint superstitions, m'love."

"Oh, not a bit," Bryony assured him, and winked at Merry. Merry chuckled, exchanging a look of perfect understanding with her mother for the first time in memory.

* * *

Gilbert Lindsay had chosen to stay with his former tutor whilst in London, and waited at Hepworth House for permission to attend Court with his sister-in-law. Sir Christopher laid the groundwork for the young man's presentation, and Merry assisted by coaching Gil in all the latest fashion trends. She had greatly missed being called upon to advise in matters of wardrobe and etiquette, and Gil indulged her. To complement his darkness and unique eyes, Merry chose a dramatic outfit of black velvet and silver brocade, inset with royal purple silk panes. Gil had no personal jewelry but Kit loaned him a magnificent silver medallion with a great amethyst in the center, and the adornment flashed almost as brightly as his smile when he made his obeisance before the queen.

Merry was not mistaken in her prediction. Gil was a natural, and his wit and charm dazzled the ladies. More than a few gazed longingly at the comely Scot by the time he finished a lively trotto with the queen. Dancing lessons were mandatory at Edzell, for Lady Darra was the family representative in the Stuart court, and sought similar positions of respect for her brothers and sons. Gil embraced anything of a social nature with alacrity, while Merry doubted Ran had ever attempted so much as a leisurely bransle. She was pleased, however, Her Majesty approved of the dashing Gil, and the Lindsay name would not be unduly mocked.

Unfortunately, Sir Jasper Wickham joined the Court for the holidays. Merry found his sudden appearance more than a little disconcerting, but he was nothing if not fawningly gallant before the queen's watchful eye. Wickham kept company with other dissolute hedonists, and most particularly Penelope Rich, the daughter of Elizabeth's cousin, Lettice Lady Essex, and hence Robert Devereux's sister. Lady Rich was arguably one of the most beautiful and exotic women of the Court, a dramatic brunette, her skin lustrous like a fine pearl, her eyes alone fascinating for the fact they did not match in hue. Merry regarded Lady Rich as one might a jewel-toned snake, both mesmerizing and repelling at once. It came to her as no surprise that Wickham counted this woman of dubious morals among his circle of friends.

Merry encountered the loathsome couple several times during the Twelfth Night revelries. The first time, Wickham merely stopped and bowed exaggeratedly, while Lady Rich inclined her head in a chilly nod, and Merry did likewise. The next time she was with Gil, and she saw Essex's sister lick her full lips and regard the youth with a predatory gleam in her odd-colored eyes. Lady Rich obviously demanded an introduction, for Wickham brought her forward.

Civilities were exchanged while Lady Rich curtsied low before Gil, her full breasts nearly tumbling out of the deeply cut bodice. One could hardly miss the fact her areolae were rouged to match her cheeks, and Gil's flush betrayed his mixture of innocence and fascination with the mature beauty.

"*Enchanté,*" murmured Lady Rich as she rose, her husky voice prompting a visible shiver in poor Gil. He put her proffered hand hastily to his lips, and even after he released it, she held it there, brushing her knuckles back and forth across his lips in a teasing fashion.

Merry frowned and did not attempt to disguise her displeasure. Gil was too young and yet a neophyte at Court; furthermore the lecherous Lady Rich was old enough to be his mother.

"We must retire for the eve, 'tis getting late," Merry said to the bedazzled Gil, who nodded and gazed after Lady Rich's withdrawing hand. She turned the full force of her cloying court smile on Wickham and his brazen companion.

"You will forgive us? I fear the family awaits our return."

Wickham arched an eyebrow. He was clad in mulberry satin, his garish outfit pinked and paned to fashion's extreme, an enormous cartwheel ruff engulfing his neck to the chin. His pale blond hair was fussily arranged in the latest continental fashion, called a bull-tour, ends held in a short queue with a pearled clasp. Merry conceded he was handsome in a foppish sort of way, but she shuddered to imagine she might be his wife now.

"Naturally we must not waylay you, milady," he said with a sweeping bow almost as mocking as his gaze. "Dear Penelope was but curious as to the identity of your escort."

"Charming escort," Lady Rich amended, her eyes gleaming with a satisfied light as she glanced over Gil one last time. "My interest has been but whetted all the more, I vow."

Merry smiled through stiff lips. "Perchance our paths will cross again."

"Oh, I do not doubt it." Sir Jasper offered an ingratiating smile. "I shall insist upon nothing less."

Chapter Twenty-Nine

Soon the eve of the Twelfth Night masque was upon them, and whilst Ambergate bustled with the preparations, Merry stepped away a moment from her costume fitting to check on Siany. Since arriving in London, the girl had been little more than a headache, slipping off every time Merry or Nell's back was turned. 'Twas useless to scold or lecture, and any assigned tasks were completed grudgingly but well, giving no complaint for dismissal. In view of Siany's relation to Hertha, Merry could hardly discharge the chit in London and leave her to fend for herself on the streets.

Still, she grappled for patience every time she must needs confront the girl. Nell needed help with the baby so she could finish hemming Merry's costume, and, as usual, Siany had vanished at the opportune time. She could hardly ever be found in the morning. When she was not sulking in the servants' quarters in the afternoon, she could oft be found wandering the halls in a dreamy daze. After some minutes of fruitless searching, Merry encountered her wayward maidservant hurrying in from the cold, wearing naught but a light shawl. Siany's skin was very pale, but her eyes had a feverish sparkle.

Merry curbed her anger for a moment. "Are you ill, Siany?" she asked.

Vigorously the girl shook her head. By then, Merry had already noted the stains on the collar of her light-colored gown. "Something did not rest well with you, I see. This is nothing to trifle with. If 'tis a chance of ague or worse, the household must be forewarned."

Siany's shoulders seemed to sag a bit. "Nay, milady." She bit her lip, avoiding Merry's steady gaze. "There is nae risk t' the others."

"I am glad to hear it. Hmm. Is that kidney pie I smell baking in the ovens?"

At Merry's idle remark, Siany clapped a hand to her mouth and rushed past her mistress, banging through the door to her room below stairs. Merry heard the girl being wretchedly ill and hurried after her, finding Siany on her knees above the chamberpot.

"Sweet Jesu!" Merry exclaimed, as realization dawned. She could not help but feel sorry for the poor girl, and steadied her with an arm around the shoulders when she was through being ill. Merry guided the shaking Siany to her bed and insisted she rest while she fetched a cloth dipped in cool water and sponged the girl's sweaty forehead. "How far gone?" she asked matter-of-factly. She had not been raised a total innocent at Court; more than one maid-of-honor there had skulked away in disgrace.

Siany turned a miserable face to the wall. "Nigh two months, milady," she whispered.

"Does Hertha know?"

"Ohh, nay!" Siany gasped to imagine her grandmother's reaction. She curled up, hugging her knees to her chest. Never had a young face looked so tragic.

"Siany, I am most disappointed. Yet it takes two to dally, even in the Highlands. Who is the one responsible?"

Siany shuddered. "I canna say, milady. Dinna ask again."

Something in the girl's manner warned Merry not to press the issue, but she chafed with frustration. "The knave can be persuaded to honor the promise his loins made, m'dear. When you're ready to tell me, I am prepared to take swift action.''

Siany shook her head. '' 'Tis nae even an option, milady.''

''Why not? Is he betrothed to another? Dear heavens, not . . . married?''

The maidservant did not answer, not those questions or a dozen others put to her, but remained in a miserable silent huddle on the bed until Merry sighed with defeat and rose.

''I must attend the masque, but we shall speak again when I return. In the while, I will tell Nell you're ill and cannot tend Ashet. Although I am sure the experience will be sorely welcomed by midsummer.'' Merry left shaking her head, despairing over the situation but at a loss for any solution. If Siany would not name the father, there was nothing she could do to extract reparation from the rogue. She wished her parents had not returned to Ireland already, for her mother was a well of straightforward advice. Merry knew Slade and Bryony had not been wed ere long before the birth of the twins, and while it had shamed her for many years, it no longer mattered now.

The theme of the Twelfth Night masque was ''Fair Virgin Thron'd in the West,'' a phrase coined by Will Shakespeare in honor of Elizabeth Tudor. Earlier in the evening, the queen went in state to St. Paul's to offer thanksgiving for the country's strength and continued blessings of the New Year. Elizabeth was drawn in a coach by white horses surmounted by a canopy resting on pillars—two of them bearing a lion and a dragon, the supporters of the English arms. She was attended by the officers of the state and a great company of ladies and gentlemen from her Court. Thereafter the company adjourned to St. James's Palace and the revelries began in earnest.

Merry was lent use of her former apartment in the royal residence. Her former tiring-woman, Jane, now served Lady Scrope but stopped by to wish Merry well, and exclaim over the costume Merry had chosen. She and Gil were attending as Clove and Orange, after the term of intimacy derived from the custom of sticking oranges with cloves and roasting them during the holidays. The resulting liquor was called bishop, a rare pun on the Church, which might only be carried off with impunity during the mischief of Twelfth Night.

Merry's gown was a lavish concoction of burnt orange satin and cinnamon velvet, huge sleeves slashed and paned with gold silk and jet beads, with a gold-embroidered chemise and petticoats visible at her bosom and hem. Her hair flamed just as brightly as her costume, dressed high and threaded with tiny citrines and seed pearls. She wore a clove-studded orange pomander and her fan was dyed to match, orange feathers with gold-dipped points. Though identities were established early by the canny courtiers, the pretense was maintained until the light of dawn. Therefore, as a last touch, Nell fastened an orange silk half-mask over her mistress's face, and clapped with delight at the results.

"Ye look fair tasty, milady!" she cried. "Beware lest one o' the *Sassenach* scoundrels tries ta sample yer sweet juices."

Merry laughed. "I daresay he should get a bit more than he bargained for, Nell." She showed the wide-eyed maidservant the little jeweled dirk she kept up one sleeve. Since her mother had reminded her of Lovelle's previous treachery, she agreed 'twould be wise to have some means of defense in close quarters. Nell nodded. Practical Highland lasses ken a thing or two o' weapons, the maid mused, or what damage a swift-placed kick could do.

A lusty gallant greeted Gil and Merry as they entered the festive, foiled dancing hall where dancers already promenaded, leaping and turning in time to the beat, the ladies' skirts swirling like bevies of bright butterfly wings. The arrival of Clove and Orange caused a ripple of interest to run through those not presently engaged with the gallant. Gil looked exceptionally dashing in his dark-brown velvet doublet, slashed with gold silk to match Merry's gown, and knee-length breeches of a tan brocade patterned with gold. The "cloves" were tiny smoky quartz sewn all over his costume, casting a glittering reflection whenever he moved. Despite his mask, his identity was obvious enough, for all the ladies of the Court had exclaimed upon his beautiful violet-blue eyes before. Merry watched in amusement as every lady's hand he bowed over caused a resulting flutter or giggle in the one so honored; despite his youth, Gil was born to courtly ways.

Uncle Kit and Aunt Isobel had already arrived, and were comfortably ensconced at a banqueting table with fellow knights and ladies of similar rank. Kit was a "fox" as every year, since Elizabeth adored it so, and Isobel came as her lord husband's pretty little snow goose. She was garbed in pristine white satin with crystals sparkling over her skirts and hair, and waved a great feather fan to combat the stuffiness of the hall. Twelfth Night was the usual crush of revelers, some reeking of perfume and others sweat or ale, but excitement permeated the air and all heads craned as each new arrival was presented.

The queen had not yet appeared, doubtless awaiting the moment when her entrance could be made even more spectacular by the suspense preceding it. Elizabeth Tudor was nothing if not shrewd. Merry was relieved she had a moment to relax and circulate, and while Gil fetched her a plate from the vast spread of delicacies, she gazed over the colorful crowd. There was still a line of those waiting to be presented at the door, but some of the costumes must needs explaining and Merry laughed a little at the furious whispering going back and forth between the announcer and the impatient arrivals.

Gil reappeared and handed her a glass of malmsey and a little plate containing roast goose, several slivers of cheese, and sections of orange. She laughed and offered him one of the slices. While they were thus engaged in playful banter, the announcer's voice rang out over the crowd.

"The Earl and Countess of Crawford."

Merry froze, the orange slipping from her fingers to the plate. Could there possibly be another? She turned and Gil grabbed her elbow, held her fast.

Her startled gaze flew from him to the couple entering the

throng, amid whispers of confusion and uneasy laughter. The man, neither so tall nor broad as Ran, was outrageously garbed in a mock Highlander kilt, sporrie, and bonnet, walking knock-kneed on his companion's arm. 'Twas obviously Wickham despite the dark wig, and Merry drew herself up with outrage.

"Bastard," Gil seethed beside her. But the worst was yet to come. For "Lady Lindsay" was not a caricature of Merry, but Blair. The sight of the blond wig and grotesquely red smiling lips made Merry sick. Lady Rich, doubtless, or one of Wickham's other paramours; she'd heard he kept company with a lusty widow, too. How could even Wickham be so cruel?

Merry leaned against Gil for support, whispering, "Take me home."

He nodded, his eyes bright with rage and disgust. "They are not worthy of your presence, Merry." His contemptuous gaze took in the sniggering courtiers and ladies as well; only Sir Christopher and his wife realized the depth of evil intent behind Wickham's actions, and soberly, anxiously, watched Merry from across the hall.

Gil wrapped his arm protectively around his sister-in-law. Though Merry was older, she was petite enough to appear a waif under his guard as they headed for the exit, giving the mock Lindsays a wide berth.

"What, canna stay for the lively reel, lad?" Wickham called out in an exaggerated brogue, and beside him "Blair" pealed with laughter. Their goading remarks trailed Gil and Merry out the door, though Merry remained remarkably composed until they reached Ambergate. There she alternately wept and raged, both for their actions and for leaving without a final cut. Too late she thought of the little dagger; she should have thrust it in Wickham's black heart in passing!

Gil patted her shoulder awkwardly while she cried, then spoke to her in soothing tones when she stormed. "Och, Merry, 'tis glad I am for my own bungling attempt at highway robbery. If I had not foolishly waylaid your uncle's coach, you would be wed to that *Sassenach* snake."

"I know. Bless you, Gil." Merry smiled a little through the

remnants of her tears, and soon composed herself again with the aid of a stout port left in her uncle's library. She considered the wasted work and expense of their beautiful costumes, and sighed. "I suppose we can always sell them before we leave London."

"What's wrong with hosting your own ball sometime at Auchmull?" Gil suggested with a wink.

"Oh, certainly you jest. I know none to invite, and, besides, Ran would be furious."

Gil shrugged. "Darra and Fiona have all the connections you need, and as for Ran, he can go hang. You've brought light and laughter to that gloomy old keep, Merry, and I for one should be quite distressed if we did not permit the same for you."

Impulsively she set down the port and hugged the youth. "Gil, I count you among my dearest friends. You've grown into a fine young man, and I trow you have a position at Court if you but seek it."

"Aye. After tonight, I've no desire to associate with such cruel folk. 'Twas amusing for a spell, with the music and dancing and bonny lasses all about, but they lost my respect when they turned on you with Wickham's act. I wish now I'd gone reiving as Ran wanted me to. I'd show that smirking *Sassenach* swine a thing or two!"

Merry took her turn at calming the other, then hugged Gil again and wished him good night. As she started up the stairs, he announced he was returning to Scotland. She turned, her momentary lift of spirits gone.

"Why, Gil?"

He shook his head, shrugged. "I miss it, I suppose. Don't you?"

"Sometimes." Merry did not feel like lying. She missed the cozy hall and hearth, the laughter of Lindsay retainers and the gruff affection they bore for her. She missed her husband most of all, but Ran neither wanted nor needed her there. Her pride rebelled against the notion of returning so soon, crawling back in defeat after Wickham's public humiliation. God willing, Ran would never hear of what transpired tonight. His fury would make a frenzied wolf look tame by comparison.

Gil nodded, realizing the answer lay in her cautious reply. "I'd like to set out on the morrow. Your uncle promised to see you home in style and comfort whenever you wish, and there are things I can attend while Ran is busy with the king's rebels."

"I understand. But could you possibly take Siany with you? I fear she hasn't been well since we arrived."

"What's wrong?" He looked alarmed.

"Homesick, I think. Nothing serious, but she is pining for the Highlands." Merry smiled to disarm his visible concern. "I am sure Hertha is missing her terribly, too."

"All right. I'll leave Hugo here for now, hire a couple of men your uncle recommended. The border still isn't safe, especially with a pretty lass in tow." Gil grinned, and Merry was delighted to see the roguish twinkle had returned to his eye. He had already moved on, dismissed the Wickham incident, and 'twas the wise and healthy thing to do. Yet she knew she would agonize over her mistakes tonight as she did the countless ones she had made with Ran.

Chapter Thirty

Merry had vowed never to return to Court after the humiliation of Twelfth Night, but Uncle Kit insisted she must quickly reclaim her dignity and secure her status. Elizabeth Tudor proved quite querulous upon inquiring after the real Countess of Crawford and was not pleased to hear one of her ladies had left without permission. The queen had not seen the mocking charade Wickham and Lady Rich enacted, and thus it appeared Merry had dashed off in some flighty fit of emotion most unbecoming to a married woman.

Merry acknowledged the sense in her uncle's advice, and after Gil and Siany left for Scotland, she effected a move back into Whitehall where the Court adjourned for the remainder of the winter months. Nell would serve as her main tiring-woman, and another girl was secured for lesser errands and relieving Nell with the babe. The queen did not summon Merry for a week, annoyed as she was to have her masque disrupted, but in the end mighty Gloriana softened and Merry was restored to favor.

As one of Her Majesty's ladies-in-waiting, Merry's primary function was providing social diversion from the tedium of daily royal duties. Elizabeth conducted business in the morning, and dealt with the Privy Council generally until noon. If the sun was out later in the day, and the weather fair, she would walk in the gardens despite the chill. Otherwise, she strolled the galleries of the palace, attended by the favored members of her Court, including Lady Lindsay. The queen devoted part of every day to study, and was faithful to her religious exercises. Supper was the pleasurable conclusion to each day, always a chance for merriment and moments of mischief Elizabeth favored.

When the queen retired for the eve, she was accompanied by the married ladies of her household, one of whom always earned the privilege of sleeping in the royal bed chamber on a little trundle at the foot of the majestic canopied bed. In addition to the guards, several gentlemen of good repute took turns waiting up in an adjoining room, so their liege might be roused in any emergency. While Elizabeth was known to storm in her council, and on occasion slap a pert maid-of-honor, she was for the most part good-humored and tolerant. Few appreciated a keen wit more than England's domina, nor loathed dullards just as emphatically.

To Merry's dismay, Wickham had not left Court but continued as a hanger-on, his usual companion the notorious Lady Rich. Before long he had joined the circle of Essex's friends at Essex House, securing his position through the absent Earl of Leicester's reputation. However, noblemen and citizens whose loyalty was of doubtful character were known to frequent Essex House as well, and thus Elizabeth Tudor never came to fully trust the man.

Since the disastrous masque, Merry took care to avoid Wickham altogether, but 'twas impossible short of leaving Court. Besides, Sir Jasper openly curried her favor now, making a point to approach her whenever possible and gushing both apology and remorse for his moment of "unthinking mirth." Merry found nothing humorous in the memory or the man, and cut him coldly at each turn. Despite her frigid nature, he continued to subject her to a flurry of flattery and regrets, making her appear the cruel one before the queen.

"What tiresome feud is this, Madam Merry?" Elizabeth demanded one afternoon as they walked the gallery, after Sir Jasper threw up his hands in a dramatic gesture of surrender and left. "I' faith, never have I known you to be unkind. The fact you did not wed Wickham should scarcely be a point of contention now."

"Aye, Your Grace," Merry agreed, wondering how much she might explain before the other got impatient with her. She paused to admire a portrait of King Henry, Elizabeth's sire, but the queen was not distracted.

"Wouldst provoke Wickham to further scenes? Offer the kiss of peace, milady, and be done with it right quick."

Merry took a deep breath, nodded. She realized 'twas a royal order, though softened by the twinkle in Elizabeth's gray eyes.

" 'Pom my word, yer as stubborn as your mother at times." The queen laughed, seeing the resentment in Merry's expression. "Is't truly too humbling, m'dear?"

"I fear so, Your Majesty. Mayhap the Highlands have made me too proud by half."

Elizabeth regarded her a moment with an indulgent smile. " 'Tis true, you've changed. I rather fancy it. Just so your newfound impertinence never exceeds your loyalty."

"Never, Your Grace. This I vow with my life."

While Merry sampled court intrigues and conversed with the most powerful woman on earth, Ran found himself teetering on the edge of quiet despair. He had never expected to miss his wife, especially given the white-hot fury with which he had all but driven her from his household, but the weeks without Merry had proven surprisingly stark and empty. It came as a shock, for he had never considered something in his nature might crave the simple domesticity she offered. Auchmull's halls no longer rang with laughter, the hearth ceased to burn bright after Christmas morn. Blair's stolid portrait was little consolation when 'twas the warmth of a living woman he missed, the playful sparkle of rain-colored eyes or an impulsive kiss on the cheek.

Absently Ran traced his cheekbone, remembering Merry's little affections. 'Twas hard to resent one with such a giving heart and honest nature, whose almost childlike devotion to a cause could humble the greatest warrior. Even the Wolf of Badanloch was not immune to a stiff dose of humility now and then. His relentless hunt for the thieves finally met with success, led to the capture of a band of outlaws posing as Padons. The penalty for stealing from the king, whether a bull or a royal stag, was execution. Kidnaping one of the king's Cabinet was just as grave an offense. Not too many months ago, Ran would have swiftly dispensed justice himself. He was still raw from the incident with the Macleans, however, and did not like to envision Merry's expression if she heard her husband executed seven men.

Fortunately the king was not too pressed to deal with the outlaws, and they were removed to Edinburgh to await their grim fate. The indignant Sir Ian Coates returned to the Stuart Court little worse for wear, considering what might have happened. With the excitement of the chase concluded, Ran found himself looking home again. Missing Merry. Her mischievous little laugh, the way she tugged at his sleeve for attention. Her sweet, spoiled, whimsical ways no longer seemed shallow. Rather, he realized she was a woman with a great capacity for love.

Gil's return, his tales about Court and Merry's enthusiastic participation in the revelries there, made Ran feel worse. Naturally she would welcome a change from this dark keep and the brooding man who occupied it. Ran had little to offer a woman who rubbed elbows with nobles and gentry and even held the ear of a queen. He had preserved Merry's reputation by wedding her, but damned them both to a life of eternal misery.

Ran knew he had reacted much too strongly to the cradle incident, but the searing pain of the moment still haunted him. He doubted Merry had it in her to be deliberately cruel, but then reason fled when he had stepped into the hall, weary and disgusted at missing the outlaws, and glimpsed the manger scene beneath Blair's covered portrait. He regretted his rage, his accusations. None of it mattered now, for Merry had fled to nurse her wounds. Eventually she must return, however, and Ran decided a truce was the only means wherein they might coexist. If he let her have run of the household, which admittedly he did not mind too much, mayhap she would be happily occupied for a spell. 'Twas the most he could offer. He had neither the means nor the desire to sustain her forever at Court, and there would be no heirs unless he kept her home. Ran smiled a little at the memory of their far too few nights together. Merry was an innocent in many ways, but no husband could complain about her enthusiasm. If only he could love her as she deserved to be loved, Ran did not doubt the English rose would flourish beyond the dreams of the practical and poets alike.

Merry realized after Twelfth Night, she had little excuse to linger in London, but the thought of returning to Scotland and further humiliation at the hands of a man who did not, would not, ever love her was far more daunting. If there was one thing every Tanner had in ample measure, 'twas pride. Ran had promised to care for her, respect her, but suddenly 'twas not enough anymore. She watched true lovers at Court, heard the romantic tales again of Raleigh defying the queen for love of Bess Throckmorton, and Dudley for Lettice Knollys, and decided she deserved as much. In truth, the fear of rejection was just as daunting as the reality. She could not compete with a ghost, nor Ran's sacrosanct memories of Blair. She did not even wish to try.

Her quiet dignity and single-minded devotion to the queen was oft remarked upon now, for Lady Lindsay was accounted uncommonly subdued. Formerly Merry had led the maids-of-honor in all sorts of mischievous outings and outrageous deeds, though always stopping short of serious consequences. Marriage had lent her a grave air in some fashion, this remarked upon with admiration by Elizabeth, and regret by her former companions. Merry still danced upon occasion, but rarely, and preferred the position of onlooker to that of participant. She could not have explained herself why she withdrew from the festivities, except it offered ample excuse to avoid Wickham and Lady Rich, the latter who seemed to have taken it upon herself to torture Merry whenever occasion arose. If Essex had been petty and cruel, his beautiful sister was crueler yet, her ingratiating smile and dismissing look calculated to humiliate Merry whenever their paths crossed. Penelope had never forgiven Merry for snatching Gilbert Lindsay away from her predatory aims; she was unaccustomed to being denied anything, especially the company of any man she chose.

One evening, the queen specifically requested Merry's presence at a minstrel and musical performance. Elizabeth Tudor was skilled upon the virginals, and oft accompanied her Court musicians. Previously Merry had served as Mistress of the Music, a position which entailed little more than turning pages for Her Grace and keeping the musical score in order. The queen expressed dissatisfaction with Merry's replacement, and wished a competent hand for the critical performance. Given little chance to demur, Merry appeared in a simple but fine raiment, an emerald-green brocade gown embroidered with the figures of the nine Muses in gilt thread. She could hardly hope to compete with Elizabeth's magnificence, for the queen had no less than three thousand robes, in every conceivable fashion and material ranging from cut velvets to butterfly-thin silks, all with requisite trim like exquisite ruffs and jeweled purpoints.

For her debut in the musical version of Spenser's *Faerie Queene,* Elizabeth wore a gown of silver tissue trimmed with pearls, small diamonds sewn across the full skirts in a starburst pattern, a larger stone nestled on her bosom in a frill of silver lace. To complete the ethereal look, she fancied a white velvet cape which flowed fully a pace behind, trimmed with pale blue and silver braid and fastened with a sapphire clasp. When seated at the keyboard, her cape was so heavy several maids-of-honor were summoned to hold up the ends and relieve the burden of weight from the queen's shoulders and effectively permit her full range of movement.

Courtiers and ladies politely gathered round for the performance. Among the flock was Wickham, though Merry did not see Lady Rich at his side. After the musical, the queen retired to her throne, resting and listening to the minstrels sing, "The Silver Swan." Elizabeth nodded off during the rendition, and Wickham seized opportunity. Merry stiffened warily at his approach, but dared not make a public spectacle.

"Well met, milady," Sir Jasper began, lifting her hand and brushing it against his lips. Merry nodded but did not feign any warmth. He smiled and held her hand a moment longer than necessary. "I see you have not yet forgiven me for the little faux pas of Twelfth Night. Perforce my regrets must follow me forevermore."

"There is no need for dramatics, Sir Jasper," Merry coolly replied. "Lest you seek position among the queen's fools, and then I should be pleased to recommend you."

Wickham inclined his head at her cut. "No less than deserved, my dear." He had adopted a more masculine appearance of late, exchanging pastel satins for jewel-toned velvets and fur-trimmed surcoates and cloaks. His topaz outfit was trimmed with scrimshaw buttons, with a faintly naval flair. 'Twas still fashionable to imitate the late Sir Francis Drake. A pouch and ornate dagger hung from his belt, and he struck a pose which might have awed any woman but Merry.

"Alas, I must inquire after Lord Lindsay," Wickham said. "Have you heard from your husband of late?"

Merry regarded him warily. "Why?"

" 'Tis but a simple yea or nay I require, milady. Have you?"

She considered lying, but suspected Wickham had several well-placed spies. "Nay."

"Ah, 'tis as I suspected. Doubtless he has been too busy . . . with other concerns."

Something in his hesitant, yet suggestive manner provoked her curiosity. "What have you heard, Sir Jasper?"

He shook his head, stroked his pointed beard as if wrestling with his conscience. "Nasty gossip, no doubt. I should not have troubled you with it, m'dear. Besides, you are far from Scotland and such petty disputes now. 'Tis advisable you remain so."

"What have you heard?"

Wickham's eyebrow arched at her emphatic demand. He sighed. "You would force m'hand, I see. Very well. There has been . . . trouble on my lands, in my absence. Someone has availed themselves not only of Braidwood cattle, but left out-buildings aflame . . . a parting blow."

"You immediately assumed 'tis Ranald." Merry regarded him with a challenging air.

"Not at first, nay. I truly believed our disagreement settled when I left Auchmull. I vowed to avoid Lindsay at all costs and have managed it admirably well, I believe. Nor am I the only one who has suffered at the hands of this mysterious villain. English strongholds up and down the border are reporting smash-and-grab assaults, though my properties appear hardest hit.

"This has been going on for nearly a fortnight, on a nightly basis. There are a few who have reported glimpses of the man, though 'tis fleeting. Instead of a band of reivers, he operates alone, making it harder to track his movements, or trap him in the act of committing such crimes."

Merry shook her head, denying the possibility, while at the same time her innards churned with fear. She had to admit, Ran had more than enough motive to hurt Wickham. If his previous hatred was not enough, the proof she had flung at him during their confrontation was enough to engender the sort of burning resentment which might well explode into flames of vengeance now.

She looked at Wickham levelly. "I fail to see what you expect me to do, sirrah. Ran has no obligation toward me, nor would he necessarily tell me the truth if I asked him."

"Aye, I realized as much myself. Which is why I did not care to trouble you. 'Tis but a word of warning you might pass on, if you should hear from Lord Lindsay, because such incidents must needs be reported to the queen very soon. I have abstained till now, for fear of incurring your further resentment when I have sought amends for previous wrongdoing.''

Merry was silent a moment. "You must do as you see fit," she said at last.

"Aye, milady. I fear I must."

Chapter Thirty-One

Shortly before Candlemas, Merry received urgent word from her uncle Kit at Court. She had retired to Ambergate for the holiday, her first relief from serving the queen since she arrived. Her peaceful retreat was shattered with the news: a border warrant had been issued by Elizabeth against Ranald Lindsay. The raids had not ceased since Wickham's complaint, but rather increased in frequency and severity until other border lords began clamoring for royal justice. The evidence mounting against Ran was serious enough that his identity was no longer in question. The Wolf of Badanloch was legendary enough in the north; accusations of outlawry seemed less outrageous than the idea he had settled down peaceably for the winter.

Hearing this, Merry flew back to Court with the intent of pleading the queen's ear, but Elizabeth was indisposed with her Privy Council and no immediate recess was in sight. While she was there, a message came from Lady Rich. Merry considered tossing it out, but curiosity got the better of her and she read it. 'Twas an invitation, rather a plea couched in flowery language, asking "the honorable Lady Lindsay" to attend Essex House as soon as possible. Merry puzzled over the message, as she knew Lady Rich bore her no lost love. Perhaps 'twas another jest, a second chance to mock an abandoned wife?

In the end, reason prevailed over paranoia and Merry went to Essex House. Lady Rich had stayed in her brother's residence during his Irish campaign, doubtless for its convenience to Court. Merry was admittedly impressed by the elegant residence, famed for its lavish entertainments. The powerful charm of the siblings who held sway over courtly events was based here, and she drank in the aura of the richly foiled hall while she waited for Penelope.

She was studying a Hilliard of the famous beauty herself when Lady Rich appeared. The two women greeted each other civilly, but Merry's attention was immediately drawn to the greenish and purple tinges beneath the brunette's exotic eyes. Lady Rich smiled a little wryly.

"Now y'see why I have not attended Court of late, Lady Lindsay."

Merry was still reeling with shock. "Pray tell, who did this to you?" She was horrified by the bruises; though obviously fading, 'twas clear Penelope had been beaten and quite severely.

"Wickham. 'Tis fortunate I did not lose more than a tooth, and that from a remote place which shall not permanently mar my looks." Lady Rich gingerly touched her jaw. She understood Merry's dazed state quite well. "Aye, I did not believe it at first . . . until he came at me in a sudden rage, and boxed me fiercely. Then he slammed me against a wall, struck me several times and later raped me on the floor." She gestured almost casually to a Turkish carpet of forest green, crimson and white before the hearth, and Merry shuddered.

"I am so sorry. What triggered the rage . . . d'you know?"

"Yea. 'Twas the night of the masque. We came back here after you left. I was still garbed as . . . the first Lady Lindsay."

Merry gasped. "Blair! You looked like Blair . . ." It made a terrible, ironic sort of sense, even though Penelope did not deserve to suffer for Wickham's evil plan.

"Aye, and Jasper was drunk. Fearfully so." Lady Rich

stroked her bruised cheek and shivered at the memory. "I remember, we were laughing. He was pleased by the success of his cruel charade and I had found it amusing also; after all, you had secured your brother-in-law from my clutches with great success." She smiled with a trace of irony. "Anyhow, we kept drinking . . . and I proposed a playful romp, never suspecting my attire might rouse the beast in the man."

Merry briefly closed her eyes, nodding. She feared she knew the rest of the story already. Lady Rich confirmed her suspicions that Wickham and Blair had been lovers; he muttered filthy phrases during their rutting, alternately laughed at Ran for being a cuckold, and cursed "Blair" for her stupidity in getting her belly up again. Apparently the two had been lovers before she wed Ran; there was mention of timely fortune in losing another babe. Sickened, Merry sank down into a chair as Lady Rich continued the tale. She trembled with indignation for Ran, felt disgusted and outraged over Wickham and Blair's actions.

"At first I did not care; I bear the Lindsays no loyalty, and Jasper has been a generous benefactor. I even found the notion of him with another woman a bit titillating. Alack, he started acting very oddly . . . threatening me. 'Twould seem Lady Blair was blackmailing him with her belly, doubtless saying she would go to her husband if he did not comply with her demands for money and favors."

Merry nodded; now it made sense why Blair had gone to Braidwood—she was determined to wrest something more from her lover. Darra was right, 'twas no coincidence at all. Blair was not innocently wandering the heather-clad hills, collecting herbs; she was meeting Wickham, demanding accounts due. Her death was still certainly suspect, judging by Lady Rich's bruises, but Merry was sure Ran would have demanded further investigation if Blair's body had shown any sign of abuse. Therefore, Wickham was guilty of nothing at this juncture except adultery, and men were hardly held accountable as women were. Going to the queen was a mixed call.

Lady Rich saw Merry's distress, and in a surprising gesture reached out and hugged the younger woman. "Count your blessings you did not marry Jasper, my dear,'' she said. ''Else I shudder at the image of your lovely face and body. He was . . . quite thorough in his abuse.''

Merry returned the hug, sensing Penelope was sincere. She might never like the woman, or approve of her morals, but she knew Devereux's sister was genuinely distressed by Wickham's behavior. So was she. Whatever had led Blair to the villain's bed, and kept her cuckolding Ran, was no excuse for Sir Jasper's foul nature. The challenge yet remained, whether she should approach the queen. Or Ran. Not that the latter would believe her even now, for any who rocked Blair Lindsay's pedestal suffered the consequences . . . in spades.

Merry never found opportunity for confrontation. Nor did she need to, for Wickham brought matters to a head within a few days. For some time, he had exceeded the queen's Chancellor Sir Christopher Hatton in his obsequious fawning over the throne's occupant, offering much amusement to the worldlier courtiers who saw through Wickham's disguise. Elizabeth tolerated Sir Jasper, but did not bear the fondness for him as she did her "sheep." She was not above boxing a knave's ears, either, and had once given Gilbert Talbot, the Earl of Shrewsbury's son, a sharp rap on the forehead when he glanced into the queen's bedchamber and saw her in her nightcap.

One eve at Hatfield House, Wickham had ingratiated himself enough that Her Majesty permitted him the honor of accompanying her in a stately pavane. By this time, Lady Rich had also rejoined Court, though Merry noted the woman avoided Wickham. At one point during the procession, Sir Jasper tread upon the queen's train, and Elizabeth was quick to react. She rapped him smartly on the knuckles with her feather fan where he gripped her arm, and Wickham flushed with rage. He snatched the fan from her grasp and flung it on the floor, and while onlookers gaped in horror, he crushed it with his heel. Elizabeth Tudor, pale but proud, pointed a shaking finger at the offender.

"One more move, sirrah, and 'tis the Tower where you will finish this pavane."

Wickham scrambled to offer reparation, having obviously succumbed in a flash of hot rage. Merry wondered if a similar loss of control might have provoked his attack on Lady Rich, and perhaps Blair as well. Yet the lack of bruises on Blair's body was mystifying. Hertha and Ran had mentioned nothing about such evidence.

Merry noticed the queen's nostrils flared with anger, her eyes flashing, even after Wickham's apology. Mayhap now was her chance. With her head held high, Merry stepped forward and stated, " 'Tis well you bear a high title, Your Grace. Else you should be the recipient of far worse than a groveling little speech."

Wickham glared at Merry, and Elizabeth's fine eyebrows arched. "By the mass! What sayeth you, Lady Lindsay? What of the kiss of peace?"

"I beg your pardon, Your Majesty. I cannot conceal my ire any longer. Not when the man who accuses my lord husband of nefarious deeds is more than guilty of the like."

She looked for Lady Rich to come forward, but was not surprised when the woman quickly melted into the throng. No mind. She would lay her cards on the table, let Elizabeth judge for herself. Penelope could always be coerced or forced under oath at a later date. Right now, she had to bluff through the inquisition. Fortunately she had always been a sharp at cards.

Meeting Wickham's glare levelly, Merry stated, "I am aware of the circumstances of your relationship with the former Lady Lindsay, sir."

"Madness," Sir Jasper snapped.

"Aye, I would term it thusly. Certainly, cuckolding the Wolf of Badanloch could not be considered an exercise in great wisdom."

Elizabeth Tudor listened intently, her gray eyes keen upon one speaker, then the other. She contrasted Merry's firm demeanor with Wickham's flushed face and trembling hands, and came to her own conclusion. Though she disliked such scenes, considered them boorish and unworthy of her Court, she knew Merry took her duties very seriously and would not have countermanded an order to make peace unless she was grievously injured.

"I'faith, what prompts such charges?" Elizabeth inquired.

Merry tore her challenging gaze from Wickham, and lowered it before the queen. "Lady Rich, Your Grace. The latest victim of his wrath."

Elizabeth looked surprised, but before the queen could summon Lady Rich, Merry added, "The lady in question has already fled, Your Majesty. I believe you will find her at Essex House. 'Tis more to this tale than meets the eye. Much more."

"Your Grace, I beseech you, do not fall prey to the clever speeches of those who would smear my good name. 'Tis an outrage, this woman who I once betrothed in all good conscience should turn on me now, to protect her kidnapper." Wickham's grimace was more a sneer, ripping all the way down Merry's rigid frame. She met him squarely on.

"Shall I tell Her Grace what you said and did to Lady Rich in detail, or perchance d'you wish the lady involved to share the sordid tale in private chambers?"

Pale gray eyes fixed on her malevolently. "Say whatever y'wish, madam," he retorted. "And be damned for it."

Wickham spun on his heel, thrust through the gaping crowd. Merry glanced at the queen, but Elizabeth made no move as yet. Rather the queen appeared thoughtful.

"I will have a word with Lady Rich, y'may be sure of it," she told Merry at last. "Yet this does not alter the grave charges brought against Lord Lindsay. Alack, it might lend further credence to m'border warrant, if your lord has such true motive for making Wickham's life hell."

Merry nodded. "I thought of that, Your Majesty. 'Twas a risk I was willing to take, rather than remaining silent. If . . . if Ran 'tis guilty of such crimes, he must pay the consequences as any who flout the laws, Scottish or English."

Elizabeth regarded her a moment, then nodded gravely.

"Yea, Madam Merry, you have grown up, indeed. Methinks you represent the House of Lindsay well."

Merry smiled a little. "I am pleased you find it so, Your Grace."

Sir Jasper slammed the door behind him, causing the woman reclining on the fringed velvet chaise longue to jump.

"How did you get in?" Lady Rich scrambled to her feet, clasping her silken robe closed with her fist. Her dark hair tumbled about her lush figure. "I ordered I was not to be disturbed!"

He heard the vein of fear running through her shrill voice, and smiled cruelly. " 'Tis pointless to hide from me, Penelope. Even your servants flee when I crook my little finger. There are none to defend you now, not with your precious bastard brother floundering about somewhere in Ireland."

She stared at him, eyes wild and dark, her breast heaving with emotion. "If you touch me, Bess will hear of it!" she cried. "I will go straight to Whitehall, I swear it."

"Bitch! D'you think I care now?" he snarled, sweeping a vase off a table with his fist. It shattered at her feet, while she sobbed with fear. "I have nothing to lose since you betrayed me. Your glaring fault, besides your vanity, is your greedy nature, m'dear. If you had accepted the reasonable sum I offered for your silence, you would be peacefully slumbering at this moment."

"Like Blair?" she hurled back shakily, her stance defiant despite her terror.

Wickham almost admired Penelope; she was a shallow, selfish, cold-blooded beauty he understood quite well. She was the perfect mistress for a dark-soured man like him . . . until she began to question his decisions. Shared her concerns with Ran's little bride.

Reminded of her betrayal, his initial flush of rage turned to calculating ice. He took a step towards her, and Penelope shrank against the velvet-flocked wall of her boudoir.

"Jesu, nay . . ." she whispered.

Jasper thrilled at the sound of her whimpers, her eloquent pleas. He did so like to hear women beg. The little servant girl he had mounted at Falkland, the ones he ruled at Braidwood with a mixture of terror and generosity, another saucy blond wench . . . he had lost count long ago, but of them all, Blair had been the best. Her sky-blue eyes, hazy with passion as she writhed upon his aroused body, still had the power to make him hard. He felt his loins stir now, remembering the wild, frantic coupling in the glen, the stables, Braidwood's bedchamber . . . wherever and whenever he could shove up Blair's skirts and tumble her. Aye, he had loved her . . . as much as he could love any woman, and she was a proud, canny Highlands lass, half bitch and half angel, too much for any man. Jasper raged with jealousy when she wed the Wolf of Badanloch.

Despite her promiscuous nature, Blair wanted nothing more than a wedding ring and a title to ease the taint of her own bastardy. Jasper had no intention of wedding the slut, no matter how enticing her wares, for he could not bear the thought of her standing mother to Wickham heirs, not when she was of dubious birth herself and willing to lift her skirts for any randy knave. *His* wife would be a virgin of good birth and generous dower, not some Highland bawd.

When Jasper refused to marry Blair, she wed Ranald Lindsay in a gesture of purest spite. Knowing she carried Jasper's seed, she still held sway over her former lover, and taunted him mercilessly. If she could not have Braidwood, she would have a third of his annual rents and tithes. Blair had only to whisper in her lord husband's ear, and Jasper knew his life was forfeit at any time. The Wolf would not be merciful. 'Twas a frenzy of frustration and rage which finally pushed him over the edge, the last time Blair visited Braidwood.

How sweet she looked, garbed in turquoise purled satin, cradling her swelling belly in silent reminder of the power she wielded. Jasper seethed, simultaneously lusting and loathing, longing to wrap his hands around her fragile ivory neck even as he kissed her fiercely.

"I do believe," Blair had said, "yer a wee bit behind in yer monthly tithes, m'laird."

Her blue eyes gleamed with a mocking light, and something in Jasper snapped. The last thing he remembered was flying at her, but in the last seconds he restrained himself, a calculating calm descending . . . almost eerily . . .

He had clutched Blair by the upper shoulders as comprehension slowly had dawned in her loch-blue eyes; she seemed almost resigned to her fate, or mayhap he imagined it. He crushed his lips down on hers, one final time, weeping with fury and lust as his hand tore the Maclean badge from her shawl and drove the pin beneath her hair . . . in the delicate point between skull and neck.

Looking at Penelope now, trapped sniveling in the corner, he felt a similar frisson of anger, though not nearly as intense. He did not love this woman as he had loved Blair. Her betrayal was a vicious blow, but nothing he could not return in kind. Penelope's eyes widened. She knew, even before he raised a hand. She did not try to flee.

Chapter Thirty-Two

"If I must, I will sell every last bit of jewelry I own, and buy a nag myself."

Merry regarded her uncle defiantly from across the desk, and after a heavy sigh, Sir Christopher Tanner shook his head with resignation. "I cannot countenance the notion of you and Nell dashing off without a proper full escort, m'dear. Remember what happened last time."

"Aye, but I have no choice. Gil already returned to Scotland, you are indisposed at Court, and 'tis urgent I reach Auchmull before disaster strikes."

"There is naught you can do, Merry, if Lord Lindsay is involved in the border raids. Plead with him, mayhap, but he does not seem particularly inclined to listen to an Englishwoman. 'Tis far safer and wiser if you remain here until the queen's men have investigated the matter further."

"Leaving Ran to face Wickham without warning?" Merry's eyes flashed and Kit realized the depth of her emotion for the Wolf of Badanloch. She was fiercely protective of a man who did not even love her. He worried her loyalty was misplaced, but he could not deny Wickham had proven an odious fellow with a devastating history. A few days ago, Lady Rich was discovered at Essex House by her maid, badly beaten, almost to the point of unconsciousness, but by the time word reached the queen, Wickham had fled Court. Back to his stronghold in the north, no doubt, or else into hiding where one of his evil cronies could shelter him.

"Nevertheless, 'tis a matter between Lindsay and Bess Tudor now," Kit chided her gently, setting down his feather pen. "Bess has heard the worst of Wickham and is surely prepared to deal with the man as she sees fit. You'll only endanger yourself and perhaps Ranald as well if you interfere."

"Interfere!" Merry exclaimed. " 'Twas those two who dragged me into their feud in the first place. Need I remind you, Kit, 'twas Ran who took advantage of my accident. An accident which resulted in the utter devastation of your finest coach."

Kit chuckled, and Merry regarded him with frustration. He and Aunt Isobel had warmly welcomed Gilbert, the very rogue responsible for the loss of their finest possession. Merry knew the fine coach had taken years of saving and excruciating service at Court to obtain. Her uncle said Ran had already sent payment, which he promptly declined. She did not understand his reasoning or lack of anger.

"Well," Kit said with visible amusement, "your new family has already handily dispensed with my best rig, and I fear I still require the services of the old, so the old-fashioned way must serve."

"A wheelbarrow?" Merry laughed despite her agitation over the situation.

Kit's green eyes twinkled. "What, and ruin those fine gowns of yours? Never . . . nay, I propose you borrow one of my swiftest mounts, and accept my personal escort in addition to Hugo's. Doubtless if I do not go along with this mad impulse, you will slip off in the night like a wraith bent upon sheer mischief and do so anyway."

Merry nodded. "Aye, quite true. Will Her Majesty spare you ere long, though? She seems agitated without her 'fox.' "

"My dear Merry, at my age, I fear I no longer quail at the thought of Bess's temper." Kit chuckled and rose from his desk, abandoning accounting for the far greater lure of adventure. He extended an arm to her in an exaggerated, gallant gesture. "Shall we away, Lady Lindsay? Before dear Bess sets the royal hounds on this fox's tail, I should like to make the border, at least."

Nell sat beside Hugo in a cart during the journey north, responsible for overseeing her mistress's baggage as well as tending the baby. She and Hugo chattered idly about the winter weather and the fine spring to come. Nell was aware of the depth of Hugo's interest in her when he asked her why she had never remarried after Fergus's death.

"I'm no spring chicken," she replied, modestly lowering her eyes, but she was secretly pleased by his question.

"Neither are ye an old hag, Nell," Hugo said, cracking the whip smartly over the team of mules.

"Why, thank ye, Hugo Sumner. I'll take that as a compliment."

"As ye should, woman," he growled under his breath. Her nonchalant air piqued his interest more. He had been fascinated with Nell the first moment he laid eyes on her at Auchmull. "Hae ye found no fellow ye fancy, then?"

Nell pursed her lips as if deep in thought. "Well, one," she admitted at last, amused when she saw his hands visibly tighten on the reins. "He dinna seem to be all that interested in me, though."

"I find that verra hard to believe. The mon's either blind or an utter fool."

Nell shrugged. "Mayhap. Anyway, I've caught him looking at me many a time, but he ne'er presents his suit. Like as nae, I'm too old for him. I'm nearly twenty-four, ye ken."

"Fool!" Hugo exploded. "Dinna he ken the seasoned lasses are the best? The riper the fruit, the sweeter the juices."

"How would ye know?" Nell mischievously teased.

Hugo's face flushed dull red under his shaggy blonde fore-lock. "Yer an impertinent wench, Nell Downie!"

"Privilege of age," she retorted, tossing her skirts over his knees. Hugo glanced down and scowled, but didn't make a move to push the material off his lap. Nell smiled to herself. Siany might have won the water draw at Goldielands, but Nell knew for a certainty she'd be remarried within the year.

Several days later, Merry stood in Ran's study again. The room held a faint scent, of leather and horseflesh and mellow tobacco. The man himself was long gone. Raiding the border or harassing Braidwood, she knew not. She was afraid to find out. With a little sigh, she ran her fingers over the glossy desk Ran used when he balanced his accounts. Unlike most lords, he did not employ a seneschal or steward to see to his affairs, but seemed to enjoy the direct experience and control that such personal accounting afforded him. Inkwell and pen were still in place where he had left them, and Merry paused to pick up the latter, balancing the elegant gold barrel in her hand. A slight rustling sound nearby caused her to drop the writing instrument, and the nib full of dark ink splattered across Ran's papers like blood.

"Siany."

Merry immediately recognized the girl standing in the deep shadows, half hidden by the velvet curtains. At first she was bewildered by the girl's furtive stance, then suspected she had interrupted something when she noted the papers askew on the desk. As she spoke, she calculated what this might mean.

"What are you doing in here?" Merry decided the best defense was an offense, for she knew those on the staff were forbidden to enter Ran's private study when he was gone.

Realizing she was caught, Siany stepped forward, and the lamplight gleamed down the length of her pale hair. "I hae a right to ken if Lord Ran provided for me and m'bairn son before he left," she boldly stated.

Merry recognized the undertone of challenge in the young

woman's words and arched an eyebrow. "I have no idea if he did or not," she replied coolly. "However, we both know Ran looks after the welfare of those in his demesne. After your reluctance to admit your plight to me, I am surprised you confessed it to Lord Lindsay."

Siany didn't answer for a moment. "Because I decided ye were right, the father owes me. If Lord Lindsay does nae come back, I want yer assurance that ye'll nae drive me and the bairn away," she said defensively. "Auchmull is my home, and I hae nowhere else to go."

"Are you implying Ran is the father of your child, Siany?"

The girl regarded her with cool blue eyes. "Will ye run me off now, milady?"

Merry felt an intense pang of doubt and pain, but was careful not to let it reflect in her expression. "D'you truly believe I'm that sort of woman?" she asked. When there was no reply, she sighed and said, "Of course you may stay, Siany, whatever the circumstances. The child is innocent. I only ask you keep the matter of your former relationship with Lord Lindsay discreet. I've no wish to be made the laughingstock of the Highlands."

Siany's blue eyes gleamed for a moment. "Former, milady? Are ye truly so naive?"

Merry's stomach tightened from the calculated blow. This time she could not disguise her distress. Noting the reaction, Siany shrugged.

"Ah, poor Lady Merry. Did ye never suspect? Yer husband took me again for his lover right after ye two were wed." She smirked at Merry, enjoying the abrupt change of control, and Merry's visible shock and uncertainty.

"Mind ye, milady, if yer planning to toss me out, I think he'll stop ye. I've no doubt Lord Lindsay loves me."

"Then why didn't he marry you instead of me?"

The girl's eyes flashed. "Because he willna wed a bastard lass again!" she hissed. "He made a dire mistake wi' Lady Blair, he says, and nearly lost his people's faith. Ye ken Lord

Ran also needs a legal heir, though he's promised to acknowledge my wee laddie as his own."

As the upsetting conversation progressed, Hertha passed through the downstairs corridor, having turned over the task of unpacking trunks to one of the lesser maids. She overheard the rising voices coming from Lord Lindsay's study, and paused for a moment in the hall. Hertha thought she recognized one of the voices as belonging to her own granddaughter. A second later, she was sure. Horrified to think Siany might be causing trouble for Lord Ran or Lady Merry, she reached for the latch and inched the door open, just in time to overhear her granddaughter's latest remark.

"He does nae love ye, milady. He could nae love any *Sassenach.*" The girl was gloating. "He wed ye on royal command, and yer just a means to an end. Gie him a legitimate son, and then get out. Yer nae wanted here. Lord Ran has Auchmull and me, and 'tis more than enough for him."

Hearing this, Hertha hurled open the door with a great crash against the wall, and rushed in to grab her wayward granddaughter by the ear. As Siany shrieked in rage and pain, Hertha exclaimed, "Ye lying little slut! How dare ye speak so to Lady Merry? Ye'll apologize at once."

"Never!" Siany cried, and shrieked again when her grandmother's palm lashed out and left a stinging imprint on her left cheek.

Stunned by the scene being played out before her eyes, Merry tried to diffuse Hertha's anger against her granddaughter, but this time 'twas the retainer who held the trump card, and who was determined to set matters aright.

"Tell Lady Merry the truth, Siany Gill," Hertha calmly threatened, giving the tender earlobe a twist which set Siany to howling anew. "Or by heavens I'll rip off yer ears, the pair of them, and feed them ta the stable curs."

" 'Tis true!" Siany defiantly cried.

"Och, ye canna expect me to believe that, little lass, when I've seen ye wi' my own eyes sneakin' back from Braidwood more than once. I held my tongue, but I will nae do so any longer. 'Tis long past time for yer comeuppance, my gel. Ye'll get it now.''

Taking a deep breath, Hertha continued. ''I never told anyone who sired ye, Siany, because yer mum was too ashamed and sickened to tell a soul the truth. Yer real father was a wicked man, a verra evil one who fancied sweet young lasses, and took his pick wi' out paying heed to the consequences. Near twenty summers ago he found Alyce to his liking, had his way wi' her, left her for dead. 'Twas Lord Ran's father who found me bairn, cleaned up her wounds, and both her an' the bairn when 'twas found she was wi' child.''

For a moment, Siany was stunned into silence. ''I always thought Rhynd Crawford was my father,'' she said at last in a stricken voice. ''I hae his features, Mum said more than once.''

Hertha laughed, a low and bitter sound. ''Aye, Alyce let the others assume what they would. Ye've always fancied puttin' on airs, my gel, and ye've run a cruel course for the other kitchen lasses wi' all yer nonsense stories about bein' a bastard Lindsay born on the wrong side o' the blanket. Dinna be too disappointed, lass. Yer gentry-blooded, all right. Just nae Rhynd Crawford's brat.''

The silence was terrible. Merry saw the explosion coming a split second before Siany herself did.

''Nay!'' the girl cried at last, a scream of pure denial, but Hertha continued in a surprisingly calm vein:

''Aye, ye foolish chit. Sir Robert Wickham was yer sire.''

Siany looked ready to swoon from the shock. Merry rushed forward, held her up on one side. Against her will, she found herself pitying the girl.

''Nay,'' Siany moaned, and a second later her eyelids flickered open on Hertha. ''I hae coupled wi' Sir Jasper only once, and he's nae the father of my bairn.''

''Neither is Lord Ran,'' Hertha said sternly.

Miserably Siany shook her head. ''Nay,'' she admitted in a low whisper, avoiding Merry's gaze. Siany sounded defensive, rather than ashamed.

''I could use a few extra groats,'' she sullenly explained

when Merry asked her why she had invented such a tale. "I hoped ye might offer me some money to leave Auchmull. I've always wished for a grand life."

"After which you would come back periodically for more funds," Merry said with disgust. The girl didn't deny it.

Though Merry was hurt and infuriated by Siany's lies, Hertha looked by far the more upset. She obviously found it hard to believe she could have raised such a calculating child.

"Ye hae yer father's bad blood," the woman said at last, turning free of Siany's ear. "I wash my hands of ye."

Siany's eyes unexpectedly filled with tears. Clearly she hadn't expected such dire consequences from her actions.

"Oh, Gran'mum," she begged, "dinna disown me! I'll apologize to Lady Merry, even Lord Ranald himself, if'n ye wish."

Hertha's expression didn't soften in the slightest. She shook her head, looking weary. " 'Twill nae be enough this time, Siany. I wanted ye heart and soul even though ye were nae a child born of love. Ye've repaid my kindness and care o'er the years wi' lies and cruelty to the few others I care about. Still ye stand here and lie to m'face. Nay, lass, I gave ye every benefit of the doubt for sixteen long years. I've nae more ta gie."

Sobs began to wrack Siany's slight frame, but Hertha was not moved. Taking Merry's arm instead, she said quietly, "Ye look in dire need of some peace, milady. Come, I'll see to it ye finally get some."

Merry was about to protest, realizing the matter was far from resolved, but she never had a chance. For a shrill cry suddenly pierced the halls of Auchmull, and as the women looked at each other in mutual alarm, Nell's voice was finally distinguishable above the rising din.

"Someone left a message wi' the guard at the gate," she cried. "Edzell is under attack!!"

Chapter Thirty-Three

Hearing this, Merry's blood turned to icewater in her veins. She rushed past Hertha and Siany, into the hall below the gallery where Nell was frantically trying to order the visibly stunned staff to organize the castle defenses. Recognizing her mistress, Nell nearly crumpled, but managed to grab fast of the iron handrail and came stumbling down the stone steps as fast as she could.

"Lady Lindsay!" she wailed, and the impact of her small figure nearly knocked Merry flat as Nell flung her arms around her waist. The maid was gasping for breath so hard Merry almost couldn't understand her. Nell's normally pink-and-ivory complexion was splotchy and red from her crying jag. Merry pried the other woman off like a limpet, and sternly demanded, "What's going on, Nell? How can Edzell be under attack? You're not making any sense." She shook the other slightly in an attempt to snap Nell out of her hysteria.

The other woman shook her head wildly. "Ye ken Hugo went back to Edzell after Sir Christopher left. He was plannin' to retrieve his things and return here so we could be wed."

"Such news does not come as a surprise, Nell. I knew you were fond of one another."

"Aye, milady, and Hugo wants to serve Master Gilbert still. Lord Ran ordered Master Gilbert to return to Edzell and finish his studies before he left, but I ken Master Gilbert has plans of his own. The message . . ." Nell gestured helplessly, "came from Hugo himself. Edzell is being ransacked by Tudor soldiers searching for Lord Ran."

Merry thought a moment, trying to stay calm. "I know the queen's hand was forced. Despite Wickham's treachery, 'tis true someone is plaguing the border. She must needs put a stop to it, and Ran picked the worst time to vanish. He looks guilty."

"Aye," Nell admitted, "but I canna believe 'tis him, milady."

"The description matches, including that of his mount, Dearg," Merry replied. She sighed with pure frustration, running a hand through her flaming locks. "We have to find him, and soon. Set with an immediate search of the entire grounds."

Merry briskly instructed the rest of the Auchmull staff who still stood there gawking, to search the keep completely from top to bottom, as well as the outer ward and yard. Someone run and check with the guards at the gate," she added. "They may have seen something. Most likely Lord Lindsay is elsewhere, but we can't take any chances."

Nell almost wept with relief when Merry took charge, and though she saw her lady's face pale with trepidation, she knew Merry would not rest, nor allow the others to do so until Ran was found and matters settled to her satisfaction.

For the sake of the others, Merry kept an outwardly calm facade, but inside she was a churning mass of fear and uncertainty. Her worst nightmare was coming true. Any moment she expected to hear the clatter of horse's hooves in the courtyard, announcing the arrival of the queen's men, or mayhap Ran himself, but the hours ticked by and there was only grim silence in the keep. Her heart became heavier and colder with each passing moment. When one of the men arriving from Edzell reported there had been sightings of a familiar horse and rider riding the border the previous evening, Merry's uneasiness turned to genuine fear.

It must be Ran. Logically there was no reason why he should seek revenge against Wickham, given Blair's complicity in the matter of their affair, but as Merry knew, logic did not necessarily prevail in this instance or any other. He had loved his wife despite her flaws, and probably still did. She had no way of contacting Ran, and though she considered sending a message to Darra or riding out herself, she realized she might foolishly blunder into the midst of the conflict, and become an unwitting pawn or a hostage herself.

By midday, Edzell's plight had spread from one end of the demesne to the other, and Merry was surprised and touched by the number of Ran's supporters and those at Auchmull who volunteered to go up against the queen's soldiers if need be. Even those who had once railed against her now drew close to offer quiet words of sympathy or advice. Where Ran was concerned, clan honor could be put temporarily aside. She set them on a search for Ran instead. While Lindsay women scoured the keep from top to bottom, the remaining men and boys rode out in four small parties, one in each direction. Nell had started a prayer circle in Auchmull's small stone chapel, along with a handful of other women who were too elderly to physically assist in the search.

Of them all, Merry felt the most helpless, though never more so when one of the guards from the gate found her late that afternoon in the Rose Tower. Stepping hesitantly across the threshold, the guardsman found her keeping her a silent vigil, and when Merry looked up and spied the folded parchment in his hands, she let out an inadvertent cry of hope. Had Ran heard they were looking for him? Was he coming home?

As if reading her mind, the burly guardsman quickly shook his head. " 'Tis nae from Lord Lindsay, milady. 'Twas fired over the wall a few minutes ago, attached to an arrow. Nobody saw who did it. It has yer name on it.''

"Mine?" Uncertainly Merry rose from the velvet settee and accepted the heavy ivory-colored vellum. 'Twas closed with a plain red wax seal. The words "Lady Lindsay" were roughly scrawled across the flap. Merry nodded to dismiss the guard, who hesitated slightly before he bowed and left. She had the terrible feeling 'twas not good news, another plea for help from Edzell, perhaps, but far more likely it concerned her missing husband.

Taking a deep breath, Merry slit the seal and unfolded the paper. The unevenly scrawled, black ink letters leaped off the page at her:

> Lady Lindsay—If you want to see your husband again, come alone to Badanloch just before sunset. Tell no others.

The bluntly worded note was unsigned. Merry's fingers trembled. What should she do? This clearly did not come from Elizabeth Tudor's men. Someone else was involved with Ran's disappearance. She realized she should alert the others, but the note had warned her not to tell anyone else. She was desperate now, worn from waiting, worrying. It might be a trick, but could she risk Ran's life? She shook her head in reply to the fleeting thought. Nay. If she was ordered to go alone, she would do exactly that. There had been no mention of ransom, and maybe the responsible party wanted to lure her into their clutches as well. Even if Merry was taken prisoner, at least she would be with Ran. She must simply have faith she would not be hurt.

Most likely, someone wanted a bargaining ploy with the Lindsays. Macleans or Padons, probably. Ran would be forced to pay a hefty ransom, no doubt, but then would be set free. Merry could only hope the rebels reasoned the same way she did. If not, she and the Wolf of Badanloch might well never set foot in Auchmull again.

It proved more difficult than Merry imagined not to confess her secret predicament to the others during the evening meal.

The curious guard had mentioned the strange note to others, but when Nell asked Merry about it, she lied and told the maid it had merely been a well-aimed taunt by a passing Maclean. It must have been consistent with the other clan's behavior, for Nell asked no more about it.

Meanwhile, the frightening note burned a hole in the pocket of Merry's gown. She had ordered supper early, so she might have time to prepare for a long journey to Badanloch. Not certain of her directions, she had casually mentioned the place earlier, and Hertha had chimed in with a bitter little laugh, saying that it was the same spot where Siany claimed to have met with her lover.

With a few more artless questions, Merry learned the burn was nestled in a nearby wooded copse, about three miles or so from Auchmull. She would set out promptly after dinner. Each bite tasted like ashes in her mouth, but she knew she would need to keep up her strength for Ran's sake. If the note was genuine, someone clever had managed to capture the elusive Wolf off guard. It seemed very unlikely they had known of Ran's exact whereabouts, unless they had an inside informant. 'Twas a chilling thought.

After the meal, Merry escaped to Ran's room and quickly exchanged her gown for a pair of his wool riding trousers and a plain white shirt. Both were too big for her small frame, but she rolled up the cuffs and sleeves and cinched the breeches snugly with a bit of corded hemp. Then she crept carefully down the hall to her own room, and added a pair of sturdy leather boots, a dark cloak, and gloves.

She felt like her bold sister Kat, donning men's trews, and almost laughed at the irony of the circumstances. She had always been the proper one, scandalized by any unladylike actions or garb, and suddenly nothing mattered but Ran's life. She felt icy resolve settle over her like a cloud. She would do what she must.

Merry knew the hardest part would be retrieving her mare from the stables, and distracting the Lindsay guard from their post of duty so she might ride out. Divine providence intervened that night, for one of the guards became ill from a stew made with tainted meat, and while Nell and the others scurried to tend the ill man, Merry was able to slip unseen from the keep and reach the stables without being questioned.

There she found the remaining mounts untended, for Brodie had already ridden out with the main body of Lindsay men, looking for Ran. Merry remembered her riding lessons at Ambergate and managed to secure the bit and bridle on her mare without incident. The saddle was more difficult, for although Orlaith was well trained, the three-year-old lacked the patience of an older horse.

After the first few attempts, Orlaith began side-stepping the irritated efforts of her mistress to heave the awkward saddle up on her back. Finally Merry managed to distract the horse and drop the saddle in place. Quickly she cinched the girth before Orlaith had second thoughts. The mare gave a disgusted snort, and nudged Merry's shoulder as if to say, "Y'must needs practice this a bit, milady!"

Merry chuckled at the mare's ire, realizing haste had made her clumsy. She paused to pat the sleek golden neck of her trusty mount, then quietly she led the mare out of the stables into the growing dusk. There was still one man on guard duty, but Merry saw him flirting with one of the young maids who was lingering by the gate. She watched and waited as the saucy minx finally lured the fellow from his post into the shadows behind the stables. The moment they disappeared, Merry dashed across the yard with Orlaith in tow, and there stopped to tug at the wheel mechanism. A moment later she closed her eyes in defeat. 'Twas too heavy! She didn't have the strength to raise the gate herself. She must risk ordering someone to do the deed, and pray he wouldn't try to stop her.

A moment later, Merry heard a muffled hollering on the other side of the gate. One of the search parties who had ridden out earlier had just returned. Their leader sounded irritable.

"Damme," she heard him curse. "Where's Sullivan?"

"Prob'ly off porkin' Agatha again," sniggered another male voice.

"Sullivan! Get yer lazy arse up here!" bellowed the first man.

Merry managed to hide herself and Orlaith in the shadows near the well house just before the rumpled-looking guard hurried out from behind the stables and back to his post. Flustered, the young man began to heft the gate up, his muscles bulging from the effort. He wasn't paying attention to anything but the disgruntled party who rode through, and Merry seized opportunity to slip out just behind them. The leader of the party began berating the lackadaisical guard as the gate descended again. Soon their heated words were muffled by the solid thud of the wooden barricade hitting the ground.

Merry's heart pounded furiously, and her mouth was dry as cotton. Nevertheless, she managed to mount her horse, realizing too late she had forgotten to bring so much as a candle to light the way. She would be racing the sun's fall in the snow. Judging by the dull reddish glow behind the gray clouds, she had little more than a half hour.

"Show me what you're made of, girl," she begged Orlaith, setting her heels to the mare's sides. She turned the animal's head in a northeasterly direction, remembering Hertha's words. Orlaith lapsed into a smooth canter, Merry's cloak flying behind her like dark wings. As they set out, she heard the distant rumble of thunder. Soon there might not only be darkness to contend with, but a storm as well.

The horse's hooves were muffled by the thick carpet of undergrowth as she entered the forest's edge. Quelling a pang of uncertainty, and fighting her own childish fears of the dark, Merry relentlessly pressed the mare for more speed. Something had unsettled Orlaith, as well, for the golden steed pranced and balked when Merry tried to urge her deeper into the cavernous gloom.

Merry brooked no disobedience from her mount. Ran was in danger, and that superseded any horse or human fancies. She slapped her palm smartly on the mare's right flank, and with a snort of surrender, Orlaith plunged into the snow and shadows. Merry clung to the mare's mane as they moved at a reckless pace through the woods. Childhood tales of evil trolls and woodland monsters rose to engulf her now; the ancient copse seemed alive with weird shadows and sounds.

" 'Tis only the trees, Merry," she rebuked herself as the mare raced deeper and deeper into the murk. "Only the trees!"

Time blended into one dark blur, punctuated only by the brief intrusion of nature when a mist began to drift down through the canopy of firs. Merry was seized by a momentary panic when she saw the first tendrils of mist curling through the boughs above, as if bony fingers were reaching to pluck her from the saddle. She was seized by a sudden, violent shiver. For a moment, she was almost too panic-stricken to go on.

When Orlaith cleared a fallen log, nearly pitching her rider from the saddle, Merry was forced back to reality with a jarring thump. The mist inexplicably cleared, and she glimpsed a smoky orange glow ahead that appeared to be rising from a pool of water at the edge of the forest. She knew it must be Badanloch, and she drew the lathered mare to a halt. Her six senses were tingling, her scalp prickled with a nameless fear. There was no sign at all of other humans. Only the loch, glittering smooth and polished as a piece of black jet, utterly tranquil and yet somehow more frightening to her than all the dancing shadows of the woods.

Merry tried to imagine Siany and her lover sharing a romantic interlude here, but all she could see was the dark water sketched before her like some bottomless abyss, surrounded by the strange smoky mists. Merry's palms dampened on the leather pommel. She remembered Nell's stories of the Each Uisge, and shivered. Sensing her rider's fear, Orlaith snorted and bobbed her head as if to say, "Aye, you little fool, 'tis dangerous. Let's get out of here!"

Before she even considered fleeing, visions of Ran flashed before Merry's closed lids, superseding the fear and even the uncertainty. Her husband was in danger. Only she could help him. She would wait. Sooner or later, whoever sent the note must come. She imagined they would hardly pass up the chance to make a passionate speech about their cause. What better opportunity than when they held the new Countess of Crawford as a captive audience?

Merry considered dismounting in order to stretch her cold, cramped muscles, but she was still far too wary. What if Orlaith should bolt and leave her here? She shuddered at the thought. She could think of a thousand places she'd rather be, even gloomy old Ireland.

Aye, Siany and the kelpies were welcome to Badanloch. Merry far preferred the comforting confines of Auchmull, and the man who had made it home for her. Ran. Her lips curved in a slight smile as she pictured his reaction to her actions in her mind. She knew he would be furious with her for riding out unescorted into such a dangerous situation. Probably he would lecture her about her flightiness, toss in a few terse comments about women in general, and then decide on an appropriate punishment. Later. If only 'twas in the privacy of their bedchamber.

While Merry mused and distracted herself, the wind suddenly shifted from the incoming storm, and she caught her first strong whiff of acrid smoke. Her eyes flew open; she realized the strange orange glow she had glimpsed earlier must be from a nearby campfire, and the smoke was drifting slowly in her direction now. Perhaps someone had been observing her all along.

She felt a sudden tingling on the back of her neck. Danger surrounded her like a dark cloak. Too late, Merry attempted to wheel her horse about. Several shadows shot from the dark woods like wraiths, and a burly hand shot out and seized Orlaith by the bridle. Merry cried out, drumming her heels uselessly into the mare's sides. Horse and rider were pinioned fast.

She stared wide-eyed into a man's face as he stepped forward into the shifting twilight. The flash of the silver badge fastened to his breccan was the first, and last, thing she saw.

Chapter Thirty-Four

An icy wind gusted around the figures gathered in the clearing, and the golden-haired man smiled a little crookedly at Merry.

"What a coincidence, milady," Sir Jasper said softly, then released the mare's bridle. Merry knew, however, she wasn't free to go. There was no point in protesting when he reached up to lift her from the saddle, and though her knees wobbled for a second when she stood, she managed with some effort to keep her head high.

"The queen has a number of questions for you," was the first thought which came to her mind. Hurled from her lips, it sounded exactly like the angry warning 'twas meant to be.

Wickham merely nodded. A green-and-black plaid breccan billowed around his shoulders, secured by a silver badge Merry had never dreamed might be in his possession. She recognized the tower decorating the badge. 'Twas the Maclean emblem. The same one she had embroidered upon a wall hanging. Clad in a Maclean tartan, Wickham straddled the earth as if he were in possession of the very soil itself. She glanced around at the others; his men all wore mock Maclean tartans. When Merry gazed into those pale eyes, she saw they were every bit as flat and ominous as Badanloch.

"Robert the Bruce, I presume?" she said a little dryly.

Wickham looked surprised, then laughed. His laughter was neither warm nor amused. 'Twas more a reflection of satisfaction from a soulless man as he glanced back over a long day's work.

"Tell me, Merry, why you don't seem shocked to find me wearing Maclean colors."

"Because it makes sense now. Cullen may be a scoundrel, but he is no murderer. Yet you find him handy for pinning your crimes upon."

Sir Jasper smiled thinly. "Aye, Scots weasels do have their uses."

"There was always something odd about Duncan's death. Too convenient Cullen was in residence at the time. Of course, you assumed Ran would blame his old adversary.

"I suspect the Padons didn't give a fig about Ran's wedding an Englishwoman, either. But you did. You sent your men to exact revenge, disguised as a Maclean sept."

Her gaze was direct and challenging. Wickham stared back at her for a long moment and then chuckled.

"You're a surprising wit as well as hellcat, milady. A pity I did not have opportunity to discover how well we are suited."

Merry refused to pursue that line of thought. "Where's Ran?" she demanded.

"All in good time. I needed to be sure I could lure him here, as he appears to have a soft spot for you. Likewise, 'twould seem."

Furious, Merry glared at him. Wickham's arrogance was maddening, as was his cool control of the situation, but even more infuriating was the fact of his involvement in the Padon attack. She had always had suspicions about Wickham's exact role in the slaughter, but there had been no proof until now. He used the fact in an attempt to either impress or frighten her.

"Come," he said curtly, sweeping his arm to indicate a

badly overgrown path through the forest. '' 'Tis far too cold by half, standing here. We've a camp just over the rise.''

For the first time, Merry glanced at the other silent figures flanking her. There were perhaps a dozen other men, she could make out that much, but their facial features were still streaked by shadows and half hidden in the gloom. Seeing no choice, Merry reluctantly followed Wickham through the woods to the Englishman's encampment. She didn't see anything until she literally stumbled upon a bunch of twigs stacked beside a small, smoldering fire. Sheltered by the thick canopy of trees, Wickham's hideaway was nearly invisible. She could easily be killed and left here, her bones undiscovered for years. She shivered.

Wickham read her mind. ''You will be safe, milady,'' he assured her without elaboration. ''As long as you obey and Lindsay surrenders himself peaceably.''

''Why should he?'' Merry demanded. ''So you can trap and kill him like an animal?''

He suddenly turned on her with the full brunt of his outrage. ''Should not a mad wolf be put down, Lady Lindsay?'' Wickham sneered when she shrank back from his mad ranting, and he raised a hand as if to strike her. ''You're as much a whore as Blair,'' he snarled. ''You promised to wed with me, promised to be a true and faithful wife, yet the moment you met Lindsay, you lusted for the Earl of Crawford in your traitorous heart!''

''I love Ran,'' Merry said, meeting his gaze despite her fear. Hearing the simple words spoken aloud only seemed to infuriate Wickham more.

''Sweet Jesu, you women all come as cheaply as Lindsay's maid,'' he growled. ''At least she'll give me a son.''

Merry stared at him a moment in shock. Then she sketched him a mocking little bow. ''Congratulations, sir.''

Wickham's expression was still thunderous. ''Shut up,'' he muttered.

''Not only did you beat Lady Rich, your charming history includes rape and seducing a sixteen-year-old-girl, your own half-sister. I wonder what Her Majesty will make of all this?''

''I wouldn't point any fingers, Lady Lindsay,'' Wickham

retorted. "You're presently wed to a traitor, and the queen's men are hot on his trail."

"My conscience is clear," Merry replied, and the meaning of her words was not lost on Wickham. With an angry growl, he seized her arm and hurled her roughly to the damp earth. An icy rain began to fall, and it pattered upon Merry's face as she scowled up at him.

"'Twon't work, you know," she said.

"Silence, woman!"

"He'll find me soon."

"Shut up!" He opened his fist as if to backhand her.

"When Ran discovers what you've done, 'twill all be over," she added as confidently as she could. "If Black Cullen doesn't rend you to pieces first."

"Tsk, tsk, are ye just going ta stand there and let the little bitch bark at you?" a second male voice inquired, and Merry gasped as a familiar figure stepped from the shadows. Hugo Sumner grinned at her as he folded his arms and struck a jaunty pose against a tree, folding his brawny arms. "Why, milady, dinna look so shocked. Surely ye ken Wickham and I are of like mind. Sir Jasper and I hae a rare sort o' acquaintance. We even made a pact to bring the Wolf down together. 'Twas the perfect opportunity when ye were tossed into his lap. Another Achilles' heel in the mighty wolf."

Bile rose in Merry's throat, nearly choking her. "Then 'twas you . . ." she began huskily.

"Duncan?" Hugo shrugged his massive shoulders. "Aye, the old man caught me plotting wi' Wickham and confronted me. Unfortunately he had to be silenced." He cracked his knuckles and Merry paled, realizing a simple squeeze of those huge hands on her throat would silence her forever.

Wickham interrupted them with a low, silky laugh. "Oh, dear, I fear you've gone and frightened the lady, Hugo. Do apologize."

Hugo grinned, his teeth flashing white in the gloom. "As ye wish, Sir Jasper."

Merry still stared at Hugo. "How could you," she whispered.

"Ran trusts you, Gil adores you, Nell loves you! What of honor?"

Hugo's grin faded to a sneer. "What would ye ken o' honor, milady? Yer a woman." Ignoring Wickham's scowl, he continued coldly. "What honor or respect does a bastard get, milady? None . . . be they English or Scots. I'm a Sumner by name, a Lindsay by birth! Aye, but for the flip o' the blanket, I could rule Auchmull now. I'm the poor bastard, the charity case o' Lady Darra, Lord Ran's dirty secret. Even Gil dinna ken I'm his half-brother . . . and his blind devotion sickens me. So many times I wanted ta kill the little rotter, or tell him the truth, but suffered in silence for the good o' the clan. Until now, silence was the right thing. I gave in to rage but once, and Ran found evidence of that, a *sgian dubh* buried ta the hilt in his pillow. I did my best ta destroy the Wolf three months ago. As 'tis, I'll just hae ta kill him now."

"Nay!" Merry's protesting cry emerged loud and sharp. It echoed throughout the forest. Wickham looked annoyed.

"I'll gag you, milady, if I must. Lindsay mustn't have any warning when he rides to your rescue."

"He's not foolish enough to come alone," Merry said desperately. "He has his loyal men, Lindsays by blood or birth, all of them—"

"Minus one," Hugo added.

Merry felt a wave of stark fear wash over her when she glanced across the pit of glowing embers and saw his cold blue eyes glinting by the firelight. He crouched down on his heels and smiled almost congenially across the fire at her.

"Some of us are nae content to wait for our rightful titles," he said.

"Swine," Merry railed angrily.

Hugo chuckled. "Macleans or their ilk will take all o' the blame for the Wolf's death, thanks ta Wickham here," he said. " 'Twill be easy enough to plant the evidence on Cullen or one of the others. When they are charged wi' the crime, surely good King Jamie will see fit ta return the lands o' Badanloch ta the last surviving Lindsay heir. Me." He grinned.

"What of Gilbert? Darra's boys? Sweet Jesu, Hugo, you can't kill them all!" Merry cried. " 'Tis utter madness!"

Hugo glanced at Wickham, and the two men shared a look that made her blood run cold.

"Nay, I don't believe it," Merry said faintly. She stared at Hugo, saw he wouldn't meet her eyes. She felt the nausea rising in her throat. "You would kill innocents. Your own relations. For lust of a meaningless title. 'Tis unbelievable . . ." Her accusing gaze swiveled on Wickham. "While you . . . you murdered Blair," she accused him in a ragged voice. "I don't know how, but I know you did."

"I loved Blair," Wickham growled under his breath. "You understand nothing."

"Oh, but I do know one thing. You're lower than snakes, both of you."

Her gaze shifted back to Hugo. "You—are far worse, I think. A disgusting traitor. When you know how the Lindsays love and trust you."

His lips curled. "Love? What's love compared to rightful inheritance?" His face mottled with rage. "Or the way a bastard bairn is scorned? Ye silly little Tudor bitch, ye ken nothing o' our ways, all ye can do is sigh and moon over the enemy! Brave men and women hae died o'er the centuries for love o' the clan, but yer so hot for Ran ye canna see past the man to the true cause. Lindsays can be restored ta their rightful power in the Highlands, but only wi' the help of yer countrymen. I see this, I ken the Ran clings ta old ways, old days . . . the Wolf's hour has run its course." Hugo's icy blue eyes hardened on her. "Ye can still help us, milady, lead the Lindsays into the future. Gie us yer loyalties now, help put Ran into the purgatory o' the past wi' the rest of them."

Merry shook her head, and felt a tear trickle down her face. "Never," she whispered fiercely. "Never."

"Then you may sit there and watch him die," Wickham said flatly. "I've no more patience for coaxing." He motioned to Hugo. "Go and set a watch for your beloved brother, Hugo. We daren't be taken by surprise."

* * *

The night passed in a slow blur of cold and misery for Merry, as she huddled beneath the extra cloak Wickham had carelessly tossed at her. Sir Jasper had even dared attempt to share her warmth, dropping down beside her as the fire died, and inching gradually closer as the wind picked up. When he tried to sling his arm around her, Merry lashed out with her fist, catching him squarely on the jaw. Wickham sprang to his feet and cursed, then stalked off into the darkness. She heard Hugo snigger softly in the shadows.

Merry rolled herself snugly in both cloaks and turned her back on her captors. Her thoughts whirled wildly with fear for Ran and the frightened clansfolk at Auchmull and Edzell, and she was sure she couldn't sleep. Stress had taken its toll, however, and despite her best efforts, her eyelashes slowly drifted shut. In the wee hours of the early morning, she awoke feeling stiff and cramped with cold. The damp of the ground had seeped through her layers of clothing, and she shivered as she sat upright and tried to work the kinks out of her neck and back. Balefully she regarded Wickham's snoring lump across the cold remains of the fire. Hugo had taken last watch. He glanced at her from his position by the trees as she stretched and stirred.

Merry was hungry, but determined not to lower herself to begging for anything from these animals. Nature, however, impressed a call of a different sort now which she couldn't ignore. She got to her feet, hugging the loose cloak about her like a blanket, and approached Ran's half-brother.

Immediately Hugo struck an aggressive pose. "Stay put," he ordered her. "Yer nae allowed ta wander about."

"I have to find some bushes," Merry said, avoiding his eyes, her meaning clear enough. He shifted a little uncomfortably on the balls of his feet. A second later, he jerked his head sharply to the left.

"Right there," he said grudgingly. "Where I can keep an eye on ye."

She flushed with humiliation. "Nay, I cannot."

He smirked a little. "Then ye'll hae ta hold it, milady."

Merry bit her lower lip. "Please. I won't go far. Just behind those bushes there." She pointed to a nearby clump of bracken. She tried to convey a sense of urgency by jiggling up and down a little.

At last, Hugo impatiently waved a hand. "Be quick about it. If ye tarry, I'll drag ye out wi' yer breeches still down."

Merry nodded and hurried off into the edge of the woods. She was aware of him watching her closely, so she stopped and took care of necessities the moment he was out of view. When finished, she stayed in a crouch and looked furtively about. She hadn't intended to run, but the temptation was too great. Wickham was still asleep, as were most of his men. There was only Hugo to worry about with any distance; mayhap she could elude him long enough to find her way back to Auchmull.

The horses were secured on the other side of the camp, so she would have to flee on foot. Quickly Merry untied and shed both wool cloaks, to make her flight easier. 'Twas chilly without any protection from the elements, and a light drizzle was starting again. Not cold enough for snow, but that might change. She heard a rustle of brush and then Hugo's low, impatient voice spoke nearby.

"Milady?"

Merry sprang from the bushes and ran. She heard Hugo swear, the crash of his big body as he came flying through the bracken after her. The trees were thick enough she was able to evade his clutches and dart off between them, her smaller frame more nimble than his. Her breathing sawed harshly in her throat as she scrambled over an endless obstacle course of fallen logs and cut an erratic, weaving path through the woods. Merry panicked she might be going deeper into the forest. Then she spied the black sparkle of Badanloch and stumbled, gasping, into the clearing where she had been captured the night before.

Hugo was not far behind. His shouts had roused Wickham and the other men, and she heard them stumbling and running for their mounts. Horses whinnied and loud curses sliced the early-morning air as the men set out in pursuit of Merry.

Spying the overgrown path she had taken last night, where Orlaith had trampled down the new bracken, Merry lurched across the clearing in a westerly direction. Behind her, Hugo emerged from the trees and hoarsely ordered her to stop. She heard a strange "thunking" sound and glanced back in time to see the big man cocking a deadly crossbow with his foot. He swung the wooden stock to his shoulder as if to fire.

"Nay!" The shout came from Wickham, who hurled himself from the back of a galloping bay and knocked Hugo sideways to the ground.

Surprised, Sir Jasper intervened, but Merry nevertheless turned and hurried on down the path. The brush closed behind her as she heard Wickham shout at Hugo, "Idiot! Without the woman, there is no bait for the wolf trap."

Chapter Thirty-Five

The simple keep of Invermark, smallest and most remote of the Lindsay possessions, had not been used since the death of Ran's grandfather, the ninth Earl of Crawford, in 1558. Since then, the castle had deteriorated, and the wild heather and bracken had crept up through the glens, effectively blending the rough stone into the background. The roof, such as it was, had half caved in, and birds nested in the cavern of what had once been the great kitchen. Once Invermark had commanded the outpost against the invading Caterans, the later castle evolved from a fourteenth-century fortress. The huge drawbridge and massive iron gate still remained operable, however, and made for strategic defense with the torrent of the Mark keeping any harriers at bay.

Here Ran had escaped, managing to elude the queen's soldiers just as they swept down upon Edzell in search of him. Kinross was away at the Stuart Court, and while Darra was left to deal with the minor Tudor inquisition, Ran did not doubt his spirited sister was equal to the task. By now, he wryly reflected, the soldiers were probably wishing they had never crossed the path of the undaunted Lady Deuchar. Fortunately,

Gil and Darra's boys had been sent to safety before the invasion, and Ran doubted even Elizabeth Tudor considered it worthwhile annoying a powerful border lord like Scott simply to question children about his whereabouts.

The isolation of Invermark suited his nature, and soothed his anger somewhat, but he knew the entire clan stood to suffer for the latest happenings. King James was well pleased with his capture of the reivers of crown cattle, but sooner or later he would cave in to his royal cousin's demand and reluctantly uphold the charges of outlawry. Ran might conceivably evade everyone for weeks yet, for the spring was too cold and young for easy traveling with troops, but he realized Invermark was but a temporary solution.

Besides, there was the matter of Merry. Thank Jesu at least he had sent her home to England, though he had done so in a fit of anger rather than concern for her welfare. He walked up the stairs of the central tower, overlooking the Gothic battlements and the distant Howe of the Mearns and let the spring breezes rush through his hair, whip his kilt and tartan about his body. Ran felt closer to his grandfather than he ever had his own sire, and here in the splendid seclusion of a rugged outpost, he could almost imagine, for a moment, he lived in easier days, a humble laird in a simple keep. Good company, hearty but basic food, a woman with a ready laugh and a sparkle in her eye . . . He shifted slightly, bracing one foot against a crumbled pinnacle, and in his mind's eye heard the silvery laughter of his wife. She burst from the castle into the glen, humming beneath her breath, turned and shielded her eyes against the sunlight as she looked up at him.

"Whatever are you doing way up there, milord?" she laughed at him. "You'll tumble and crack your thick Scots noggin, and I'll not be a bit to blame . . ."

Ran felt his breath leave him in a sudden rush, for the vision in the sunlit glen was not Blair, but Merry . . . Merry of the blazing hair and rain-colored eyes, the ready smile and dazzling wit, a heart open to him with such innocent appeal he felt a corresponding ache in his own breast. The pain was almost as daunting as the joy as he realized what he had been denying for many months . . . how hard he had fought against the notion of loving anyone, much less an impertinent *Sassenach* lass with the power to make Blair's memory fade. 'Twas the source of the true terror, this gradual understanding there might be another who could ease his grief, bring him happiness when he wanted so desperately to cling to old wounds, never let them heal. 'Twas terror had prompted him to lash out, push her away.

Ran took another shuddering breath, scouring his surroundings through new eyes as the red-haired woman faded into the mists of dreams and furtive hopes. Love . . . he had felt love for Blair Maclean, of an intensity so fierce it almost counted for obsession. This emotion with Merry was different, softer, more blurred and indistinct, yet oddly comforting just the same. He knew somehow he could turn to Merry, lay his head on her shoulder. She would hold him, never question the need for it, nor his strength. *Could this not be love also?*

Mayhap love was not always the finely honed passion of a blade; maybe 'twas the gentle brush of a fingertip across a cheek, or warm laughter flowing across the room, gazes meeting and sharing a smile, all of these and more. He sat down suddenly, as if stunned, upon the edge of a caen stone turret, and never even heard the mocking laughter of a white raven in the wind.

Three days later, Ran risked a quick return to Auchmull for more supplies, and there heard the news of Merry's return and subsequent disappearance. By then, she had been missing a day. When he realized she must have ridden out and met with disaster, he swore under his breath and smacked a balled fist into the palm of his other hand.

"By all the bloody hounds of hell! Doesn't the woman have half a brain?" Ran, seeing the genuine alarm in Nell's face, softened his tone just a bit. " 'Twas the height of foolishness for her to return at such a time. D'you have any idea where she went?"

Nell shook her head. A second later, she ventured, "I do remember she kept asking about Badanloch last night, milord."

"What about it?"

"Lady Merry wanted to ken exactly where 'twas. When I asked why, she said she had a fancy to visit it sometime."

"Badanloch," Ran mused softly. He was still taut with rage from being hunted by the Tudor soldiers; encountering a pack of Macleans trespassing on Lindsay lands on the way here had not improved his temper any. Though the supposed "enemy" had turned out to be nothing more than a handful of youths intent upon some mischief-making in another clan's territory. Despite their breaking up into separate groups and fleeing, he'd caught a couple of them, and even obnoxious as the boys were, Ran believed their story that they knew nothing about Merry or any possible kidnaping. One of the older lads, named Malcolm, had particularly impressed Ran with his cool head and obvious intelligence. He appeared to be only about ten or so, but his natural Highland defiance had tickled Ran. Malcolm had been utterly unimpressed finding himself the prisoner of the Earl of Crawford. At least until Ran had given him a good switching, and then at last there had been a grudging respect in the lad's eyes.

Ran finally set the Maclean lads free after questioning them at length. Back at Auchmull he quizzed the guard who had delivered some kind of note to Merry, but the man admitted he couldn't attest to the contents of the urgent message she'd supposedly received. At this news, ominous chill gripped Ran. Someone had deliberately lured his wife away from Auchmull. But why?

The rain was a solid downpour by the time Merry finally straggled from the forest, shivering and soaked to the skin. She was exhausted and dispirited, stricken with fear. Faced with the ruthless elements, she'd almost turned back and offered herself into Wickham's hands again. She had never been of strong constitution, and the weird shadows and sounds of the primal forest sent deep chills wracking through her. It seemed she had been walking, or stumbling rather, for hours. Time ceased to matter, for the mist never completely burned from the woods.

Once free of the meadow, she fell to her knees in the slick meadow grasses and pressed the painful stitch in her side. Her hair hung in sodden ropes around her, and her shirt and breeches were torn from the many thorns and branches she'd encountered during her flight. She wondered if she could ever get up again. Yet she knew she must get back to Auchmull somehow.

After a respite, Merry heaved herself up again and staggered on. She had barked her shin on a lichen-covered boulder sometime earlier, and her bruised knee throbbed and burned with every step she took. She knew she must look a sight. Fashion had never been farther from her mind, however, and somehow she doubted 'twould ever mean much again.

Gray sheets of rain had changed the landscape into a murky, indistinct canvas of threatening cliffs and deep gullies. Merry soon lost sight of the washed-out trail left from Orlaith's hooves. Uncertain of her directions, she was soon forced to admit she seemed to be going in circles. Auchmull was nowhere in sight. Only the icy rain, beating a steady tattoo upon her head, provided any company for a lone woman wandering through the hills.

At last Merry could go no further. She stumbled, slid, collapsed in a heap on the wet ground. Her shoulders shook from the cold. A second later, she heard the drumming of hooves, even over her pounding heart.

Peering out through her waterfall of wet hair, Merry saw horses galloping across the meadow towards her. Her fingers dug into the mud with fury, resignation. The desperate flight, risking her life, had all been for naught. Wickham had found her again.

Merry waited, weary with resignation. She could not even summon the strength to plead for mercy; there was nothing left now but a cold hollow ache and the remnants of a bruised heart.

When a horse slid to a stop in the damp grass beside her, she looked up dully, like a trapped animal. She let out a spontaneous cry. Ran! He vaulted from the saddle, dropped to his knees in the mud and grabbed her in his arms. Merry was wracked with dry sobs as he clutched her fiercely against his heart.

"Ssh, sweetheart," he soothed her in his soft Highland burr, "you're safe now. Safe . . ."

"How did you find me?" she sobbed.

"Nell remembered you asked about Badanloch. I was following a hunch, nothing more."

Ran unfastened his badge, swept off his breccan and wrapped it around her. Merry clutched at the edge of the tartan, which was so large it nearly enveloped her like a blanket there on the grass and mud. She spoke through chattering teeth.

"Wickham. m-murdered B-Blair . . ."

Something flashed in Ran's eyes, no doubt the same agony preventing him from ever loving her, and Merry drew the breccan tighter as if it might shield her from further pain. Ran did not speak for a moment, simply held her clutched against him. After a while, he nodded.

"I always knew, lass, but could never prove it."

"Hugo . . ." she whispered, dreading word of this betrayal even more than the other. "He turned, Ran. To Wickham." She licked her lips, wondering what else she might say to ease such a devastating blow. Ran whitened and drew in his breath, but didn't look as shocked as she expected.

" 'Tis the matter of inheritance?"

She gave a jerky little nod " 'Twas all planned, Ran. Badanloch . . . the massacre came about because Hugo killed your messenger. Nell's husband. Later, Wickham staged the attack upon the wedding party, hoping you would blame Macleans and inflame the feud even more."

She inhaled deeply, trying to measure what his brooding silence might mean. "Hugo has joined up with Wickham now, and I saw a few other disgruntled Lindsays among the lot. They held me there in the woods, hoping to lure you into a trap.''

Ran threaded his fingers through her damp hair, drawing her tightly against him. "Sweet Jesu," he whispered roughly. "I thought I'd lost you."

Merry exulted in his embrace, but feared to respond. Mayhap the emotion of the moment, the shock of Hugo's betrayal had unsettled his reasoning. He still did not know about Blair and Wickham, the depth of their real relationship, the fact the child had not been his. Merry opened her mouth to tell Ran everything, but his lips silenced her. Gently yet urgently, with the depth of intensity she had only dreamed of henceforth, the Wolf of Badanloch kissed her. She clung to his broad shoulders, weeping, and suddenly nothing mattered but the union of two lost and hungry souls in the mist.

Chapter Thirty-Six

"Well, 'tis surely a scene worthy of courtly accolade."

Wickham's snarl was precipitated by horsemen bursting from the wood, and Merry shuddered as the Englishman's soldiers surrounded her and Ran. Ran came to his feet, still holding Merry, his dark gaze never wavering from the man taunting him from horseback.

"I thought a wolf was only capable of rendering others, not offering succor," Sir Jasper mused as he cast a disparaging glance upon the couple. "Or would you say this wolf, in particular, has a soft spot for red-haired lassies?" He gave the edge of his tartan a mocking flip in Ran's direction, but the latter did not react. Wickham shifted impatiently in the saddle.

"You saved me the trouble of returning to Auchmull with a ransom demand, milord." Sir Jasper smiled coldly at his adversary. "How nice to find both my objects neatly clumped together. Most considerate, wouldn't you concur, Hugo?"

The blond man riding at his side nodded, but Merry noticed Hugo did not seem to be of quite the same swaggering bent as before. Mayhap Ran's cold, dark stare unnerved him more than he cared to reveal.

"I'm sorry," Merry whispered to her husband, but he brushed his lips against her hair.

"Lass, I would have come for you at the ends of earth," Ran murmured, and she sensed his relief that matters were almost resolved, however daunting it miqht be. Within minutes they were taken into Wickham's custody, without visible protest on Ran's part, for he knew the odds of one man against two dozen. Yet their destination was not Auchmull nor Braidwood. Wickham had discovered the queen's soldiers left Edzell, and deemed it more suitable for his purposes. He was certain the lovely Lady Deuchar would not refuse him admittance once she saw the other guests he brought.

The captives rode double on Dearg, Merry clinging to Ran's waist and trying to keep her seat on the animal's sweat-slicked back. She wore Ran's breccan, but still shook from the cold.

Merry tensed with fear as each mile passed and they drew nigh their destination, for she knew what awaited them was far more deadly than the queen's displeasure. By contrast, Ran seemed resolved, his jaw set. Hugo had removed Ran's claymore earlier and slung it across his own back, the deadly blade glittering a bright silver in the late-spring sunshine. Weaponless, Ran was as vulnerable as any man. The mix of anger and devastation on his face when Hugo took his weapon had wounded Merry almost as deeply.

She understood his bitterness, wondered if Hugo would ever feel safe venturing anywhere alone again. Doubtless, Ran intended to sink Scathach home in the traitor's breast at first opportunity. Though she shuddered at the terrible thought, she knew the unwritten code of the Highland vengeance was clear. Hugo had betrayed his kin, bastard or not, and revenge would linger on every Lindsay's lips until the giant fell.

Dearg plodded on through the damp undergrowth, straining a bit from the unaccustomed burden. All around them small forest creatures chirped and chattered, falling silent only as the horses passed. Then the noises would resume, cocooning them with a cacophony of sound. At last the rain slowed, then stopped. They all knew it to be only a temporary respite.

During the journey, Merry recognized a few places where she had rested and hidden from her pursuers. When they reached Badanloch, the clearing was empty, the encampment deserted, but she felt the same ominous sensations which had stalked her here before. The urge to escape was overwhelming.

The Wolf glanced at his namesake, the glittering black waters as impenetrable as his gaze. No emotion showed on his profile, except possibly a quiet resolve. She prayed 'twas not surrender. Merry squeezed his waist with her linked hands, reminding him she was there.

Edzell's medieval battlements and turrets had never looked more ominous, sketched against a rumbling gray sky. The storm had followed them, winging swiftly in from the west, roiling above them now like an omen of darkest intent.

Ran's mount was spent, and limped the last half mile. Wickham forced the couple to walk. Merry never knew how she found her own last reserves of strength, but somehow they were there when she most needed them, and she was able to keep up with Ran as they abandoned the horse grazing on the hill and slowly picked their way down through the rocks with their escort.

The castle loomed strangely silent and forbidding above them. There seemed nobody on watch. They were able to reach the gates without sounding an alarm. 'Twas a sign something odd was going on within Edzell's walls, Ran thought, but Wickham was too cheered by the lack of defense to care.

"Obviously Lady Deuchar is a bit wiser than her brother," the Englishman chuckled as he drew his mount to a halt in the courtyard. "Else the Tudors took the fight out of her, and I would hardly complain in either case."

Ran shrugged, somewhat nonplussed by the eerie silence. Perhaps the residents had escaped by some unusual means. He remembered his mother complaining about a secret passage used by the original Lindsays. It hid been sealed off once, but the wood boards had rotted away and the children had found and used the old tunnel in their games of hide-and-seek. He tried to remember exactly where it was. In later years, he had roamed around Edzell several times, trying to find it again, but unable to find any sign of a hidden door. While Wickham and the others dismounted and secured their captives, a few men poked around in the hall and returned to report the keep was deserted.

Wickham frowned and stroked his goatee, then nodded. ''The lady and her household have obviously fled, but it matters not. I have everything I need right here, and the queen's men are unlikely to return after such a thorough inspection.'' He chuckled as he kicked at a ripped tapestry left lying trampled in the mud. Merry was horrified by the obvious ransacking which had taken place during the English occupation, but Ran squeezed her arm reassuringly, a silent reminder objects could be replaced, people could not.

At least Darra and her retainers had escaped, doubtless halfway to Edinburgh by now and appealing to James Stuart for protection. The true danger came now not from the queen, but a madman posing as English gentry.

The first order of business for Wickham was accessing the dungeons. When he ordered Hugo to the task of escorting the prisoners there, Merry paled but remained stalwart beside Ran. The giant prodded them forward with the tip of his blade, with Ran at a healthy distance.

''I'll go first,'' Ran said, silently holding Merry back above the stairs descending into the gloom. '' 'Tis dangerous when you don't know the way. Stay close behind.'' He gave her a faint, reassuring smile, and started down the stone steps, her hand securely in his.

''There are steps to the bottom, but some are broken.'' Ran's voice was muffled as he helped her down after him, Hugo's weapon urging them both. Merry clutched at Ran's and they crept carefully down the crumbling steps into the black void below.

An icy wind sighed and moaned around them, propelled by some unseen force beyond the abyss that loomed ahead. Only

Ran's hand—strong, solid, and warm with life—kept Merry from turning and trying to flee back to the safety of the familiar world above, Hugo's sword be damned. Finally they reached the bottom of Edzell's dungeons, the damp, musty smells embracing them like death itself. Merry shivered. As they moved cautiously onward, down narrow corridors, bits of earth and rock debris began to crumble from the rough walls around them. Merry felt several clods strike her.

Ran's voice echoed back to her. "There's a torch up ahead. Just a wee bit farther."

Merry fancied the unstable walls around them were beginning to collapse inward. Her breathing quickened, every step seemed to bring her inches closer to the edge of losing control. Panic swept over her like a cold, suffoccating fog. She held Ran's hand in a vise like grip. Sensing her terror, he spoke again, very softly in his Scottish burr:

"Easy, m'love. Almost there. Concentrate on the light, Merry. The light . . . the light."

Step by step her fears receded as Merry fixated on the faint, single glow from a torch at the far end of the dungeon and listened to her husband's soothing voice. Soon only the wind was left to tease at her hair and wrap its icy, invisible tendrils around her heart. Memories of being accidentally shut up in the cellar as a child, of screaming until she was hoarse, until she vomited with fear, rose to choke her now. She was terrified of the horrid darkness, of dying here sealed up in a living tomb, but she feared being alone more. With Ran, 'twas almost bearable. She forced down the hysteria, scrabbling for a grip on sanity if only to rub her dignity in Wickham's face.

Suddenly they were free of the twisting corridors. The cold, damp walls of Edzell's dungeon surrounded them instead, but these walls were almost comforting compared to the narrow confines of the steps coming down. Merry took in great, deep gulps of the dank air. She saw Ran regarding the wildly flickering torch fixed above them in an iron sconce with something akin to fascination.

"Somebody's just come and gone this way," he said, frowning. "Look, Hugo."

The giant regarded him suspiciously. He waved the point of the blade at Ran. "Step over there."

Ran shrugged, started to move. The moment he pulled his hand free of Merry's, he pushed her back behind him and leapt for the bigger man in a calculated gamble. Hugo swore, stumbling back a few paces but managed to keep his grip on the weapon. Merry heard the impact of bodies, the whistle of steel screamed . . .

"Nay . . . !"

Ran did not fall before her dazed, terrified eyes. Instead, the arc of a blade from the shadows knocked the claymore from Hugo's two-fisted grip, sent the heavy weapon spinning end over end. It came to rest with a clatter upon the dungeon floor, seconds before Ran met his end at the point of the same blade.

A chuckle rang off the mossy stone walls. "Why, Hugo, I never dreamed the disarming trick you taught me would come in so handy one day."

Stunned, Hugo stared at the shadows where Gilbert Lindsay materialized. So did Ran and Merry. For the innocence of youth had been replaced by a grim demeanor they hardly recognized. Gone was the laughing lad with the twinkling eyes, in his stead a young man determined to preserve his family at any cost.

Nothing resembling empathy flickered across Gil's face as he looked at Hugo, though his voice shook slightly. "You were as a brother to me," he said. "I trusted you with my secrets, my very life. This is how you repay us all . . ."

"Ye snivelin' little cur, I *am* yer brother," Hugo sneered back, when he regained his composure. "Bastard kin, aye, but nae less a Lindsay for it." The giant pointed a thick finger accusingly at Ran. "The Wolf of Bandanloch ken it all along."

Gil's blade did not waver from Hugo's throat. Merry had never imagined violet-blue eyes could be so icy. "I know not what you speak of, Hugo," he said almost congenially. "I am the Wolf of Badanloch." He acknowledged Ran with a nod. "With all due respect to my honorable predecessor."

Comprehension dawned. Ran stared at his younger brother.
"Gil—"

"I'll brook no quarrel about it, Ran," he said calmly.

"Take Merry now, and go. My men have secured Edzell
from without. We are thrice in number. Darra and the staff are
safe at Auchmull."

"Wickham?"

"Dead." Gil's voice was flat, cold. "He will not trouble
you again."

Ran nodded, gazing at Gil a long moment as if to memorize
the youth he had been, or the man he had become. Merry, too,
sought the handsome young man's face for a vestige of the
Gilbert Lindsay she had known, but he had vanished. Part of
her mourned, but another realized 'twas inevitable.

Gil was waiting for them to leave. "Go, please." His gaze
had dismissed them, now rested unwavering upon Hugo.

His order brought Merry from her reverie. With a final look
at his brother, Ran gripped her tightly by the elbow, guiding
her out past the men back down the narrow corridor. Merry
fled, stumbling and gasping, across tile dank dungeon to the
spiral of steps leading upward into the main hold. Just as she
gained the first stair, she heard a man's piercing scream of
agony.

"Don't look," Ran commanded her grimly, and with a sob
of quiet despair, Merry obediently turned her head and denied
herself any further knowledge of the justice being exacted in
their wake.

Ran glanced up at his wife in surprise. "You are certain?"
he asked. "You don't wish to return to Court?"

Merry looked at the man facing her in Auchmull's great hall.
She shook her head.

"Nay, Ran. With your permission, I would very much like
to remain Lady Lindsay. And occupy the family residence, as
well."

A few servants, including Nell and Hertha, watched in sober

silence as the laird considered his lady wife's request. None made a single move to interrupt the moment. They were wise enough not to ask questions. Especially questions concerning the continuing legend of the Wolf of Badanloch, said to suspiciously resemble Gilbert Lindsay, nor would they voice their curiosity about a rumor of a strange pile of ashes supposedly found in Edzell's dungeon, or what had happened to Sir Jasper Wickham. 'Twas said the Englishman had fled to the Continent to evade the queen's wrath, and that of the Earl of Essex's, but his household had been left undisturbed, and many found it odd.

"Are you certain, lass?" Ran repeated, sounding almost . . . worried.

Merry smiled and held out her hand to him. Ran reached out, enfolded her fingers in his warm, calloused hands and brought them to his lips. She looked at their intertwined hands, and couldn't tell where his flesh ended and hers began.

"Aye," she whispered. "As certain and true as the raven flies, m'laird husband."

Epilogue

March 1603
Richmond Palace

Harington emerged from the queen's bedchamber, shaking his head with grave dismay. "She will not rest, nor eat, nor bestir herself even for chapel."

Merry looked up from her tangled embroidery, quickly set it aside. She had not been able to concentrate upon a single stitch all the morn, now she knew why. 'Twas something in the air, some foreboding come to fruition she had sensed for a long time. She saw the despair sketched in the eyes of Elizabeth Tudor's godson and knew the hour was nigh.

She and Ran had come for Twelfth Night at Westminster, despite her husband's worries over the lengthy journey and its toll on Merry. She had pointed out Fi was quite accustomed to traveling about during all of her pregnancies, Darra had danced until the day of her deliveries, and besides she would not be outdone by her own twin. Lady Kat was still a neck-or-nothing rider when she had a great belly. Ran could hardly argue with her logic, and indeed he had wisely stopped arguing with Merry at all when it came to their bairns. He had no complaints with Alasdair just turned three, and Malcolm one. Both were spitting images of their dark-eyed sire; both had been born under highly inconvenient circumstances. Alasdair made his indignant appearance a month early, as she and Ran had ridden out to picnic at Invermark in the meadow. The great Wolf of Badanloch panicked, and Merry still laughed whenever she teased Ran about his midwifery skills.

Malcolm tried to outdo his brother on Burns Night in the middle of a roaring blizzard. This time the midwife could not reach Auchmull, and though Nell was skilled, poor Lord Lindsay was reduced to tearing out his glorious hair by the time the babe showed at dawn. This third child would be born on English soil, a harsh fact for any Highlander to swallow, but word of Elizabeth Tudor's failing health brought Merry far and fast. Ran could only serve as escort, for he knew his wife would accept no restraint on this matter.

On a stormy day in January, the queen was moved from Westminster to Richmond, and this rare public appearance after months was enough to stir gossipmongers. Superstition was rife because the coronation ring which Elizabeth had never removed before was ordered filed from her finger, as 'twas cutting off her circulation. Furthermore, her face had become haggard and her frame shrunken, not unexpected at her age and after such a harsh lingering illness, but the courtiers were cruel and quick to turn, like mongrels on a wounded cur. Merry overheard some of the maids-of-honor laughing when Her Majesty refused to change her gown, the once-vainglorious Tudor queen now reduced to indifference over her toilette. She had rapped the ninnies smartly for their mirth, but secretly fretted over the sign. There would be more to come.

The queen's fierce temper made her more difficult to deal with than ever. She insisted upon keeping a sword at her bedside, and from time to time waved it about and thrust it menacingly at any who distressed her. Quinsy seized her throat in February, she hardly ate, and her fevered fancy led her into muttering of golden days past and calling for Cecil or Dudley.

At such moments Merry was one of the few who could ease her distress, and though great with child, the undaunted Lady Lindsay managed to bustle about with cheerful efficiency and banish the shadows and sickness with her smiles.

She met Harington's sober gaze now, and rose. "Her Grace is restless again?"

"Aye, fearfully so. There is naught which seems to bring comfort or ease."

The young man was visibly distressed, and Merry patted his arm in passing. He was a spoiled coxcomb, like Essex had been, but in the last hours he was loyal, she saw. "Bring your books," she said, and entered the queen's chamber without further aplomb.

He scurried to obey, with a puzzled air. Merry did not wait, but approached the great canopied bed draped with heavy curtain frowning a little at the silence she encountered. "Your Majesty?" she softly inquired, drawing back the curtain and letting a pale shaft of light fall upon the bolsters there. The head with thin gray hair shifted a bit. Merry gently touched the withered cheek, and nodded at Harington. Fumbling with his book a moment, he began to read, understanding what was needed. His verses had oft amused Elizabeth, and his clear strong voice put the shadows at bay, if but for a moment.

Merry eased herself down into the chair beside the bed, and listened as well. When he finished, and the page crackled over, a querulous but surprisingly firm voice issued from the bed.

"When thou dost feel creeping time at thy gate, these fooleries will please thee less. I am past relish for such matters. Thou seest my bodily meat doth not suit me well. I have eaten but one ill-tasted cake since yesterday night."

Harington's eyebrow arched, but Merry smiled a little at the familiar tart tones. "Mayn't we summon something from the kitchens to break your fast, Your Majesty?"

A thin, spotted hand waved impatiently above the bed. "Conspire as y'will, Madame Lindsay. But let not the bread be stale."

For a few days there was renewed hope, yet on the fourth

Elizabeth's strength ebbed again, and in desperation her Council and attendants sent for Admiral Lord Nottingham. He was the queen's closest surviving relation, the oldest of her friends. He coaxed Elizabeth into swallowing some broth, and indeed she reminded Merry of a child with her trusting air in those moments. She felt her own babe stir, and laid a protective hand upon her belly. Sir Robert Cecil entered then and told Elizabeth she must go to bed, 'twould please her people greatly if she slept, rested. Always the queen had considered public opinion critical, and yet his request was met with a spark of high dudgeon this time.

Elizabeth turned upon Cecil and sharply reminded him "must" was not a word to be used with princes. "Little man, little man, if your father had lived, you daren't not have said so much, but thou knowest I must die, and that maketh thee so presumptuous." The Tudor spirit never truly flagged, Merry saw, though Sir Robert's jaw was seen to sag a bit.

A short time later, Nottingham coaxed the queen to retire, and when she did not sleep, the Council decided the matter of succession must be firmly established. They assembled round her bed, and though Merry was not privy to the discourse, she later heard they had mentioned the King of France, testing Elizabeth's wits, but she did not react. They suggested Lady Catherine Grey's son, Lord Beauchamp. The spark flared again.

"I will have the son of no rascal in my seat," Elizabeth indignantly rasped, and the wits were declared intact at such juncture. At last King James was mentioned, and accounts varied on her reaction, but 'twas gathered one of approval by remark or sign. When the archbishop was sent for, Merry closed her eyes, wishing Ran was there with her. 'Twas hell pacing the antechamber with the other women, most of them sniveling maids or wailing old hens. Merry had little respect for most of them. Many had forsaken the aged Gloriana, weary over the loss of gaiety and trifles so rampant in the early years of the reign. Oft Merry had heard the queen mutter, "There are none left whom I can trust." The mere fact she stated such in Merry's presence seemed a compliment, and indeed she preferred Merry and Mistress Southwell to any of the other ladies.

The last time Merry saw the queen 'twas in the wee hours before Lady-Day, and she had entered one last time with a cup of warm broth. Robert Carey waved her away, and Merry's gaze fell upon the shriveled figure in the bed as she turned. She felt a shiver of premonition then, and touched the amulet at her throat. Within an hour, the bells tolled.

Merry pushed through the knot of weeping women, hurried into the hall and was met with the open arms of her husband. She flew into his embrace and Ran clutched her tightly, letting the sobs roll through her and steadying her as best he could.

He ran a hand over her hair, soothing her, whispering endearments until she calmed. Finally Merry drew a ragged breath, but not for the reason he expected. Her water had broken. Her fine hose and slippers were soaked. She looked at her husband wide-eyed, and despite the sober moment Ran chuckled.

"Not again, lass."

Merry giggled a little. "Aye, milord. Again."

While Elizabeth's funeral procession passed through the streets to Westminster, and throngs gathered in witness to the passing of a great sovereign and a marvelous era of discovery and romance, one woman labored in a small Richmond apartment, alone but for an unfamiliar midwife.

Merry grit her teeth with each rising contraction, cursing the plague of being female. Her sons had been relatively quick, easy births, but this one had ebbed and flowed for hours, and she was exhausted. Kat was en route to London, but she knew her sister would not arrive before the blessed event, and her mother was in Ireland. She felt alone and distressed over missing the tributes and honors being paid Elizabeth. She was fretting when a shadow fell over the bed. Merry glanced up, panting still from the last contraction.

"Ran!"

Her husband winked. In a thick Highland brogue he said, "Now we canna be breakin' wi' Lindsay tradition, lass."

Within moments he had banished the unfamiliar midwife

and assumed quiet, surprisingly calm control of the situation. Merry was astounded and delighted, but never more so than when he cradled their slick, newborn daughter in his hands, gazed down into unfocused blue eyes and softly declared, "Elizabeth Meredith Lindsay, meet your sire."

The Wolf of Badanloch grinned.

Author's Note

Dear Reader,

I hope you have enjoyed SNOW RAVEN, the final book in the Raven series. I was compelled to write this story after reading several touching accounts of Lindsay history and legends of Edzell. The ruin of the family came with the fall of the Stuarts, reported as follows, from *Lives of the Lindsays:*

"The Laird, like his father, had been a wild and wasteful man, and had been long awa'; being engaged with the unsuccessful party of the Stuarts. One afternoon the poor Baron, with a heavy heart, followed by one a' his company, came to the Castle, almost unnoticed by any. Everything was silent—he gaed into his great big house, a solitary man—there was no wife and no child to gie him welcome, for he had never been married.

The Castle was almost deserted; a few old servants had been the only inhabitants for many months. The broken-hearted ruined man sat all night in the large hall, sadly occupied—destroying papers sometimes, sometimes writing, sometimes sitting mournfully silent—unable to fix his thoughts on the present or to contemplate the future.

In the course of the following day he left the Castle in the same manner in which he had come; and, turning round to take a last look of the old towers, he drew a last long sigh, and wept. He was never seen here again.''

I invite fellow readers and history lovers to write me at P.O. Box 304, Gooding, ID 83330. If you desire a reply, please include a self-addressed, stamped envelope (No. 10).

Best regards,

Patricia McAllister